KEY

THE REDWYN CHRONICLES

BOOK 1.5

KEY

THE REDWYN CHRONICLES

BOOK 1.5

MADISYN CARLIN

This installment in *The Redwyn Chronicles* is dedicated to the Master of Mayhem, also known as K.R. Mattson.

*Peace I leave with you; my peace I give to you. Not as the world gives do
I give to you. Let not your hearts be troubled, neither let them be afraid.*
John 14:27

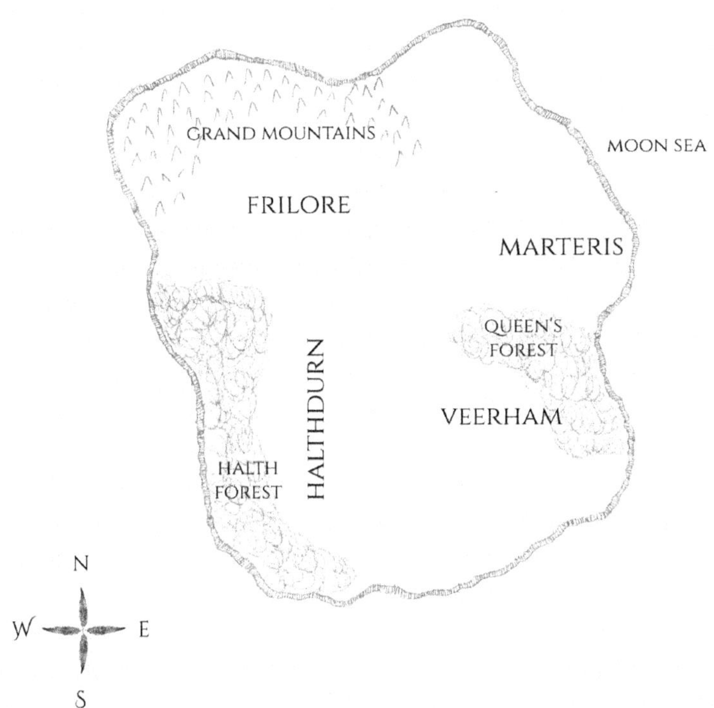

GRAND MOUNTAINS
MOON SEA
FRILORE
MARTERIS
QUEEN'S FOREST
VEERHAM
HALTHDURN
HALTH FOREST
N
W
E
S

CHAPTER ONE

DENTON

LOVE WAS CONDITIONAL.

Denton Yindell reined his horse to a stop atop a sloping hill covered in waving prairie grass. Land stretched before him, dotted with wildflowers and leading to the Moon Sea's light blue waters. The distance could neither hide the gentle surges of foam-capped waves nor the faint sound of them descending upon the shore.

He exhaled and closed his eyes. The warm sun and the whispering breeze would offer peace to most. But not him. No, as long as Father's icy blue eyes and harsh voice haunted Denton's memory, he'd not be obtaining peace.

He turned Cinders, directing her northward. His path led him toward Marteris' rolling hills, not its famed shores and waters.

At Denton's command, Cinders eased into a trot. He grit his teeth as the jolting gait jostled his wounds. Half a year of recovery and still the pain persisted.

He could handle physical pain. The stabbing, the burning, the throbbing. It was the emotional pain he wasn't fond of.

Love was conditional. That was what twenty-three years of life had taught him. That's what Father's fist, harsh tongue, and continually-burning temper taught him. One wrong word, one wrong action, one disagreement led to him no longer being qualified to be Father's son.

According to Father, Denton was no longer worthy of being acknowledged as a Yindell.

Not that Father's statement now mattered. He had met his end courtesy of a noose, hung for the very crime he so arrogantly believed he would never be punished for.

The leagues passed by with only the cry of seagulls and cardinals and the jangle of Cinders' tack keeping him company.

Red's letter of introduction burned him despite being tucked in his saddlebag. Denton hadn't read it, but he could well imagine the ink splatters and rips adorning the paper. The detective's face had been as red as her hair as she penned the missive, her temper almost physically manifesting by way of steam whistling from her ears.

She hadn't been pleased at the doctor's verdict of four more months of light work, which did not include traipsing across the land in search of criminals.

It mattered little whether or not Red had been cleared to travel. Denton would go anyway. He owed Jonah that much. Owed it to the numerous children he could have helped but didn't.

He flinched as a deep rumble split the air. Chill bumps rose on his arms as a stiff, cool breeze whipped through the weeds and grass.

Cinders snorted and tugged at her bit.

Denton stroked her neck as he scanned the landscape. He had long ago left the area inhabited with palm trees. No trees or bushes were around to bend in the wind, but the waves rose and crashed with what promised to be a deafening roar if he was any closer.

Heart plummeting, Denton stared at the sea. A long, narrow object bobbed about, tossed to and fro by the waves in frantic fashion.

He ground his teeth. With his luck, someone needing rescue was in that object.

Just ride on. It doesn't concern you.

The apathy he had subscribed to for so long threatened to again claim him. It would be so easy to ride on, and he had more than adequate practice ignoring his conscience.

No. No more cowardice.

Exhaling, Denton reined Cinders toward the wave-battered shore. As he neared, his heartbeats increased to an almost ferocious cadence. Stomach in a solid knot and skin cool and clammy, Denton forced himself to dismount where the shore met the grass. Deep gray storm clouds gathered above and obscured the horizon from view. Faint flashes of cloud-to-cloud lightning preceded deep rolls of thunder that sounded more ominous than Red when her temper was beyond riled.

Turn around. You owe no one anything.

It would be so easy to leave. If anyone *was* in that object, which looked like a boat, it wouldn't take much to let them deal by their lonesome with being adrift.

No.

That was what Father and Antony would do—if they hadn't placed the poor soul there in the first place.

The last people Denton wanted to emulate were his late family members.

He inhaled through gritted teeth and told Cinders to stay before making his way toward the white-capped, foaming waves. His legs forewent their bone and muscle and turned as limp as uncooked flatbread.

This was absurd. He—a twenty-three-year-old man who had faced down kidnappers, been shot twice and survived, and who had dealt with a cantankerous Redwyn Deathan on more than one occasion—shouldn't be afraid of waves.

Man-eating waves.

Okay, maybe being afraid of the monstrous surges of water was normal.

Whatever the case, Denton would be beyond grateful when he found Jonah and returned to Veerham, where the only waves were those caused by the Roaring River and Red breaking etiquette rules.

Even if there was really nothing there for him to return to.

Denton shook away the thought and advanced. Churning water lapped at his boots, then his knees, then his waist as he trudged through the water toward the object, its shape gradually shifting into a canoe.

The water's iciness stole breath from his lungs and spray and raindrops pelted him with bruising force.

Beginning, please guide me.

Whether or not the Beginning heard him was debatable, but it never hurt to try, especially when another life was at stake.

Denton clenched his teeth and forged ahead. The current and resistance stole his breath, another reminder of how out-of-shape he still was after his injury.

More thunder rumbled and lightning continued to flash. Denton slogged out of the way of an incoming monster wave and grabbed twice at the canoe, only to miss both times. His third attempt proved successful.

Straining, Denton pulled the canoe through the tempestuous water. His shoulders and back muscles ached and the scar in his side throbbed. Though the stitches had long been removed, right then it felt like they were still in and threatening to tear.

Time passed marked only by the storm and the draining of Denton's strength. He finally stumbled ashore, muscles all but useless as his legs threatened to give out. Groaning, he managed to pull the canoe from the sea's clutches.

Gasping for air, Denton braced himself on the canoe's edge. Saltwater soaked his clothing and the rain only worsened the matter.

Denton's throat clogged as he stared at a bundle of blankets wrapped around what was surely a person. Images he'd dwelled on many a dark, painful night flashed through his mind.

Children encased in blankets. Swords. Blood. Screams. An arrow flying toward him. Carter's bruised face and Princess Chamonix's rumpled appearance. Red being thrown off a quarry's edge. And the agonizing impact as two broadheads entered his body.

Snap out of it, Yindell.

Now was not the time to dawdle.

Denton hauled the limp bundle from the canoe and drew his knife. The wet wool resisted the honed edge. What if the blade slipped and he cut the person beneath? What if *he* killed them due to incompetency?

Beginning, please guide me.

Cinders whinnied.

"I know, girl. I'll be done in a bit."

Sand crunched, barely audible over the waves and storm.

"Cinders, stay." Denton squinted and readjusted his grip on the knife. With his other hand he pulled away part of the blanket to reveal part of a pale forearm.

Bile burned his throat.

Cinders snorted.

"Cinders, I told you to stay."

The hairs on the back of his neck rose as a harsh chuckle sounded in his ear.

"I'm not Cinders. Now stand up and back away."

Denton froze. Of course this would happen. His luck wasn't really luck—more of a curse that caused him to attract trouble nearly as often as Red.

"Stand. Up." A blade hovered near Denton's throat. "Or the waves will wash away more than one body today."

Instinct demanded Denton run the other way, bolt for Cinders, and ride for safety—both from the man and the storm—but the memory of dirtied, worn faces lodged in his mind and stayed his feet.

No, no more running. No more cowardice. Denton was done with looking the other way.

He was tired of being his father's son.

"I want no trouble. This person could be injured."

"You're going to be hurt if you don't do as I say."

Again, the instinct to run away settled deep in his bones. The other way was safe, free of harsh fists, cruel words, and parental disappointment.

No more cowardice.

His spinelessness already cost innocent lives. That couldn't happen again.

Denton inched his other hand toward his sword.

The man grunted and growled indiscernible words.

The air behind Denton shifted, and the last thing he saw as something solid slammed into his skull was the figure still trapped in blankets.

Chapter Two

NERISSA

TWO BODIES IN ONE day. If she didn't know better, Nerissa would say she was cursed.

She sighed as she poked the man with her walking stick. Combing the beach for valuables or objects that washed ashore during storms generally did not supply her with dead bodies.

The usual amount of flotsam dotted the shore—nothing more than usual. If a ship had wrecked, splintered wood would be everywhere and the unfortunate souls who hadn't been carried out by the tide would be well on their way to attracting birds of prey.

Nerissa scanned the shore. Daffy and Elberta were picking flowers, their backs to the waves. She could only pray her younger sisters hadn't seen the corpses. Most things evaded Daffy's comprehension since she thought of little else besides puppies, flowers, and cookies. But Elberta...Elberta, as Mamma would say, was sharper than a freshly-honed kitchen knife.

Meaning the precocious eight-year-old saw and understood more than she should.

A blessing at times, but not so much when death rested only fifty paces away from the little whippersnapper.

"Another one?" Edver's shadow fell across Nerissa as he joined her near the body. Sweat glistened on his dark skin and discolored his sand-colored shirt. "Honestly, Ner, you find the weirdest things when we come out here."

Nerissa exhaled. "At least he's not smelling of decay yet." Her stomach turned as she stared at the man. Facedown in the sand, dried blood matted dark blond hair and stained the jerkin and shirt stretching across broad shoulders. His boots were black, a definite indicator he was no Marterisi.

Edver whistled. "I'm going to check on the other poor sap. See if this one's alive, will you?"

"Why would I want to touch a dead body? *You* see if he's among the living." Nerissa had seen enough death to last her an infinite amount of lifetimes, and she refused to gaze upon another face claimed by expiration.

Edver graced her that flat-lipped, narrowed-eyed expression he often donned whenever he thought her absurd. "Because I'm busy checking the other poor soul."

"I don't see you doing any such thing." Nerissa dug her nails—what was left of them—into her palms to keep her desperation from showing. How could she handle more death? She still hadn't managed to erase the last few instances from her mind.

Holding a baby as it gasped its last inhales had a way of shattering a soul and embedding the fear of evil into a heart.

Life was precious. So, so precious and valuable. Everyone, from the babe in the womb to the oldest person alive, was individually formed by the Beginning. Life was a priceless gift and blessing, yet so many were too eager to snuff it out.

Edver raised a brow and took three exaggerated steps backward. "I'm walking away. Last I checked, that counts as being *occupied*."

"Edver, so help me…"

"What, Ner? What will you do? Deprive me of sugar in my coffee?"

Nerissa scowled. "I hope your clothes get doused in saltwater and shrink."

"That's not very ladylike of you." Edver tsked. "It's just a dead body, Ner. Nothing you haven't seen before. Now, I really do have to go get the other one before high tide comes in and it's time to return home."

Nerissa sucked in her breath as Edver left her with the body. Gnawing her lip, she scanned the grass. When no blonde-haired children entered her vision, something hollow filled her chest and her heart jumped before plummeting.

Her sisters were gone.

In the span of five minutes, they had vanished.

How, though? They hadn't been near the water and Marteris' largest animal of prey was a bobcat, and most bobcats she'd seen weren't interested in two targets at once.

Most.

Oh, what if someone had snuck up and kidnapped them?

Please, Beginning, don't let that be so.

"Nerri!"

The coiling terror dissipated. Nerissa lifted a trembling hand to brush away stray hairs tickling her face as she turned toward the voice. Elberta and Daffy—Daffy's head barely visible over some of the taller grasses and weeds—moved toward her, a tall, black-and-white horse trailing slowly behind.

Nerissa placed a hand over her heart. "What are you two doing?"

"Exploring."

"I told you two to stay close." What if something happened to them?

Elberta shrugged and snagged Daffy's wrist as the little one prepared to dart off after a butterfly. "We did stay close. We could see you the entire time. And we waved, but your back was to us." Petulance punctuated her words.

Nerissa sighed. "Where did you find the horse?"

Elberta's grin revealed a missing tooth. "She was grazing. Isn't she pretty? I've never seen a horse with a spotted rump before. Do you think she's his?" She pointed at the body. "And is he sleeping or dead? I didn't think that's what a dead person looked like."

Goodness gracious, Nerissa hoped not. It would be complicated enough to bury the man, much less determine what to do with whatever belongings his saddlebags contained.

Daffy squealed as the horse nosed her hair. "No, horsey. Hair doesn't taste good."

"Elberta, grab your sister and take her to the pile. No, the horse may not go with you. I don't want either of you to move a muscle, understand? You just stay right by the pile until I tell you otherwise."

Nerissa's middle sister scowled at the scant pile of interesting finds they had discovered. "That's boring."

"Then tell Daffy a story."

"Why?"

"Because I told you to." Why must her sister be so mulish?

Elberta crossed her arms, a motion Daffy copied. "I want to help. Mamma said I was old enough to help."

"Mamma said you were old enough to help *gather*. Not...deal with other things."

"Like what? Dead people?"

Elberta was smart for her age and often baffled folks with her advanced vocabulary and scholastic abilities, but she was still so young and naïve and innocent. Nerissa would pay any price to keep her as such. "Elberta, death is a serious matter. The man was badly injured before he died and I don't want Daffy to see the wound. It is your job to keep her occupied, alright? You know how easily things scare her."

Shoulders slumping, Elberta released a dramatic exhale. "Fine. But I'm telling Mamma you were really bossy and unfun to be around."

"*Unfun* is not a word."

"Bossy. I'm not in school right now, and even if I was, Mamma is the teacher. Not you."

"Elberta..."

Eyes rolling, Elberta snatched Daffy and carried her to the pile, all the while uttering a list of grievances at least five leagues long.

Nerissa swallowed another rise of nausea when she again faced the body. Of all the times for Edver to be ungentlemanly, it had to be today.

Gritting her teeth, she advanced on quaking legs. Sand shifted beneath her and the gentle collision of waves upon shore offered comforting background noise.

Hopefully she wouldn't lose her composure and shriek, cry, or upheave her breakfast.

Please, Beginning, don't let this be gruesome.

Nerissa held her breath and situated her walking stick's end beneath the man's shoulder before attempting to roll him over. No way was she touching a cadaver. That far exceeded her limits and Edver would simply have to be okay with that.

By the time Nerissa's fifth attempt occurred, sweat stung her eyes and soaked her dress. Groaning, she gave one final push with the walking stick, and the man was finally turned onto his back.

She wiped sweat from her forehead and took a deep inhale. A sizable gash spanned the man's forehead. Sand crusted the injury and clung to his skin and the blood smeared around the wound. He looked around her age.

Her heart sank. Would anyone miss him? Was he a husband? Brother? Son? Nephew? Had he known the Beginning? Why had he stepped foot into Marteris?

"Well?" Edver dusted off his hands as he claimed the space next to Nerissa.

"I rolled him over, just like you wanted."

"So I see."

"See what?"

Nerissa jumped at Elberta's question. She spun and glared at her sisters. Daffy returned her displeasure with an innocent expression as she hugged her stuffed seahorse doll. "I told you to stay by the pile."

Elberta tipped her nose in the air. "We were bored."

Nerissa could guarantee they wouldn't be bored at home. Elberta would find her list of chores tripled in length for the next month.

Edver tried shooing them away before his serious, deep brown eyes met Nerissa's. "The kid is dead—has been for quite some time."

Bile rose. "He was a child?"

"Yes. Ten or so, I think. It's hard when rigor mortis has already set in and the decay is well-advanced."

Daffy tugged on Nerissa's wrist. "What are rig tortoise and decay?"

"Ask Mamma when we get home." Nerissa wasn't explaining rigor mortis to a four-year-old. Goodness, she herself was twenty-three and the concept gave *her* the willies.

Edver hummed as he knelt beside the man. His expression shifted from wary to surprised when he placed his fingertips on the side of the man's throat. "Ner."

More nausea, followed by a sinking feeling of premonition. "Yes?"

"He's not dead."

"I beg your pardon?"

Edver's eyes again met hers. "This man is alive."

Nerissa's shoulders ached as she dug the oars into the water. It wasn't so difficult with Edver's help, as the bulky Marterisi could row twice as fast and with thrice as much strength as she could, but by herself?

Rowing was difficult. Little wonder the fishermen were big and strong. By the time she and the girls arrived home, Nerissa would likely have thrice the amount of muscle in her arms and upper back.

More sweat stung her eyes and caused her bodice to cling to her. The hairs escaping her braid stuck to her skin, causing a mighty itch. And she was hot, tired, and thirsty.

Of course the man had to have a horse. Of course Edver would insist upon riding that horse back home. And of course the man would be alive.

She chastised herself for that thought. Hadn't she just been lamenting how so few valued life? Yet here she was, bemoaning the fact someone lived.

As the canoe glided along, Nerissa peeked over her shoulder. Edver had placed the man atop an extra blanket in the back of the canoe. The sand had been brushed from most of his face, but Edver refused to touch the wound.

A grim bit of satisfaction arose at the memory. Edver, a strapping, six foot-two inches tall Marterisi, had paled at the sight of blood.

It was a good thing he hadn't fainted, for Nerissa would surely be squashed if she attempted to catch him.

Edver hadn't found that comment amusing.

Inhaling a deep lungful of clean, sea-scented air, Nerissa resumed rowing.

In front of her, Daffy and Elberta remained surprisingly still as they gabbed and stared out at the water.

"Nerri?"

"Yes, Daffy?"

A cherubic face, complete with chubby cheeks and sparkling sea-blue eyes, turned toward Nerissa. "The waves must be rich."

Nerissa grunted at the strain in her shoulders and back. "Why do you say that?"

"Because they have diamonds. See? On the waves? Are those sea diamonds? Do you think I could have one?"

"Those aren't diamonds, Daffy."

"What are they?"

"That is the sun's reflection. If you try scooping it up in your hands, all you'll have is water."

Daffy pouted.

Nerissa returned her full attention to rowing. The lack of death explained why there was no stench of decay, but how had the man survived? Providing he had washed ashore during the storm two days ago, that was a long time to survive the heat and lack of food and water. And with wounds like that…blood loss often played a deadly variable when it came to survival.

The discovery Edver found in the man's saddlebag caused a roiling storm of emotions. Who was this man? What was his story? Would he survive long enough for her to find out? Did she *want* to find out?

"Can we name the horse?"

Elberta's question drew Nerissa from her thoughts. "I think the horse has a name."

"It's probably a stupid name."

"Elberta…"

"What?" Elberta shook her head. "Really, Nerri. It probably is. You know all the stupid names the others want to name Uncle Morris' horses. People just don't know how to give horses good names."

"And you do?"

Elberta nodded. Her thin, light brown eyebrows bunched with the expression she always made whenever she felt strongly about something. "I would name the horse Magpie."

A chortle lodged in Nerissa's throat.

"She and magpies are the same colors, plus she's kind of noisy, just like magpies are."

Elberta and Daffy commenced listing all the names they thought worked for horses. For her pride's sake, Nerissa hoped they would never own a red roan, lest it be named Lobster per Daffy's suggestion.

Nerissa breathed a prayer of gratitude when fluffy white clouds obscured the sun and blocked part of its heat. Aside from the violent storms often thrown their way, Marteris was a beautiful land.

To Nerissa's right, the sea, now a calm aquamarine-gray, met the horizon. To her left, rocky cliffs topped with scraggly pine trees and even scragglier underbrush rose high, proud, and protective. Unlike Southern Marteris, no palm, coconut, or banana trees inhabited the northern portion.

Another prayer of gratitude arose when the canoe's bottom scraped across the sand stretching into her village's shore. No dark smoke tainted the pale blue sky, every building looked intact, and there was no sign of distress.

A smidgen of the weighty anxiety inhabiting her chest eased. Her family was okay. Her friends were okay.

"Girls. You are back." A broad-shouldered behemoth of a man exited the humble shack plopped right on the shore. He strode toward them, his league-long strides consuming the distance. "Where is Edver?"

Daffy giggled as she was lifted from the canoe. Happy as a clam, she perched on Lemuel's shoulder, gabbing and gesturing as he did the same with Elberta.

"How was it, Little Miss Nerissa?"

"Unexpected."

"What do you mean?" Lemuel's eyes were as black as the agate Marteris was known for. Though his sixty years of age showed in his whitening hair and wrinkling skin, he could wield a sword as well as, if not better than, a man half his age.

"We found two bodies and a horse." Daffy held up her hand, her index and middle fingers forming the *two* indicator. "Edver doesn't think the one man's dead. He's a royal detector, you know."

"*Detective*, Daffy. Detective." Nerissa accepted Lemuel's hand and relished the feeling of being on solid ground again. She followed the man's gaze to where the royal detective remained still and unmoving. If not for the slight rise and fall of his chest, she would think him deceased.

"Just what does she mean?" Thunder edged Lemuel's words and a storm glinted in his eyes. Though not the oldest soul in the village, he was a valuable member and respected by all. And he was as protective as a mother cat to her kittens. No one harmed a villager without experiencing Lemuel's wrath.

Nerissa wiped her palms on her skirt and winced at the contact between material and raw skin. "Edver searched his saddlebags and found a letter of introduction. Assuming the letter wasn't stolen, this man is a Veerhamer royal detective."

"He's too young. Even I can tell that."

"Edver is riding the horse back here." A lump lodged in Nerissa's throat. "We found someone else, too."

Lemuel glanced at the girls before setting them down. "Could you please fetch Doc for me?"

Elberta giggled and tugged Daffy along. "Maybe Hauni will have made cookies."

"I smelled them baking, so I'm certain she did. There you go, now. Off you get. And tell Hauni I give my greetings."

The two dashed off without any indication of hearing him.

Lemuel's expression promised a tempest-sized interrogation for the man if he ever awoke. "Well?"

"It was a child. He…he was dead. Had been for some time, too, if Edver is right."

And he probably was. Edver was rarely incorrect in such matters.

Lemuel's shoulders sagged. "Another victim?"

"He did not say."

Grumbling about outsiders and the problems they inevitably caused, Lemuel lifted the man from the canoe and set him on the shore. "He really is young. No older than you, I'd say."

Doc arrived then. Where Lemuel was balding, Doc owned a full head—and face—of graying dark-blond hair. Where Lemuel was the tallest man in the village, Doc's lackluster height caused outsiders to look down on him both figuratively and literally.

But that did not stop the man from remaining firm in his convictions, and he could stare down a hurricane and win if he so pleased.

"The little ones said there was a half-dead body? Is this it?" Doc stared at the outsider with an inscrutable expression.

"Of course he's the one, Guy. No one else looks like they're courting death."

Doc pinned an unimpressed glare on Lemuel before kneeling and evaluating the man. "I don't cotton to half-dead young men being brought here. That usually means trouble is on its way." He sighed. "He requires immediate care. I do not like the look of that injury. If infection has not already set in, it soon will. Lemuel, help me, will you?"

Nerissa watched the waves lap at the shore as the men carried away the outsider.

The shack Lemuel exited had been accosted by all manners of ill weather, yet it stood strong. She found a nail and began picking. If only she could be like that shack. Steady when the storms arrived. Unflinching despite the hardships and maelstroms of life. True to her faith no matter what trials the Beginning decided she must endure.

With a knot in her stomach, Nerissa gathered her sisters and walked home. The outsider was far too young to be a detective, and royal one at that, and what would a detective be doing in Northern Marteris?

The only explanation was the letter was either stolen or forged and the outsider was, as Doc said, a precursor for trouble.

Nerissa grimaced and tightened her clutch on her sisters' hands. What type of danger had she brought to her village?

CHAPTER THREE

DENTON

PAIN, RED HAD SAID, was the unspoken part of the job description. Denton already knew that from watching Carter and the feisty detective be carted off to the physician's more than once. He also knew that the deep throbbing engulfing his skull, the desert-dryness of his mouth, and the general aching that embedded itself bone-deep into every part of him was outside the bounds of what Red meant.

Somewhere between his mind and his fingers, the command to move his hand was lost. Instead, the aching intensified, worsening until it seeped into his marrow.

Living wasn't supposed to hurt so much.

Had he been found guilty like Father and Antony and sentenced to the same fate? Was he still in the Queen's Forest and resembling a pincushion as two arrows protruded from him? He didn't feel the same type of wooziness like what the blood loss caused, nor did he smell loam, leaves, and the coppery stench of blood.

No, the sharp, herbal scent burning his nose did not belong to the Queen's Forest.

Perhaps he was still in the infirmary, then? The salves, tinctures, and remedies Federigo insisted giving Denton for his injuries smelled similar.

A scraggly male voice, decidedly not one Denton ever heard before, spoke barely loud enough to be heard over the roaring rush in Denton's ears.

A roaring rush much like what he remembered hearing on the shore.

The shore.

As fragmented memories returned to his addled mind, Denton mentally scowled. He should have listened to his intuition and not gone after that canoe. Those waves were deadly and man-consuming, and now he was probably inches away from a sea predator eagerly awaiting to consume him.

But that explained neither the herbs nor voice.

This is why helping others is dangerous, the poisonous voice said.

Time after time, Denton had struggled to silence the voice, which sounded just like Antony's. He didn't want to be his brother. Didn't want to even resemble his father.

"I think he's stirring." The second voice sounded much deeper than the first—and much closer. "Should we let them know?"

"Let's see if he even comes to first."

The men continued speaking and, in spite of the darkness tugging Denton back into nothingness, he strained to hear their words. Were they kidnappers? Did they feed trespassers to sea monsters? What had they done with Cinders?

Despite his efforts, the darkness engulfed him.

Like the waves lapping at the shore when Denton first saw Marteris' beaches and sea, recognition of being alive gradually eased him from the swirling mass of darkness.

Voices, faint in the background, set his heart racing. For all of Father's cruelty, he seemed nice enough compared to Antony. Denton's brother delighted in causing pain, even more so than Father. Denton was in no shape to protect himself, not with the sudden dizziness and nausea.

Denton sought his limbs with no luck. Had he lost his arms and legs? Or was his spine broken and he now could neither feel or move the rest of his body?

A burst of inflected voices set his heart into a fierce cadence. He needed to fully awaken, arise, and escape before Father or Antony entered wherever he was.

Attempting to lift his head felt akin to trying to lift a bucket of boulders with his neck only.

And why did his throat feel so raw? Hadn't he nearly been consumed by the waves?

Perhaps everything would make sense if he could find some water—freshwater—and ease the agonizing dryness in his mouth.

Intervals of weight clomped against a hard surface before pressure landed on Denton's forehead. "He's stirring," a woman said.

More intervals of weight—*were they footsteps?*—before another voice answered. "Fetch some water, please. Son, can you open your eyes?"

Denton forced his eyes to crack open. Blurred brown met him.

"A little more, please. There you go. Yes, all the way. Good job, son."

As his vision shifted into focus and gained clarity, Denton found himself staring at a man with a massive beard and a head of gray-streaked blond hair. Even after he blinked away the grittiness, the man remained hovering above him.

A woman joined the man. Deeply tanned skin, light blonde hair, and gentle turquoise eyes that invited Denton to trust her. Something about the way she carried herself reminded him of Queen Isadora.

"Here." The man slid an arm beneath Denton's shoulders and helped him sit.

The room swam. Denton grasped at the navy coverlet to keep from toppling from the narrow bed. His stomach churned with the spinning.

"Easy, easy. Here, take a drink."

The cool water soothed a bit of the desert that was Denton's throat and cleared the fog from his mind.

Everything hurt. Ached. Bone-deep and persistent.

The man drew up a wooden chair and sat while the woman perched at the very end of the bed. Apparently Denton was no threat. He could see why. Right then, he hadn't the strength to lift his hand halfway to shoulder-height.

"I am Guy and this is Hauni, my wife." The man gestured to the woman. "What is your name?"

Something in the man's eyes told Denton they already knew, but his mind was still too muddled to make sense of anything beyond the most basic questions and phrases. If they wanted to know his identity, why was that an issue?

Unless…unless they worked with Father and Antony. Then that most definitely was an issue.

"Do you know where you are, son?"

Son. He'd not been called that for a long, long time. "No," he croaked.

"You are in Marteris. Do you mind telling me why a Veerhamer with no goods to trade, no news to impart, and no royal markings would be this deep into Marteris? We're not a place most intentionally visit."

Perhaps Denton could answer if he knew where in Marteris he was. For all he knew, he had somehow been carried by the waves back to the Veerham-Marteris border.

"Guy." Hauni inclined her head toward her husband. "Why don't you fetch the chief? I will get our guest some sustenance while you do so."

"I don't think—"

"He is no threat to me," she responded quietly, "and I am quite certain he will be more amenable to answering your barrage of questions after he has some food in his belly."

Guy scowled but listened to his wife. After he left, Hauni graced Denton with a slight smile that strained around the edges. "Let me bring you some food."

Denton blinked to clear the shadows framing his vision. Was it his imagination or did the husband-and-wife duo now treat him like he was a potential threat despite Hauni's offer of food?

His stomach lurched as he managed to inch his fingertips up to his forehead. Cloth provided the answer to why his head felt like it was being constricted.

Cinders. What had happened to his horse? Was she alright?

Brain throbbing, Denton settled back into the pillows between him and the headboard. Wooden beams crossed overhead and the walls were constructed of stone. The only stone building in Veerham was the palace, and that was finely-cut, smooth rock. These stones were all shades of gray, and some were even black. Mortar of a hideous tan shade kept them together. A door made of what looked like pine wood matched the simple nightstand next to the bed and the chair Guy had vacated.

Only the open door and a slight window cut high into the wall allowed natural light in.

Beyond the door, Denton could see part of a table and a window festooned with sea-green curtains.

Must everything have something to do with the sea? If Denton never saw it again, he would consider himself blessed.

Hauni entered with a bowl in her hands. Her simple gray dress brought to mind the storm clouds Denton had seen forming over the churning waters.

A boulder rested in his stomach. "Ma'am?" His voice was more rasp than articulate phonetics.

Hauni's brow furrowed and she inched a step away from the bed. "Yes?"

"Where was I found?"

"That will be discussed when Guy returns." She placed the bowl in his lap. "Clam chowder. It is a Marterisi specialty."

It was a specialty for Denton too—the type of specialty that caused his gag reflex to be almost too efficient. His taste buds revolted at the smell, taste, and texture. He never had been fond of fish, and while there wasn't an overabundance of fishy flavor, it was still enough to make him struggle to withhold a retch.

Only through the manners instilled in him by Stepmother did Denton manage to finish the meal.

Never again.

He loathed himself at times, but never to the extent that he would ever force himself to consume clam chowder again.

A man could only take so much, after all, and it was bad enough smelling the fish, let alone eating them.

Hauni reappeared in the doorway. "Would you like some more?"

"No, ma'am, but thank you," he croaked. What he wouldn't give for Aldyth's beef stew or even the palace cook's blueberry muffins. Simple, hearty, normal fare. Not this fishy, sea-vomit nastiness.

Brow still furrowed, Hauni inched toward him and took the bowl. Despite her claim about Denton not being a threat, she clearly believed the opposite.

His blood iced when a door creaked open and thumps and voices barged inside the cabin.

Denton ground back a snarl as he reached for weapons that were no longer there. He stilled. The pale blue shirt wasn't his, nor were the dark brown pants. Had whoever taken his clothing also stolen his weapons?

What about the rest of his supplies and belongings? Had they been washed away, stolen, or stored by whoever hauled him to this fish-infested place?

Guy, two other men, and two women entered the small room.

Denton's heartbeat quickened until pain almost shot through his chest. Aside from Federigo, Guy, and Hauni, the last Marterisi he saw had dealt Red a grievous injury, participated in trafficking, and had kidnapped a child.

These people had bandaged his wounds and kept him alive, but why? Who were they and what did they want? Red had warned him about the rumors—carried along by merchants and tradesmen—sweeping in from Marteris.

Veerham wasn't the only land affected by trafficking.

Guy crossed his arms. Though the shortest person in the room, his gaze penetrated with the ease of a broadhead arrow. He nodded at the dark-skinned Marterisi. "This is Chief Talart. His son was one of the ones who found you."

Chief Talart's eyes did not contain the cold greed and hatred as the traffickers', but Denton couldn't push away his unease.

"This is Jarrel Wessen, his wife, Veri, and his daughter, Nerissa. Nerissa was the first one to locate you."

The youngest woman stood half a head taller and was a replica of the older woman beside her. Lighter blonde hair pulled back in a braid that encircled her head, and even the distance could not disguise her vibrant green-gray eyes.

Though she stood straight, her fingers flitted between picking her nails and wringing her hands. Red would say the lass was as jumpy as a cat in a bathing chamber.

Guy sighed. "I feared you would suffer memory loss due to your injuries, but I am relieved to see that has not occurred. Whoever attacked you gave you a nice gouge across your forehead and I think you sustained some bruising when you fell. Not to mention the ramifications from dehydration." He shook his head. "Truly, lad, the shore is not the best place to be felled."

Like Denton requested to be attacked on those wretched shores. And perhaps it was because he was from a different kingdom, or that his mind wasn't congested with salty air, or he wasn't addled from living next to human-consuming waves, but *nice* and *gouge* did not belong in the same sentence.

Chief Talart claimed a spot near the other side of the bed. Tall and brawny, he looked like he could choke Denton with just his pinky finger.

A possibility Denton had no desire to test.

"What is your name?"

"Denton Yindell, sir." Best not anger the giant.

Heavy eyebrows lowered over piercing, dark eyes. "Why are you in Marteris?"

"I'm looking for someone."

Chief Talart's expression thinned. "Are you sure you weren't sent here because your presence was requested?"

Denton's eyes throbbed, but closing them would indicate weakness. "As far as I know, no Marterisi correspondence has reached Veerham in the past eight months."

A muscle in the chief's jaw ticked. "Are you certain?"

"As certain as I can be."

It hurt to speak. Why must they ask him questions requiring more than simple, monosyllable answers?

Chief Talart exhaled. "You said you're looking for someone. Why here? Few Veerhamers come this way."

"The person I'm looking for isn't in Southern Marteris." Or, if he was, he wasn't breathing.

"Who is this person?"

"A child."

Everyone stiffened and more than one surreptitious glance was passed around.

Denton's spine crawled. Had he landed himself in the middle of traffickers? Kidnappers? Those similar to the evil souls who destroyed so many lives back in Veerham?

Chief Talart's glower deepened. "Why are you looking for this child?"

"Because I promised him I wouldn't stop until I found him."

"He's missing?"

Mrs. Wessen sighed and shook her head. "What the chief means to ask is why are you looking for this child in the first place?"

Denton may not be as shrewd as Carter or experienced as Red, but even he could tell when he was being interrogated—and Mrs. Wessen's "gentle" question was just another form of grilling him.

What should he do? Answer their question with one of his own? He couldn't get up and wobble his way to freedom, not to mention he had no idea where Cinders was. And he wasn't exactly the most self-sufficient individual. Plop him back in the middle of Veerham and he could probably survive. But in the middle of Marteris? A land deadlier than anyone realized?

He'd perish for certain.

A touch of frost edged Mrs. Wessen's tone as she repeated her question.

Denton exhaled. "I made a promise."

"So you said," Chief Talart rumbled. "We need more information than that before we decide what to do with you."

How comforting.

Red gave Denton an introduction letter. A shame she hadn't given him some of her gumption as well.

"I'll ask this one final time, young man. Why is this child missing and why are you, one man—and a young one at that—looking for him?"

The attitude Denton had kept under lock and key so he wouldn't incur Father's wrath flared. "If a child under your protection was missing, wouldn't you go looking for him? Or would you sit around twiddling your thumbs and asking inane questions?"

So maybe he had more in common with Red than he thought.

The chief's face darkened. "Do you talk to your king in that tone, young man?"

No, but Denton *had* snapped at Carter—the king's son-in-law—quite a few times. And he'd also taken to task the king's ward numerous times as well.

Red hadn't appreciated his attempts at keeping her safe.

A muscle in the chief's jaw ticked. "I will ask this one last time, *Detective* Yindell, and if you do not answer, I'll haul your wimpy hide to the village jail. I care little if you look like you tangled with a shark and barely won. Why is this child missing and why are you, one man—and a young one at that—looking for him?"

A shark? Horses and horseshoes, what was a shark?

"You've seen the introductory letter. That means you know who I am."

Great. That rap to the noggin really messed something up in his mind. Usually he left the snappy replies to Red.

"You could have stolen that letter."

Denton stared at the chief. Did this man really think him capable of such a feat? "The letter was neither wrinkled nor dirtied in any way. If I had stolen it, it would be all those things. I was right there when Detective Deathan wrote that, and I can assure you I stole it from no one."

Though he wouldn't mind if it went missing. He had no desire to be a detective. All he wanted to do was right a wrong.

A wrong that never should have occurred.

"We have your word and your word only. For all we know, you were the one who murdered the boy."

Denton's heartbeat thrummed in his ears as his chest tightened and numbness swept over him. Did the chief mean the body he found? It had been on the smaller side, but surely not small enough to be a child.

"You know what I'm talking about." The chief's cool tone cut into the haze surrounding Denton. "The child wrapped in blankets. The child with you on the beach. The child you murdered."

"It was a child?" His voice croaked. The numbness evaporated, leaving emptiness in its wake. How many more innocent children would perish at the hands of evil? How long would it take before people realized what was happening?

Why, Beginning? Why are You allowing this?

"Did he have red hair?"

The chief looked at him like he was a few horses shy of a full stable. "No. As far as we could tell, the victim was Marterisi."

"Did he have any identifying marks on him?" Red's instructions filtered into his memory. He should ask these questions first and not let emotions overtake him.

Horrific as it was that another young one had perished, he still thanked the Beginning it wasn't Jonah. That meant there was still a chance the boy lived.

Before the chief could reply, Denton managed to hold up a shaky hand and stall him. "Some of the others had rope burn on their wrists and were covered in bruises."

Red's reports still made him nauseous. After the battle to free the captives, he'd been unconscious during the journey back to Veerham, but Red took intense delight in making him memorize the reports.

And there were plenty of them.

The chief's countenance darkened. "Just how do you know this?"

"Like the letter says, sir. I'm a detective."

Detective. The word tasted unpleasant. He was no detective. The Beginning neither gifted him the knack of finding clues nor being intelligent enough to solve mysteries.

"You're a waste of my time, Denton."

Father voiced that particular opinion more than once.

Was Denton a waste of the Beginning's time? Was that why the Creator gave him no gift? Nothing that enabled him to truly help where it was needed the most?

The thought embedded in Denton's mind like a tick burrowing into a deer's hide. He hadn't mattered to Father. Hadn't mattered to his birth mother, either, if Antony was to be believed.

If he did not matter to his earthly father, there was no chance he would matter to the Beginning.

Chapter Four

NERISSA

"Do you think he's telling the truth?"

Nerissa kept her attention on the peas she was shelling. Her skin prickled beneath Mamma's gaze. Mamma knew full well the ramifications if Denton Yindell, if that was truly his name, worked with the traffickers. Everyone knew what could happen if they trusted the wrong person.

The skeletal remains of the village Tilb were proof that misplaced trust could result in a heartless massacre. The broken souls of countless children and young adults were proof.

Please, Beginning, if I made a mistake bringing him here, do not let my sisters suffer for it.

Good intentions often brought deadly consequences, something Nerissa couldn't risk.

She should have left that man on the beach. His fate mattered little to her.

"Nerissa?"

She exhaled. "I don't know, but what will we do if he is lying? What will we do if he tries harming us?"

Mamma set down the bowl of peas she was rinsing, dried her hands, and framed Nerissa's face. "My darling girl, worrying about *what-ifs* will not change the future. We may know neither this man nor his true intentions, but the Beginning does. Nothing that happens is outside of His control."

"I know." Nerissa stared at her fingernails. Bitten, picked to the quick, and their ragged edges evidenced how she physically dealt with the continual fear and pressure in her chest.

No matter what she did, no matter how much she prayed, and no matter how often she recited verses from the Scripts, the heaviness remained.

"We've so much to lose. I honestly do not know if he is worth the risk."

Mamma sighed. "We cannot let fear and anxiety direct our steps."

Nerissa had heard the admonition time and time again. "I know." And she did. She really did. But she could no more stop the anxiety than she could halt a hurricane.

With another sigh, Mamma returned to rinsing the peas. "We best work on supper. Your father will be home soon."

Swallowing the lump in her throat, Nerissa shelled the last of the peas and turned the fish filets. Had the man been speaking the truth? Was he truly a detective? The traders who passed through mentioned the important Veerhamers wearing something that signified their status—flowers or bracelets or something like that. The man arrived with no adornments and nothing but the supposed introductory letter to indicate who and what he was.

He could be a murderer. Your sisters could be endangered right now. What if he's with the traffickers?

Nerissa's heart quailed. Once kidnapped, it was rare for the victim to be recovered and rescued. If they were, they could never return to who they once were. How could they? Even the young ones who hadn't been captive for long were forever scarred by evil's machinations.

She rubbed the area just below her left clavicle. If this pressure did not soon relent, she would lose her mind.

No earthly remedy could cure the storm within. *Please, Beginning, settle and calm me.*

Supper passed with the conversation crafted to revolve around topics Daffy and Elberta could discuss. Once the dishes were clean, the sand washed from Daffy's hair, and the leftovers tucked in the cellar, Nerissa made her way outside.

Past the garden she walked until she reached the fence separating their land from Uncle Morris'. The rickety wooden fence wouldn't last through the next thunderstorm, but Uncle Morris' horses were well-trained and rarely ventured so far away from their water trough.

She rested against the only sturdy pole and stared at the rippling green grass. Ginormous pine trees edged the land and at the far end, light streamed from the single window in Uncle Morris' cabin. The first few stars twinkled against the orange-and-purple colors of sunset gradually fading from the sky as a gentle breeze whispered through the grass.

Nerissa closed her eyes and took a deep breath. She lived in the prettiest part of Marteris. Why was she so chronically jumpy? It wasn't like the raiders from across the Moon Sea ever reached her shores. In fact, the only raiders her people had to contend with were magpies and the traffickers.

A gentle snort sounded in her ear.

Cracking an eye open, Nerissa stared at the outsider's mare. The equine returned her gaze for but a moment before whuffling Nerissa's hand and wrist.

"Sorry, girl. I have no carrots for you."

The mare's ears flicked.

Nerissa crossed the fence and held her breath as she approached the horse. Uncle Morris worked with horses—rehabilitated, trained, and sold them—but his admiration of the equines had skipped Nerissa and landed on Elberta. Daffy just liked horses because she thought they sounded funny.

Horses were not Nerissa's favorite animal, but she did admit they were elegant creatures.

Holding out her hand, she slowly advanced until her fingertips met the mare's neck. Uncle Morris reported faint scars marred the mare's shoulders and withers. Despite the trauma the poor thing endured at some point in her relatively short life, she did not act afraid of humans.

Had the outsider been the one to harm her? Or had he saved her?

The mare bobbed her head before returning to grazing.

Nerissa stroked her neck and untangled a knot in her mane. Uncle Morris said the mare was in excellent condition—her hooves were cared for, she was groomed regularly, and no saddle sores marked her back. The saddle and saddle blanket were in good repair as well.

But just because the outsider took care of his horse did not mean he was a good man.

Still moving slower than a frozen fish, Nerissa leaned her forehead against the mare's neck. "Who is your owner?" she murmured. "What is his story?"

"And there you were, sprawled out and more resembling a corpse than someone still breathing."

Edver's enthusiastic voice boomed through the infirmary. Nerissa cringed as it startled a flock of cardinals from the nearby trees. Why was he so friendly? Of course, Edver could easily hold his own against the outsider, but that did not mean he had to be congenial to the man.

Wiping her hands on her apron, Nerissa forced herself to enter the infirmary. Father and Chief thought the outsider might be more willing to offer information if he spoke with those who saved his life.

Nerissa did not see the logic in that, but she said nothing.

The floorboards creaked beneath her, announcing her arrival before she was ready. Edver spoke in a lower voice before bellowing her name.

Knees knocking, Nerissa slipped into the room. Edver lounged in a plain wooden chair, his long legs extended and crossed at the ankles. His fingers laced behind his neck and he sported an amiable expression.

Traitor.

Smoothing her apron, Nerissa nodded to her childhood friend before directing her attention to the outsider. The sunlight streaming through the long, small window darkened the shadows beneath his eyes and the weariness etched in his countenance. Blond hair in dire need of cleaning stuck up every which way. Unlike yesterday, no bandage obscured his head wound. Eyes she vaguely remembered being blue dully watched her movements.

No emotion crossed the man's face.

The chair squeaked as Edver stood. "Here, Ner. Have a seat."

"Thank you, but no."

"Why not?"

Nerissa made a vague gesture toward the chair. "I see those sand grains. You may like having them all over your clothing, but I do not."

Edver scoffed and dusted off the seat. "Happy?"

"That would depend. Are your hands clean?"

"What does that have anything to do with this?"

Nerissa crossed her arms and pinned Edver with what Elberta called her *big sister expression.* "Do you remember the last time you offered me a seat?"

Edver squinted. "No. Why?"

"You had brushed it off while icing was still on your hands. You smeared it all over the wood. Father had to sand for an hour until he was able to remove it."

With a pshaw, Edver rolled his eyes. "You're making a sea out of a small puddle. That was one slight smear of frosting. You're acting like my entire hand was covered in it."

"Because it was."

The slightest grin touched the outsider's expression and lent life to his eyes.

"Just sit down, Ner." Edver glowered at her.

Nerissa raised both brows. "I think not. It is safer to stand, thank you."

"You're not welcome." After one final harrumph, Edver gestured to Nerissa. "I think you met Lady Stubborn yesterday. We're the ones who found you on the shore waiting to be shark bait. Just what were you doing, anyway?"

"Being unconscious." The stranger's voice rasped as though remnants of salt from whatever sea water he previously swallowed still lodged in his throat.

Edver snorted and hid a grin behind his hand as he faked a cough. "I meant before that."

The outsider shrugged. "I was trying to see if the child was alive."

"Child?"

"Yes, the child. The one you brought back for burial. The one who was wrapped in several layers of woolen blankets. The one your father said you pronounced dead at the scene. The one who was probably kidnapped and then abandoned in that canoe-thing."

Nerissa inched back to the doorway as her stomach churned like a storm-tossed sea. Chief Talart said nothing of that sort in the man's presence.

Edver crossed his arms, likely attempting to intimidate the outsider.

Who didn't look one bit cowed.

"Just how do you know I'm the chief's son? Pa didn't say he told you that."

An eyebrow rose. "You just admitted as much, plus you look like him."

Edver spluttered and stammered. "I...that...well, that doesn't mean you're right about anything else."

The other eyebrow joined the first and a flat, almost wry expression claimed the outsider's face. "No, it doesn't, but I overheard your father and the rest of his cohorts discussing it after they questioned me."

"My father does not have *cohorts*."

"No? Then what do you call them? Minions? Lackeys? Henchmen?"

Nerissa found herself stepping forward as Edver's fists clenched. Her friend only exhibited outbursts of anger when he encountered traffickers or his favorite pie was left off the menu.

Apparently it was time to add the outsider to the list of things that irritated him.

"Those indicate Father is evil."

The outsider merely stared at Edver. "Is he?"

"Of course not!"

"Then how and what do you know about the traffickers?" The outsider's gaze sharpened and his posture straightened.

"We *rescue* the victims—not kidnap them."

Nerissa located a nail that wasn't quite picked at enough. Edver offered too much information. Chances were the outsider was a spy and sought any way to destroy those who opposed evil.

"Then have you seen a red-haired boy? He's about seven or eight with an abundant sprinkling of freckles. He's short for his age and is named *Jonah*."

Edver slouched back in the chair and blinked. "Was this Jonah kidnapped?"

"Yes." Iron edged the outsider's voice before it faltered. "Last year near the beginning of autumn. We retrieved the ones we could, but he had already been removed from Veerham by that time. I've been physically searching for him for about a month now."

"Why only a month?" Nerissa willed the words to fade into nothingness before they reached the outsider's ears, but such fortune was not granted.

His eyes flashed. "I don't know what the weather is like here, but in Veerham, we have what's called *winter.* That means we get a lot of snow and dangerously cold temperatures that make it impossible to travel. Plus, I was unable to walk at the time, and I couldn't really go hopping about the kingdoms on one leg now, could I?"

Edver stood, drawing to his full height. "You don't speak to Nerissa that way."

The outsider's jaw ticked, but after a moment his stiff shoulders eased. "I apologize, miss."

Nerissa swallowed and nodded. "You are forgiven."

The man had some semblance of manners, but that did not mean he was law-abiding.

Edver pulled a rumpled square of paper from his pocket and shook it out. The sunlight glittered off the royal emblem affixed at the top—a cardinal in a diamond. "This says your name is Denton Yindell. What kind of a name is that?"

The outsider's brow furrowed before he regained his stubborn mien. "What kind of a name is *Edver*?"

"It's a good name."

"So is mine."

Edver glared, again shook out the missive, and peered down his nose as he read aloud.

"'*I, Redwyn Deathan, Royal Detective for their majesties King Calvin and Queen Isadora Seyden, do so introduce my fellow detective, Denton Yindell. Under the alliance between Veerham and your fair kingdom, he is to be assisted with any matter he brings to your attention.*'"

Surely Nerissa's eyes deceived her when she saw the outsider wince.

"Who is this Redwyn Deathan?"

"Like the letter said, she's a royal detective." The outsider tilted his head, still maintaining his unamused expression. "She wouldn't like you very much."

Edver harrumphed. "She sounds like a joy."

"She's a terror."

Nerissa choked. Did all Veerhamers speak with such bluntness?

She squirmed when she caught Edver's plaintive glance. He would one day be chief, and therefore really should be conducting this interrogation by himself. It would serve him right as well since he forced her to turn over what she thought was a dead body.

She relocated that nail and worked to smooth its rough edge. Her heart threatened to cease operations as her eyes met the outsider's. Would he seek revenge if she angered him? Would he harm her sisters? Her parents? Her village?

Please, Beginning, stay his wrath.

After working moisture into her dry mouth, Nerissa managed to speak "How do we know you're not lying?"

The outsider held her gaze. Something lurked in his eyes, but Nerissa could not discern the emotion. "Ma'am, I have seen some of the purest forms of evil. I know what the traffickers are capable of. And the way I reckon it, you folks have two options. One—believe me and help me find an innocent child who has met malevolence far too soon in his young life, or two—disregard the truth and do nothing to stop the vile wretches who are chronically destroying innocent lives."

Anyone could say that. Anyone could try guilt-tripping her village into helping. Words were merely a façade for the true intent behind them.

Edver tucked the letter back in his pocket. "Talk to you soon," he mumbled before ushering Nerissa toward the door.

"Did you find my horse?"

The question halted Nerissa's feet. She risked turning. Unlike earlier, furrows grooved into his forehead and he sat forward, one hand pressed to his side and the other gripping the coverlet.

Edver spoke. "What does it look like?"

"She's a black-and-white appaloosa and is about fifteen hands high. There are faint scars on her shoulders and withers and her bridle is inscribed with Veerham's emblem."

"She is safe." Nerissa forced the words out. Did he just admit to harming his horse? Or had those scars come before he owned her?

The outsider relaxed against the headboard. "She's not limping, is she? I had to ride her across some rocky terrain and didn't have a chance to check her hooves and horseshoes before…" His voice trailed and his features tightened.

Nerissa clenched her hands to warm her cold fingers. The pressure in her chest remained a steady presence. Something had to be wrong with her. No one else became unsettled when nothing was amiss.

"What happened?" She wasn't shy, nor was she timid and a quiet speaker, but her voice sounded timorous even to her ears. "What happened to you on the beach?"

Shadows crossed the outsider's eyes and he eyed her and Edver with what could only be mistrust. "I saw the canoe-thing about to be capsized as I was riding. The storm was about to hit when I managed to pull it from the water." He shrugged and cast his gaze downward. "I removed the bundle from the canoe and then…"

"And then what?"

A hurricane settled in his eyes. "And then someone held a blade to my neck and that's the last thing I remember."

Chapter Five

DENTON

During his time healing from the arrow wounds, Denton had mostly stayed in his old room. The sunlight had filtered in, warm despite autumn's crispness. The blanket Stepmother sewed for him helped him keep his thoughts on happier times—and not the fact that his father and brother would soon join their counterparts in the criminal graveyard. It hadn't helped the loneliness or the inexplicable sense of loss, though. After all, Carter was now wed and busy with his new bride and taking on kingdom-related tasks. Aldyth, the housekeeper, was only there to clean the house and not engage in much conversation, a job she took with utmost seriousness.

Navigating stairs with crutches was not counted among the wisest choices he ever made, but when the heartache and emptiness became unbearable, Denton would somehow manage to descend the stairs and hobble his way to the stable. Where he would sit in Cinders' stall and stare at the ceiling. And fight back tears.

The gaping hole in his heart never filled. Never healed.

Love is conditional.

How far did he have to go until he earned the Beginning's love? What more could he do to ensure that love, once he earned it, remained?

Or was the Beginning like Father? Would any goodwill grow stagnant over time?

Quietly exhaling, Denton stared out the window. The slight size enabled him to see only a few stars twinkling against the black expanse of night.

Was the Beginning as far away as those stars were? Was He unreachable?

Love is conditional.

Perhaps he should give up on this quest for the Beginning's favor. After all, if he couldn't earn a mortal's approval, how could he possibly gain the Creator's?

Morning arrived at about the same speed as Red's ire cooled.

Grit obscured Denton's vision as he blinked once again to bring the ceiling into focus. Lack of sleep wouldn't help his mood any, and if they thought to interrogate him again, he'd not be as considerate as before.

He had seen horses cribbing before—a habit brought on by boredom—and he was mighty tempted to take it up just so he had something to do. With only his thoughts for company most of the time, Denton was sick of them. They led him down paths he strove to ignore and whispered unwelcomed reminders when he tried focusing on the few good things in life.

Grinding his teeth, he convinced himself to ease from the bed. According to Guy, Denton suffered from more than a head wound. Dehydration, near drowning due to the high tide, and numerous other smaller cuts and bruises sapped his strength and slowed his response time.

The room spun as he rose. Rough stone met his fingertips as he lurched to the side.

"You're pathetic." Father's sneered insult again revisited. *"Real Yindells aren't wimps."*

Pathetic was right. Who else would still suffer from dizziness and weakness two days after being rescued?

Biting his tongue to keep from losing his stomach's contents, Denton shuffled to the doorway. His skin felt tight, likely from the seawater, and his joints creaked like he was ninety instead of twenty-three.

If only he could sneak away and find a freshwater stream nearby. Then he could wash away the blood, grime, and salt.

With a hand on the doorframe, Denton peered into the infirmary's main area. A door and kitchen filled the area to his right while a table, a few chests, and a window lay straight before him. To his left, two more doors and a fireplace took up the rest of the space. The scent of fresh bread mingled with that of herbs.

His stomach growled, but now wasn't the time. Escape was key—right after he located his belongings. Specifically his weapons and boots.

The clothing he had been changed into hung loose, and though it was soft enough, it stung when it brushed against his scars. The tender skin made even the gentlest sensation feel like a thousand needles pummeled it.

Limping, Denton crossed the room and peered out the window. Pine trees and buildings filled his view. His gut twisted. Surely they hadn't stolen Cinders. He needed her for his travels, and beyond that, because she was a good listener. Cinders never laughed at him for feeling emotions Father thought were puny and demeaning. Cinders never called him a weakling when his leg buckled and his muscles gave, resulting in him toppling over due to the strain where the second arrow hit his leg.

And she was a connection to Veerham. While no home awaited him, he did love his kingdom. The trees as they turned in the autumn, the snow as it glittered in the cold sunlight, and the sight of horses grazing in the lush green pastures.

He had no home, yet his heart belonged in Veerham.

Love was conditional. Apparently belonging somewhere was too.

"You're up." Hauni's voice jolted Denton back to the present. She joined him at the window. Now that he stood, he could see just how short she was. The rumors were true, it seemed. Marterises were either short or quite tall.

"How do you feel?"

Was the concern in her voice genuine?

Very few had ever been truly concerned about his welfare.

"I feel fine." The lie and his sore throat caused his answer to croak. He felt just the opposite, but he couldn't—wouldn't—say that. Hauni and Guy had cleaned his wounds and ensured he survived the night, but he knew neither them nor their intentions.

Hauni's cool hand pressed against the part of his forehead that wasn't decorated by a gash. "You don't have a fever. That is good. Do you notice any other symptoms of a concussion? Really, you shouldn't be up until Guy clears you."

"I'm fine, ma'am." No telling what they'd do if he revealed a weakness.

Father certainly would use it against him. Antony, too. Alone, both were insidious. When they schemed in tandem?

They were monstrous.

Hauni's brows drew together. "You do not look *fine*. In fact, you look terrible."

Denton barely stopped himself from retorting. Hauni wasn't Red, and though he traded mild barbs with the detective, Stepmother's training dictated he be polite to his elders.

And polite he would be until he learned they wanted to do away with him.

"Sit down, please, and I will fix you a meal."

"Ma'am…"

Hauni held up a hand. "I have four sons. I know a hungry boy when I see one."

"Ma'am, really…"

She pinned him with a look Denton vaguely remembered Stepmother giving him—the look warning him he should just hush and accept whatever gift was being given.

Father drowned Antony in presents while Denton was forgotten like an unwanted pair of gloves discarded in the attic. He hadn't minded, as being in Father's good graces wasn't worth the cost of his conscience, but it'd been so, so long since someone considered him worthy of a gift.

Besides Carter, that was. His stepbrother had been gracious enough to allow Denton to keep Cinders.

Denton's throat still thickened at the memory.

"Sit down, young man."

"Yes, ma'am."

Hauni raised a brow as she bustled toward the kitchen. "Are all Veerhamers so polite?"

"Most of us, ma'am." Denton eased into a chair. His joints again groaned, but he shouldn't complain. He was out of bed and able to walk around.

After serving Denton a cheese sandwich, Hauni sat across from him.

Denton stared at the meal, hesitantly and mentally saying grace. He'd been to the chapel enough times to learn how important it was to offer gratitude for one's blessings, even if those blessings were few.

Although, he *was* mighty grateful Hauni hadn't served him seafood. That was one pickle he had no idea how to escape.

Denton's stomach welcomed the sandwich. And it was on homemade bread. He hadn't had that since Stepmother died.

Hauni leaned her elbow on the table, resting her chin in her hand. "Who are you?"

Not this again. "I'm who the letter said I am, ma'am. Royal Detective Denton Yindell." The title tasted sour.

"Aren't you a mite young to be a detective? And a royal one at that?"

"The other detective is even younger than me, ma'am."

Hauni pursed her lips. "My goodness. Are there no qualified detectives in your kingdom?"

Wouldn't *that* question pitch Red into a tizzy. "Ma'am, the other royal detective is one of the greatest currently alive. Not much escapes her notice." And not much danger evaded her either. Red attracted danger like a corpse attracted flies.

"Oh?"

"Yes, ma'am." Denton's pulse quickened. Was he sharing too much information? Unintentionally exposing secrets?

Blast it all, he wasn't meant to be a detective. Snooping and spying and knowingly walking headlong into danger weren't his fortes.

"If you want to search for Jonah, you'll need the crown's protection." King Calvin had been blunt about the unlikeliness of Jonah being located, but something in his eyes hinted at understanding. The king was a good man and an honorable and just leader. Still, Denton had almost ceased breathing when he was brought before the royal couple for the first time.

"And just what has this other detective accomplished?"

Denton resisted the urge to close his eyes and rub his forehead. That was surely a sign of disrespect. "She uncovered one of the largest trafficking and black-market rings Veerham has ever dealt with. She hunted them down and made them pay for their actions."

"She did this single handedly?"

Was Hauni mocking him? Denton bit back a scowl. "She led the charge, ma'am, and that qualifies her to be one of the greatest detectives in this period of history."

"Would this detective happen to be Redwyn Deathan? The same one who wrote your introductory letter?"

"Yes, ma'am."

Hauni nodded, then stood. "Enjoy the rest of your meal. I will heat some water so you can wash up. You truly do look terrible."

Perhaps Red wasn't the only one gifted at doling out insults.

The sight of waves crashing against the shore stole Denton's breath and turned his legs into appendages as limp as the fabled octopus' arms. Was it normal for his heart to feel like it would break through and escape his chest?

Marterises, he decided, were lunatics. Not only did they amble along the shore without a care in the world, they allowed their children—their *children*—to play in the dastardly water. What would they do if one was swept away? Could they rescue the child before sea monsters consumed them?

"We have a proposition for you." Chief Talart's deep voice reminded Denton of Captain Bedros. Commanding and demanding full attention and respect.

Denton eyed the large Marterisi from the corner of his vision. Chief Talart could squish him like an ant and not even have the decency to break a sweat while doing so. Being on the man's bad side was not a destination Denton wished to reach, but neither would he willingly assent to any plans. Not until he knew just who these people were and what they were up to.

And they were up to something. He felt it in his bones.

Or perhaps that was just the residual pain from his shore experience.

A squeal caught Denton's attention. A little lass with light blonde hair zipped toward them, running as fast as her short legs allowed. Two pigtails flopped with her bouncy gait and a grin bunched her chubby cheeks. She halted before Denton and stared up at him with large blue eyes.

Denton ignored the urge to smile. Children could be used to manipulate—he'd seen that during the whole trafficking debacle back in Veerham.

"You're the royal detector." She took a step closer and looked at him from head to toe. "What's a royal detector?"

Her childish accent tugged at his heart, which threatened to melt as she graced him with another wide smile. This lass didn't know him, yet she welcomed his presence.

It had been a long time since anyone had been happy to see him.

Ignoring his command, a smile broke free. "A royal detective helps important people find things."

"Like what?"

Before he could answer, a passing butterfly snagged her attention and she darted after it.

"Daffy," the chief called. "Stay in sight."

Daffy paused and turned, offering a wave before resuming her butterfly hunt.

Chief Talart shook his head. "Little ones make me feel like a whale compared to a minnow"

Denton knew what a minnow was, but he'd never heard of a whale. Based off the chief's comparison, he didn't want to.

The giant of a man faced him, arms crossed and expression hard as tempered iron. "You claim to be against trafficking."

"Yes, sir."

"Why did your king send you to find this Jonah? Isn't one man too few for such an endeavor?"

Denton drew himself as straight as he could and looked the man in the eyes. He was tired of people questioning his motives. Tired of being reminded of his failures. Tired of being haunted by Jonah's wan face and terrified voice.

And he was tired of explaining himself over and over. These people's skulls must be made from granite, because nothing was reaching their minds.

"One man is better than none, and efforts are still continuing back home. I volunteered to go, sir, and that's all I will tell you."

Two bushy brows rose. "Do you speak to your king in that tone, young man?"

Denton grit his teeth. "Sir, with all due respect, King Calvin listens. And he understands. The *first* time something is said."

The king certainly understood when Carter wished to marry Princess Chamonix. Denton had never seen Carter shake in his boots like when he recounted King Calvin's interrogation.

"So you become disrespectful when someone does not understand the first time you say something?"

What did this man think Denton was? A toddler who required reprimanding?

"Sir, there is a difference between honestly not understanding and purposefully acting dense."

The second the words left him, he wished he could snatch them back. Father would be backhanding him by now for such insolence.

Steeling his spine, Denton braced himself for potential impact. Would the chief break his face? Or just his nose or cheekbone?

Instead, the man tapped his left fingers against his right bicep. "I took you higher-up Veerhamers as snobby, soft folks. Perhaps you do possess some mettle." He grunted and muttered, "You'll need it."

Wait. The man wasn't going to strike?

"Come with me."

The words barely registered before Talart turned on his heel and strode toward the church perched at the end of the barely-there street. Like the majority of other buildings, stone constructed its walls. The humble exterior was nothing like the palace's chapel, yet when Denton stepped inside, a familiar sensation of awe washed over him.

Because here the Word was taught. Here the truth was told. Churches were sanctuaries, reminding attendees that, even though evil riddled the world, hope was not lost.

The desperation Denton always experienced when in a church revisited. What could he do to earn such favor? To acquire such hope, even? Surely he had to immerse himself in the Beginning's good graces in order to be noticed—to even be considered.

Movement shuffled to his right, and the awe fizzled, replaced by the weight of thirty draft horses combined.

Five other men sat in the front pews, their voices low.

Denton's stomach turned.

Talart cleared his throat.

The conversations ceased, replaced with stifling silence as six sets of eyes pinned Denton in place.

Breath squeezed from his lungs. He couldn't do this. The last few times he stood before a group, he was waiting to be condemned for his apathy about the black market and slavery.

Though he'd done nothing to be convicted by Marteris law, cold still traveled along his arms and neck.

He could still run. If he made a surprise break for it, he could reach Cinders and escape. It'd set him back in his search for Jonah, but he'd persevere.

Heaviness landed on his shoulder.

"Breathe, boy. Collapsing won't help your health."

Denton twitched. The last time someone clasped his shoulder like that, it was Captain Bedros wishing him well on his journey. Before that...

Before, Father always gripped his shoulder with such intensity bruises were left afterward.

The chief motioned Denton toward a pew before taking a seat in the one across from him. "We're expecting a surprise tomorrow," he said in a low voice, "and we have a proposition for you. If you help us, we'll help you find Jonah."

Denton reared back. "I refuse to help you traffic innocent human beings," he snarled. How *dare* this man think he'd turn on his convictions. A shame he had no law-abiding connections, else he'd turn this pathetic village in.

And he may not be as brawny as Talart or as knowledgeable as the men surrounding him, but surely he didn't come across as so insipid that they thought they could pressure him into accepting. No group was large enough to force him into that.

He wouldn't. He refused to be like Father in any way.

And Father would buckle. Though a leader of sorts in his own way, he always thought sidling up to the ones in charge would gain him more profit.

Talart scowled. "Boy, one of these days that affliction of yours that causes you to jump to conclusions will result in your death—or a good beating. Are you that daft or do you just have selective hearing? How many times have I said we don't cotton to traffickers and do everything to stop them?" He shook his head. "Yald, do you wish to tell him our plan?"

A dark-skinned Marterisi with more height than width eyed Denton like he carried a contagious, flesh-eating disease. "We are embarking on a rescue mission. Are you sure you want to take him, Chief? He looks like those soft Veerham nobles we've heard so much about. I wager the only type of blade he knows how to use is a butter knife."

Denton sent a squinty-eyed glare toward the man. While he wasn't thick with muscle, he wasn't a twig-armed worm.

The man closest to Denton did little to hide his guffaw. "He has a point, Chief."

"Which is fine and well, but Yindell comes with us. Continue explaining, please."

Yald scowled, but refocused on Denton. "We're going on a rescue mission. At least six children have been taken from neighboring villages, and we're going to rescue them. Apparently, Chief thinks you'd be beneficial to drag along.

Denton slowly inhaled. Like the chief, Yald didn't act on his annoyance. Unlike Father and Antony, who delighted in applying fist to flesh. "What will you need me to do?" He'd help them in exchange for finding Jonah.

Then he could return the lad to his family and mend the broken promise.

And, possibly, begin mending his broken self while he was at it.

"Only cowards and idiots fail." One of Antony's favorite insults, and one Denton knew applied to himself.

He was a coward. And he was an idiot. For he always hesitated to do what was right. And he had failed Jonah. Failed the others they couldn't recover. He even failed Carter by allowing him to be kidnapped. He failed Red through his incompetency to keep her from harm. And he failed his kingdom by not doing more to help rescue Princess Chamonix from Lord Riley's clutches.

"Return to the present, boy."

Denton blinked. "What will you need me to do?" he repeated.

The chief exchanged a look with the other men. "Listen carefully, because I'm only saying this once."

CHAPTER SIX

NERISSA

"HE DID *WHAT?*" NERISSA ceased kneading the dough and gaped at Edver, who sat calm as could be at the table, munching on a square of banana bread. "Please tell me you jest."

"Nope." He popped the *p.* "Father invited the outsider to help us tonight."

All those years in the sun had dried out Chief Talart's brain. Accepting the outsider's assistance was a horrendous idea. For all they knew, he could turn on and slay them.

Nerissa clamped her mouth shut as nausea stirred at the thought. Her sisters loved to roam and play in the fields, but until the outsider left, they would simply have to stay inside or within the initial yard. That was the only way she could keep them safe.

"Easy, Ner." Edver rose and placed a heavy hand on her shoulder. "I can hear you worrying."

"Of course I am worrying. Your father just endangered my sisters."

Edver eyed her like she was an inch away from flying off her rocker.

Perhaps she was.

"Don't you think that's a bit overdramatic?" He held up his hands when Nerissa spun on him. "Look, all I'm saying is this outsider is still recovering from his injuries. He has a gash the size of Shore Canyon spanning the length of his forehead and he can't walk ten paces without coughing, courtesy of the water he likely ingested on the beach. He has no weapons and he's as wobbly as a newborn fawn. He's not a threat."

"He could be in league with the traffickers."

Edver nodded. "He could be, or he might be who he says he is. Father wants to test him. While this isn't foolproof, it will provide insight regarding this man's intentions. Father says he's tougher than he initially comes across."

"That's comforting."

"It is."

"I was being sarcastic." Nerissa sighed as she leaned against the counter. "I can't let any harm come to Daffy and Elberta, Edver. I can't. I couldn't live with myself. And are you really comfortable working with a man who could very well have...well, you know, hurt *him*?"

Edver tilted his head. His eyes, so dark and calm, studied her. "*He's* fine and sometimes I wonder where you get your crazy ideas."

"What do you mean?"

"I mean you fabricate all of this duty and blame and don it like my sisters do new dresses." He shrugged. "Think on it, Ner. Life's events are not in your hands."

Nerissa stared at the pale lump of dough. Perhaps they weren't, but she would do her best to ensure nothing happened that wasn't supposed to.

"Everything will be fine tonight," Edver murmured. "You'll see."

"The last time you told me everything would be fine, you were shot."

"So I was wrong for once in my life. I'm allowed to stop being perfect ever-so-often."

Nerissa swatted his arm. "Get out and go prepare for tonight. I expect a full report when the rescue is over."

Her stomach churned. Unless she and Mamma were called to help Hauni at the infirmary, they wouldn't receive a report until tomorrow.

Please, please, please, Beginning. Keep everyone safe and unharmed.

At least Father and Uncle Morris were in control of the horses and transportation. That meant they rarely entered the action.

Icy wisps of fear brushed her heart and a myriad of *what ifs* flooded her thoughts.

So much could go wrong. So many innocent lives could be lost.

"Let not your hearts be troubled, neither let them be afraid."

Would the Scripts' admonition ever sink into her worry-worn heart?

When they saw Father and Uncle Morris off, Nerissa knew the answer—it would take a long time, if it happened at all, for her to comprehend the Scripts' directive.

Soft linen glided beneath Nerissa's fingers as she unrolled and then rerolled the bandages. Daffy and Elberta played checkers in the corner and Mamma and Hauni chattered in low tones as they sat at the table, sipping coffee.

Please, Beginning, keep them safe. Please keep the enemy from inflicting more harm than it already has.

An informant from one of the other villages kept them updated when suspicious boats were seen off the coast. The kidnappers all used similar watercraft and the amount of bundles—which were really their victims wrapped in blankets and sacks—always gave them away. Oftentimes, they would then transfer their victims to wagons and traverse Marteris' roads during the night, leaving only wagon tracks to be found come morning.

Stomach cramping, Nerissa located a nail and picked at its ragged edge. This night, her village wouldn't be heading out to rescue the victims.

They'd be attacking the wagons.

While sea fighting was deadlier in many ways, there was something worse about battling on solid ground. In the sea, you couldn't fire an arrow if you fell overboard. On land? Even if you injured your leg, you could still shoot.

Her father and uncle were in dangerous tides when fighting in the water, but on land?

They were almost as defenseless as a fish washed ashore.

Please, Beginning.

No amount of prayers could adequately convey the fear bubbling within and threatening to erupt in a spout of shrieks and hysterical sobbing.

Abandoning the bandages, Nerissa relocated to the small table shoved in the infirmary's far corner. Joining her sisters, Daffy snuggled into her lap and Elberta mumbled something about her chances of winning now plummeting.

Nerissa rested her chin in Daffy's hair as the four-year-old moved her checker piece. She'd held another young one recently, a child taken by the traffickers. The little boy was covered in filth and bruises and he cowered in fear of anyone who came within ten paces.

Only after he fell asleep, worn down by fatigue, had Nerissa been able to pick him up. Father and Uncle Morris cleaned him up and when he awoke, he was greeted by Uncle Morris' exuberant lab, who proceeded to eventually draw a smile from the boy after trying to sneak a piece of fish from Uncle Morris' plate.

Others hadn't been so fortunate, though. For every child rescued and sent either back to their families or to a home where they were adopted and loved, two perished.

Nerissa's heart broke every time. What kind of world did they live in where evil prospered and innocent lives were snuffed out?

Daffy giggled as she shoved Elberta's piece off the square. "My move."

Elberta rolled her eyes. "That's not how it works, Daf. You know that."

"But I want that square."

"You can't have it because I already took it."

Nerissa smoothed Daffy's hair and murmured a request for her to behave. Her eyes misted as she watched her sisters. She loved them so. How could she ever forgive herself if harm came to them? If they were kidnapped and trafficked?

The only way to ensure that did not happen was to keep them close and within sight whenever they weren't with their parents.

"Nerri?"

"Yes, Elberta?"

"What happens if they have to chase the bad guys into the sea? Will a shark eat them?"

Nerissa offered what she hoped was a comforting smile. "The bad guys are too far away to run to the sea. And, even if they weren't, sharks rarely come so close to shore, and you know everyone is capable at swimming."

"Yeah, but what if it's stormy outside?"

"Then we should pray they do not have to go near the water."

Elberta moved her checker piece. "I hope they don't. I saw a huge shark once. It was so big I thought it would eat all of Marteris."

Nerissa sent Elberta a warning look. If only Mamma overheard. She wouldn't let Elberta get away without anything less than a scolding. "Do not tell falsehoods. There is no such thing as a shark so big it can consume Marteris, and I know full well you've never seen such a thing."

Nose scrunched, Elberta refused to meet Nerissa's gaze. "It sounds cool."

"But it is wrong."

After shrugging, Elberta moved her piece.

As though to add veracity to Elberta's prior worry, thunder rumbled. Two minutes later, the wind picked up. Five minutes after that, the rain hit.

Nerissa's attempts to smother the rising pressure in her chest did not meet success.

Please, Beginning.

Ten more chess games passed before the infirmary door slammed open.

Nerissa jumped to her feet, all but throwing Daffy behind her. It was a common worry that the village was left unprotected when the majority of the men left for a rescue.

And it was so early. Too soon for them to be back. They had to travel at least a league to reach the wagons, and with the muddy roads and ill weather, it would take a while to cover such an amount of ground.

Edver's dark head appeared first, followed by a shorter, staggering man whose face Nerissa hadn't expected to see.

The outsider stumbled in, arm slung around Edver, who slumped against him. Rain soaked their clothing and pooled on the floor, creating a puddle that wouldn't be fun to mop up.

Mamma sprang upward. "What happened?"

"He was shot," the outsider grunted. "Cowards hid behind the trees and fired on us." Harsh pants interrupted his answer, and his visage, paler than Nerissa remembered, drew taut as his jaw set at what could be a stubborn clench.

Mother and Hauni dashed forward. "Are there any other casualties?"

"A few. They're on their way." The outsider grimaced and placed a hand to his side before his eyes met Nerissa's. A mask shuttered over his expression and he dropped his hand before spinning and stalking outside.

Not even bothering to close the door behind him.

Nerissa instructed Daffy and Elberta to play another game before shutting the door and joining Mamma and Hauni. Somehow they managed to maneuver the block of a Marterisi onto the table and on his stomach so they could inspect the arrow protruding from the back of his arm.

Edver coughed. "I feel terrible," he rasped.

Nerissa held down his arm as Mamma cut away his shirt and Hauni began cleaning away the blood and grime. "That is what happens when you become an arrow's target."

Groaning, Edger cracked an eye open. "Shoulda seen me out there, Ner. I was the stuff of legends."

"I'm sure you were."

He scowled. "I'm being serious."

When he tried rising, Nerissa placed a hand on his shoulder and pushed him back down. "This is why you never say everything will be fine."

"We were ambushed. It's not like I jumped in the line of fire waving my arms like a madman and willing one to hit me."

As far as Nerissa was concerned, Edver *was* a madman.

Not that she would tell him that. There would be a time to scold him, but that time was not when he writhed on the table, sweating and shivering and bleeding. "Your mamma won't be happy."

Edver coughed, sucking in a sharp breath as his skin lost a shade of color. "She'll blame Father. Tell 'im I shoulda stayed behind."

Nerissa shook her head and helped Edver onto his back before easing her hand behind his head while bringing a cup to his lips. "Drink."

He sniffed and gagged.

"Drink, Edver, or I'll tell your mamma who ate that coconut pie at the church lunch."

"Don't you dare."

"I'll dare if you don't drink."

After grumbling about hard-headed women who wanted him dead, Edver choked down the tea, gagging no less than ten times and whining no fewer than fifteen. "That's nasty."

"You'll survive."

Despite his grumbling, Edver's eyelids soon drifted downward until his snores competed with the thunder. Mamma and Hauni then commenced removing the arrow.

Nerissa jumped when the door again crashed open. This time, Lemuel barged in, carrying a limp young woman. The outsider and Uncle Morris followed, each with a child in their arms.

"What happened to her?"

Lemuel shook his head. "I don't know, but she's out cold. There are five more children being brought in as well."

Hauni bit her lip. "We'll have to lay out bedrolls. Nerissa, would you do that?"

"Yes, ma'am."

Nerissa's hands trembled as she snatched thick blankets and pillows from every chest and laid them out as hastily as she could. Prayers abounded—prayers for every victim to survive. Prayers for Edver's expedient recovery. Prayers no one else was injured.

At Hauni's instruction, Elberta and Daffy relocated to Guy's office. Once they were within and the office door closed, the young woman was settled in the room the outsider inhabited until mid-afternoon, when he was moved to Uncle Morris' residence where he would be kept under scrutiny.

Nerissa shook the young woman. "Miss? Miss, can you hear me?"

The woman offered no response.

Mamma and Hauni entered, closing the door behind them, Hauni carrying a slip of a girl. As Mamma helped the little girl change, Nerissa and Hauni switched out the woman's sodden, torn dress with a thick nightgown.

Hauni muttered an indecipherable word before lifting the woman's wrist. "Look at this. Rope burn."

"She has open wounds on her fingertips too." Nerissa squinted. "And rope fiber beneath her fingernails." Not to mention the copious bruises marring the rest of her.

Hauni's hands shook. "May those lost souls turn to the Beginning, because if they don't..."

Mamma patted Hauni's arm. "Revenge is not ours," she murmured.

"I know. I wish it was, though."

Once they received the go-ahead from Lemuel, they reentered the main area. The outsider still held one of the boys, who clung to his neck. Uncle Morris distracted the other with checkers.

Lemuel sighed. "I'll go see what's holding the rest up. We didn't find any injuries besides a few bruises, so unless the lass needs Guy, I'll tell him to stay on the frontline."

"She'll be fine." Hauni pulled two bowls from the cupboard. "Her breathing was steady and I heard nothing suspicious in her lungs. Edver will be fine as well if he behaves himself and stays out of trouble."

The outsider crossed the room to the checkerboard and convinced the boy to let go. He spoke to both children in a quiet voice before leaving without a word to anyone else.

Nerissa took the filled bowls from Hauni and sat with the boys. The first lad was a dark-skinned Marterisi. The second's bright turquoise eyes were round with the fear causing him to cower in the corner.

A Halthdurnite.

"You are a long way from home, little one," Nerissa murmured.

The boy nodded and sniffled.

"What is your name?"

"Noko."

She held out the bowl. "I promise it's just soup. Fish-and-noodle soup."

A grimy hand inched toward the bowl before snatching it from her. Once Noko began inhaling the meal, Nerissa turned to the other child. "What village did you come from?"

The boy's eyes darted to where Mamma and Hauni checked Edver's wound. "Tysla, miss."

"You are far away from your home as well." Nerissa settled in the chair opposite him. "Who took you?"

Thin shoulders jolted in a hiccup. "My teacher. He said I needed to stay after school because I scored a bad grade." Watery dark eyes met Nerissa's. "I tried my hardest. I really did. Mathematics is just so hard."

"Numbers aren't my strength either." Nerissa worked to keep her tone calm and light as she spoke. Giving vent to the anger building within would only scare the boy.

"He told me to stay afterward and when I did, something hit me on the back of the head. When I woke up, I was surrounded by what felt like blankets." He shivered. "It was really warm and I could barely breathe."

"What is your name?"

"Utku, miss. I'm named after my great-grandfather."

Nerissa took Utku's hand. "Utku, I will see to it that we will do everything we can to return you to your home, okay? And when we do, we will warn the authorities about your teacher."

Utku sent her a miserable look. "That won't do you much good, miss. He's the chief's brother."

Heart empty, Nerissa sat back and stared. How could someone be so vile?

Just how large was the trafficking ring? And just how deep did its corruption run?

CHAPTER SEVEN

DENTON

FIVE CHILDREN, TWO TEENS, and one adult survived the rescue.

Three children and one teen died.

And only three traffickers remained alive.

Denton leaned against Morris Wessen's rickety pasture fence and stared at the trees on the opposite end. A handful of horses grazed, unconcerned with the world and its trials.

Snapping grass blades warned of someone's arrival, and soon Morris joined him. "If you put any more weight on that pole, it will snap. Then I'll have to haul you to Guy, and he'll be mighty cross with you. He doesn't like it when fools injure themselves, especially when he already has a full clinic. And he'll really not be happy if he finds out you already hurt yourself."

Denton spared a glance at his raw knuckles. How was he to know punching someone hurt more than the tales let on? And how was he to know he'd have to climb a tower—a cursed tower—in the rain?

Intelligence was in short supply in this land.

First, they converged upon an area without checking every nook and cranny. The tower, built into the side of a cliff, had few handholds and fewer steps. How the children were ushered within mystified Denton, because he could barely climb, and he was in better shape than most of the children.

Then he had to scale back down the tower with a child strapped to his back. Four others joined him on the tower's slippery side, the chief's son being one of them. Why Denton was selected, he had no idea. The other men were stronger and able to partake in such an activity without their arms feeling like they were falling off.

Then the fighting. Talart had thrust a weapon at him, but a knife was hardly sufficient when it came to engaging addlebrained monsters. The mud hadn't helped.

Yes, Marterises possessed little to no intelligence.

Morris tapped his fingers against the wood, the cadence drawing Denton back to the unfortunate present. "Have they told you anything about your horse or the boy you're looking for?"

"No."

"I know where your horse is."

Denton spun. Thrill threatened to course through him, but he fought it. He couldn't give these people anything to use against him, and who knew what they would do to Cinders if they discovered how much she meant to him? Tamping down his elation, he asked, "Where?"

"Before I answer that, I want some answers." Morris' eyes—the same green-gray as the blonde-haired young woman who looked at Denton like he was a varmint to be avoided at all costs—hardened. "Where did the scars come from?"

Denton relayed the story of where Carter found Cinders. "I ended up being the one to work with her and she just…became mine."

Morris' eye twitched. "What about your own scars? Guy said you have a wicked one on your side and on your upper thigh."

Denton ground his teeth as he pinned his attention on the nearest horse. When he came face-to-face with the traffickers last night, he'd froze, fully expecting another arrow to embed itself in him. His limbs still trembled from the effort of staying upright when all he'd wanted to do was give in to the lightheadedness making everything spin.

Helping others required so much effort. Perhaps Father was right when he said no one was worth it.

No. That was what Father and Antony wanted him to believe.

Others were worth it. The children were worth it. The suffering families were worth it. Earning the Beginning's favor was worth it.

"Well?"

"I wasn't paying attention during a rescue mission."

Morris grunted. "Tell me more about yourself. Not the detective part, but about the boy behind the title. You seem to love horses. Does the rest of your family share that trait?"

The taste in Denton's mouth soured. "My stepbrother is a farrier by trade."

"What about your parents?"

Had Stepmother liked horses? Or had Carter's father been the one to pass that love onto his son? "My father only saw them as a steady source of income."

"How old are you, lad?" Morris' tone softened.

"No disrespect meant, sir, but why is my age relevant?"

"Malarky. Just tell an old man, will you?"

Morris could hardly be considered *old*. Likely in his mid-forties, he stood shorter than Denton but taller than Guy. Gray lightly streaked his blond hair and full beard. And, though he was slighter in stature, Denton reckoned Morris could take on any Veerham noble and win.

Without breaking a sweat.

"I'm twenty-three."

"Ner's age, then." Morris grunted and stood straight, cracking his back and neck before releasing a sharp, deafening whistle.

Denton grimaced and rubbed his aching ears, but his motions slowed as a small herd of horses thundered over the pasture's crest.

The day always took a better turn when he was able to see the Beginning's most glorious creatures.

His breath caught as a familiar equine pulled ahead of the others. Cinders was neither the fastest nor sleekest horse, but right then, she galloped faster than a thoroughbred and looked showier than an akhal-teke.

When the herd slowed, Denton slipped through the fence and jogged toward Cinders. His mare trotted to him and nudged his shoulder with her nose.

Denton couldn't withhold his broken sob as he buried his face in her neck. Cinders was the only thing that remained of his former home, and right then, she was the only normalcy he had.

Cinders whickered and nibbled at his shirt.

Closing his eyes, Denton grit his teeth to hold back the tears. It was unmanly to cry, and he had no reason to shame himself in such a way.

"You're an embarrassment. No wonder Father wishes you had died instead of Mother."

Antony hadn't held back while voicing his opinions. Opinions Father shared.

Well, they were now dead, and the only person Denton could embarrass was himself. Cinders certainly didn't care.

Pressure expanded through his chest and a pounding ache rooted just beneath his skull. Why must emotions exist? They did nothing but cause pain and inconvenience.

When he finally lifted his face, the shadows stretched longer and a slight chill sent a shiver up his spine.

Dragging his sleeve across his eyes, Denton blinked himself back into reality. The birds still sang, the breeze still rustled the grass, and the horses continued to graze.

His stomach dropped when he turned. Morris still stood there, arms crossed and expression thoughtful.

Of all the weaknesses to show.

"Come, lad. Let's see if they need help with the victims."

Morris said nothing else, but the man wasn't blind. Denton knew he saw his blotchy face.

His steps slowed as fatigue smacked him. What he wouldn't give for a good night's rest in his own bed, in his own home, in his own kingdom.

But out of those three, he only had one.

And there was no place in Veerham for him.

The path from Morris' cabin to the village cut through a copse of towering pine trees. Pine and salt scented the air.

Denton willed his legs to continue moving. His gut churned as they neared the village. Voices rose in laughter and calls. The people sounded *happy.*

Happiness had long eluded him.

"We always are on guard after a rescue," Morris said. His brow furrowed as he stared at where breaks in the trees showed patches of sand. "Evil doesn't like being upended."

The rest of the walk passed without another word. Denton's chest tightened when the path led them to the beach. His legs stalled and he found no necessity to will them to work.

How could these people be so calm—even exuberant—about the shore? About the sea? Didn't they know it was murder in water form? Didn't they know how easily one could die—drown—in its depths?

"Come along, lad."

One minute Morris looked at him like Denton was planning on setting the village ablaze, then the next he was being affable. What changed? Why?

"You can't trust commoners. They're filthy, vile, and lazy."

How ironic. Father had embraced the traits he thought only applied to those beneath him.

"Come on, Denton."

"Come on, Denton."

Red had said that phrase numerous times while pleading for him to stand up for and protect Carter.

Just another area Denton failed in.

No, he was fine right where he was, and if Morris didn't like that, then he could call Lemuel and the chief and have them try to drag Denton closer to the destructive waves.

But he wouldn't go without a fight.

"They won't hurt you."

Denton's attention snapped from the unending expanse of water to a young girl who had somehow crept up on him. Wisps of light brown hair floated about her face and sand and grass stains decorated her plain pink dress.

She looked vaguely familiar, but Denton couldn't place why.

The girl tipped her head to the right. "The sea won't hurt you if you don't go too far out or get caught in the tide."

What was he supposed to say? Admit to a *child* that she was right?

"Elberta." Nerissa materialized behind the girl and placed her hands on the child's shoulders.

Just what was with these Marterises? How were they able to move so quickly and quietly?

Denton held himself still and silent as wariness flashed through Nerissa's eyes. Even though Edver presented a friendlier demeanor, something about Nerissa put him at ease. Perhaps it was her gentle eyes, the way she cared about others, or how she interacted with her sisters.

He turned and scanned the scene before him. A ramshackle hut slouched near the waterline. A short wall of rock, topped with pines, rose beyond it. Villagers of all ages played on the shore, though the majority were children under twelve.

A shift of movement at the edge of the area snagged his gaze. A young lad sat, arms around his knees, watching the ongoings. With black hair and pale skin, he certainly wasn't a Marterisi.

He vaguely recalled the boy and the fear in those brilliantly-hued eyes.

"Has he told you anything?" Denton nodded toward the child.

Nerissa's lips pursed as she eyed him. After a long stretch, she finally answered. "Yes. Noko is from Halthdurn. He refuses to tell me his story."

"Is there a dog a villager could lend him?"

Elberta huffed and scowled at Nerissa. "Don't even bother. Daffy and I have pleaded for a puppy for years and Nerissa always argues against us."

Nerissa sighed. "As our parents have said time and again, you and Daffy must learn responsibility before you get a puppy."

"I'm plenty responsible."

"You still forget to take off your shoes when you get in bed, and now's not the time to discuss your penchant toward stretching the truth."

"I'm busy and don't think about removing my shoes." Elberta lifted her chin. "Besides, I need to show Marteris how to *really* name a dog. The rest of you are terrible at naming animals."

Amusement flickered across Nerissa's expression. "You wanted to name a horse *Magpie*."

"That's a perfect name."

Nerissa shook her head and glanced at Denton. "That horse already has a name."

"Which is?"

"Cinders."

Denton recoiled. Magpie? For *Cinders*?

Nerissa gave her sister an exasperated look before turning her toward the buildings. "Go find Mamma and see how you can help her."

Elberta scowled. "I'll get stuck helping Daffy with her chores. That is not a wise use of my time."

"Then you get stuck helping Daffy. It was not that long ago that *you* required assistance." Giving her sister a gentle push, Nerissa sighed. "Go, Elberta. Please cease dawdling."

Muttering beneath her breath, Elberta stomped away.

"Why are you smiling?"

He'd been smiling? Denton snapped his attention toward Nerissa. He forced himself to speak as his amusement drained away. "She reminds me of someone."

"Who?"

Why must her tone be sharper than Federigo's scalpel? "Red."

"The royal detective?"

"Yes. She can put anyone in their place and I don't recommend ever engaging in a sarcasm war with her, because she'll win. Every time."

"How is it you know her so well?"

Denton exhaled and leaned against a nearby tree. The sharp scent of sap burned his nose, but that meant he was alive, and aside from pain, he welcomed every reminder that he still drew breath. "She's my stepbrother's best friend and I helped her with a mission."

"A mission for what?"

Horses and horseshoes. Must everything turn into an interrogation? "It was a rescue mission. Now, is there a villager with a dog to spare?"

Nerissa's eyes narrowed, but she accepted the bait for a topic switch. "I'll ask Uncle Morris. He would know."

Just Denton's luck that Morris would be her relative.

By then, Morris had made his way to where the chief and an older man stood near the shack. Ignoring everyone else, Denton wove through the crowd of children and made his way to Noko.

Eyes the color of bright turquoise trained on him before Noko froze.

Denton eased to the ground and ignored the tremulous thumping of his heart. He was so close to the waves—definitely close enough that a massive swell could drag him into the bottomless sea.

You know nothing. How could you possibly help? Father's derision was ever present.

False. Right? Denton interacted with Lycus and Ruid—much to Red's dismay and disapproval—when the king and queen hired the wolfmen to hunt down the traffickers. Something told him all Halthdurnites were taciturn, but surely a child would be easier to converse with than adults.

A quick scan catalogued the visible bruises on the boy's arms and neck. The dormant sparks in Denton's gut flamed into an inferno. No child deserved to be harmed, and may the Beginning have mercy on the souls of those who injured children, because he certainly wouldn't.

"I think collies are my favorite type of dog. What is yours?"

Noko side-eyed Denton like he was a few horseshoes shy of a full set.

Denton forced a laidback grin, though his facial muscles protested. "Unless you prefer cats? I'm not too fond of them myself. Personally, I don't care to suffer from heart failure because I turn around and see their glowing eyes glaring at me from the shadows."

Noko's mouth tipped upward.

"Or maybe you prefer parrots? I heard they're considered the pet to have if you live in Frilore's lower regions."

A snubbed nose scrunched.

Denton inspected a healing scab on his knuckle. "I even heard some kids like keeping squirrels as pets. Between you and me, my stepmother never would have allowed that, but the concept is intriguing." He glanced at Noko, and something in his chest warmed at the sight of the slightest twinkle in the lad's eyes. "Don't tell me you have a pet squirrel."

Noko huffed a chuckle. "No, Ma wouldn't like that."

"Do you have a mouse, then?"

"Ew. No. Ma hates them."

"What about a kitten? Or a tiger?"

"We have a mouser." Noko rubbed his nose. "But she don't have a name. I don't know what a tiger is."

Denton reclined on his elbows. "So, if you don't have a mouse, squirrel, or a cat with a name, what type of pet *do* you have? A fish?"

Noko shook his head. "I eat fish."

Kid's tastebuds were wonky, but Denton wouldn't say that. "Then do you have a bird?"

"I eat those too." Noko scratched his shoulder. "I have a lab. I'm not old enough for a wolf yet, but Pa says soon." A wave of darkness dulled his expression.

Denton shifted and leaned his elbows on his knees. "Aren't you allowed a wolf when you do an act of bravery?"

Thin shoulders shrugged.

He nudged Noko's arm. "Then you should get a wolf. Enduring what you have is one of the bravest things a man can do."

Watery eyes met his. "I'm not a man, though. I'm just a boy."

"A boy would be screaming and be unable to keep a clear mind. From what I heard, you were able to help a fellow captive from the boats, then keep everyone together on the shore." Denton waited to continue until Noko looked at him. "That's being a man. Helping others even when you're scared."

"I'm really scared," Noko whispered.

"And I'd be concerned if you weren't. But you kept your calm and even managed to help. That's not only brave, that's heroic."

A shadow flitted across them, and Denton looked up to only to catch a wary expression from the chief, who then ignored him as he knelt before Noko. "How are you doing, lad?"

Noko recoiled.

Denton rose, forcing the chief to take a few steps back. Offering his hand to Noko, he scanned the shore. This village exuded happiness. Why? They witnessed suffering whenever they rescued victims. They risked losing their own at the very worst and sustaining injuries at the very least. Due to their desire to help others, they put themselves at risk.

But they didn't care. They were still prepared to sacrifice themselves.

"Yindell." The chief's deep voice rumbled like the warning of thunder just before a terrible storm. "A word, please."

Denton shot Noko a reassuring smile and followed the mountain of a chief to a secluded area. His skin prickled. It would be so easy for the man to smash his skull in then either hide his body or throw it into the sea.

Chief Talart crossed his arms as something frosty entered his bloodshot eyes. "You agreed to help rescue the victims, yet you went beyond and kept my son from dying. Why?"

Why? Did Denton *look* like a cold-blooded killer? Did he ooze malice like Father and Antony had? Did his eyes hold the same cruelty as the kidnappers' and traffickers'?

He convinced his teeth to unclench. "What kind of man would I be if I stood by and did nothing to help those harmed by evil? I'd be just as bad as the enemy. And I can't sit back and do nothing."

The words tasted foreign. When was the last time he willingly helped others with no thought of his own gain? The Yindells were not known for their philanthropy or kindness.

"You're different from your father and brother."

Red had spoken the words begrudgingly, like she hadn't wanted to believe them.

One of Parson Gil's sermons revisited. *"The Scripts call us to seek justice, love mercy, and walk humbly. That means we must fight for those who cannot fight for themselves."*

He couldn't stand by and do nothing. He couldn't willingly allow children to be taken into a life of slavery. He may be many things, but he refused to idly watch evil be unleashed upon children.

Chief Talart tilted his head. No emotion claimed his neutral expression. "Do not make me regret allowing you into my village, Yindell."

"Don't make me regret not getting rid of you at birth, you worthless wimp."

Denton ground his teeth and lifted his chin. No external weakness allowed. "You don't need to worry."

"See that I don't."

And with that, Chief Talart strode away.

Denton sagged against a tree and ran a hand down his face. The appendage trembled with the same terror infusing his heart and pumping through his veins. He needed to escape and flee. That was the safest option.

But that would make him a coward. That would make him just like Father.

CHAPTER EIGHT

NERISSA

GRASS AND WEEDS SNAGGED at Nerissa's skirt's hem as she approached the cabin she'd visited more times than she could count. Pine trees framed the clearing while the cabin and two other structures—a well and a shed—dotted the area. To the cabin's left, an expansive garden burst with the beginning blooms of numerous plants.

The door opened before she could knock, and Kanni's hoary-haired head poked out. "Come in, dearie. Come in."

Nerissa offered the old woman a smile as she crossed the threshold. The fresh scent of baking onion rolls tempted her stomach to grumble, but if she allowed that to happen, Kanni would insist on feeding her.

"Lloyd, Nerissa is here."

"I heard." Kanni's husband stood and grinned at Nerissa. Winkles formed a fine network around his eyes and mouth and his dark skin made what little hair he had left look all the grayer. "How fares your day, young one?"

"It goes well, thank you. And yours?" It wasn't hard to smile around the sweet couple. They exuded love and exhibited their faith in everything. They were practically the village's grand-parents.

"Oh, fair, fair. What brings you here?"

Nerissa held up the basket. "And I need to see Jonah."

Kanni ambled about the kitchen. "Lloyd knows where he is. Last I saw, the child was to be weeding the garden."

Lloyd chuckled. "He's infatuated with the leatherwork. I bet you an onion roll I'll find him in the shed."

"You'll already receive an onion roll, you old coot." Kanni shooed Lloyd from the cabin, laughing and shaking her head as she closed the door behind him.

Nerissa smothered the whisper of longing that arose. What would it be like to have a marriage like her parents' and Kanni and Lloyd's?

But all of the men her age were either already betrothed or those she couldn't imagine ever joining with in matrimony.

Lloyd soon returned, and with a shout, the redheaded child beside him dropped an armful of kindling and sprinted toward Nerissa.

She smoothed Jonah's flyaway hair as he clung to her. Every rescued child tugged at her heart, but Jonah had wormed his way in and brought out every bit of her protective instincts. "How are you?" she murmured.

"I'm okay. Kanni and Lloyd are still nice."

Nerissa's heart threatened to shatter. Jonah had been rescued four months ago, and still the child struggled with believing everyone would eventually hurt him.

If only she was a warrior like Father and Edver. Then she would hunt down those who forever broke his ability to trust and give them just what they deserved.

"And they will continue being nice. They are a good couple, Jonah. Nothing like those monsters who harmed you."

Blue eyes, so wide with childlike wonder yet ancient and weary beyond his years, teared up. "Promises can be broken, though. I was told I would never be kidnapped again, and look what happened."

Nerissa bit her lip as tears stung her eyes. Was Denton Yindell part of those who fostered Jonah's unending mistrust? Had the outsider harmed Jonah in some way?

Best not to ask the child about the unwanted, temporary inhabitant, though. Things had to be taken slowly with Jonah else she risked frightening him back into the silence he'd recently broken free from.

"Is something wrong? Did Elberta get caught sneaking banana bread again?" Wistfulness claimed Jonah's freckled face. "I got in trouble once for filching some of Ma's cookies. I know I shouldn't have, but they were gingersnap and she makes the *best* cookies."

Nerissa attempted to laugh. "No, Elberta is currently free from any punishments brought about by misbehavior. I am here to deliver these." And check on the boy, but she didn't know how he'd react to hearing that.

Jonah gasped when he dug into the basket. "Banana muffins with glaze!"

"Yes."

"May I have one, Mrs. Kanni? Please?"

Kanni laughed. "I suppose. Just one, though, else you'll destroy your appetite for supper."

"There's no way that can happen, ma'am. Ma says I'm a bottomless pit."

As Jonah dug into the muffin, Nerissa's eyes met Kanni's. The woman clasped her hands beneath her chin and watched the boy with a heartbreaking expression. Lloyd joined her, placing an arm around her shoulders.

Only the Beginning could heal a wounded soul.

Nerissa just prayed it was in His plan to do so. Jonah did not deserve to struggle with such trauma for the rest of his life.

Voices chattered and dishes clanged as supper commenced. Banana bread, salad, and breaded fish filets were passed around and jovial conversation enveloped the participants.

Well, all but one.

Nerissa eyed the outsider as she forked a piece of banana bread. He stared at the plate, which held one small square of the delicacy. He was far from Edver's size, but neither was he frail and skinny. He needed more than a few crumbs to sustain him.

Yet he took not one bite.

Perhaps Veerhamers embraced snobbery over good manners.

Uncle Morris sat to the outsider's right. He hadn't said anything negative about the supposed royal detective, and Nerissa dared think Uncle Morris' tone turned *fond* while discussing the young man.

Heaven forbid.

Uncle Morris was supposed to be smarter than that. He knew what happened last time they allowed an outsider into their midst.

Her stomach twisted and turned with dangerous turbulence. Nausea wasn't a stranger when her chest tightened and her throat constricted. Nor could she ever eat much when her mind escorted her to perilous thoughts and dark places.

She could still lose her family. Still lose her friends and village.

A whisper of a laugh snagged Nerissa's attention toward her left. Edver and the young woman Lemuel rescued sat side by side. Wide, luminous eyes accompanied a sweet smile, but the woman, who wrote that her name was *Afya*, refused to say one word.

Nerissa's heart leapt from her chest as a crash silenced the conversation. Daffy blinked from where she sat between Mamma and Jilin, Chief Talart's wife. Bottom lip quivering, Daffy sniffled as Mamma took one look and gasped.

Craning her head, Nerissa sighted the ocean of gravy that had previously taken residence in the dish that now lay scattered about the floor.

Daffy wailed.

Mamma sighed and stood, picking Daffy up. "Hush, now, darling. Everything is fine."

Movement in Nerissa's peripheral redirected her attention. The outsider stared at Mamma, expression hard and eyes harder as he then glanced at those around the table. His hand hovered near his left hip and he half-stood, his other hand clutching the table with such ferocity his knuckles were white.

Sparing one more peek at the outsider, Nerissa fetched cleaning supplies as Mamma whisked Daffy away to help her change.

"It's alright, lad. Daffy is fine."

Why did Uncle Morris pronounce his words with added clarity and emphasis? Anyone with a quarter of an eye could tell Daffy sustained no injuries.

The outsider remained stiff and unapproachable throughout the meal's duration, even when Daffy returned with fresh clothing and an appetite to rival a shark's.

After few crumbs remained and the littles were put to bed, Nerissa cornered Uncle Morris when he took a quick break to check on a mare close to foaling.

Uncle Morris rested his arms on the stall door's edge. "What's going on in that mind of yours?"

"Do you trust the outsider?" The words spilled from Nerissa without hesitation.

"If you're asking if I trust Denton Yindell, then the answer is I'm beginning to."

"Why?" Oh, how she wanted her fretting to be for naught. But one had an intuition for a reason.

Uncle Morris ran his fingers through his bushy beard. "He wasn't the one who harmed Cinders. I know because I watched them reunite." He shook his head. "A man who hurts animals doesn't cry when he again meets his favorite animal."

"What do you mean?"

Uncle Morris answered with a levelling look. "I'm not telling you this so you can hold it against him or think him weak and unmanly, but that boy cried—honest-to-goodness sobbed—when I allowed him to see Cinders for the first time. Denton has a past, and I don't think it's all sunshine and roses."

Nerissa located a nail and began picking. "You don't think he's planning to destroy the village or is working for the enemy, do you?"

"No. You didn't hear him with Noko. That level of concern can't be faked." Uncle Morris fully faced her. "Ner, there's a difference between worry and your sixth sense."

A lump rose in her throat. "I know."

After studying her for what felt like an hour, Uncle Morris finally nodded. "Well, I'll let you return home. I heard your ma put in another loaf of banana bread to bake, and I don't know about you, but I can't get enough of that." He patted his belly.

Managing a wobbly smile, Nerissa bade him farewell and hastened back home.

Uncle Morris was intelligent in many areas, but he could well be wrong about the outsider.

Just because everyone else was softening toward the man didn't mean she had to.

She couldn't. She couldn't risk putting her family in harm's way.

It was never a good thing when three different chiefs and their warriors converged upon Nerissa's village. Nor was it a good thing when they came decked in more weapons than usual. With war paint. And expressions so grim one would think a great calamity was upon them.

No amount of praying could quell the nausea constantly churning as Nerissa finished four more loaves of bread and a few pans of biscuits. Not even helping Daffy search for eggs so they could make banana bread eased the tide of fear thrumming through her.

The last time such a meeting occurred, it had been about a potentially-hostile village. The time before that, it'd been to interrogate the outsider who tried poisoning them all. Even the babies.

The Beginning had been gracious enough to turn aside the attack, but would He extend his grace to keep her people safe once again?

"Everything will be fine, Nerissa." Mamma wrapped a loaf of banana bread in a clean cloth and handed it over before gently brushing stray hair from Nerissa's face. "My dear girl, you must not always fret so. It will gain you nothing. Now, would you mind taking this to your uncle? A mare is foaling so he'll not be over tonight."

Nerissa managed a wobbly smile before setting off down the path. The breeze carried the sea's scent, and she allowed herself to stop, close her eyes, and inhale.

Just as the waves glided onto the shore before sliding back into their watery home, so did the sea course through her blood, pumping in time with her heart. Something about it made her feel *alive.* Sent energy trembling through her—energy that made her want to be brave and face the causes of her fear head-on. To never blink in the face of trial. To remain as stalwart and unflinching as the sea during a storm. To remain as inmovable as the cliffs as rain and frothing waves battered them.

She wanted to be brave and bold and strong.

But she wasn't.

Instead, shadows could send her skittering, and she put Uncle Morris' most skittish horses to shame.

A branch cracked, and her heart leapt to her throat as a thin yelp tore from her lungs.

Of course something would happen when she was unarmed.

Unless the attacker liked banana bread. Perhaps she could throw the loaf at it and escape as it snacked.

Heavy panting preceded the sway of underbrush and deep green fronds before Uncle Morris' dog emerged, pink tongue lolling and tail wagging.

Nerissa pressed a hand to her chest and sagged against the nearest tree. The sharp scents of pine and sap filled her nose. "Oh, thank the Beginning."

The dog yipped. While a sweet thing with soft, dark brown fur and floppy ears Daffy loved playing with, Uncle Morris never gave the canine a proper name.

Well, if he let it continually roam around and give innocent women heart failure, perhaps a change was necessary.

"I will name you Bluet." The pale purpley-blue flowers would go well against the dog's rich coat.

And, oh, Uncle Morris would not be happy his dog was named after a flower, but that was what happened when one neglected to name their faithful companion.

Hand on Bluet's head, Nerissa resumed walking. Bluet's tail continued wagging, the assurance of nothing amiss soothing over her like a balm to a wound.

Bluet barked as they neared the corral, where a man urged a red roan to a trot.

But it wasn't Uncle Morris.

The calmness evaporated, and Nerissa clenched her teeth. Where was her uncle? The barn doors were shut, so he wasn't in there. The cabin was closed up, too, and he always left the windows and door open.

"Easy, girl." The outsider slowed the mare to a walk, then a standstill. "Morris isn't here."

Did he think her eyes were in the back of her head and obscured by her hair? "I can see that."

"He said he'll be back in a while." The outsider squinted at the sky. "Whatever that means. He's been gone for a few hours."

Which meant he was in the village. Just lovely.

Nerissa inched toward the cabin's front steps and placed the banana bread down, keeping her attention on the outsider as she did so. He offered her a cursory glance before continuing training. Sweat marked his shirt, causing the fabric to cling due to the heavy mugginess infusing the air.

She sniffed. Salt, pine, and something else. The slight scent of a storm building just beyond the horizon. They'd receive rain by no later than tomorrow, by her reckoning, and like most Marterises, she was rarely incorrect in guessing the weather.

Snorting, the red roan tugged at the lead rope before sluggishly obeying the outsider's commands and easing into a trot. After a few rotations, she increased her speed to a canter.

The drumming of hooves and the smooth glide of the roan across the packed earth almost drew Nerissa into a lull. Some horses looked like they flew when they ran, their manes catching the wind just like flags and their carriage proud and noble.

She could admire the steeds from a distance, but only that.

A faint burn spread through her elbow, as though her body desired to remind her what happened the last time she really attempted to ride.

Broken bones were no fun, especially during the stormy season.

"Come on, Dancer. Stop fighting me." The outsider flicked the rope. "You know what that means. Slow it down."

Dancer kept cantering.

"Dancer…" When the horse again ignored him, the outsider tugged repeatedly on the rope until the stubborn equine listened.

"You're worse than Kline, and I thought that was impossible."

Dancer snorted.

"Or maybe you're just a mule in a horse's hide." The outsider shook his head and patted Dancer's nose. "I think that's what it is. You're just an ornery little rascal, aren't you?"

Nerissa paused inching toward the path when he looked her way and froze, blinking like a raccoon caught in the chicken feed.

Was it her imagination, or did he lose a few shades of color?

"Why are you training her?" The question left Nerissa before she comprehended the fact the words were forming.

He shrugged. "Morris asked me to."

"I watched them catch her. She doesn't take kindly to being removed from roaming the plains." A shudder crawled up her spine at the memory. This roan mare—Dancer—hadn't been pleased. Father received a chunk bitten from his arm and Edver had been thrown what looked like a league.

All Uncle Morris had done was rope the persnickety beast and gently lead her home. For his efforts, he received a horse with the most hostile personality Nerissa had ever witnessed.

The outsider shrugged. "They never do at first."

Why in all of Marteris would Uncle Morris ask this man to train the worst horse to step hoof on Uncle Morris' land? While Uncle Morris said something about the outsider having a knack with horses, surely he wasn't *that* good.

Watching the outsider stroke Dancer's neck, Nerissa was forced to reconsider. Perhaps he was.

He caught her eye once more. "You can come closer. She's past the kicking stage."

"I'll stay where it's safe."

His slight laugh lightened his countenance and removed the strain from his face.

He had a nice smile. How unexpected.

You are addlebrained, Nerissa Veri Wessen.

Truly addlebrained for noticing such a thing.

Nerissa cleared her throat and turned her back on the sight, scampering for the path as hastily as her skirts allowed.

"There's been a change in plan."

Nerissa loathed that term. She hated it even more when Chief Talart was the one breaking the news.

Even worse was the way the three other chiefs glanced at each other, like said change was all bad with not even a smidgen of good sprinkled in.

After the service ended, Chief Talart requested a handful of attendees remain behind. Now, arms crossed and stance wide, he stood at the front of the church, bearing his sword and a grim expression.

Her stomach dropped. The last time those words were uttered, Father almost lost his life rescuing victims.

Such a claim never boded well.

"We've received word that a village south of Chief Nadli's has been decimated. Those who weren't slain were taken as captives. We can assume those who attacked will use the women and children in the trafficking." Chief Talart exhaled and ran a hand over his beard. "We're scrapping the idea of retrieving children from Losibar. Instead, we will join with these three villages, plus Losibar, to rescue the victims."

Yald, the village's postmaster, shifted and sent a wary glance at the other chiefs. "No disrespect meant, Talart, but why have you summoned this particular bunch? Half of us are neither warriors nor fighters in any sense of the word."

Nerissa located a nail and began picking at its rough edge as other murmured agreement. Yald spoke true. The postmaster, Nerissa, Hauni, Afya, and four others were not warriors. Edver, who perched in the corner stuffing himself with banana bread, still wore a sling and would for some time. While he was a good swordsman, he wasn't experienced enough to fend off ill-willed ne'er-do-wells with one functioning arm.

"There's more."

If there was a phrase Nerissa despised to a greater depth than, "a change in plans", it was, "there's more".

That always meant more bad news. More fear to face. More worry to shoulder.

A glance was swapped amongst the chiefs before Chief Talart continued. "We have reason to believe Keller is involved in these attacks."

The breath left Nerissa, leaving her lungs struggling and empty. *Too close.* Keller was too close to home. Too close to her sisters and family. So close that, if they desired to wrought war and devastation, it wouldn't be difficult for them to do so.

Please, Beginning, spare us.

"You all were asked to this meeting for a reason. In such a rescue endeavor, we need more than warriors. We need wagon drivers, physicians, and those to tend to the children."

The words sank through Nerissa like an anchor through water, yet instead of water, they cut through a dense fog of premonition that only worsened as the meeting continued.

Twenty minutes later, a plan was in place.

And Nerissa bolted outside so she could expel the contents of her stomach in private.

She couldn't do it. Couldn't help with the rescue. She was just…herself. Average in everything except fretting and fussing. In those she was a master.

She drew a shaky breath as a hand rubbed her shoulder. Father's eyes, the same sea-blue as Daffy's and Elberta's, scanned her face before he frowned.

Nerissa hiccoughed a sob.

Father's sympathetic smile did not help. "Come here, Ner."

One sob turned into five, and five into fifty as she cried on Father's shoulder. What if she returned and he was dead? What if Mamma and the girls had been kidnapped? What would she do if the village was ransacked and burned down?

Beginning, I can't do this. Please don't make me do this.

"You are stronger than you think." Father patted her head. "Talart wouldn't have selected you if he did not trust you wouldn't do a good job."

"I have no special skills. Edver is still in a sling. Hauni and I are mediocre at best with weapons. There's no protection. We're decent hunters and fishermen, but what if something happens to us? The children will be lost and helpless." Bile burned her throat at the thought of transporting a third of the victims.

Father chuckled. "You're acting like we're preparing for an invasion. This is a rescue attempt. The scouts have reassured us there are only a handful of guards. You know there's little reason to fear."

Nerissa pressed the heels of her palms against her eyes. She was making a fool of herself, but no one else saw the danger in this plan, so she must bring it to light.

Father placed an arm around her shoulders. "I have confidence in you. Your mother and Talart have faith in you. You can do this."

"This is a mistake."

"Look at me, Nerissa Veri Wessen."

At the stern shift in Father's tone, Nerissa looked up. Blond brows shot with gray lowered over his eyes and he wore his famous Wessen glower.

"You've let fear rule you for far too long. You are more capable than you think. You are smarter than you believe. And you are needed on this journey. Edver would walk off a cliff if he wasn't paying attention. Hauni is getting along in years and is only there for medical purposes, and Afya doesn't speak. You're needed."

Nerissa hugged herself and stared at the ground. Shoots of grass bravely grew along the well-tread path, and pine cones and pine needles littered the dirt, interspersing with tree roots. Father was wrong. He meant well, but he was wrong.

She offered a brittle smile. "Yes, sir. May I be excused?"

Father's eyes softened. "I know you can do this, Nerri. Yes, you're excused."

Nerves more tangled than thread rescued from Daffy's clutches, Nerissa paced outside the Talart cabin. Male voices rose from within, carrying through the open window and accompanying the sweet scent of Mrs. Talart's famous cookies.

"If I help with this relocation, will you tell me where Jonah is?"

"Why would you think we know where he is?"

"Because I know the signs of withheld knowledge."

A growl deepened Chief Talart's voice. "How would you be of any help? You know neither our land nor terrain, you're terrified of the water, and you're little more than a potential enemy to our allies."

"I—"

"What would you give to find Jonah?"

"Anything." The outsider's words hardened. "I would give any-thing."

"Even your horse?"

Not even a pause before, "Yes."

Silence permeated the air for several minutes before Chief spoke. "I will make you a deal. Your sword for information about Jonah. You will defend the group at any cost. In exchange, I will tell you everything I know about the boy. Is that acceptable?"

"Yes, sir."

Chief grunted.

Nerissa jumped as the door opened.

"Just the girl I wanted to see. Come in, Nerri."

Feet heavy as bricks, she obeyed.

The Talart cabin boasted the typical furnishings—a table and chairs, a kitchen, two rocking chairs, a few cabinets, and a bookcase. Crisp curtains adorned the windows while weapons decorated the far wall.

The outsider stood near the fireplace, fingers clenching and unclenching. His clothing had been returned to him, and he looked far better in clothes that fit instead of Edver's, which swam on his shorter frame. His gouge was fading to a scar and his color was better, but fatigue still lined his face.

She resisted the urge to study his face and see if she located any indication that this was one of the men who hurt Jonah.

"Nerissa, Yindell is going to help Edver protect the group. Yindell, you better do what Edver says and only what Edver says. Any backtalk or problem-causing will result in the negation of our agreement. Understood?"

The outsider nodded.

"Nerissa will also brief you on what's going on. She can do that while you all are riding. The journey begins in a week. Is that understood?"

Another nod.

At Chief's gesture, the outsider left.

Mrs. Talart emerged from Chief's office as the door slammed shut. She offered Nerissa a wink as she withdrew the cookies, ignoring Chief as he all but salivated.

"Wait until they cool, dear."

"I don't know if I can wait that long." Chief gazed longingly at the delicacies.

Nerissa resisted a smile. The way to Chief's heart was, indeed, through his stomach.

Finally, he shook his head and tore his gaze away. "What can I help you with?"

She took a deep breath that did nothing to settle her stomach. "I can't go on the mission."

"Why not? You're not ill, are you? You're walking fine so I assume you haven't injured your ankle." Chief scowled. "Don't tell me Daffy ate too much sugar again."

That particular episode would forever be in the village's Tome of Infamy. "No, sir. I...it's not that."

"Well, then? What is it?"

Mrs. Talart looked up from where she chopped lettuce. "Be nice," she warned.

"I am, dear." Chief motioned to Nerissa. "Well? I need you to answer, Ner."

"I can't go," she rushed. "I...I'm hopeless at things like this. I need to stay here." To protect her family. To help Mamma in case Father got injured.

Chief opened his mouth, but when Mrs. Talart raised her hand, he snapped it shut.

Mrs. Talart took Nerissa's hands in her own. Flour dusted her dark face and her large, deep-brown eyes held perpetual kindness. "What my husband is trying to say is you need to go because you bring something unique. You keep Edver from being too cocky, you can speak whfere Afya won't, and you have enough medical knowledge to assist Hauni." She patted Nerissa's cheek. "They need you, dearest Nerri."

Sure. About as much as she needed a broken toe.

"Please stop underestimating yourself, dear."

Mumbling a promise that really wasn't a promise, Nerissa excused herself and fled.

Fresh, salty air dragged her toward her favorite spot overlooking the ocean.

The waves rebounded off the cliff, white-capped and foaming. Tall weeds and grasses caught at her skirt's hem as they quivered in the breeze coming off the sea. Dark clouds gathered on the horizon, a premonition of storms to come.

Nerissa closed her eyes and inhaled. Why couldn't she find peace? Why must worry hound her every step and heartbeat?

"Peace I give to you..."

The verse, one of her favorites in all the Scripts, repeated through her mind. Still, nothing settled her uneasy spirit.

"Let not your hearts be troubled..."

She tried. She really did. But it was just so impossible.

Exhaling, Nerissa turned to go home. Perhaps chores would remove her attention from the upcoming task.

An empty cabin greeted her when she finally reached home. The faint scent of breakfast lingered in the air, but the windows were closed, the back door locked, and no shoes were in their designated areas by the front entrance.

Nerissa's heart pounded against her chest with unequaled ferocity. Mamma and Father had mentioned something about going out, but Elberta and Daffy were to remain at home and focus on their schoolwork. Mamma even made extra banana bread to bribe them into long-lasting obedience, something the girls hadn't quite grasped yet.

An ashy taste in her mouth, Nerissa bolted to the back and called her sisters' names.

Only birds and cicadas answered.

No. No, no. Please, Beginning, do not let it be so.

Her sisters had disappeared.

Fingers turning icy, Nerissa locked the front door then flew down the path leading to Uncle Morris'. The silent pine trees and the twittering birds mocked the maelstrom of worry and apprehension welling in her chest.

Her prayer became a chant, matching the rhythm of her feet against the hard, packed earth. The surroundings blurred into a mixture of pine-green, brown, and gray.

Uncle Morris' booming laugh barely broke through the haze miring her thoughts.

Nerissa pulled in an unsteady, shallow breath. "Uncle Morris!"

She followed his hollered response. Sounds of faint giggles reached her ears as she approached. Surely that wasn't…no, it couldn't be. Best not dredge up any hope lest it was dashed and her heart splinter with disappointment.

Nerissa's heart plummeted then soared as the far pasture came into view. Uncle Morris leaned on one of the vertical rails comprising the corral where he usually put troublesome horses. Elberta stood beside him, doing her best to copy his stance despite being incredibly shorter.

And there, on the back of Cinders, perched Daffy.

Nerissa pursed her lips and clenched her hands. The outsider had Cinders on a lunge line and walking in a circle.

What in all of Marteris was *wrong* with Uncle Morris? How could he allow Daffy anywhere *near* a horse they knew little about?

Gathering her skirts, Nerissa stomped toward her kin.

Her temper rarely made an appearance, but it was high time she unleashed her tempest-like wrath upon her unsuspecting—and quite addlebrained—relative.

Uncle Morris shot her a smirk as she stormed toward him, having the audacity to not once look concerned.

"What are you doing?"

Uncle Morris combed his fingers through his beard. "I'm just standing here, Nerri."

"That's not what I meant. Why are you allowing Daffy's life to be at risk?"

"What do you mean?" Uncle Morris gestured to the horse. "Cinders is as trained as a horse can be and Denton is an expert horseman."

"Who told you that?"

"I witnessed it. Lad knows what he's about." Uncle Morris sighed. "Look, Nerri. Daffy is as safe as can be. Cinders is a calm horse and Denton and I both have the situation under control."

There wouldn't be a situation if Uncle Morris didn't insist on endangering Daffy.

Nerissa clenched her teeth to keep from spouting disrespect. The outsider could not be trusted. Cinders looked like a nice mare, but any animal could snap without warning.

Daffy squealed.

Nerissa's heart nearly left her chest when Cinders' ears twitched.

The outsider laughed as he halted Cinders and lifted Daffy from her back. His smile eased the weariness embedded in his countenance.

Nerissa scowled. He was an outsider—a potential enemy. He wasn't allowed to have a nice smile.

"Did you see me, Nerri? I rode a horse." Daffy sprinted over, ignoring the outsider's warning to walk, and tugged on Nerissa's skirt. "Did you see?"

"I saw." Nerissa transferred her consternation to the outsider, but he conveniently had his back turned as he untangled a knot in Cinders' mane.

"Come, now, Nerri, Daffy is fine, Elberta is as ornery as ever, and your parents are on a picnic. Stop glaring holes into the man's back and looking like you're willing him to spontaneously combust."

Inhaling through clenched teeth, Nerissa grasped her sisters' hands. "We are going home, and there we shall stay until you two finish your homework."

Elberta pooched out her bottom lip. "That was boring."

"Boring or not, that's where we're going."

Ignoring Uncle Morris and the outsider, Nerissa swept her sisters away, paying no heed to their protests.

Her lungs fought to draw in ragged breaths as she slammed the front door shut after ushering the troublemakers inside.

Please, Beginning, help me learn to trust in You.

For her need to control where her sisters were was likely just that—a lack of faith and trust.

Please keep them safe. Please keep my parents from harm. And please keep anyone with hostile intent from attacking the village.

CHAPTER NINE

DENTON

"PEASANTS ARE BENEATH US and are merely a waste of time." Antony's disdain for those he deemed of less worth than his oh-so-important self remained attached to Denton's memory long after he first heard the oft-mentioned quote.

What would his father and brother say if they knew he rode beside those they'd deem *peasants*?

He cringed. It didn't take much guessing or imagination. Father would spew a litany of profanities and Antony would sneer at Denton's ineptitude and worthlessness before throwing in a few choice words of his own.

Denton would be declared hopeless, an embarrassment, and a stain on the family name.

He scanned those around him. According to the plan, he would join Nerissa, Edver, Hauni, Afya, and three soldiers from another village and take a longer route to where the captives were being held. There they'd help extract the victims and take them to Or-ryth.

What the plan hadn't accounted for was Noko.

As Denton prepared to mount and the group readied to ride out, Noko had burst from Lemuel's cabin, squawking unintelligible words and skinny arms waving. A small pack had bounced against the boy's back and he gave no heed to the stones beneath his feet as he flew over the sandy terrain.

"Don't leave me."

Denton's throat closed. While he had never been physically left behind, the emotional and mental abandonment by Father and

Antony had driven a shard in his heart, and that was nothing compared to what Noko endured.

How could he refuse?

Still, his heart felt as heavy as a thousand cliffs. He'd promised to save Jonah, to never let anyone harm the lad, and he failed. Would the same happen to Noko? Or was this an opportunity to redeem himself?

A child wasn't safe near a fight, and while he could defend himself, he wasn't good enough to protect Noko too.

Father and Antony were wrong in many things, yet in one they were completely correct—Denton was a failure in every way. He would only cause Noko more hurt. It was inevitable.

What did he know of protection? Everyone he'd tried to safeguard always ended up wounded or kidnapped.

And now Noko sat next to him on a stalwart dun trained by Morris.

Beginning, please help me. The prayer fumbled in his mind. Was it acceptable to pray for oneself? Best not risk it. *Please keep Noko safe on this journey. Please don't let harm befall this group.*

"Be safe."

Mrs. Wessen's concern drew Denton's attention back to Nerissa, who clutched her mother's hand.

A pit opened in his gut. What would it be like to be cared about? Worried over?

After final instructions from Talart, the burliest soldier waved his hand and commanded they be off.

Cinders bobbed her head as Denton guided her behind Nerissa's horse and next to Noko's. It felt good being in the saddle—the one place he belonged.

Once they crested the road leading past the village, Nerissa twisted in the saddle and stared over her shoulder. The longing in her gaze almost drew Denton to her side. If only he could offer some form of hope that she'd return. That the mission would go as planned.

But he couldn't, because life never went according to plan.

"What happens if the olcs recognize me?"

"The what?"

Noko stared at Denton with eyes surpassing the width of the pastry platters the king and queen used. "The *olcs*. The bad guys."

Denton swallowed. Here he went, about to make another promise he likely couldn't keep. "Even if they do, I won't let them take you."

The words burned his tongue, and he'd do his best to ensure they held true. But he was just a man of mediocre intelligence and fighting skill. Perhaps the soldiers should be the ones riding with the boy. They could protect him.

"You're a failure—always will be."

Father's reminders revisited at the worst of times.

Denton swallowed, ignoring the echoing whispers of sure failure. "I promise I'll do my best to keep you safe."

But what if, once again, his best wasn't enough?

The days passed with only the chatter between Edver, Nerissa, and Hauni mingling with the jangle of tack and the quiet conversations between the soldiers. Afya, of course, did not speak and Noko remained nearly as quiet as a chapel mouse, uttering only a peep or two when he needed reassurance all would be well.

Denton's attention lingered on Afya. Red still tinted her thick, black hair, a hint of the malnutrition she was gradually recovering from. Her cheekbones still protruded, but to a much lesser extent, and she no longer tottered about on unsteady legs.

A chuckle rose in his throat when Edver glanced her way and blushed as she smiled at him. Who would have thought the irritating chief's son would fall so soon and so hard?

The clatter of hooves rang in his ears. Darting squirrels and birds caused the underbrush to shift, but there was no sign of anyone lurking behind the trees.

He tugged on Cinders' reins and guided her to Nerissa's right. If looks could kill, he'd be as melted as a candle placed on a hunk of red-hot iron. Something about him just rubbed her the wrong way, he supposed.

It wouldn't be the first time someone disliked him, and he doubted it would be the last.

"What is so important about Keller? Your chief practically uses it as an imprecation." He'd ask Edver, but the man didn't know how to shut off his yapping, and Denton's ability to deal with an unending barrage of chatter was nil.

Nerissa pursed her lips. "The Keller village is known for their apathy when it comes to the trafficking situation. They outright stated they don't care as long as nothing interferes with trade. We suspect they may be assisting the kidnappers and participating in attacking the villages."

"Why?" The shred of curiosity Father hadn't stamped out of him arose.

Distrust painted Nerissa's expression.

Denton sighed. Perhaps he should pull a Red and set things straight—in the most tactless manner possible. "I'm not the enemy. I have the scars and the monarchial support to prove it. We're riding into what could potentially become a war. Anything you can tell me will be helpful."

Edver snorted. "For pity's sake, Ner, just tell him. Father trusts him and your uncle does too. Divert your suspicions elsewhere."

Yes, like to Afya.

Denton tuned out the discussion between the two and focused on the young woman. She stared at Nerissa as her complexion dulled. Her posture more resembled a schoolmarm's ruler and she clutched the reins with such force her horse snorted and sidestepped.

Nerissa huffed. "Every time they have visited a village, at least three children are kidnapped during the following week. This has happened to eight villages so far. I've no idea why Chief Talart and the others suspect them for the attacks, but it doesn't surprise me. They're not allies, but they're not enemies either."

"Are there any distinguishing features about this village?"

Edver piped up. "Yes and no. *Yes* because they have accents and we don't. *No* because everyone who lives in Western Marteris has an accent."

A chill prickled Denton's spine, but he brushed it away.

Nerissa gazed at nothing as she continued, though her words were mumbled, like she forgot about those around her. "Why they don't just send warriors is beyond me."

Denton could tell her why. The rescued needed the touch and care and kindness only a woman could offer. They needed to feel comforted and safe. From what he'd seen, most of the traffickers were men. To the victims, a woman would pose less of a threat.

"The chief also said something about a key. Did he mean a physical object?"

Nerissa's eyes were wider than a draft horse's hooves when she glanced his way. "When did you hear that?"

He actually *overheard* it—unintentionally. "A few days ago."

Her lips pursed. "The farther north we travel, the worse the terrain becomes. That's why supplies are often delivered via boat. The far-northern villages are also a bit...reclusive and odd, so they don't mind. There's a gate that is carved from a cliff that leads to their holdings. To get through the gate, you need a key."

"Let me guess. There aren't many keys."

She shook her head.

Denton exhaled and returned his attention to his surroundings. How he longed for Veerham's simplicity.

He huffed. Red would say Marteris was simple, too. After all, what was so difficult about a rescue mission?

He'd thought that same thing until about a year ago. There had been nothing simple about dragging his stepbrother from the gaping maw of a shed set ablaze. Nothing simple about jumping from horse to wagon. Nothing simple about awaiting for his fate to be decided in the aftermath.

As the days passed, the terrain grew rockier, steeper, and less inhabitable. Scraggly pines clung to their precarious positions atop and alongside cliffs and the path narrowed until Denton questioned how the horses fit. Nights were spent out in the open if the weather cooperated and beneath overhangs when it didn't.

He exhaled and leaned against a boulder as he stared at the rod in his hands. For some reason, Edver thought fishing from the edge of a cliff a grand idea. If there wasn't an almost certain option of death, the nearly-inevitable risk of the rock crumbling beneath them, and the chance of falling over the edge, Denton might agree.

Might.

Behind him, Nerissa and Hauni chatted as they prepared the fire. Apparently, they too believed fish milled about the base of cliffs, as did the three soldiers, who still hadn't provided their names.

Marterises were lunatics.

Edver sighed as he stretched out his legs and leaned his head against the back of the same rock Denton leaned against. His pole hung loose in his grasp and it wouldn't take much of a tug on the line to drag him into the water.

If Denton ever returned to Veerham, he was warning everyone away from the sea. It scrambled one's brains and turned their common sense into mush.

"Tell me about Veerham."

Denton side-eyed the man. "What do you want to know?"

"Are the rumors true?"

"What rumors?"

"That, well, you know…"

Shifting, Denton placed his attention fully on the Marterisi. "No, I don't know, which was why I asked."

"Is it true your rulers are monsters?"

"Excuse me?"

"Yeah." Edver scratched his jaw, audacious enough to meet Denton's eye and not look one bit ashamed of being daft enough to believe such ludicrous murmurings. "I've heard the monarchs are monsters. You know. Bad temperaments, longer-than-normal teeth, hair that's not been washed for their entire lives, and fingernails that have grown out of control."

That certainly did not describe the king, queen, Carter and Chamonix. "Who told you that?"

"Traders, maybe? I don't remember."

"And how old are you?"

Edver shrugged. "Twenty-six."

Denton scowled. "Then you should be old enough—and mature enough—to realize how ridiculous it is to listen to scuttlebutt. Furthermore, the king and queen are as opposite from monsters as can be."

"How do you know?"

"Because I've met them."

Ate with them, spoke with them, was interrogated by them, attended a wedding with them—*participated* in the wedding, which he doubted he'd ever be asked to do again. A catastrophe had almost occurred when his and Red's crutches disagreed with the thick rug.

"Oh, right. *Royal* detective." Edver stared at the sea, still as relaxed and calm as before. "I thought royals wore something symbolic to indicate their royalty."

"Most wear feathers. White feathers indicate singleness and red indicate noble status."

"Right. So why aren't you wearing feathers?"

"Because I'm not a noble." The words lodged in Denton's throat. Less than a year ago he'd worn the feathers. But he hadn't been nobility. Not really. Not when it was stolen from Carter.

Nor did he bother wearing the white feather. What woman would want to tether herself to a coward and a man who'd turned a blind eye to the evil committed right beneath his nose?

No, it was best to remain single. Besides, he was unlovable. And he couldn't survive another heartbreak.

"But you're a royal detective."

"It's a title. Doesn't mean I'm anyone special."

Silence fell, and Denton stared at the vast stretch of sea before him. When looking at the stars, he felt as insignificant as one ant. Looking at the sea, he felt as powerless as a single drop of water. What could one man, about as far from a hero as one could be, do against the evil overwhelming the world?

Edver's voice, quiet and low, interrupted Denton's musings. "It's a sad thing when someone's worth is based off their man-made status. The Beginning created all of us. He knitted us in our mothers' wombs, forming us individually and with perfect crafts-manship. Every life has value because we're created by Him. That alone determines our worth. Not some human-contrived rank that's actually worthless in light of eternity."

Denton drew his knees to his chest as Edver rose and walked away, pine cones and needles crunching beneath his boots.

The concept of the Beginning taking the time to actually *create* him was laughable. A worthless man, a coward, a sinner, one who would never meet perfection...why would the Beginning care?

Maybe Denton was a mistake. Someone who wasn't meant to be alive. Maybe he should have died instead of his birth mother.

Ignoring the hopelessness gnawing his heart and soul, he once more fastened his attention on the sea.

CHAPTER TEN

NERISSA

SHADOWS CREPT ACROSS THE path by the time they reached the outskirts of Marterisi's northernmost boundaries. A warm wind edged with the scents of fish and salt brushed loose strands of Nerissa's hair across her face. Pine trees topped the stone wall overshadowing the now-silent band of travelers. Years of storms, sun, and wind had battered the gray façade and smoothed its surface.

And still it remained stalwart.

So unlike her wishy-washy self.

Please, Beginning, guide us. Protect us.

Glitn, Valti, and Xandr tensed as they stared at the massive stone wall looming over them. For as fierce and determined as their stoic countenances portrayed, Nerissa swore she saw fear carving a new expression on their faces.

It wasn't every day someone came across the wall.

"Is this your first time?" She stood beside Valti, smothering the swell of premonition at the sweat gathering on the warrior's dark brow. If he—a man no stranger to fighting and battle—experienced such nerves, how could she face what lay ahead? A warrior she was not unless one wished to engage in a battle of making banana bread.

"Not for me, but it is theirs, yes." Valti's deep voice rumbled like thunder in the distance. Gray hair and the lines around his eyes marked his age, he stood as tall and strong as a man half his years. His reputation as one of the best warriors in north Marteris was not won without reason.

"Where is the tower in proximity to this wall?" Glitn matched Father in age, and his average, wiry stature made him look like a sprout compared to Valti.

Nerissa shook her head. "We'll have to ask Losibar." If they allowed questions. One never knew with that village. Valti was Losibaran, but he rarely offered input.

Out of all the northern villages, Losibar was the one Nerissa would fear most if they weren't allies. The adults were nearly as tall as the pines—or so they seemed when Nerissa met them when she was a wee one. As thick as boulders and as strong as twenty whales, they used curved swords and axes and could kill you with one glower.

In fact, it was quite difficult to discern between their murderous glares and pleasant grimaces.

If nothing else, Losibar wasn't known for its ability to create easy-going individuals.

Glitn frowned as he surveyed the deep gray mass rising before them. "Where is Losibar in proximity to our current location?"

"About three leagues." The queasiness returned. Barring any complications, they would reach Losibar before the sun met the horizon.

They would be that much closer to the tower. To fulfilling the plan.

Beginning, please...

Not her first prayer, and certainly not her last.

Valti uncrossed his arms, one massive hand resting on his sword as he nodded toward the wall. "Let us proceed."

Willing away the lump in her throat, Nerissa walked toward the gate inset in the stone. The breeze eased the sun's warmth, but sweat still tickled her neck.

The key had remained threaded on a thin chain around her neck, and while the object weighed no more than a thicker locket, but right then, it felt heavier than a whale.

Hands trembling and fingers as cold as they were during winter, she removed it from beneath her shirt and slid the chain from around her neck. The metal clacked against the keyhole's edges as she struggled to insert it.

Seas and sands, why was she so shaky? She'd done this before.

But those times, Father, Chief, and Uncle Morris had been with her. She'd been safe. Not joined by a one-arm-working klutz and an outsider.

The key slid in and, with a soft click, unlocked the gate.

Bracing her hands against the cold iron bars, Nerissa pushed. It slowly swung open.

A solid, naturally-occurring rock wall separated the northern area from the rest of Marteris. It could be breached and climbed, but that took more time and effort than most cared to put forth.

Chills rippled across her skin. They were now in the northern tip of Marteris.

Once the others crossed the gate's threshold, she locked it up. No one said a word as they resumed their journey. Perhaps they too felt that sensation of *different*. That same prickle up the spine that made one sit a little taller and be a little more aware of their surroundings.

Not that Northern Marteris was different topographically. The same pine trees, the same ledges, the same cliffs, the same waves, the same animals.

There was just something...different about the area.

Something that brought to mind the premonition they were walking into a trap and wouldn't emerge alive.

"You must trust, my dear. Remember that one verse? 'And those who know Your name put their trust in You, for You have not forsaken those who seek You.'"

Would Mamma be proud of her for remembering the verse, or would she think Nerissa should have recalled it *before* the journey?

The ride continued in near silence until they reached a little cove hidden from the path. Thin etchings decorated the deep gray stone walls, hints of prior residents who made the spot their permanent residence.

Valti dismounted his rangy gelding and surveyed the area. "We will camp here tonight."

Nerissa hugged herself as Edver and the outsider started the fire and the warriors occupied themselves with a perimeter check. Her stomach knotted and twisted at the gravestones topping the hill and overlooking the cove offered eerie silhouettes in the waning light. She did not consider herself a people person in the least, but right then, she wished for the noise from her village's craziest night.

The cove and nearby beach hadn't always been so calm.

"What's with the graveyard?" the outsider asked.

Edver answered. "What do you know about Marteris history?"

"Not much."

"Then, long, long story short, about eighty years ago or so there were two different villages who were, for some unknown reason, enemies. They agreed to parley and this area was the meeting spot. Only there were no talks of truce and peace. Another village tried mediating, but before any good could come of the meeting, something—probably a muttered insult or the like—set the two villages off and a massacre occurred."

Nerissa glanced at the outsider. He stared in the direction of the gravestones, a pensive expression on his face, though his gaze was distant.

"Don't tell me Veerham doesn't have graveyards." Edver grinned and elbowed the outsider.

"We do."

With that, the outsider turned his back on the group and joined Cinders, who was tethered to a nearby tree.

Hauni grumbled as she placed down a blanket, then lowered herself onto it. Firelight played across her face, highlighting her wrinkles and the concern in her eyes. "That boy has many a secret." She watched him stroke Cinders' neck. "And I'm not so certain his heart isn't fractured as well."

Nerissa watched Edver explain something to Afya, hand waving about as his features became animated. "What do you mean?"

"He has more than his fair share of scars. Nasty ones, too. His eyes are so sad sometimes and he flinches whenever someone nearby makes a sharp gesture." Hauni shook her head. "I don't know. I could be wrong, but I rarely am, so I doubt it. If only there was a cure for emotional pain."

"Do you think he's experienced that?"

"I do. Far more than anyone his age should." Hauni placed her hand atop Nerissa's. "Dear, there's a difference between being on guard and being excessive. He's bled for the innocent and fought beside our own to rescue victims. I don't think he's tricking us. Regardless, be on guard, but do not let worry direct your life."

Nerissa traced a pattern in the sand. Did everyone notice her propensity to fear the worst?

"Nerri, what steers a canoe?"

"The oarsman."

A slow, gentle smile bunched Hauni's wrinkles. "Give your canoe to the Beginning, young one, and relinquish your grip on the oars. Let the Knower of all—not your fear—steer you."

Chapter Eleven

DENTON

LIKE EDVER AND NERISSA'S village, Losibar was situated near the shore. Fenced with towering trees and looming cliffs and rocks, it radiated wariness where Nerissa's village exuded warmth and welcome.

Well, *most* exuded that. The reception from a select few could freeze the sea to its bottommost depths.

Denton reined Cinders beside Edver's horse. "Why didn't your father and Morris come?"

"We've seen folks snooping around, and it needs to look like everything's normal so these unknown individuals won't get the harebrained idea of attacking."

Denton scanned the area ahead of him. That was one upside of living in Veerham. The nobles never physically attacked—only verbally while wielding expert passive-aggressiveness.

Unless they were Father or Lord Riley.

The taste in his mouth soured as, unbidden, memories of Father's and Antony's gravestones leapt to mind. What they did was inexcusable, and he knew King Calvin was right in condemning them, but still, it was difficult to fathom they were dead.

He couldn't muster the stomach to attend the hangings—not that the public was invited.

"Sea to Denton. Hey, man, come back to the present."

Blinking, Denton reverted his attention to the dark hand waving in his face. How Edver managed to do that while not falling off was beyond him.

"Where'd you go? You just tuned me out and mentally traveled somewhere else."

Denton forced his voice to remain normal and not strained, although the onslaught of emotion and recollections left his very core feeling shaken. "It was nothing important."

Edver harrumphed. "Has anyone ever told you you're a lousy liar?"

"Has anyone ever told you you talk too much?"

"Ner, did you hear that? He insulted me!"

Nerissa spared a thin, unamused glance Edver's way before resuming staring at the nearing village. Loose strands of dark blonde hair fell in tangled tendrils about her sunburnt face. Though she looked exhausted and harried, she easily put most of the noblewomen to shame. Where the majority relied on powders and such to "enhance" their appearance, Nerissa did not fall into such vanity. Nor did she appear to care that she wasn't put-together and looking "perfect".

Red would like her.

Denton's hand flew to the loaned sword as armed men streamed from the huts and cabins. His heartbeat quickened. The last time he'd been approached by armed men, they tried killing his brother and somewhat-of-a-friend.

Edver said something, but the ringing in Denton's ears drowned it out. In the far, untouched recesses of his mind, he felt Cinders move, following Nerissa's horse as she urged it toward the advancing horde.

He had to do something. The last time he didn't, children were kidnapped and innocent people almost died.

Commanding Cinders to a canter, he overtook Nerissa's horse. Snatching its reins, he slowed Cinders before drawing his sword. "What are you doing?"

"What do you mean?"

He kept his gaze fastened on the nearing men. Hard expressions made them appear carved from black granite.

Beginning, please keep them from attacking.

"They're armed. They could kill you."

"I'm fine."

"No, you're not." Denton yanked the gelding's reins. The horse snorted. "I know what angry men can do. I've seen them in action. We need to get out of here as quickly as we can. They don't have horses, right?"

He'd have to ride in the back so the others wouldn't be hit with the spears and arrows glinting in the sunlight. Even the soldiers should go before him. Their brawn and intelligence could be used in the war against the traffickers. He was expendable. They were not.

Oh, horses and horseshoes. *Noko.*

Denton twisted in the saddle. The boy's face, painted with terror, tore at him. He already failed Jonah. He couldn't fail Noko as well. "Listen. Get Noko and leave here as quickly as possible. They can only throw so far and the archers won't be in a good position to shoot once you reach the bend."

"*What* are you *talking* about?"

Though warm fingers latched around his wrist and attempted to pull his hand from the reins, Denton held firm. He couldn't fail these innocent souls. Not like he failed the children who were kidnapped and trafficked beneath his very nose.

"Have you ever seen Marterises fight? They almost rival the wolfmen. You don't want to face them. You won't stand a chance."

Nerissa spluttered incoherently before snapping, "The man in front is Losibar's chief. This isn't a war party—this is how they greet their allies. It's Losibar tradition to ensure welcomed visitors receive the traditional greeting and reassurance of safety for the duration of their journey, however long or short that may be. And, yes, I have seen Marterises fight because *I* am a Marterisi. Now, if you don't sheathe your knife and stop acting like an addlebrained squirrel, you might become their next enemy, which I wouldn't recommend."

Denton glanced at her. Surely he misheard. This...this gang of armed, angry-looking men couldn't be friendly. Who in their right mind welcomed their allies with a death glare?

Nerissa sighed. "They're friends. Well, as friendly as Losibar can be, anyway." Her features softened just a smidge. "We know what we're doing. Stay with Noko and keep him calm. He's probably frightened."

Noko. Keep Noko calm.

Yes, Denton could do that. After he mastered his own surging fear, stashed it away, and donned his, "I don't care what's going on" expression. The one he always wore around Father and Antony.

Dropping back, Denton blanked his expression as he took his place beside Noko. "Do you travel a lot back home or do you stay in your village?"

"We don't have villages." The boy's words squeaked and he watched the mass of men with wide eyes. "We have clans."

"Which clan do you belong to, then?"

"The Spiros Clan. My best friend's father is the chief. I'm gonna marry her someday."

The kid had high aspirations and lofty relationship goals—Denton had to give him that. "Why do you want to marry her?"

"Because she's my best friend." Noko gave him a *duh* look. "Why wouldn't I?"

There were many things Denton refused to give advice on. Relationships was one of those. "Hope all goes well for you, then. What's her name?"

"Syca."

Not only did wolfmen have weird eyes, they had weird names. To be fair, *Ruíd* wasn't too bad. But *Lycus*? *Noko*? *Syca*?

Unless Frilore was normal, Veerham was the world's only hope.

A voice deeper than Federigo's called out in a language Denton did not recognize. In front of him, Edver and Hauni halted their mounts.

He brushed his fingertips across his sword. For once, Nerissa did not look concerned. That should comfort him, right? The worrier being unworried?

Then again, she was flanked by three massive men who could give the wolfmen a fair fight.

Nerissa dismounted and walked toward the foremost man, who did the same. They met in the middle and he inclined his head to her, an action she mimicked.

Once they returned to their horses and began toward Losibar proper, Denton flagged Edver's attention. "Why weren't you the one to greet? You're the chief's son."

Edver shrugged one shoulder. "Nerissa has done this more often than I so they recognize her. Plus, she has earned Chief Mossen's respect, and in Northern Marteris culture, the one most respected acts as the spokesman for the group."

"So she's not in danger?"

Edver snorted and Hauni chuckled. The soldiers smirked and Afya, from where she rode on Edver's left, smiled. "No. Losibar is extremely safe. As safe as a shoreline village can be. They're renowned for their fighting abilities."

Small comfort.

"You'll always make a fool of yourself, whelp. It's your curse. You ruin everything."

So Father said in a drunken rage one night, applying his stein to Denton's noggin.

The resulting bruise hadn't been easy to cover up, but he managed to fool Red and Carter into thinking nothing was wrong.

Denton clenched his teeth as they passed the first cabins. Best he stay silent and do only what Edver did. That way he couldn't destroy this crucial attempt at saving lives.

Shadows shifted across the rocky terrain, the only movement besides the erratic thumping of a heart doing its best to pummel its way from Denton's chest. The trees towered above, their pine needles doing their best to obscure the sun.

It was too early to attack, but if they waited until sunset, the darkness would hinder them.

He hunkered down behind the boulder, willing himself to become smaller. How did the soldiers do it? They topped him by a foot, at least, and made the strongest Veerhamer look skinny.

"It's too quiet," Edver whispered.

One of the soldiers slashed a hand at him, a deep scowl indicating Edver would never make another sound if he didn't hush up.

Cool sweat coated Denton's grip as he clutched the hilt of his borrowed sword. The square pommel bit into his palm and the weight drew his arm down, but at least it was an actual weapon, unlike the sewing needle first offered him.

A smidge of what could be satisfaction bolted through his chest. He may be a Veerhamer, but he wasn't half bad with a sword.

A shuddery breath drew his attention to where Nerissa leaned against the same boulder. Face as pale as snow, she stared at her shaking hands. The confidence exhibited while interacting with Losibar had vanished as quickly as an apple given to Cinders.

He couldn't blame her for the nerves. Not really. Not when he himself likely was, as Edver said about five times in the last day, "green around the gills". Whatever that meant.

The breeze picked up, bringing with it an ominous chill that drew upward the hairs on Denton's arms. As though in response, the shadows hastened their speed, briefly dotting the massive stone structure not fifty paces away before flitting elsewhere.

When the Losibar chief said the children were in a tower, a stone cylinder carved from the side of a gargantuan cliff hadn't been what Denton expected.

Three windows dotted the space just below the roof's edge, the only visible entrance.

The other tower had been just that: an actual tower Edver said had been used to watch for boats adrift in storms.

"How will they retrieve the children?" Nerissa's voice sounded as thin and brittle as a frozen top layer of snow.

"They'll find a way." Edver flashed her a smile that didn't reach his eyes.

Denton ignored the weight of a thousand horseshoes taking root in his chest. He'd made a promise, and he would keep it. Then he'd force Talart to uphold his end of the agreement and help him find Jonah.

A bird trilled, its call heralding the emergence of dark-skinned Marterisi soldiers, who crept from the tree line with so little noise if Denton wasn't watching them, he wouldn't know they were there.

Movements swift and containing a confidence Red would envy, they met at the base of the cliff-tower.

May the Beginning have mercy if Veerham ever warred with Marteris, because the land of feathers and deciduous trees wouldn't survive a week against such expert fighters.

"How will they get up there?" His whisper sounded louder than the largest, tolling bell.

A sharp pain sparked through his side as Edver introduced his elbow—his extremely pointy elbow.

"Quiet," the chief's son hissed. "And they'll use hooks and ropes."

"They don't even know if someone is inside."

"That's the risk we must take. We haven't the time to look around. You heard the reports. The kidnappers are on their way to collect them."

The lack of details didn't help the queasiness. If the scouts were right, why couldn't they determine the general time of the kidnappers' arrival? Why couldn't they provide a report of their appearance? The horses? The type of wagon? How many children could it transport? That would give the rescuers an idea of how many were kept captive within the unnatural tower.

"Even the smallest details hold significance." No irritation or impishness had flickered in Red's eyes. *"Never underestimate the power of one seemingly-unimportant fact. It could save someone's life."*

If only Denton had come to his senses earlier. Then perhaps Jonah wouldn't have been taken—again. Perhaps Carter would not have been nearly killed. Perhaps Princess Chamonix would not have been kidnapped.

And perhaps Red would not have been injured and almost murdered.

Failure's crushing weight threatened to pin him in place.

Denton ground his teeth and fought it. He couldn't buckle beneath the pressure. The only way to succeed was to tap into the miniscule amount of bravery the king and queen believed he possessed.

He could do it. He *would* do it.

For Jonah. For Carter. For Red.

For everyone else he failed.

He dried his palm on his pant leg and set his jaw. No failure for this Yindell. He'd disprove Father's claim a thousand times over.

Three Marterises separated from the group and withdrew thick coils of rope from their packs. The hooks on the ends glinted as they were launched toward the windows.

With a screech followed by a clank, the hooks caught and held fast.

Denton exhaled. Was it normal for his heart to beat faster than a Thoroughbred's on race day?

With smooth movements, the men began scaling the ropes.

If Denton had a quarter of their physical strength, maybe he would have been bolder in standing against Father and Antony.

No, no he wouldn't have. Cowardice came from the heart. Not the external.

A horse whinnied.

Denton's spine itched at the distinct rattling of wagon wheels upon the jutted path.

It came from the wrong direction—north instead of south. Losibar made it clear they had no wagons to contribute, and no other village on this side of the wall had been alerted to the rescue.

Chills covered his arms. "They're coming," he whispered.

The first Marterisi reached the top and shimmied through the middle window.

A shout rang through the forest just as an arrow clacked against the tower's side.

The singular ring of seven swords drawn in unison temporarily drowned out the sound of the approaching kidnappers.

Denton's fingers flexed. Even now Valti's and Glitn's expressions left one to wonder what the men were thinking.

As silently as the men before them, the groups from Nerissa's and the other three villages barged from the trees, weapons waving and countenances fiercer than a furious stallion's.

Valti gripped Edver's shoulder. "Go warn the others," he hissed. "Tell them we will meet opposition."

Just as another arrow clattered against the tower, the second Marterisi emerged from the far left window with a child on his back.

Denton's pulse thrummed. The first rescue.

But if the arrows kept coming, it would be their last.

A war cry filled the air.

Nerissa pulled in a ragged breath. Her pallor put snow to shame. "That is the traditional Marteris battle cry." She shuddered. "Why would...why would they be using it?"

"Because we're upsetting their plans?" Denton scanned the area. The attackers weren't yet visible, but they soon would be. They would grow impatient at the arrows continually missing and would engage in hand-to-hand combat.

A twig snapped in the lower area of the slope they rested on.

His stomach urged him to relocate his last meal.

They hadn't counted on the kidnappers coming *around.* Only going straight through.

A storm claimed Valti's gaze when his eyes met Denton's.

Grinding his teeth, Denton clenched his sword's hilt. They wanted him to be a hero, and a hero he would endeavor to be. "Do you want me to see who that was or get the child?"

"The child. Xandr will take care of the ones below us." With that, Valti signaled to Xandr, who slipped down the slope as quietly as could be.

Exhaling, Denton drew his sword and skirted the tree line, sidestepping the Marterises gathered near the tower's base.

He locked his focus on the child. Red would say to always know your surroundings and to constantly swivel your attention, but the Marterises' height blocked him from the kidnappers' view. No need to worry about what he couldn't see. All that mattered were the sobbing children strapped to the two men's backs.

The men removed the children and placed them in Denton's arms. "There are many more," the shorter said. "At least fifteen."

"What ages?" Denton could carry a toddler, but anyone over ten?

Sometimes being a weakling really stunk.

"From two to sixteen, I'd say." The man shrugged before his gaze turned flinty. "We must continue our mission. Keep them safe."

It wasn't just an order. It was a warning. Denton's blood would be spilled if he allowed harm to come to their fellow countrymen.

He nodded and spun, slipping back into the trees as hastily as possible. Nerissa glanced up at him as he approached, and he dumped the smallest child, a crying toddler, into her arms. "Let's go."

Divots and exposed roots made the path an obstacle course Denton never wished to traverse again. One calf muscle aching and his opposite ankle mildly twisted at least four times, he ignored the need to limp as they wove between trees. In front of him, Nerissa's skirt tangled with every grass blade and speck of dirt.

Red would say wearing such a long skirt to such an occasion was foolish.

Then again, Red had no right to disparage anyone's fashion. She believed mud, twigs, and a haphazard crown of dried leaves were perfectly acceptable adornments.

Pulse thrumming, Denton breathed a prayer as they reached the slight clearing where the others congregated while awaiting the children.

Afya snatched the child from his arms, her mouth puckered and her forehead furrowed as she stroked the little boy's hair and made crooning noises in the back of her throat.

Nerissa handed the girl to Hauni, who promptly offered the little one a cornhusk doll.

Denton rolled his shoulders. "There are at least fifteen kids." They needed a quicker way of transportation. "Is there a smoother path?"

Edver grimaced as he drew his sword. "Yes, but it's exposed."

"That's a risk we'll have to take."

Denton turned his back on them and let loose a soft, lilting whistle.

A moment later, Cinders trotted toward him, her dangling reins snapped in half and mud splattering her legs.

"Hold on, now." Edver bit out the words. "You're wasting time, outsider. Time we don't have. Just go on and retrieve the children."

Denton glared up at the man. Red would likely call Edver a wishy-washy rat. "I don't know how big the enemy's forces are, but we need a quicker way to remove the children from their clutches."

Edver's eye twitched. "You're just an outsider. I'm the chief's son. What do you know of this? You've probably only ever spent your time being spoiled rotten and made to think you're the greatest hero this century will see."

Bile burned the back of Denton's throat. "You asked what I know of this. I may have only ever participated in one other rescue, but I'll tell you what I know. I know horses. I reckon I'm a better rider than you. You stay here and guard the women and kids. Let me work with what I know best."

"And what's that?"

Denton bared his teeth in what could be interpreted as a grin by others, but what felt like a snarl. "Like I said—horses."

CHAPTER TWELVE

NERISSA

THE OUTSIDER WAS INSANE. Plain and simple.

Or perhaps her fear just colored him in an unfavorable light.

"This is a bad idea." Instead of sounding commanding like Ed-ver or calm like Hauni, she squeaked like a mouse being stepped on.

The outsider unhitched the ornery red roan from the wagon and mounted her without blinking, effortlessly pulling himself up on her back without the assistance of saddle or reins.

Yes, he truly was insane.

Eyes bluer than a late-August sky pinned her in place. "Do you want us to succeed?"

"Yes."

"Then mount up."

Stomach knottier than Mamma's thread after Daffy got hold of it, Nerissa stared at the black-and-white behemoth beside her. Elegant, yes, but deadly just the same.

Her chest tightened. She could barely ride at a walk, much less a canter, which was probably what the outsider would demand. She would do no good if she fell off and broke another bone. No good if her flailing and shrieks startled the mounts.

Nerissa swallowed. Her parents would want her to be brave. To do what her family and village needed.

Please help me, Beginning. Give me courage.

The outsider urged Dancer forward a step.

Nerissa scrambled toward Cinders. Fingers so icy they almost refused to grip the saddle horn, she clutched at whatever she could and managed to fit her boot in the stirrup. Air wheezed from her lungs as she gracelessly hauled herself atop Cinders.

"Follow me."

With that, the outsider commanded Dancer to a trot and swept past her.

Whispering another plea, Nerissa trailed him.

Taking a smoother, although just as narrow path, the ground passed beneath them at what felt like a speed both too slow and too fast.

Nerissa pressed a hand over her mouth as clanging and shouts filtered through the trees. What if her people were overrun? What if the children were stuck? What if they were slaughtered?

The outsider never faltered from his course, and when they reached the edge, he held up a hand before dismounting. "Stay here. I'll bring them to you."

"This is hardly ideal."

He shrugged. "What else can we do? I don't know where the other group is, and hopefully the attackers will ignore us in favor of fighting. Stay here. Prepare to go as soon as I tell you."

Nerissa squeaked as Cinders snuffled and shifted. Clenching the reins until her knuckles popped, she risked attempting to peer around the trees. Flashes of color and glints of reflections offered no indication of whom was winning.

Please keep my people safe.

Why couldn't the Beginning allow them easy recourse? Why must doing what was right meet with so much resistance?

The outsider returned after what felt like eons, two more children in his arms. He settled the youngest in front of Nerissa and the older one behind her, providing strict instructions to hang on.

Nerissa's lungs temporarily forgot how to work when he looked at her. Could such earnestness be fake? Did he truly care that much about those not even from his own kingdom?

"All you'll need to do is twitch the reins on occasion. Cinders knows what to do." He patted his mare's withers and nodded to Nerissa. "Go. I'll be right behind you."

Mouth dry, Nerissa reined Cinders about-face and commanded the mare to a walk. At a whistle from the outsider, Cinders broke into a trot.

Nerissa choked back a cry of surprise and clutched the little one to her. Thin, dirty arms wrapped around her ribs and clung with all the strength a weak child could muster.

The path stretched onward, skirting the road's edge and allowing the sun's warmth to heat her skin. The sounds of battle waged nearby, blessedly outside the children's line of vision.

"Horse." The little boy in front of her pointed to the side.

"No, honey. The horse is beneath us."

"Horse."

"That's right," a deep voice slithered. "A horse."

Nerissa's heart threatened to cease working as she jerked her attention to her right.

A bulky, dark-skinned Marterisi, more than a match for Chief Talart, stared at her from where he sat on his horse just off the road's opposite side.

Beginning, help us.

For if He didn't, this rescue mission was over.

The man reined his horse so the beast—plain brown and probably the ugliest horse Nerissa ever saw—was close enough to occasionally bump her foot with its side. "Here's what's going to happen, miss. You're going to hand over the reins and keep nice and quiet as we go for a little ride."

There was no way she could escape. If she rode by herself, there was a slim chance, but with two children? Anything faster than a trot would throw them off and possibly injure them.

The child behind her whimpered.

Cold icier than the streams during winter flowed through Nerissa, sludging through her veins until shadows edged her peripheral and short, hasty exhales escaped her. How could she protect the little ones? No weapon would save them from this man, and no one would hear a plea for assistance.

A large, gloved hand reached for Cinders' reins. "Hand them over, miss. I don't want to hurt you."

And yet here you are.

A whistle trilled just before the man grasped the reins.

Cinders sidestepped beyond his grasp.

The string of curses burned her ears.

Another whistle preceded Cinders backing up two paces.

The man released more vehement oaths.

A steady drumming pulsed in time with Nerissa's heartbeat.

Please, Beginning, give me wisdom.

Ever fiber dictated she whisk away the little ones, but how?

Her throat closed at the whimper of the child behind her.

My throat.

Fingers as stiff as a frozen tree trunk, Nerissa brushed her fingertips over the smooth stone pinned to the neckline of her bodice. The dull black stone and surrounding quartz possessed sentimental value only, but if left unlocked, the pin could cause a great amount of discomfort if one didn't watch out.

She undid the brooch as hoofbeats drummed in the far distance.

The man reached over once again.

Flipping the pin's pointy edge downward, Nerissa stabbed.

The man howled as the point penetrated his glove and met resistance.

Four sharp whistles.

Cinders broke into a trot.

"I don't think so, you pathetic little—"

The hoofbeats sounded like thunder when just overhead.

A sob stuck in Nerissa's throat when she peeked over her shoulder. The outsider, perched astride Dancer, hurtled toward them, riding with the grace she only witnessed in professional racers.

And without a saddle, no less.

Nerissa yanked her attention back to the man. He removed the pin, cursed it, then flung it over his shoulder. Crimson trickled from within the glove and smeared along the leather exterior.

A curved sword caught the sunlight before Nerissa found herself looking at the tip of a weapon that could easily gut a whale.

"Hand over the reins, girl, or I'll—"

"Or you'll what?"

The man snarled as the outsider interrupted him. "I should make you fish food first, you stupid little—"

"Save the compliments." The outsider slowed Dancer to a trot, then a lazy meander. "I've heard your sorry attempts at describing us. And, frankly, I've met dead worms who comprehend the basics of language better than you." He drew not his sword, but a knife Nerissa remembered seeing hanging on Chief Talart's wall. "I doubt this will be appreciated, but I'll give you a chance. Put down the sword."

The man laughed. *Laughed.* Like Denton Yindell was no more than a pesky, irate fly. "Boy, I could run her through before you figure out how to use that thing."

"Are you sure of that?" Frost laced the outsider's voice. "Because the last person who doubted me ended up dead."

"I have the upper hand, boy. You'd do best to sheathe your weapon and ride away. I'll even let you live."

Nerissa clutched the little boy. The man wasn't looking at her, but if his reflexes were as quick as the outsider's wit, he could miss Nerissa and stab the child behind her.

Beginning, what do I do?

"Listen, you half-eaten louse," the outsider growled, "do you hear that? It's the sound of your people losing. It's the sound of good overcoming evil. It's the sound of justice."

The sword flicked.

Nerissa gasped.

"You're one word away from watching your woman be run through."

"Am I? You may want to check your perspective."

The man blinked and squinted.

The outsider offered a cold grin and nodded to his right.

When the man glanced that way, Nerissa again nudged Cinders into a trot.

A soft *thwap* followed by the unmistakable impact of arrow entering flesh drew a lump to her throat. Another peek over her shoulder provided adequate reassurance the man would never utter another threat.

The sobs building in her chest threatened to erupt when Father stepped from the trees, bow in hand and a hurricane of wrath etched across his features. He sent the outsider a scathing glare, likely already plotting how to kill him.

With a few steps, the outsider drew abreast of Nerissa. "Here. I'll take a kid."

"You'll do no such thing," Father hissed. He pointed an arrow at the young man. "You're going to make sure my daughter and the young ones get to safety. Then you're going to resume your job. No dilly-dallying, no more leaving my daughter unprotected."

Nerissa willed back the need to cry. This wasn't the time for emotions, and a far more important task was at hand. "We're going, Father." Her voice broke.

Father's eyes softened. "Be safe, Starfish."

"I will."

She hoped. She prayed.

At the outsider's whistle, Cinders walked.

The path passed in an unintelligible blur. For all Nerissa knew, they could have traveled all the way back home before her eyesight cleared.

The little boy was removed from her grasp before the rib-busting grasp around her ribs was alleviated. Then hands, warm and calloused, helped her from Cinders' back.

"You did well."

Eyes watery, Nerissa blinked at the outsider. Dirt smudged his face and a slight cut nicked near the corner of his left eye.

"My brooch," she whispered.

"Played an instrumental part in keeping both you and the young ones from being taken." His tone softened, and he gently grasped her elbow, leading her to who-knew-where. "You were brave and did your job well."

"He almost had us." The shadows infiltrating her sight thickened.

"Yes, but you stopped him. Not everyone would have thought to stab their assailant with a piece of jewelry."

Another set of hands grasped Nerissa's as the outsider continued speaking. "I think she may be going into shock. I'll be back with more kids."

"Do you need help?" Hauni's voice floated in the distance.

"Just stay here. Edver, have that sword ready. Noko, be on the lookout for anyone you don't recognize."

Hoofbeats drummed away, echoing through Nerissa's mind like the drums played at village meetings.

Should she feel like she was frozen in place? Short of breath? Rather woozy?

"Oh, dear girl."

If that was pity in Hauni's voice, Nerissa didn't want it. She needed to be strong. Brave. Her family—her village—counted on her.

What could she do to dissipate the stagnant sensation overcoming her? She'd helped Hauni many a time in the infirmary. She should be able to recall the methods.

Breathe. Her lungs felt like air hadn't entered them in a day.

A few big, gulping breaths helped clear the fogginess. A few more dissipated the wispy darkness.

Nerissa blinked as her surroundings came into full focus. Hauni stood before her, face pinched with the worry in her eyes. Edver paced off to the side, lips moving as he no doubt cursed his injury.

Noko stood atop the wagon, head swiveling and small fists balled at his sides. And Afya sat with the children, somehow keeping them quiet.

Everyone was doing their part but her. The wimpy, anxiety-ridden mess who did nothing but fret.

Nerissa lifted her chin and ignored its wobbling and the burn in her eyes. No more. She could be brave. She *would* be brave. "I'm going back."

"Are you sure that's wise? You looked ready to pass out for a minute."

"Denton cannot do it on his own." His name felt strange and emerged rather garbled. "I was brought for this purpose. I can do it."

Father thought she could. So did Chief Talart. Surely that should impart some form of comfort.

Before Hauni could respond, Nerissa spun on her heel. Legs as wobbly as Daffy's when she began learning to walk, she hurried toward Cinders and managed to mount. "Come on, girl."

Dryness filled Nerissa's mouth as they neared where the man was shot. Her father had slain him to save her, but how long would he be haunted by the blood he spilled? For all his bravado, Father was a gentle soul who preferred to first attempt talking things over.

Her shoulders sagged as she came across the spot. Only a blood smear marked where the man fell.

Thank You, Beginning.

Small favors were always welcome.

The collision of blades and shouts still marred the air as Nerissa neared. Her heart leapt to her throat when Dancer rounded the corner, Denton on her back with a lad sitting behind him.

"You're okay?"

That an outsider would be concerned about her was stupefying, but Nerissa would contemplate it later. "Yes."

He inclined his head. "We'll wait for you."

Blood's stench thickened the air as Nerissa reached the tower. Despite the mayhem, only a few bodies littered the ground. The men still scaled the tower while Xandr guarded a collection of children huddling near the bast.

Her heart twisted at the torn shifts, stained shirts, and shoeless feet. While the littlest ones clung to the older children and either cried or watched the ongoings with wide eyes, haunted pain dulled the older children's countenances.

She couldn't leave them there to wait, wondering if they'd be rescued. It would take too long to go back and forth.

"Where are the others?"

Xandr nodded to the fray. "Every available man is fighting. You, Hauni, and the other girl were the only women in the three groups."

Which meant rescuing the children fell solely on herself, a mute woman, an outsider, another child, a middle-aged woman with a questionable knee, and a chief's son with a bum arm.

Beginning, please show Your favor upon us.

The Scripts were clear He neither abandoned nor forsook those who believed in Him, but that didn't mean He wouldn't use this experience as a life lesson.

And while Nerissa did not doubt His might and infinite wisdom, she couldn't see how a lesson at such a time *wouldn't* involve pain or emotional anguish.

Both of which she was too weak to endure.

With the tallest children's help, she placed two toddlers and one eight-or-nine-year-old on Cinders. "Those of you with the strength to do so, grab a little one."

Scooping a gaunt-faced youngster into her arms and bracing him against her hip, Nerissa snatched Cinders' reins. "Follow me."

Xandr nodded at her. "I'll keep anyone from following."

An arrow smashed against the tower.

The need to flee both the battle and all rational thought sank its claws into her fracturing façade of assurance.

Beginning, give me strength.

Not the strength to move, but the strength to remain immovable. Strong and unflinching against the fear and confidence to lead these tortured souls to safety.

Guide me.

She placed one foot in front of the other. The clop of Cinders' hooves joined the tumult.

Go before us.

She glanced behind. The children followed like goslings trailing after their mother.

Surround us with Your protection.

What could be a smidgen of relief slowed her heart's unnatural pace. Denton stood in the middle of the road, sword drawn and expression hard.

That hardness melted when he saw the children. "I was about to come get you."

"Everyone else is fighting." The words squeaked, likely due to the lack of air in her poor lungs.

"That will give us some time, then." He placed another child on Dancer's back. "Let's go."

She shouldn't feel safe, but as she walked next to the man not from her land, Nerissa couldn't deny that perhaps his presence was, just this once, a gift from the Beginning.

Chapter Thirteen

DENTON

To say the children were overwhelmed was an understatement.

Denton resisted the urge to cover his ears as more crying began. Two days had passed since the rescue. He wasn't annoyed by the sharp, piercing noise, as he well understood their fear, but if it continued, his ears would be ringing until the day he perished.

"Here. Hold him." A dark-skinned Marterisi with more wrinkles than Red had freckles handed Denton a scrawny toddler. She then pinned him beneath a gaze of equal parts doubt and unease.

He dipped his chin her way. "Ma'am, I know how to hold a youngster."

Granted, he only learned two days ago, but it wasn't that hard if they remained still.

She pursed her lips and eyed him before bustling back to Losibar's church, which was doubling as an expanded infirmary.

Six men dead. Twelve wounded. Thankfully, those from Nerissa's village only sustained minor injuries. Although, if Mister Wessen kept glaring at Denton, it would become seven dead.

Nerissa flitted about, a young one on her hip and at least two following her every step. Hauni and Afya had the rest of the rescued children settled beneath a large tree and kept them entertained with stories. Edver was with the men, doing manly things like cleaning weapons. The matrons cooed over Noko and stuffed him with food Denton had no hope of recognizing.

When clam chowder was offered, he forced himself to choke it down lest he insult Losibar's chief, who watched him like a cat watched a fish.

The chowder tasted as nasty as it had the first time it assaulted his taste buds.

And Denton sought solace with the horses. Every hoof had been cleaned and checked, every equine groomed and rubbed down, and all were adequately fed, even the scar-littered gelding Nerissa's attacker had rode.

Denton patted Cinders' muzzle and huffed a laugh as she nibbled at his shirt. "It's not edible, girl."

The young boy's hand joined Denton's.

Many saw horses as only beasts of burden, but they were so much more. They were the Beginning's most incredible animal. Watching them run was therapeutic. There was something special about earning a young foal's trust. And there was nothing like feeling the wind whip against one's face as they rode across meadows at a gallop.

Perhaps horses could help this child heal from whatever trauma he endured.

The relaxed, yet guarded casualness dissipated at the next sunrise's arrival.

Cinches and bridles were double checked as horses were saddled and prepared for the journey back to Nerissa's village and warnings and "take cares" were issued a few times over.

"Ride safely," Valti said.

"Do you think that group is still a threat?"

While a few were captured, most attackers fled into the woods, somehow evading their pursuers.

Valti shrugged. "They went opposite of the wall. I would say be on alert, but the chance of an attack from that particular group is low."

At Mr. Wessen's call, the horses shuffled forward.

Valti walked alongside Cinders and gripped Denton's knee. "You're a decent swordsman. Keep honing your skill." Then he let go and returned to his village.

Only when they vacated the iron gate did the new children break down. One girl sobbed and the youngest child, a boy of three, refused to be consoled no matter what Hauni, Afya, and Nerissa tried. He eventually wore himself out, falling asleep while cradled in a makeshift sling as Afya rode.

Denton scanned their surroundings. The looming trees and shifting weeds could hide any number of assailants. Defending the group wouldn't be easy, especially now that everyone save Denton and Edver rode double, and several of the children were paired together. Noko was constantly reassuring a little Friloran boy everything would be fine, and Nerissa didn't seem to mind the ten-year-old girl clinging to her and startling at every noise.

In all, eight children had been added to the group, with the rest being dispersed between Losibar and the other three villages.

Denton twitched as his mouth dried. He wasn't equipped to protect such young lives. Wasn't prepared to do whatever it took to save them.

He helped where he could, but comforting frightened children was not his forte.

What he *could* do, though, was tend to the horses, and that was exactly what he did. It kept him busy, kept his mind off the lack of home and family awaiting his return to Veerham, and helped him focus on something other than his desperation to find Jonah.

The following day, Hauni kept the little ones entertained with stories from her youth and the promises of a warm meal once they reached their destination for the night.

The destination turned out to be a cave.

A cold cave.

A dark cave.

A cave that looked like it'd only been inhabited by bats and birds.

Denton eyed the gaping maw. It was almost as dark as the warehouse he and Red rescued the children from.

He tried not to remember that day, nor the following days of agony, but life seemed determined to force him to relive it.

With a good-natured whistle, Edver and Nerissa's father gathered the older children and ushered them off on a firewood search.

Denton clutched Cinders' reins. This was ludicrous. No, more than ludicrous. This was pure lunacy. Who in their right mind stayed in a *cave*? "Is this safe?"

Nerissa spared not one glance at him as she began withdrawing supplies from the numerous saddlebags. "If you have an issue, go home."

Where is that?

A year ago, he would ask that in jest, or just to rile up Red, but now?

Now he would very much like the answer.

Nerissa paused at the entrance, a load of bundles in her hand. "Does it honestly make you uneasy?"

"When someone asks if something is safe, that's usually the reasoning behind their inquiry."

She eyed him before disappearing into the cave.

If only he never offered to join.

No. Jonah was worth it.

Denton tethered Cinders to a nearby tree then approached the entrance. He grimaced at his clammy fingers as he gripped the loaned sword.

If only he had his own weapon, but the blade was either sold, being worn by his attacker, or at the bottom of the sea

Nausea announced its existence as he entered the cave. Cool air tainted with salt and decaying grass brushed over him.

Definitely a creepy cave. All it needed was a stench of decay and a few bones scattered about or tucked in various nooks and crannies.

Nerissa motioned for Afya to take the youngest child before planting her hands on her hips and facing Denton with a most unamused expression. "Could you tend to the horses?"

Denton jerked a nod and retreated back into the outdoors and fading sunlight. Horses he could do. Horses were his friends and confidants.

After unsaddling them, he lost himself in brushing down and cleaning hooves. If only he could remain there forever.

Denton had just finished watering the horses when the rest returned from wood hunting. The children offered hints of no longer fearing their rescuers—the occasional giggle, a flash of a smile here and there, and allowing the women to hug them.

After supper—rabbit and biscuits—was consumed, Denton settled at the edge of the firelight' reach. The children huddled around the contained flames, the dance of shadow and light making their faces appear gaunt.

Nerissa perched next to her father, who put his arm around her shoulders and gave her an affectionate squeeze. Was the man truly a good father, or just putting on airs so others wouldn't see past his lies? Neither Nerissa nor her sisters acted afraid of him. That type of fear was difficult to mask, especially when one was caught unaware.

Edver settled back and rested his one good arm behind his head. "Alright, kiddies. Who wants a story?"

Denton remembered story time. Stepmother had pulled him and Carter into the solar when they were young and read them stories. Some were fanciful tales, others were from the Scripts.

The overwhelming sensation of being loved, even if Denton wasn't her child by blood, had almost knocked him off the settee.

He longed for those days, where things were simpler and Father's hatred wasn't as pronounced.

Edver's voice deepened and he began making over-grand gestures with his good hand. "Have you ever heard how a shepherd boy slayed a giant?"

Denton stared at his hands as Edver shifted from one Scripts story to the next. He was saved—he knew that—but that didn't mean he had the Beginning's love, did it?

After all, love was conditional, and if his earthly father hated him, why would his Heavenly Father be any different?

CHAPTER FOURTEEN

NERISSA

DENTON YINDELL WAS A mystery. The fatigue etched in his countenance and eyes seemed perpetual, yet the few smiles the children drew from him lit his demeanor. He spoke to the adults only when he had a question, yet he'd taken Noko under his fin, so to speak, and readily engaged both the boy and the other young ones in conversation.

Nerissa huddled within the confines of her cloak and gripped the hands of the young girl clinging to her. Unrelenting rain muddied the trail and lambasted them with unrivaled fury. Thunder cracked and lightning did little to illuminate their path.

Please, Beginning, keep us safe. Do not let us stumble.

Hauni had limited medical supplies, and their horses trod a trail that meandered atop a cliff. If someone fell over, they would be dashed upon the rocks below. If they wandered left, they would land on a completely different trail that took them to who-knew-where.

One wrong step could cause so much trouble.

Please, Beginning.

Nerissa glanced over her shoulder. Father should be just behind her, but either the rain blocked him from sight or he had gone over the cliff.

Breath punched from her lungs at the thought. *Please, Beginning. Don't let that be so.*

She inhaled a moisture-soaked gulp of air. If she focused on what could be, she'd drive herself insane.

Still, the prayers tumbled about her mind with increasing fervency.

A gasp escaped her as the horse halted, and she froze, clutching the child's hands even harder. The best thing to do was stay still. If an enemy approached, perhaps the rain would blind them and they'd miss the ragtag group.

Unlikely, but it could happen.

That familiar pit again yawned within her stomach and chest.

Fingers brushed her arm and she squinted to her left. A blurry, male form stood to her side, facing her. Too short to be Edver, so it had to be the outsider or Father.

Oh, Beginning, please let it be Father.

The wind carried his words away.

Nerissa screeched when the girl vanished. Twisting, she stared at the empty space behind her.

Pressure on her wrists guided her off the horse. The figure picked up another shape, took Nerissa's elbow, and escorted her to an overhang. Only a slim strip was dry, but the shelter was better than being in the open.

Nerissa hunched and fisted her hands to warm her fingers. That cloak was not Father's. Nor did Father limp.

Oh, where is he?

Biting her tongue to keep her teeth from chattering and the welling tears from overspilling, she counted the little faces who either gawked at the rain or cowered against the wall.

Only seven children, Afya, and Hauni.

She grabbed Denton's arm. "Noko is missing."

"Who?" He leaned toward her. Rain slicked off his cloak and dripped down his face, dampening the strands of hair clinging to his forehead.

"Noko. I don't see him."

Edver rushed into the cramped area. "We're missing one kid and the rest of the adults."

Denton spun. "Nerissa says it's Noko." Without waiting for a response, he began to stride away.

Edver halted him. "Where are you going?"

"To find them."

"You don't know the land. I do. You need to stay here."

Denton yanked his shoulder away. "You have one good arm. *You* need to stay here."

Without another word, he charged into the downpour.

Nerissa grit back tears as thunder again cracked the air. When the little girl began to cry, she picked her up, ignoring the cold moisture seeping into her shirt.

Please, Beginning, let them be okay.

Edver pasted on a false smile as he went from child to child, reassuring them all would be fine. Hauni joined him, her soothing voice calming the more terrified ones.

Nerissa jolted at the pressure on her arm. Afya offered a wisp of a smile. Understanding crinkled the skin around her eyes and the sympathetic cant of her mouth told Nerissa what the woman did not verbalize.

The rain intensified, sounding like a thousand hoofbeats against stone. The pine trees on the other side were now faint smudges as a wall of pale gray obscured everything from clarity.

No one could find their way in such a downpour.

Please, Beginning.

The squelch of boots against mud and pine needles jerked Nerissa from an unsettled doze. Heart leaping to her throat, she felt for her knife before Edver's whispered, "You look atrocious," drew her fully from the dredges of near-sleep.

Her stiff joints creaked as she rose. The rock's chill had seeped into her skirt and frozen her muscles and joints.

Not the best situation when they could be attacked at any minute.

Stone slick beneath her still-damp shoes, she crept around the slight bend, drawn knife in hand. The children huddled with Hauni and Afya, who had somehow cocooned them in a nest of spare blankets. It wasn't much, but it would mostly ward away the chill.

Nerissa barely bit back a gasp. Denton stood just beneath the overhang's protection. Noko, bundled in a cloak suspiciously the same color as the outsider's, was clinging to Edver.

Blood and torn flesh arrayed Denton's left forearm and his sodden shirt bore numerous tears and countless, small bloodstains. Scratches dotted his face and neck. He looked worse than when they rescued him from the beach.

But he and Noko were alive, and that was all that mattered.

Nerissa blinked at the revelation. Since when had she cared if Denton survived? If he lived? If he even existed?

Since you found him on the beach, a no-nonsense voice in the back of her mind said with a "duh" tone.

She rarely wished death on anyone, she supposed. Only the kidnappers and traffickers and those who aided them.

"Where did you find him?"

Noko whimpered, and Denton gave him a slight smile. The boy quieted.

"I found him a level down."

"What do you mean?"

Nerissa joined Edver. This close, it wasn't hard to miss Denton's pallor, nor the exhaustion in his eyes. Mud's stench clung to him and he wore enough pine needles on his boots and the knees of his pants that a pine tree was surely bald.

He shrugged. "The second tier, then. The jut of cliff just below the edge of the top."

Noko sniffled. "I dismounted like I was told to, then I couldn't see anything. I thought I heard someone call my name, so I went in that direction. Then I fell."

Nerissa felt herself melt at his choked sob. Brushing hair from his face, she murmured a nonsensical nursery rhyme.

"How did you get back up?" Incredulity laced Edver's words and he looked from Noko, to Denton, and back, like he couldn't believe they existed.

Another shrug. "We made our way."

"Barely, from the looks of you. Well, however you did it, thank the Beginning you're okay."

Denton glanced at his hands, grimaced at their equally-shredded state, then shrugged once more and shoved one through his hair. He made a face at the mud and debris that came away. "I think Noko sprained his ankle at the very least. He couldn't walk."

The child released a hiccupping sob. "I'm sorry. I wasn't very manly."

Denton looked him straight in the eye. "There's nothing unmanly about what you did. Accidents happen and that rain is nothing short of diabolical. It could have happened to anyone."

Edver grunted. "Let's pray it doesn't happen again. Come on, kiddo. Let's get you into something dry. Nerissa, I'm going to fetch Hauni and you two can look at Sir Battered's injuries."

"It's just a few scratches."

Edver raised his eyebrows. "Sure, and I'm a midget. Look, Yindell. I may not be the smartest man alive, but I do know how to count, and the amount of gouges you have far exceeds *a few*. Just behave and let them fix you up, alright?"

"It's nothing to worry about."

"It is if you get infection."

Denton pinned Edver with a glare most would cower from. "I've had worse and I'm not interested in being patched up. I have some extra bandages in my saddlebags and will use those."

"I don't think so. You're supposed to do what I tell you, remember? *Anything* I tell you. Father won't like it when he hears of your disobedience. Besides, everything in your saddlebags will be swimming in rain. Bandages are no good if they're soaked."

Something flashed through Denton's eyes. "It won't be the first time I've disappointed someone. You'd do better focusing on Noko's injuries. If his foot heals incorrectly, he has to deal with that his entire life."

"No reason why we can't catch two fish with one net, as the saying goes. Nerissa, carry on. Don't let Mister Grumpypants deter you."

Soon Hauni was up and bustling toward them with her satchel in hand. She eyed Denton and tsked. "Seems like it was just yesterday that I patched you up when Ner and Edver dragged you from the beach. Seas, boy. If you were mine and Guy's only patient, you'd keep us busy. Remove the shirt."

"Ma'am…"

"Nope. Don't you go using those Veerham manners on me, young man. Just do as I say and we can get this over with."

Scowl deepening, Denton pulled off his shirt with a hiss.

It wasn't the bruising, cuts, or blood that drew Nerissa's attention. No, it was the pale, vile scar on the lower right portion of his abdomen.

She'd seen that type of scar only two other times.

Broadhead arrows were often deadly, and a gut shot was almost always fatal. He hadn't been in jest when he said he'd experienced worse.

He said nothing as Hauni cleaned the injuries. Nerissa handed her the needed supplies and tried keeping her mind from wondering when and how he had taken a broadhead. News reached their village a few months late, so if war had embraced Veerham, they hadn't yet heard about it.

"You're not feeling faint, are you?" Hauni pressed a hand to his forehead.

He frowned. "No."

"Do you even know what that sensation feels like?"

"Yes." His jaw clenched. "Acutely."

"Very well. Let me know if you feel any worse than you already do, if your wounds begin to itch in the next few hours—that indicates an allergic reaction to the salve—or if you feel lightheaded and more out of sorts than you usually are." With that, Hauni gathered her things and bustled back to the children.

Nerissa alternated between clasping and unclasping her hands. The impression upon her soul she'd been ignoring flared with vengeance. Not all outsiders were vile scum. Just most of the ones her village encountered.

Perhaps this man could not be counted among them.

Denton helped rescue the children, delayed the kidnapper until Father could end the miscreant's life, and had rescued Noko.

But someone with ill intent would help just to save face, her logical side reasoned. *You can't lower your guard. What if he returns and harms your family?*

True, but as much as Nerissa loathed to admit it, perhaps her logical side was incorrect. Just this once. Plus, she well remembered his terror in Losibar. He honestly thought them in danger, and if his drawn weapon was anything to go by, was prepared to defend them. And the panic in those August-blue eyes...that could not have been contrived.

If he was a criminal, he certainly wasn't emotionless. Numerous times had Nerissa witnessed fear, uncertainty, and—dare she admit it—pain flash across his face. The times he genuinely smiled made him look like a different man, one who wasn't burdened and bearing more secrets than a fish had scales.

This man, this Denton Yindell with his numerous cuts and bruises, did not act like any of the criminals she'd been warned of.

Nerissa swallowed. It might be time to reconsider her opinion of Denton, but the new opinion would take time to form.

Hopefully they would complete the mission and return home, whereupon he would leave them in peace.

Yes, that was most optimal.

Unfortunately, life never traveled the most optimal course.

Chapter Fifteen

DENTON

THE RAIN ABATED HOURS later, leaving behind run-offs, the potential for mudslides, and a path so slippery and muddy no one could safely traverse it.

Denton scowled at the impassable mess. Fate surely hated him, for this trip had been filled with problems from the beginning.

"We can plan our path all we'd like, but it is the Beginning who determines our steps."

Or so Parson Gil claimed.

Denton exhaled and rested against the imposing stone surface. The overhang, while cramped and too inhabited, *had* offered shelter, but it also restricted any hope of solitude.

That had been one good thing about home. He could go to the stable, pastures, or river and be alone. No one hounding him. No one giving him tasks he would only fail at. No one asking him to break the law and harm others. No one trying to mold him into a monster like his father and brother.

He did miss the chapel, though. Parson Gil possessed a comforting presence and his voice was one of the few that didn't make Denton tense. Perhaps because he'd never witnessed the man raise his tone, not even when interacting with Red, who could test the patience of the kindest soul in existence.

He missed the sermons even though he did not understand them. There was something different about the chapel. Something reverent. Something that called to his spirit and tempted him to ponder questions there were surely no answers to.

If all fathers were like his, then the Beginning had no time for his inquiries.

Denton swallowed the lump in his throat and watched leftover raindrops kerplunk from the overhang's protruding edge to the puddle below.

He drew his gaze away as laughter burst from the group to his right. Afya stood in the middle of a ring of children, cheeks puffed out and eyes excessively large.

"A fish," Kinm, one of the older girls, guessed.

Afya nodded and smiled before wrinkling her brow and pressing a finger to her chin. After a moment, she snapped her fingers and pantomimed another animal.

Denton allowed a sliver of a smile. What he wouldn't give for half that energy. A void had opened within, sucking away his drive to move, interact, and even think.

He felt...empty.

Hollow.

His spine stiffened when Nerissa eased to the ground beside him. There was no denying she was pretty with her green-gray eyes, dark blonde hair, and the gentle way she cared for the children, but her expression always soured when she looked his way and her gaze turned colder than the chilliest winter day. Her courage added to that prettiness, a thought compounded during the rescue. She'd been trembling and as pale as a white daisy, but still persevered.

She also disliked him more than Red did, and that was saying something because Red held no love for him.

"Thank you for your help with Noko. And...and for your help during the rescue."

Horses and horseshoes, perhaps he'd swallowed too much mud yesterday while scaling the cliff. Or maybe he concussed himself and didn't realize it. Had she actually *thanked* him?

"You've reached him in a way no one else is able to," she continued in a soft voice.

Well. She truly was thanking him. Wonders never ceased.

Heat flushed up Denton's neck and he shifted his shoulders. He wasn't compassionate, loving, and tender like his kind-of sister-in-law. Chamonix was adored by most due to her quiet demeanor. Nor was he unassuming and patient like Carter. Come to think of it, he wasn't bold and protective like Red, either.

What did that make him?

Coward.

Red had spit the accusation at him more than once, and every single time he deserved it.

"Something about you makes him feel comfortable. I don't know what. His people and yours are so different."

Denton wagered a new saddle Nerissa hadn't met one Halthdurnite aside from Noko, but he wouldn't say that aloud. "I've interacted with his kind before."

"Oh?" She tilted her head. "I've only seen a few when they came for trade. Are they as wild as the stories say?"

What was wrong with this woman? No one ever had such an abrupt change in disposition. Not unless they wanted something and were trying to butter him up.

He eyed her. She watched the waterdrops with a pensive expression while picking at her thumbnail.

He sighed. What harm could it do to answer?

Too much. It could cause too much harm. That was what Father taught him. The wrong answer or an answer with too much information only brought about pain and trouble.

"I'm sorry." She shifted away. "I did not intend to pry."

"You're fine. I worked with them back home. King Calvin hired them to help find the traffickers." He shook his head. "They're different. That's all I can tell you. Wild and calm at the same time. They're puzzles."

He huffed a laugh at the memory of Lycus carrying an injured Red up the stairs. The detective had fussed, fretted, and threatened, never once realizing she resembled a puppy who thought it looked ferocious, but was really the opposite.

Afya again caught his attention. The first true smile he'd seen from her brightened her face, and despite not using her voice, she somehow engaged each child.

"Edver is quite fond of her." An edge laced Nerissa's words.

Did she think he admired Afya? Did she think he'd attempt to gain her affection and draw her from Edver?

Denton almost snorted at the thought. "She's hiding something."

"What do you mean?"

"She's alarmed whenever you speak of the key and passage and she always stares at the ground when the traffickers are discussed."

Nerissa's lips thinned. "That does not mean she is concocting some nefarious deed."

For a woman who jumped at an unexpected shadow, Nerissa was awfully protective.

Denton shrugged and returned to watching the weather. "You asked."

"Perhaps." She sighed. "What is Cinders' story?"

At that, Denton couldn't help but smile. "My brother found her at an auction. She was in terrible condition and was so people-shy it took me weeks to gain her trust and cooperation." Cinders was also a faithful companion, and Denton rather have her than a dog any day.

A shift in his peripheral drew his attention to his left, only to find Nerissa watching him, a wrinkle in her brow.

"She's safe," Denton said. "As safe as a horse can be. I trust her around your sisters. Around any child, actually."

"What happened on the beach?" Eyes the color of the stormy sea latched onto him. "There was no shipwreck, you were the only one alive, and a dead body was no more than fifty paces away. There was no sign of anyone else. You say you were ambushed, yet your horse and belongings were untouched."

"I—"

"I need to know if my sisters are safe," Nerissa interrupted. She picked her thumbnail with such ferocity Denton didn't know how it didn't hurt. Her hands trembled and she hunched, breaking her gaze from his.

Denton leaned back against the stone, ignoring the stinging pain across his shoulders. "Nothing I say will convince you, will it?"

She shrugged, staring at her ragged fingernails.

Throat thickening, Denton closed his eyes. He could tell her the truth—the full truth—and try proving his intentions, but what good would that do? Preconceived notions were difficult to break and even harder to replace.

Or he could keep silent, pull the same tactic he did with Red and Carter and let them think what they wished, without attempting to set things straight. It had served him well enough then, but he also hadn't been responsible for a life.

A life that never should have been put in harm's way. A life he should have protected with his own. A life he shouldn't have failed.

No, it was best to remain quiet. That way less could be used against him. Words were just as powerful a weapon as a sword or arrow, and he had no desire to be on the receiving end once again.

Chapter Sixteen

NERISSA

How was it possible to be excited yet terrified at the same time?

Nerissa clenched her teeth to keep from losing her breakfast. Familiar landmarks had dotted the area for about half a day, meaning they neared home. It would be beyond lovely to be back, but how could she tell Mamma about Father? Neither Edver nor Denton had seen any sign of anyone going over the edge, but it wouldn't take long before the waves swept away the bodies.

Please, Beginning, have mercy.

What now felt like the permanent urge to sob almost overwhelmed her as breaks in the trees provided flashes of her village. How could she explain what happened? If she'd been listening instead of internally fretting, would she have heard the others as they fell off?

A sob wracked her shoulders.

They entered the village, but all Nerissa could see was a sea of blurry, misshapen colors. Father was gone. Her family's protector and leader was gone.

"Edver!" Chief Talart's voice boomed through the air.

Edver responded in kind.

Fighting to keep the tears from falling, Nerissa slid off and helped down the child behind her. Would Elberta and Daffy understand? How could one explain death to children?

"Thank the Beginning."

Her limbs froze. That voice...no, she was merely hallucinating. Grief and fear had warped her mind.

"We thought you all had fallen over."

"We thought the same of you."

A strong hand clasped Nerissa's shoulder, and she swiped at the tears before turning. Though they still distorted her sight, there was no mistaking the man before her.

"Father!"

"Nerri." He swept her into a hug. "Oh, my dear girl. I thought you were missing or dead."

A hiccup stole her breath. "I—I thought you were dead. When I didn't see you in the storm, I thought you had fallen over."

Father stroked her hair, much like he had when she was little. "We thought we kept straight, but when the rain cleared, we found we had turned. We returned home to gather a search party. Are you alright?"

"I'm fine." Emotionally wrecked and mentally exhausted, but fine.

Thank You, Beginning.

"What about the others? It looks like everyone is here."

"They're fine. Denton's scratched up from rescuing Noko, but we're fine."

Father grunted, and Nerissa looked up just in time to see him shoot Denton a crusty scowl. "Speaking of that boy, he and I need to talk. No one puts my girl's life in danger without punishment."

Ah, Father. Always so protective. A week ago, Nerissa would have said nothing to waylay him, but Denton hadn't been in the wrong. "He kept that man from killing us."

"He was a pansy."

"All he had was a sword. The man would have ended us by the time Denton was close enough to engage."

Father harrumphed. "I'll speak to your mother about it." He craned his neck. "Speaking of..."

"Praise the Beginning." Mamma's voice sounded as choked as Nerissa's, and before Nerissa could turn, the familiar scent of flowers and ocean air engulfed her. "Praise You, Beginning. They're both safe."

Managing to turn, Nerissa reciprocated the hug and again resisted the urge to cry.

The tears ignored her.

As the sobs emerged, she buried her face in Mamma's shoulder.

Father cleared his throat. "Why don't we go home and talk there? That way we can get out of the way."

Mamma nodded and pulled away before framing Nerissa's face with her hands. "You are alright?"

"I am fine." Nerissa swallowed the tears and offered a weak smile. "Truly, Mamma. How are the girls?"

Mamma studied her face before smoothing the flyaway hairs tickling Nerissa's forehead. "They are fine. Eating more banana bread than is good for them, but overall in good health and spirits."

Father clapped a hand on Nerissa's shoulder. "Ready to go home?"

"Most certainly."

They met Uncle Morris near the street's edge, and at his beckoning, Denton joined them, Cinders' reins loose in his grasp despite the tense way he held himself. The edge of unease in his eyes almost made him look like a different man than the one who had revealed such an unexpected smile.

Perhaps Hauni was right. Perhaps he had endured more than she realized. His scar certainly suggested so.

Though birds trilled and squirrels chattered, chills climbed Nerissa's spine as they traversed the trail to the Wessen cabin.

Cease being a ninny. For only a ninny worried for no reason.

Yet, she couldn't stop. No amount of praying, mentally reciting verses, or taking deep, steady breaths quelled the storm raging in her heart. The worry and anxiety...they were a part of her as much as her fingers and toes were.

A tad of the pressure in her chest eased when the cabin came into view. The goats grazed, the chickens clucked, and the crops stood tall and healthy. Everything was as it should be.

Mamma halted before they reached the porch. "There is something you need to know."

The pressure returned.

Uncle Morris traded a look with Mamma before resuming. "Unknown men have been snooping about the area. We've never seen them before and they wear nondescript clothing with hoods, so we can't tell where they're from or even what they look like. Chief found one nosing through the church one night and Lemuel caught one trying to enter the supply shack. Kanni and Lloyd saw a shadow flitting through the trees one morning. They said it had to be human."

Nerissa found no nails long enough to pick, so she clutched the key still hanging around her neck. "What do they want?"

Uncle Morris shrugged. "I don't know, but we think they may be connected to the kidnappings. Some of the neighboring villages reported disappearances in the past three days. Messenger birds have been flying in and out of Chief's office all week. That's why children and you women will be escorted by at least two men whenever you go anywhere."

Cold consumed Nerissa. Her sisters were in danger. If they were attacked, there was no way she could protect them. She possessed no particular skill with any type of weapon, nor was she strong enough to fight off a man with ill intent.

What if they were caught unaware? What if Father was injured trying to protect them? What if Mamma was harmed or Elberta or Daffy taken?

Uncle Morris crossed his arms. "Tomorrow, Denton and I will be over to escort you ladies to the village so you can do whatever it is you need to do. That'll allow you, Jarrel, to catch up on work." He wagged a thick finger. "I don't want to hear of either of you disregarding this warning and gallivanting off so you can go chat with your friends. Understand?"

Like Uncle Morris needed to worry. Nerissa would stay in the cabin for the rest of her life if it meant keeping her family safe.

As the two men left, a knot formed in her gut. Why must her sisters worry about the chance of being kidnapped? Why must innocent children be stripped from their homes and forced to endure trafficking? Why must evil overwhelm the world?

"He only is my rock and my salvation, my fortress; I shall not be greatly shaken."

The parson had spoken on that verse a few months ago, and later, Father had joined Nerissa on a walk. He had taken one look at her unkempt nails before speaking about how the Beginning needed to be the focus of every believer. Hard times would come, difficulties would arise, yet no matter what, those who put their faith in the Beginning needed to keep their hearts and mind on the Scripts and His commands.

The battle was not against the visible, but the invisible. And the only way to endure life without being dragged down by the worries and burdens of the world was to remember Who was in charge.

But that was so, so hard. It didn't feel like the Beginning was in charge. It felt, instead, like everything spiraled from His control. Like an island that had broken loose of its foundation and was now drifting along in the sea, battered and buffeted by the inescapable storms of life.

Warm wind tore free Nerissa's hair from her braid as she walked the shoreline. To her right, grasses waved in the breeze and to her left, waves brushed the sand.

She closed her eyes and tilted back her head, relishing the sun's heat as it soaked into her skin. The scent of salt and grass filled the air, accompanying the sounds of Daffy, Elberta, and Uncle Morris as they played tag.

If she blocked out the reason why Denton and her uncle were with them, she could trick herself into believing this stroll was like the olden days.

Back when she thought the world untouched by evil.

Back when she did not question the Beginning.

Something snagged around the toe of her boot, and she pitched forward.

Only for fingers to clasp her elbow and haul her upright.

Nerissa found herself looking into summer-blue eyes edged with secrets and pain.

"Careful," Denton murmured.

Why was her face burning? Her face shouldn't be burning.

Her heart leapt to her throat when he scanned the area. "Is something amiss?"

"No, but you can never be too careful." Denton made a face. "At least, that's what Red says. Funny thing is, she never follows her own advice."

"Is this your detective friend?"

"I doubt she'd claim me as a friend." A slight smirk graced his features for a brief moment, and at his motion, Nerissa resumed walking. Mamma and Father lingered behind them, no doubt relishing the few uninterrupted moments together.

"Why is that?" Why Nerissa cared, she didn't know. Perhaps it was the overwhelming sadness dousing any hints of happiness when he thought no one looked. Perhaps it was how he watched her family like they were a few fish shy of a full net. Perhaps it was the gentle way he interacted with Noko, and even Daffy when she barraged him with questions.

Denton shrugged. "Red despised the very concept of my existence for a while, I think." Shadows dulled his eyes for a second. "Not that I blame her."

"Why do you say that?"

He shrugged again and studied the pale grains of sand. With his coloring, he could pass as a Marterisi until one saw his eyes.

Nerissa tamped down the sudden rise of panic. "You're not a criminal, are you?"

"No."

"Is this child you're looking for a family member?"

"No."

"Then why are you searching for him?"

Denton sighed. "I made a promise and failed to keep it. Others made promises to him and failed to keep them. An innocent child has been kidnapped because of our carelessness—*my* carelessness—and I aim to fix that.'

Nerissa resisted the urge to squirm. What would he say if he knew she might know the whereabouts of the child he sought?

Regret claimed Denton's expression. "Never make promises you can't keep."

"How did you get your scars?" The question left her before she could contemplate if it was a good idea to ask.

"From arrows."

"I know that."

He smirked. Actually smirked. "Broadhead arrows, to be specific."

Well. Someone thought himself amusing. "Yes, I know. I've pulled broadheads from Edver before. I meant what was the occasion?"

"A bad one. A *very* bad one."

This man gave a new definition to *exasperating.*

Nerissa cleared her throat. He also knew how to make a situation awkward. "This child you are looking for—what does he look like?"

"He's tall for his age and was scrawny back then, so he's definitely skinny now if he hasn't already been rescued. Bright red hair. I think he has gold eyes. And freckles. Lots of freckles. He also liked to talk once he warmed up around you. But he was serious, too. Too serious for a child. Said his parents were merchants."

"How was he taken?"

Storm clouds filled Denton's eyes. "The first time? I don't know. But the second? He was stolen from the palace during a dance."

Nerissa had heard of palaces, with their tall spires, grand interiors, and cold-hearted rulers. Denton did not act like someone who belonged in a palace. "What was he doing in a palace?"

"The king and queen thought that would be the safest place for him."

"But it wasn't."

"No," Denton answered grimly. "It wasn't."

Nerissa stared at the sea. In a way, she felt like the sea during a storm. Appearing calm from a distance, yet in obvious turmoil the closer one neared.

Mother was so steadfast. Hauni and Mrs. Talart were brave and bold. Even Elberta and Daffy exhibited signs of staying strong under pressure.

"It's okay to be concerned, you know."

Pushing away her musings, Nerissa blinked at Denton. "What?"

He nodded toward the girls. "It's okay to be concerned. Shows that you care."

Nerissa exhaled. "I just want them to be safe."

"As you should."

"This world...it is so evil. So dark and deadly. I've seen what demented minds conjure. If I can keep my sisters from that, I will."

Denton stuffed his hands in his pockets, gaze downward, like he found his boots and passing grains of sand fascinating. "They should be grateful. Not every older sibling is so dedicated to their younger one's wellbeing."

"I don't understand why the Beginning would allow children to be sold into slavery. And I don't understand why more people do not rise up and fight against this evil."

Denton sighed. "Nerissa, the one thing I have learned in this past year is apathy is a curse most folks willingly partake in and embrace. If they don't bother themselves with another's problems, then they can continue their comfortable life."

Nerissa huffed. "Everyone is apathetic until they themselves desire help or rescue."

"This world is so self-centric." Dark undertones laced Denton's words. "We're so wrapped up in ourselves that we're blind to what's really going on. And if that's not the problem, then we're either too afraid to speak up or too pathetic to care."

Nerissa couldn't agree more with the *self-centric* statement, but she didn't hear any egocentricity in Denton's tone. Instead, she detected self-loathing.

It was obvious in how he spit out the words, emphasizing *we* like he included himself among those individuals. It appeared in how he glared at the beach, jaw tight and shoulders stiff. And it emerged in how he gave no care to himself.

Uncle Morris said the Veerhamer ate too little and slept even less. Nor did Denton act like he cared if his injuries caught infection.

She laced her fingers. When had she become comfortable sharing her heart with a stranger? "How many siblings do you have?"

"I have tw—one. I have one. Carter, who found Cinders."

"Are you close?"

Denton shrugged.

And he was back to being a man of few words.

Elberta's and Daffy's laughter and screeches filled the air and frightened a flock of sandpipers, who made known their irritation as they flew away.

If only life could remain so idyllic.

"Why are you so terrified of horses?"

"I'm not terrified of them." Not really. She just...wasn't fond of the stately animals.

Denton raised a brow. "Really? Because you shy away whenever you're near one, you ride as stiff as a frozen board, and you're terrified whenever one is in a league's vicinity of your sisters."

Nerissa restrained a scowl. "I am not terrified. I am cautious."

"There's being cautious and there's being paranoid."

She was not in the mood to be lectured by an outsider. Stopping, Nerissa whirled to face him, hands on her hips.

Denton met her with a blank expression, but something shadowed the edges of his eyes. Something that looked a lot like guilt.

What would this man feel guilty about besides being a bother?

The shadow disappeared. "Your sisters do not realize how fortunate they are to have you looking out for them, but they will be fine taking riding lessons from your uncle."

"Horses are unpredictable."

"So are humans."

She couldn't argue with that.

And, for some reason, that rankled. She *liked* keeping her sisters in a safe bubble. *Liked* keeping them close so she could protect them. She did not need to be reminded how that tenuous control could easily splinter within an hour's time.

"Give your canoe to the Beginning, young one, and relinquish your grip on the oars."

Nerissa did not want to relinquish her oars. Doing so meant she relinquished control.

"They need to know how to ride."

Ignoring how Hauni's advice kept replaying through her mind, Nerissa resumed walking. "What are you? The advocate for horseback riding lessons?"

"I could be. Knowing how to ride has saved several lives. Plus, there's something liberating about the wind in your hearing and the vibration of hooves against the earth. It almost feels like freedom."

The wistfulness in his tone once again drew Nerissa's attention. Denton stared at the stretch of swaying grass and weeds, longing etched in his countenance.

What did he yearn for? He only mentioned his brother. No other family. What secret pain and turmoil did he nurse in the dark of night?

Nerissa's throat tightened. The man beside her was more than an outsider. He had bled for a lost child. He put his life at risk to help another. He sought a child he believed he wronged. He obviously carried weight or guilt that anchored him to pain.

He was more than an outsider. He was human.

Flawed and capable of emotion, just as she was.

And lonely. He looked so, so lonely and lost.

Nerissa understood that sensation. Instead of stable and secured to an immovable cliff, it was like a ship being tossed about in the worst maelstrom.

"Love heals most wounds, Nerri."

Mamma had said that during one of the first rescues. There was more than the romantic love. There was the sacrificial. The friendship. The familial.

But I don't want to.

Even as she sent the mulish protest heavenward, Nerissa knew the action required of her.

Perhaps what this outsider needed wasn't to leave her village, but to remain.

Perhaps...perhaps he needed to be shown the love only those who experienced the love of the Beginning could bestow.

"The greatest of these is love."

The verse, one of the most memorized from the Scripts, replaced Hauni's admonition.

Her spirit still rebelled. She wasn't the one to show him, and she wanted no one in her village who could attract any type of love.

"The greatest of these is love."

No. No, someone else could do it. Another village could do it.

She needed to watch over her sisters and the rescued children. Not help a man she did not know.

"The greatest of these is love."

Fine and well, but it wasn't her job.

No matter the reasoning she wielded against the prompting, it remained, stubbornly persisting.

"The greatest of these is love."

Chapter Seventeen

DENTON

"Again!"

Denton allowed a smile as he watched Mr. Wessen lead Daffy around the corral. The patient, ancient gelding ignored the ear-piercing squeals and kept plodding along.

His amusement grew when he caught sight of a most unhappy Nerissa. Wearing a ferocious scowl and with arms crossed, she watched the ongoings with an air of thunderous contempt. Beside her, Elberta clapped and urged Daffy to jump the gelding over the rail.

To Denton's left, Morris chuckled. "That Elberta. Ever eager for an adventure."

"I don't think Nerissa agrees."

"Nerissa is the calm one out of the three. If you kept her on the family farm until she died, she'd be happy."

Denton braced his forearms on the top rail and stared at the field stretching beyond the corral. What would it be like to love your home and family so much that you never wanted to leave? What would it be like to be *wanted*?

"You know, you could give Elberta lessons."

The thought crossed Denton's mind many a time, but his experience with children stretched to Jonah and Noko and not a child more. For all he knew, his father's hatred could be lurking just beneath the surface.

For all he knew, he could become his father.

An icy shudder seized him. *Please, Beginning, don't let that happen.*

"I've seen you ride." Like the resident magpies, Morris kept chattering. "You and that horse are quite a team. You've got excellent equine sense."

"Cinders is a good horse." Shame still stung him at the recollection of Morris witnessing the reunion, but the man hadn't said anything about it since, so Denton could only hope he'd forgotten.

Morris grunted. "And you're a good horseman. One of the best I've met. And I was serious about teaching Elberta. In fact, Chief may just have you teach all of the youngsters. He thinks you have a knack too."

Denton ground back a snarl. He had upheld his end of the bargain, but the chief was nothing more than a lying, decaying snack for flies. The man still refused to provide Jonah's location.

It wasn't like Denton could arm wrestle the man either. The chief's bulky muscle mass made Denton look like a toothpick.

"People aren't worth the effort."

Wrong. Jonah was, and whatever the price, Denton would pay.

He exhaled and made his way through tall weeds and grass and around piles of mole hills to where Nerissa and Elberta stood. Perhaps Morris was right and doing this would convince the chief to keep his end of the bargain.

And, perhaps, helping would convince the Beginning to be merciful to a man who deserved no mercy.

Nerissa eyed him like he was one of Halthdurn's wolves as he approached. Elberta copied her sister's stance. The short bundle of attitude and flyaway hair reminded him of Red.

"Morris sent me to teach Elberta how to ride." The words tumbled from him in an awkward avalanche.

Nerissa pursed her lips. "She knows how to ride."

"With someone leading the horse in circles. At a walk. Contained in a corral."

"That's a safe riding environment."

"Safe is fine for the basics, but if all she knows how to do is plod along on a horse that was ready for pasture a decade ago, then how will she ride away from trouble and those with ill intent?"

Those green-gray eyes flashed. "Just because you know how to ride doesn't make you an expert on what is best for my sister."

One glance at Elberta's wide eyes told Denton the kid was far too astute for her own good and that what he needed to tell Nerissa would not only be understood by the middle Wessen daughter, but would scare her too.

He inclined his head and led Nerissa several paces away, frowning at Elberta's attempts to follow. After a stern reprimand from Nerissa, Elberta pouted and returned to the coral.

"Well? What is so important that you insist upon privacy?"

Denton clenched his hands. "You were wrong."

"I beg your pardon?"

"You were wrong. In this case, I do know what is best for Elberta." He swallowed, but the memories continued to surge. Even a year later, he could still recall with horrific clarity the unspeakable agony of the arrows turning him into a pincushion. "You asked where my scars came from. My brother was kidnapped by slave traders. We went after them, but they weren't inclined to accommodate our request to return the captives." The sensation of jumping from Cinders' back onto the wagon still coursed through him. "Only by knowing how to ride—and ride *well*—was Carter able to rescue the princess. And only by knowing how to ride was Red able to rescue numerous children."

No sense in detailing his participation in those endeavors. She likely wouldn't believe him, and the recollection of such heroic actions still made him uneasy. Surely someone from Father's bloodline couldn't enact such feats. Bravery, courage, and selflessness were extinct in his heritage.

If looks could murder, Denton would be dead at the bottom of the sea.

Nerissa shook her head. "It's not safe."

"If you think about it, nothing's safe. You could choke while eating, you could trip and hit your head while walking, and you could die in your sleep."

"That's different."

"Is it?"

"Yes, it is." Nerissa lifted her chin in what he assumed was defiance, but the act couldn't disguise the raw fear in her eyes.

"Weakling."

Father's venomous hiss echoed through Denton's mind and almost spilled from his tongue.

He clamped it back. He *wasn't* Father. He *refused* to be like the man who taught him the meaning of fear and left him wanting for just one hint that he was worth someone's love and time.

What was it Parson Gil once said? Something about a gentle answer and wrath?

"Elberta could get hurt riding. There's no use attempting to ignore the potential dangers." He hardened his expression before again facing Nerissa. She needn't know the tempest within far surpassed any storm that befell Marteris' shores. "But the negatives of her not knowing how to ride are far surpassed by the positives. Your father and uncle are working with Daffy. I have been riding since I was old enough to stay upright, and I promise you I would never do anything to harm her."

A coward he may be, but a killer he was not.

At least, not now. His prior actions certainly allowed many to suffer.

Nerissa bit her lip and glanced at Elberta, who skulked near the corral and shot them continual glowers.

Something told Denton Elberta was the stubbornest of the three.

"Your fears are not unfounded." Horses and horseshoes, how did Carter console Chamonix? Being kind and gentle and understanding did not come naturally. "But Elberta will be in greater danger if she doesn't know how to ride."

"She's small enough to hide." Uncertainty laced Nerissa's tone.

A pang the size of the ocean speared Denton's chest. What would it be like to be loved so much that your well-being was worried about?

"She won't always be. Listen, let's go find a horse you're comfortable with, then we'll proceed with Elberta's lesson."

Nerissa backed up a few paces. "Why would *I* need a horse?"

"Because you're joining us. There is no room for antics while on horseback, and your presence will keep Elberta behaving."

A soft laugh left her and for one heartbeat amusement flared in her eyes. "Elberta will do what Elberta wants to do, and nothing else."

Perhaps instructing the impudent youngster wouldn't be so difficult. It sounded like she was similar to Red, and Denton had been dealing with the ornery detective for years.

He inclined his head toward the pasture. "Let's get the horses, then." He called to Elberta, then fell in step beside Nerissa as they followed the girl toward the fence separating the pasture from the rest of land. "What do you know about riding?"

Elberta tossed a saucy grin over her shoulder. "I know the faster you go, the funner it is. Unless you're Neri, that is."

Nerissa hissed her sister's name. "First, *funner* is not a word. Second, speaking of that incident is forbidden."

"For you, maybe, but Mamma and Father never said I couldn't talk about it." Elberta turned so she faced them as she walked backward. "Ner's never liked horses. Mamma said it's because she fell off one when she was little and broke her arm."

Denton didn't need perfect eyesight to see the crimson flushing Nerissa's face.

"And she's horrible at riding. Uncle Morris says the horses can sense when she's nervous, and that's why they act up."

"Elberta…" Nerissa warned through clenched teeth.

Currently deaf to everything but her own voice, Elberta continued. "And one time a horse Nerri was trying to ride spooked and jumped the fence. She didn't stay on."

"Elberta Jan Wessen, so help me, if you don't stop…"

Denton halted Elberta's continued tattling with a replica of an unamused expression he'd seen Carter pull many a time. "Riding may not come naturally to your sister, but she did well during the rescue."

Elberta scowled. Nerissa's shoulders slumped, and if he wasn't mistaken, a slight blush tinged her cheeks.

Red would call him foolish for noticing.

But the pretty Marterisi wasn't, to borrow one of Edver's phrases, off the hook yet. "Both of you need to hone your skills."

Elberta pouted. Nerissa graced him with a glare that could kill the toughest warrior.

Oh, yes. He reckoned he'd be at the bottom of the sea right then if she had her way.

"Come on, ladies."

"Where are we going?" Elberta's voice still pitched high with a whine.

"To find your horses."

Nerissa stopped and crossed her arms, still offering a glare Denton was sure she'd perfected on her sisters long ago. "I am *not* stepping foot in that pasture."

When someone resisted riding, it was usually for good reason. But as understandable as her fear was, there would be consequences if she did not take the first steps in facing it.

Denton sent Elberta ahead, warning her not to get too close to the horses, before facing Nerissa. "I meant what I said about the rescue."

"That is kind of you, but I will not change my mind."

"Your skillset is adequate for daily life, but you know things can change in a blink." He'd heard some Marterisi saying about tides of change or whatever, but didn't care enough to commit it to memory. "What if the village is attacked and the only way to escape is on horseback? They won't slow their pace just because you can't ride at a canter."

The storm in her eyes deepened even as her color paled.

"What if you need to fetch help? Things could take a turn for the worse before you even make it halfway at a trot."

Sparks flashed in her eyes, reminding him once again of Chamonix. A quiet and ladylike demeanor hid a spine of tempered steel.

"Don't you dare guilt-trip me into this," she hissed, her finger darting out and jabbing his chest. "It's hard enough living in...it's bad enough knowing an attack may happen. I don't need you rubbing my failures in my face. I know I'm incapable. I know I'm incompetent. I know I'll never be near the horseback rider you or Uncle Morris are. But don't you *ever* think I'll not do what it takes to save my family."

Ignoring the prick of pain from her fingernail, Denton lightly placed his hand over hers. Nerissa blinked before withdrawing her nail from his chest.

"I'm not guilt-tripping. I'm stating facts." Horses and horseshoes, comforting people was not his gift. *Nowhere* near his gift. "And I know what it's like to live with that weight in your heart. It's suffocating even on the peaceful days."

Surely those weren't tears. He could handle a crying child, but how did one comfort a crying woman who wanted to make him fish food?

Her jaw trembled as she looked away, blinking rapidly. "I'll watch from the fence."

"You'll do exactly what I tell you or I'll strap you so hard you won't be walking for a month." Father's snarled threat emerged for the first time in years.

Denton fisted his hands to keep from flinching. He wouldn't be like Father. Wouldn't force Nerissa to join. "Fine. Then I'll make you a deal."

"Oh?" Skepticism painted her tone.

"I won't push you to join us if you tell me where Jonah is."

Wide eyes and an opened mouth were not the answer he expected.

Nerissa looked away, picking double-time at a nail. "Why do you think I know where Jonah is?"

Clever girl, evading him with what most would deem an answer declaring her innocence in the matter.

"Because everyone I've asked—you, your uncle, your parents, the chief, Edver—you all either shift and look away or stare." Both were signs of dishonesty, or so Red claimed. And, though Denton wouldn't tell them so, they acted shiftier than Red caught leaving the kitchen with her hands behind her back. That usually meant she had crept in and filched a few cookies.

Nerissa pursed her lips as a battle, unheard but not unseen, played in her eyes. After a quick glance at her father and uncle, who still helped Daffy, she stiffened her shoulders and met him with a cold, haughty expression. "I will ride."

That was what he thought.

Denton nodded to the pasture and the slip of a miscreant who waited with less patience than Red. "After you."

Chapter Eighteen

NERISSA

S HE WAS NEVER RIDING again.

Never. Ever. Getting on a horse again.

She wouldn't even *look* at horses again.

Not bothering to withhold her moan, Nerissa sank onto the cabin's porch, bowl of peas clutched to her chest. May Cinders never allow Denton to saddle her again, and may Denton always fall off of every horse he rode. Multiple times. Straight onto a sticker weed.

No, *multiple* sticker weeds.

She'd never hurt so bad before. Every leg muscle cramped, her lower back ached, and she was fairly certain the bruises discoloring her entire right arm concealed numerous fractures.

"Wretched outsider," she hissed, forcing her sore hands to begin shelling peas.

Never again would she allow Denton to manipulate her into riding. First, he made them choose their horses. *Made them!* Then he forced her to saddle her own—despite her semi-incompetency in such matters—as he helped Elberta. Then he lectured her on everything she was doing wrong while riding.

"Keep your heels down. Keep your posture relaxed—you look like someone tied a slab of granite to your back. Stop strangling the reins. A simple bit of pressure will do."

Nerissa had wanted to strangle *him*.

Then, Elberta decided a trot—that wretched gait—wasn't fast enough. Applying her heels to her gelding's sides with enough force to crack a cliff, she had shrieked like a maniac when the horse—named Sir Marlin by the "expert of naming ani-mals"—took off at a dead gallop.

Denton then had to play the hero and go after her.

And that had caused the spitfire menace beneath Nerissa to think they played a game of tag.

She hadn't seen Elberta fall, but her ears still rang from the shrill shriek. All she knew was Cinders effortlessly jumped the fence, with Denton having the audacity to stay on, and then the demented demon named Dancer sped up and over the fence.

Nerissa went up too, but she didn't go over.

No, instead she went down. Down with such force it felt like her lungs were forever emptied of air and the deep throbbing spreading throughout her body attacked every nerve with agoniz-ing ferocity.

To worsen matters, when her vision cleared and the ringing in her ears dulled to a muted trill, she was able to make out a certain man's features as he knelt over her. His mouth moved, but his words did not reach her ears.

The sting of humiliating tears hadn't remained blessedly unno-ticed, though.

Nerissa pressed a hand to her cheek as her face heated at the memory. Denton had all but carried her home as Elberta told Father and Uncle Morris. He had deposited her on the chair in her room, said she'd be sore for the next few days, then fled.

Sore was the understatement of all time.

She hurt. Ached. Throbbed.

And no amount of willow tea completely removed the pain.

Mamma emerged a few hours later, wiping her hands on her apron. "How are you?"

"I'm fine."

"Nerri..." Mamma sat and placed her arm around Nerissa's shoulder. "How are you really, my dear girl?"

"Sore. Humiliated. *Right.* This is why I don't ride. I warned Denton. I really did. He just refused to listen." She sighed and leaned her head on Mamma's shoulder. "He asked again about Jonah."

"What did you say?"

"I elected to ride." Which was a mistake, but not nearly as bad as revealing Jonah's location.

"You know why we can't tell him yet, Ner," Mamma said quietly.

Nerissa stared at the wall of pine trees obscuring the village and ocean from view. "I know."

"Do you think he'd willingly hurt someone for no reason?"

"He is an outsider. Who knows what they're fully capable of?" Releasing another exhale that caused her ribs to spasm, Nerissa shook her head. "His eyes are kind and I've watched him with Elberta, Daffy, and the victims. Do I think he'd hurt a child now? No. Back then before Jonah was kidnapped? I have no idea."

Mamma squeezed Nerissa's uninjured shoulder. "Try learning more about him, specifically his past. Your uncle thinks he's trustworthy, but your father, Edver, and Chief Talart think he's hiding something."

"Then why allow him to help?"

"To test him and see if he knew any of the kidnappers. It doesn't sound like he did."

Nerissa located a nail—black and blue from her fall—and began gently smoothing the ragged edges. "He did act genuinely concerned when we entered Losibar."

"I remember you saying that. Just because he's an outsider doesn't mean he's of ill-will, my dear. And just because other villages have been attacked doesn't mean ours will."

Nerissa looked up. "You know there's a possibility."

Mamma's eyes, green-gray just like Nerissa's, always brimmed with the love exhibited in her smile. "It is always a possibility. We are on the coast, far away from the universities and learning centers—more civilized areas as far as fewer attacks go."

"I'm scared." The words escaped her. "I'm so scared. When we were returning from the rescue, I thought...I thought I'd come back to Father not only being dead, but the village up in flames and you and the girls taken." For the third time in two days, tears dared to fall.

"Oh, Starfish." Mamma pressed a kiss to Nerissa's hair.

"It's wrong to be afraid, I know the Scripts say that, but I can't help it, Mamma. I *can't*." The sobs did come then, unrelenting and with the intensity of a spring storm.

When the final sobs died away, Mamma spoke. "It is not a sin to fear, Nerissa. The sin is when we doubt the Beginning's capability to keep us safe. It's wrong when we question His infiniteness and power. The One who formed us will never remove His hand from us, my sweet girl. We may break, we may feel like we cannot go on, but He is always there. There is nothing we cannot endure with His grace and power."

"But the Scripts say not to worry." Nerissa's words emerged as hiccupping squeaks.

"And we're not supposed to. Do you remember that verse about the sparrows?"

"Yes."

"My dear, dear child, if a sparrow does not fall without His knowledge, how can anything else happen without Him knowing? He ordered the world, Nerissa. He knows when every wave crashes and every tide changes. He knows each time a fish's fin moves and whenever a leaf sways in the breeze. And He knows every beat your heart will take, my dear."

Nerissa swallowed, but the lump in her throat remained. The parson once said the Beginning allowed believers to be tested, and those tests either strengthened faith or exposed cracks in the foundation.

Compared to others, she hadn't endured terrible tests.

And the ominous premonition slowly creeping through her promised that was about to change.

"This is the path we'll take." Edver jabbed his finger at a collection of scribbles adorning the near-middle of a map so old Guy and Hauni barely remembered it being drawn. "We'll be unseen that way yet still have a good view of the tower."

Across the table, Denton frowned and crossed his arms, yet said nothing.

Nerissa returned her attention to the map, gluing it there. Since the fall, she hadn't spoken to him, and any attempts from Father, Uncle Morris, and Elberta—once she was free of her punishment for pulling such a stunt—were rebuffed.

"This will need to be a small group," Chief Talart said. "We're on our own for this."

Nerissa located a nick in her thumbnail and began working at it. The letter carrier had arrived last night, quaking like a child seeing a shark for the first time. Just before passing out, the skinny, middle-aged man managed to tell them about a string of slaves near one of the older towers.

That morning, the man had gathered the papers and scrambled off, declaring he wanted to be as far away from such accursed activity as possible.

Nerissa couldn't blame him. Three more villages had been decimated, and while rescuing the children was important, the village needed to be kept safe as well.

Her stomach twisted and churned, housing a maelstrom rivaling those of late summer. Edver was a good warrior, and Lemuel, while old, was not one with whom to trifle. Denton was, in Uncle Morris' words, invaluable with horses, and supposedly his detective skills would come in handy.

While the others expressed optimism, the curdling worry keeping Nerissa awake at night refused to settle.

Yald, the village postmaster, scratched his stubbled chin. "Wasn't that girl from that area? The mute one?"

"Stop talking about her like she's an unwelcomed rash," Edver growled. The tendons in his forearms bulged as he placed his fisted hands atop the table, ignoring the crumpling map beneath them. "Afya is intelligent and sweet and kind. Just because you avoid her like she's an illness doesn't mean you get to deride her."

"Hold your temper, Son," Chief Talart muttered. "Yald meant no disrespect.

Nerissa placed her hand on Edver's arm. When he turned a stormy gaze her way, she inclined her head toward the map.

Shoulders slumping, he backed away.

"Your father is correct. I meant no ill words toward the girl. But I would like an answer to my speculation."

Edver shrugged. "I don't know. We can ask."

"I'll fetch her." Nerissa backed from the room. As soon as she reached the letter office's front room, she scurried out. Warm air carrying hints of the seaweed soup simmering in Lemuel's wife's kitchen drifted through the air, tempting a grumble from her stomach.

Children played on the shore, women washed clothing, and men mended nets and canoes. Friendly chatter and bird song ebbed and flowed in volume, often punctuated with laughter.

All was as it should be.

Inhaling and allowing her smile to come forth, Nerissa searched the village for Afya. There was something freeing listening to the waves gently brush the shore and watching the trees stand so tall and proud.

Her home was the prettiest place in the world, and if she had her way, she'd never leave.

She found Afya helping the candlemaker and beckoned the young woman outside. "Would you mind coming with me? There's something Edver needs to ask you."

Her friend would kill her for it, but it gave Nerissa amusement, and that amusement helped her keep her mind off the aches and pains making her feel ninety instead of twenty-three.

Afya slowed as they neared the letter office until she came to a complete stop. Eyes wide and edged with what looked like fear, she shook her head and backed away.

"What's wrong?" Nerissa scanned their surroundings. No one lurked in the brush or behind trees and other buildings, and the birds continued chirping, signaling nothing was amiss.

Afya shuddered, her breaths emerging in such fast huffs Nerissa was surprised she was breathing at all.

"What is it?" Nerissa barely ignored the need to startle when Afya gripped her wrist.

"Afya, I can't help if I don't know what's going on."

The dark-skinned Marterisi shook her head. Lips pursed, she tugged Nerissa back.

"Afya..." What was going on? Why the reaction? "I promise there is no one evil in there. That's where I just came from."

The door swung open.

Afya inhaled and jumped behind Nerissa, fingers digging into Nerissa's arm.

"Is everything okay?" Edver and Denton emerged, both with hands on their swords.

Nerissa shrugged. "Afya senses something amiss."

Edver staked his place by Afya's side and offered her his most winning smile. "Would it help if I looked around? I'll take Denton with me. No guarantee he'd be of any help, but maybe he can scream louder than me."

Denton scowled. "You're the one who screeched like a frightened owl when we saw that snake."

"I did not screech."

Denton shook his head. "Liar."

Edver huffed and patted Afya's hand. "Ignore him, please. His mind is still scrambled and filled with sand."

Denton muttered something about Edver's being filled with air.

A hint of a smile eased a few lines of Afya's worry from her face.

"Please, milady." Edver offered his arm, still wearing the smile that enabled him to worm his way out of punishments and gain more cookies when everyone else was banished from snitching them from the platters. "There is nothing wrong in that building. See? I just came from there. I would never knowingly allow you to enter a dangerous situation."

Afya stared at Edver for a long moment before hesitantly placing her hand in the crook of his elbow.

"Let us go in, milady."

Nerissa followed her miscreant of a friend and his crush through the door, with Denton on her heels. "Since when do you know what *milady* means?"

"I do read, you know."

"Oh? When? You're too busy stealing my banana bread to do anything productive."

"I'll have you know thieving banana bread is one of the most productive activities in the world."

Afya shuddered when they reached the backroom, the pressure of her grip causing Edver's sleeve to wrinkle.

He again patted her hand. "It's okay, milady. I won't let anyone hurt you."

Yes, Edver was besotted.

Chief Talart and Uncle Morris offered Afya kind smiles. "Good afternoon, Afya. I'm sure you heard the letter deliverer last night." At Afya's nod. Chief Talart continued, gesturing her closer and pointing at the map. "He came from this area. We're sending out a small group to see if his claims are true and, if they are, rescue the children. Since you were rescued in this area, are we correct in assuming you passed through there while kidnapped?"

Afya's posture went so stiff Nerissa feared she would sustain spinal damage. A choppy, hesitant nod provided Chief Talart's answer.

"Excellent. Is there anything you can tell us about it?"

She shook her head.

Yald braced his hands on the table and leaned forward. "Better yet, why don't you just go with the group? Take them there yourself. You know the way, I presume, seeing how you were with the victims."

Afya again shook her head, but inched toward the table and peered at where Chief Talart's finger rested on the map.

A sharp scream punctured the air before the young woman turned and fled.

Chapter Nineteen

DENTON

At his command, Cinders switched from a canter to a gallop. The horse ahead, while a fine equine in its youth, could no longer run long distances.

Something Afya hadn't realized when she stole the horse and rode away.

Denton lifted his chin, allowing the rush of air to whistle past his ears. They still rang from Afya's scream, and it'd be days before her haunted, tormented expression left his memory.

What happened to elicit such a reaction?

"Come on, girl."

Cinders' powerful strides carried him along a path seen only by Afya. With such reckless riding, she was sure to rein the horse into a hole and cause the poor thing to stumble.

The old, gray-specked sorrel slowed, the sweat darkening its coat visible even with the distance between them.

Cinders covered that distance in a few minutes. Bracing himself as they approached, Denton leaned over and snatched the reins from Afya, slowing both Cinders and the stumbling equine to a trot.

The glace at Afya threatened to break his heart. Tears streamed down her face and dampened her bodice's collar. She could be in the middle of a windy onslaught for as hard as she was trembling, and her eyes, reddened and shiny with moisture, contained a vacant look Denton had seen in his own a few times.

Once the horses were given adequate time to cool down, he dismounted and assisted Afya off her horse. She stared straight ahead, expression empty and hopeless.

Beginning, please give me the words.

Perhaps his prayers would be answered since they were for someone else.

"Afya?"

No answer.

Denton squinted at the two, blurry shapes in the distance. Edver had ribbed him and then some about training Cinders to respond to certain whistles, but Denton wasn't the one who had to scramble to get a horse when Afya took off.

A shuddering sob shook the woman's thin frame.

Denton gently turned her around, facing her toward the village, and took two steps. "Let's go back, Afya."

Woodenly, she followed. Not as a person, but as a beaten-down soul who had been abused into compliance.

Denton had seen it in some of the children he helped rescue back in Veerham.

Please, Beginning, help her.

"You were held in that tower, weren't you?"

Afya sobbed.

Denton paused, clenching and unclenching his hands. What should he do? He'd leave the hugging up to Nerissa and the other women. He'd also leave the whole charming element to Edver.

What did that leave him to work with?

Very little.

"My brother—stepbrother—was kidnapped by traffickers." He'd never forget the dread and fear filling him when he heard Carter's fate. "They tried burning him alive."

Afya hiccupped.

"Afya, I don't know what you went through, but you experienced so much at the hands of these vile pieces of trash. I know you don't want to return to that tower. I can only imagine what happened to you there. But I also know these children must be rescued."

She flinched.

Fool. Way to make her feel like he blamed her reticence. "I'm not...I'm not saying I think *you* think they should be left there. I know you don't want that. That's not what I'm saying." Blast it all, he was horrible at this. Where was Nerissa? Even Chamonix would be excellent at this. Horses and horseshoes, *Red* would be far superior to this blundering attempt.

Afya pressed the heels of her hands to her eyes.

"I won't ask you to go. I won't ask you to relive the pain. But could you draw a map? Or maybe give us some tips about the tower or the surrounding land? That way you don't have to go, but you'll still be providing invaluable advice."

Afya's bloodshot eyes fastened on him, The depth of sadness almost undid Denton. Had he caused such agony with his apathy and cowardice? If so, no wonder the Beginning ignored him.

He offered what he hoped was a reassuring smile. "I see Nerissa and Edver coming. Don't tell Edver I said this, but I think he's head over heels for you. He's acting like an enamored dope, much like my brother did before he married my sister-in-law."

A whisper of a smile tipped Afya's mouth, and Denton was fairly certain he wasn't imagining her blush.

"We should probably go meet them. I think Edver is about to have heart failure."

Her shoulders shook, but not from tears.

It wasn't long before both horses were trotting toward the approaching dust cloud.

"You know, you're the only person who's able to get Nerissa to ride. I tried and she looked like she wanted to stake me to the beach and let a shark eat me. Whatever that is." All he knew was it was some behemoth, sea-faring monster.

Afya covered her mouth with her hand.

"Maybe you can do this again—take off without warning, that is—so she'll get on a horse again."

Afya snorted.

Denton allowed a sliver of a smile. If nothing else, perhaps he could help alleviate whatever caused her such turmoil, if even for a few brief minutes.

Nerissa and Edver reined their mounts to a hasty, unsafe halt when they drew within a few paces of Cinders and Afya's poor horse. Sweat lathered the horses' coats and Edver was covered in a layer of dust.

"Are you alright?" Nerissa slid off and ran to Afya, who shrugged.

"I am so, so sorry. If I had known, I wouldn't have retrieved you."

Afya patted Nerissa's shoulder before hugging her.

Edver groaned and wiped sweat from his head. "Are you okay? Please tell me you're okay."

Afya tilted her head and looked at him.

"She's fine, Edver, but you look like you're going to faint."

Edver scowled at Denton. "I am a man. I do not faint."

"Forgive me. *Pass out.*"

"I don't do that, either."

Denton met Nerissa's gaze. "Has he?"

She laughed. *Actually laughed.* "Yes, and I'll regale you both with the multiple stories as we head home."

And regale them she did, ignoring Edver's protests until Afya was laughing and Denton considered allowing his mirth to show through. It was almost like old times with Red and Carter. Listening to the two bicker had been the best part of his days besides working with the horses.

When they reached the village, the men from the meeting converged around them, joined by Hauni, and peppered Afya with questions, all of which she answered with the barest nods.

After they dismounted and the horses were taken away to be cooled and rubbed down by Noko and some other younger boys,

Chief Talart exhaled. "My deepest apologies for forcing you into that situation, Afya. I did not think of the repercussions you may experience."

Afya looked down, fingers lacing and unlacing.

"Nerissa, why don't you and Hauni take Afya and—"

"I will help."

Denton blinked. He didn't recognize the voice. The direction it came in, yes, but not the voice belonging to a woman who made a trepidatious mouse sound loud in comparison.

Edver gawked at Afya, eyes as wide as a draft horse's hooves. Nerissa smiled and squeezed her hand. And Afya hunched her shoulders and hugged herself, repeating, "I...I will help."

"I've never been this way before."

Denton eyed the wide path grooved with exposed roots and divots deep enough to create mini seas. The chill creeping up his spine for the last few days crept higher. Lemuel, Morris, and a box of a dark-skinned Marterisi whose name escaped his memory were the only real fighters. Edver, he'd heard, was good with the sword, but Denton hadn't witnessed anything convincing him to agree.

And Nerissa and Afya, while also armed, were not fighters.

Horses and horseshoes, he shouldn't be with this group. But Talart had hemmed and hawed like an old man when Denton confronted him about Jonah. After what felt like a years-long argument, the finicky man said if Denton helped with this rescue, he would tell him where Jonah was.

Completely forgetting—or pretending to—about making that same promise earlier.

Perhaps most Marterises were daft.

"What did you say to Afya?"

Nerissa's quiet question drew Denton from the quagmire of thoughts. He glanced over to find her watching him, a slight tilt to her head and an inquisitive expression perhaps indicating she no longer wanted to enact those threats toward him he heard her muttering during the aftermath of the riding incident.

"What do you mean?"

"You said something that helped her feel comfortable enough to begin talking. You were the one who convinced her to speak."

Denton shrugged. "She likely trusted you enough to begin opening up."

"No, she told me you convinced her to trust us enough to begin speaking."

"I said nothing special, if that's what you're asking."

"She said it was like you knew her pain."

"I could see her pain."

"Did you use some detective skills or something?"

Denton jerked his attention her way once more. "What?"

"That's what Edver thinks. That you used some detective trick."

Oh, for the love of horses. "That type of *skill* is called interrogation and usually involves some method of pain or other persuasive techniques, most of which come from a weapon. And you know I didn't do that to her."

Silence settled as the horses shuffled along the path. Trees towered, branches interlocking at points and blocking the sky from view. Squirrels and chipmunks scampered about, halting just long enough to watch the intruders before darting away.

It was so...free. So calm.

Denton closed his eyes and allowed the peaceful sounds of birds, rodents, and the impact of horse hooves to wash over him. Would he ever find the peace he longed for? *Thirsted* for? Would anything ever fill the unending hole within him?

He'd seen a piece of flotsam bobbing atop the waves a few days ago. Untethered, unmoored, all it could do was go where the water carried it.

He felt like that. Nowhere to hide, nowhere he could go to heal from the emotional wounds left perpetually raw. Just tossed about by life's whims and taken wherever the waves of fate dragged him.

What must I do to earn Your favor? And not even the Beginning's favor, but the mere acknowledgment of Denton's existence?

I'm trying. I promise. What else must I do?

When he opened his eyes, a thin sheen blurred his vision.

And he couldn't wipe away the wretched tears because the edge of his peripheral alerted him that Nerissa still watched.

Of all the times for her to want to chat.

"Was slavery bad in Veerham?"

"Terrible. Children were snatched almost every day. Red was run ragged trying to solve all the missing persons cases. Then the attacks on the princess happened, and it all spiraled into even worse chaos."

"Were you on the cases as well? Since you're a detective?"

The weight of twenty anvils filled his chest and pinned down his tongue. Parson Gil said the truth was important—that lying was a sin and something the Beginning did not condone. But he also needed to find Jonah, and if he spilled the truth about who and what he really was, they'd chain him to a boulder and send him to the bottommost depths of the sea.

"I...I was around the situation."

"What did you do? Or is that confidential?"

It's confidential, alright. "I'm afraid I can't...I can't divulge that information." The words tasted foul and his conscience screamed at him, but he couldn't risk jeopardizing his search for Jonah.

Denton shook himself from the darkening thoughts. If he showed any signs of weakness, this bunch may still turn on him. He had to be strong. Appear unmovable.

He looked at Nerissa and forced a smirk. "You're riding."

She frowned.

"I didn't mean for you to get hurt."

"I know."

When she refused to expound upon her simple statement, Denton returned his attention to the path ahead.

The weight in his chest never dissipated, however, and even as he attempted to sleep, the condemnation thrummed in his ears and mind, in sync with his pulse. *Liar, liar, liar.*

There was no way he would secure the Beginning's favor now.

Not when he willfully disobeyed Him.

Denton stared at the pinprick points of light glittering against the soft nighttime sky. The wind rustled through the pines, and they were too far from the shore to hear the waves against sand.

The peaceful setting should soothe him, but it only added layers of guilt.

Why must he doom himself in an already-tenuous situation?

Why couldn't he just be loved?

Perhaps...perhaps because he was unlovable.

With that thought simmering and the accusations—Father's, Antony's, Red's, and his conscience's—thrumming through him, he stared at the sky until the first colors of sunrise brushed it.

Chapter Twenty

NERISSA

SOME TOWERS WERE SHORT and squatty, their surfaces rough and obscured by black moss. Others were tall and smooth, with green moss and vines stretching up their cylindrical exteriors. Looking at the remains, one would never guess the towers were from a time when war consumed Marteris.

After the final war, the towers became residences and places for travelers to stay the night…if they could find the entrances.

"Just how are we to get in?" Uncle Morris scratched his beard as he stared at the map stretched out on a rock. "There are no stairs, and if the letter deliverer was right, the enemy will be swarming the place."

"If they're still there," Lemuel rumbled. Next to Denton and Uncle Morris, he looked like a hulking black cliff, overshadowing the shorter, paler men beside him. "That was over a week ago. They may have taken the children and left."

Afya shook her head. Although she now spoke, those instances were uncommon. Yet, no words were needed to convey the fear widening her eyes and causing her to tremble like a sapling in a storm. When she glanced over, Nerissa offered what she hoped was a comforting smile.

"According to the map, we're less than half a league away." Edver toyed with his knife. "If they're swarming the area, we'll be outnumbered."

Lemuel shot the younger man a flat look. "Your father's training went in one ear and out the other if you think we will just barge in. Get your head attached right, boy. We're going to scout, then we'll determine a plan. This will do us no good if we're ninnies and think with our swords instead of our minds. Edver, Norm, and I will scout. Morris, you and the kids stay here. You know the distress call."

Leveraging to his feet, Lemuel rolled his shoulders and started for the trees blocking the rest of Marteris from view.

Nerissa pulled her knees to her chest and watched the waves brush the shore. Her stomach twisted and turned, knotting with a ferocity that caused her last meal to dangerously stir. What if the men were ambushed and murdered? Uncle Morris was a strong warrior, and Denton fair, but they were no match for more than two mediocre swordsmen or one archer with any amount of aim.

Please, Beginning, keep us safe.

Uncle Morris engaged Afya in conversation, capturing her attention with stories of Elberta's and Daffy's antics. Gradually, the tension in Afya's shoulders eased, and she even laughed once.

Nerissa leaned her chin on her knees and fastened her gaze on Denton. He stared at the sea, his blank expression doing little to mask the longing she often witnessed in his eyes. Sadness resided there too, along with what she thought was self-loathing.

Mamma said a broken soul was easy to spot if you knew what to look for. And Denton had a broken soul.

"Has your opinion of the sea changed at all?" Since he sat almost within arm's reach, it wasn't necessary to raise her voice.

He shrugged. "Kind of hard to like something that almost killed you."

In theory, she could understand the concept of disliking the vast body of water, but such a thought was foreign. The waves had been her companions during some hearty cries, and they would never reveal her secrets. "You have to admit it's beautiful."

"I suppose it is in a deadly, swallow-you-up-and-drown-you way."

"There is danger in everything if you look closely enough."

Denton picked up a tiny, pink-tinged shell and traced his finger over the ridges. "Doesn't hurt to be aware of what's around you."

"Then doesn't that extend to the beauty, too?"

He raised a brow at her.

Nerissa shifted, rubbing her icy fingers. She shouldn't be cold in the humid heat, but such was the affliction caused by nerves. "If you're only thinking about danger, then that's all you'll notice. But if you realize there is beauty as well, you'll see that too. There is beauty in the sea. The way it sparkles when the sunlight catches it, the shells and starfish that reside in it, and the beautiful fish we sometimes catch. The Beginning did not withhold His creativity when He designed the world."

"Yeah, well, some of His designs went awry."

"Because we have free nature. He can do no wrong, and He is the Beginning—that means no imperfection."

Denton shrugged. "Sometimes I think He made a mistake creating certain things. Certain people."

Those words weren't spoken from a skeptic's heart, but from a hurting one. The pain lacing his tone was so potent Nerissa felt it herself. And she had no idea what caused it. "What do you mean?"

He waved his hand. "The traffickers. Those who harm innocents. Other people. You know. The ones who only cause heartache and suffering."

A sharp ache permeated Nerissa's heart. Did he believe himself to be included in that category? The derision in his voice and tension in his jaw and shoulders suggested so.

"What happened?" The words were spoken before she approved them.

"What?"

"To you. What happened?"

He ran a hand down his face. "Some of us don't have near-perfect lives, okay? Leave it at that."

"But—"

"No, Nerissa." Denton stood and brushed off the sand. "I'm going to check on the horses."

"They look fine to me."

"Appearances can be deceiving."

While that certainly held truth, Nerissa knew one instance where appearance *wasn't* deceitful.

Despite his efforts, Denton couldn't disguise the fact he ran from his past.

The question was *why*.

The thick scent of loam and wet pine almost strangled Nerissa's lungs as she knelt behind a thick tree trunk. The shift of shadows marked the passage of time—and the duration Lemuel, Edver, and Norm had been gone.

It also marked the amount of time since an arrow had punctured the sand not ten paces away from where Uncle Morris and Afya sat, skidding until it nearly entered the sea.

She clasped her fingers and tucked the icy digits beneath her chin. Uncle Morris had almost been hit. He could have died.

The thought of watching life drain from her uncle wrenched her shoulders in a silent dry heave.

Please, Beginning, keep us safe.

She'd expected danger. Just not so soon. And not targeted toward those innocently perched on the beach.

Warmth formed around her shoulder and gently squeezed.

After the arrow, Uncle Morris had yelled for them to take cover. Since Nerissa was not a crab and could not burrow in the sand, nor was she a fish and find refuge beneath the water's surface, she found herself seeking shelter behind the largest tree nearby since the cliffs were at the other side of the shore, where Uncle Morris and Afya hid.

One minute Uncle Morris had been shouting, and the next a strong arm looped around her waist and hauled her to the tree. Denton all but pinned her against the trunk, his breath tickling the back of her neck.

She looked down when something smooth was pressed into her hand. One of Uncle Morris' knives—she'd seen him use the plain blade with a bone hilt before.

"Someone's coming." The whisper barely brushed her ear.

Nerissa bit her tongue as a big, hulking figure sauntered to their left. A dark-skinned Marterisi glided through the forest, his scythe swishing through the underbrush like it was butter.

Please, Beginning, keep us safe.

She held her breath, not daring to even breathe lest something go wrong and a coughing fit befell her.

The man continued his course until he reached the edge, where the sand met the trees. Looking at the horses, he hollered, "I found their mounts."

"Then get them, you lump of decaying minnow," snapped a voice from Nerissa's right.

She closed her eyes. How many were there? Where had they come from? Had they harmed the others?

Sand crunched, and the man ambled toward the horses. "They look like they're quality."

Why was he shouting? Was he daft? Or was he trying to lure them out?

"I get the appaloosa."

"Over my dead body," Denton hissed.

"You can have whatever horse you want after we find these barnacles."

A twig crunched dangerously close near the tree.

Denton's fingers tightened around Nerissa's shoulder.

A shout sounded from the cliff's direction, followed by the clang of swords.

Please, Beginning. Help Uncle Morris.

What if he was outnumbered? What if they killed him? Afya would be taken back into slavery, and that would kill the young woman.

Another snap.

Nerissa dug her nails into her palms. If she didn't soon bring her heartbeat under control, her chest would be shattered from the ferocious thumping.

Sand shifted beneath weight.

Denton's hand left her shoulder, leaving the area strangely cold.

A solid thump cut off an expletive.

And Nerissa's head was snapped back as harshness wrenched her braid.

Forcing her to look, almost upside down, into the cold blue eyes of a sunburnt man she did not recognize.

Nerissa couldn't withhold her cry as the man yanked her to her feet. Her scalp burned, throbbing as her hair threatened to take its leave.

Her breath hitched when something cool brushed the underside of her jaw.

"Nice try, boy. Try sneaking up on me again and your woman is all mine."

Another dry heave wracked Nerissa.

No. She could not lose her cool now—what little she possessed, that was. She had to be like the heroines who did more than scream and cower in the corner as the hero was whaled on and beaten to a pulp.

She had to be smart. Her parents raised her better than to be a whimpering pansy.

When the blade left her neck, she risked turning her head. Denton stood seven paces away, steel and teeth bared. Crimson splattered his shirt, though she saw no source for it.

From her peripheral, she watched the man sneer.

"You're nothing more than a minnow, whelp. One more step and she's a goner."

The tendons in Denton's forearms twitched and a muscle in his jaw pulsed. "You're not the first kidnapper I've faced."

"Lying isn't becoming, and neither is your attempt at stalling. Put down the sword and we'll tie you up nice and peacefully. You'll make a decent profit for a mine owner. A little on the scrawny side, but you'll not last long anyway."

Nerissa's eye caught Denton's. Beneath that bravado lurked panic. Did he worry about Cinders? Himself? Or...or was he worried about *her*?

A roar came from Uncle Morris' direction.

The man cursed.

Beginning, I need strength.

And a hearty amount of courage.

Spinning the best she could with her hair still in a tight lock, Nerissa slammed the heel of her palm into the man's nose with all the strength she could muster. She wasn't strong for a woman like Edver's mamma, but she had hauled enough buckets of water and milk and kneaded enough bread to not be completely helpless.

Blood spurted from the man's nose as he reeled back, his hold on her hair disappearing as he clamped his hand over his face.

Denton's shoulder brushed hers as he darted past, applying his sword's pommel to the man's noggin with such ferocity Nerissa expected more blood to emerge.

The man dropped with a dull thud.

Denton grabbed the knife and handed it to Nerissa. "I'll trade you."

She stared at the proffered weapon. He wanted to trade? Why? A blade was a blade.

And where did that ringing come from? Was there some shrill bell in the area, or was that a bird she'd never before heard?

Calloused fingers tilted her chin up and gentle blue eyes bored into hers, somehow penetrating past the lazy, incoming fog blurring her vision.

"Breathe, Nerissa."

A sharp, yet sweet breath refreshed her lungs.

"You did well."

"You did most of the work," she managed to mumble. The wooziness slipped away, shuffling out of sight like the fog when the sun finally broke through.

"It was a team effort." He looked over his shoulder. "Want to help get the horses?"

"That man is a brute."

"No bigger than this once." Mischief twinkled in Denton's eyes. "Besides, Cinders has a few tricks up her saddle."

Nerissa inhaled again and straightened her shoulders. No passing out for her. She was a Wessen, and Wessens stared danger in the face.

At least, Father and Uncle Morris did. Her inclination was to scream and hide.

But she wasn't doing too bad. Right?

Oh, Mamma would not be happy when she heard about this.

A smile, genuine and brief and warm, momentarily relaxed the tension radiating from Denton. "Ready?"

She liked his smile.

Nerissa smothered the thought. Now was not the time to notice such things.

Even if it was true.

Edver would never let her live it down if he found out.

Which he wouldn't. Because Denton was an outsider and would leave after finding Jonah.

"Ready," she squeaked.

With another mischievous grin, Denton turned toward the horses and released a long, lilting whistle.

Cinders tossed her head and whinnied.

The other thug turned, bellowed an oath that made Nerissa's ears burn, and waved his scythe.

Denton whistled again, a different one that drew a different reaction from Cinders. With a strong tug, she broke her lead rope tethering her to a tree and took off toward them, forcing the man to dodge out of the way at the last second.

The sight would have been comical had the situation not been dire.

Nerssa's exhale wheezed as the man charged them.

"Get on."

"What?"

"Get on." Denton helped her mount. "Here's what you're going to do. Take a wide berth and ride past him. Untether the horses and be prepared for my signal. Understood?"

"No." His instructions sounded like gibberish. What signal? For what purpose?

"Just go."

Cinders leapt forward at his whistle, and Nerissa clutched her mane, a shriek rising in her throat.

Oh, heavens, she was going to fall off. She was either going to hit her head so hard she was knocked out or the man would come upon her while she was still stunned and run her through.

If I die, Denton Yindell, I'll kill you.

Knuckles white from clinging to Cinders' mane, Nerissa risked looking behind her shoulder. Denton was nowhere to be seen.

Though Cinders took a wide circle around the man, he still charged them, scythe pulled back like he prepared to throw it at her.

A flash of gray, then Denton tackled him down.

Nerissa fought back the urge to upheave her last meal. Denton wasn't weak, but neither was he big and brawny like the man.

Please keep him safe.

Chapter Twenty-One

DENTON

"THIS IS IT." AFYA'S hushed whisper sounded like a crack of thunder. She pointed at the tower before them with a trembling hand. "That's...that's where..."

Denton eyed the tower. Stone smooth from enduring the elements, only one window allowed entrance. Patches of bright green moss spotted its exterior, and the vines clinging to the surrounding cliffs were absent. "Are there any other entry points?"

"None we could find." Lemuel's deep voice rumbled through the air. "I thought I told you to stay on the beach."

Denton whipped about-face. The three men stood a few paces away, clothing rumpled, dirtied, and smeared with blood. A gash lined Edver's left jaw, blood dripped from Lemuel's arm, and the other man bore what looked like a shallow slice along his side.

Morris coughed. "After the attack, we thought it best to move along. What happened to you?"

Lemuel fingered his sword. Pain could not dull the annoyance in his expression and voice. "They did not appreciate our intrusion. The ones who are not dead have fled. We do not have much time before they return with reinforcements." He eyed Morris, who looked like he'd rolled down a bumpy cliff and through a patch of the largest sticker weeds known to mankind before swimming with piranhas. "I could ask the same of you. Jarrel will be most unhappy if you do not return alive."

Morris offered a wan smile. "My brother always has been over-protective. To make a long answer short, we were attacked. Now, back to business. You found no other way inside?"

"None except scaling the tower."

Denton ran his fingers through his hair, ignoring the grime they returned with. Using Nerissa's takeoff with Cinders as a distraction, he'd snuck through the forest's edge and tackled the man from behind. Subterfuge had been the only option if he wanted to beat his opponent. His ribs still screamed and he was fairly certain his cheek would be the color of bruised grapes in a few hours, but the man would no longer hurt innocents.

Should he thank the Beginning for the victory? Or attribute it to luck?

"One of you will have to climb. We are unable to."

A few minutes later, Denton was scaling the rope hooked just within the open window. He just adored how *one of you* was code for, *the one who has poor upper body strength and who really isn't fond of heights.*

But he was the only one. The women couldn't—Afya especially since she hadn't stopped shaking since the attack—and the other men bore worse injuries.

He hissed as the rope burned through the gloves Morris loaned him. The man's hands were stubbier than his, and the fingers did not fit Denton's.

"It'll be easy, boy. Just climb the rope, use your weight to provide a push against the wall, and walk up the side."

Because walking up the side was *so* easy. What did Lemuel think he was? A spider?

The burn in Denton's shoulders assured him he was most certainly not an arachnid.

He also didn't need to look at those below to know they weren't prepared to catch him should he fall. His protests about someone waiting within, ready to stab him or sever the rope, went ignored.

Apparently, he was as expendable to them as he was to Father.

Arms as limp as soggy weeds, Denton groaned as his fingers latched onto the wooden windowsill. Pulling himself up, he rested his stomach on the ledge and peered within. Stone was supposed to keep buildings cooler, yet hot, humid stuffiness over-whelmed his lungs.

Edver expressed worry that the open window meant the tower was empty, but that wasn't true.

Not true at all.

When he helped pull Carter from the burning building, hauled Red from the quarry, and helped rescue the kids, crimson laced his vision.

Now it washed over, coating everything he saw as fire, hotter and fiercer than ever before, flared through him.

The open window did not mean the tower was empty.

It meant the tower's occupants were bound and gagged.

Choking on the rising emotion, Denton hauled himself in the rest of the way. No one guarded the children, although bundles and extra weapons indicated someone had recently been there.

"Well?" Morris called.

"There are eight." Denton's voice cracked. "Eight children."

One whimpered.

"You'll have to bring them down."

Yes, like he hadn't thought of that already. What did they think he had? Wings hidden beneath his shirt? There was no way he could continually climb. He simply was too weak.

Coward. Red's hiss reinforced his patheticness.

A muffled scream came from his right when he unsheathed his knife.

Denton held up his hand. "I'm here to rescue you. I promise."

Please, help me keep that promise.

Perhaps the Beginning would listen.

After sawing through the ropes and gags, Denton investigated the room. A bundle of papers, supplies, weapons, a shelf of stale bread—kept out of the children's reach but not their sight—and an overturned basket.

"Well?"

Marterises would win the award for the most impatient land. "I'm working on it."

"Are they all alive?"

"Yes. And quit hollering. You're too loud."

Denton knelt before the eldest child, a hunched boy no older than nine, and placed a hand on his shoulder. "I'm going to lower you down, okay? The others will help you."

The heat throbbed even hotter. When he found whoever dehydrated these little ones and made them so weak they could barely stand, he would kill them. Mercilessly.

Placing the first child in the basket, he managed to lower it. Each time a child was lowered, the strain and ache in his arms grew until his shoulder and back muscles cramped.

Please keep the rope from slipping. So far the rescue attempt went well, but that would end if Denton lived up, once again, to his cowardly title and let the basket drop due to exhaustion.

The final child was a slip of a girl with tangled black curls and dull brown eyes. Her dark skin helped her blend with the shadows, and Denton almost overlooked her the first five times.

He crouched to her level. If only Chamonix was here. She would have this precious little one trusting her in no time. "It's time to leave this place, okay?"

She stared beyond him, clutching tatters of what looked to be the remains of a cloth doll.

Leather scuffed against stone.

Denton leapt up and spun, his sword clearing the sheathe before he realized it was in his grip.

The shadows obscured the woman's face, but nothing could hide the glimmering knife in her right hand. Her deep green skirt swished as she advanced.

Denton whisked the child onto his hip and angled her toward the window.

The woman laughed, low and too calm for such a circumstance. "You fight a losing battle, darling. Do you really think we will allow your continual interference?"

Horses and horseshoes, how had this woman gotten in? She certainly hadn't climbed through the window.

"I'll make you a deal, young man. Return my daughter and I will not tell the others of your...excursion today."

Denton tightened his grip on the girl. "You don't deserve to be a mother."

The woman again laughed, only this time it was light and tinkling. "No, no, that little one is not mine. No, I spoke of Afya."

If this woman was responsible for the torment Afya endured, the silence she wore as protection, and the fear she still exhibited at times, Denton would face an army alone before handing her over. "I don't make deals with the spawn of evil." He inched toward the window. How he'd lower the girl without being knifed in the back, he didn't know. But he'd figure something out.

"Oh, dear. I am afraid you misunderstood. Or perhaps I did not make clear my offer. You return Afya to me and I won't have you killed."

"Coward." Red wasn't the only one who called him that.

"Those beneath us are not our concern. They deserve neither your pity nor care, and it is below a noble to even acknowledge their existence." Or so Father had said.

Denton silenced the whispers of the past. He may be a coward overall, but not this time. And he may have once been a noble's son, but not now. "You're not getting her."

"Stubborn, I see. Very well. I suppose you'll take that trait with you to your grave." The woman stepped into full view. Her dark hair absorbed the light even as it glimmered on her medium-dark skin. Her dress more befitted Veerham's nobility instead of a run-down tower in the middle of Marteris.

Edver called to him, but Denton dared not remove even an ounce of his attention from the woman.

"I admire bravery, but is this cause worth your life?"

"Yes." The word spilled from him with more conviction than he realized he possessed. "It is worth everything."

The woman sighed and the fine lines around her eyes deepened. "Very well. I do so detest blood staining the floor, but discomfort is often part of life."

Her knife flashed.

Denton twisted aside, keeping himself between the child and deranged lunatic. He didn't want to hurt a woman. They were to be treated with respect, and Stepmother ingrained it in both him and Carter to always be polite and mannerly.

But he doubted a civil, "Beg your pardon, good woman, but could you please cease your attempts to slay me?" would prove effective.

Instead of again lunging, she remained near the window, knife poised to fly.

Denton dodged to his right just as her fingers released the blade. It clattered behind him.

The woman bared her teeth when he slowly advanced, her hands gripping the window's ledge. When she twisted and raised a leg to swing over the edge, Denton snagged her arm with his two free fingers and yanked her back before spinning his sword and bringing the hilt upon her head.

She collapsed in a heap of velvet.

Heart hammering with the intensity of a horse stampede, Denton hastily lowered the basket before descending himself.

"Who was that?" Morris glared at the window like he expected the woman to reappear at any moment.

"I'll tell you later. We need to leave."

"That's fine and well, but we'll not be traveling efficiently." Morris swept his hand toward the clustered children, who gnawed on the dried fish Nerissa and Afya handed out. "What was it, son?"

Son. Morris had no idea how Denton longed to hear those words. Typical they would come from a man he didn't know well instead of Father.

But Father never directed that word his way.

"There was a woman." He kept his tone low. "She claimed to be Afya's mother."

Morris' eye twitched. "And?"

"And after she tried to kill me, I knocked her out." Denton swallowed the revulsion. "I couldn't bring myself to...to..."

"I don't blame you." Morris squeezed his shoulder. "We'll talk more about this later, okay?"

Denton exhaled and nodded. Despite the chaotic attempts to get the children up on the horses, wondering if the other men could travel on foot with their injuries, and if they had enough supplies to last the journey. Four or five children had been anticipated. Not nine.

Warmth covered his shoulder, and he jumped.

Nerissa's gentle smile did little to soothe his nerves. "Are you okay?"

"Yes."

"You are covered in blood."

Denton blinked at the dried, browning spots splatting his clothes and hands. No wonder the kids thought he was there to harm them. "I don't think any of it's mine." He placed his hand over hers. Comfort wasn't something he easily recognized, and it certainly wasn't something he experienced much of, but he'd seen it offered enough times to emulate the actions involved. "How are *you?*"

Her smile did not reach her eyes, and the iciness of her fingers spoke for her. "I'm okay."

"It's okay to be frightened."

Her smile dimmed and she pulled away. "Uncle Morris says it's time to leave."

"Nerissa—"

"I don't need my shortcomings discussed at this time. Let's just go."

CHAPTER TWENTY-TWO

NERISSA

"Praise the Beginning you're okay." Mamma all but broke Nerissa's ribs with her hug before ushering her from the infirmary. "Let's get you home. You look exhausted."

Nerissa didn't bother thinking of a reply as she stumbled after Mamma. Her legs hurt, her back hurt, and her head hurt. In fact, all of her hurt. Ached. Who knew walking for four days straight would be so demanding? Or perhaps she was just in poor shape.

Yes, that was likely it. She did prefer needlework and gardening to chasing the ornery goats and chickens.

"Wait up, Veri. Give us a minute, then Denton and I will escort you home." Uncle Morris handed something to Chief Talart before beckoning Denton.

Mamma planted her hands on her hips. "You should be in the infirmary. That gash looks awful."

"Hauni and Guy are tending the children. I'm fine."

"Morris, you know what Jarrel would say."

"Yes, I do, which is why I'm attempting to forego this conversation."

Uncle Morris' mulish expression managed to draw from Nerissa a tired laugh. Though the two brothers were pushing late forties, they still acted like children sometimes.

Mamma tsked. "I suppose you have some injury you're ignoring as well, Denton."

"No, ma'am."

Uncle Morris slapped Denton's shoulder. "He was one of the few who emerged physically unscathed. In fact, he may well have saved Nerissa's life. Twice."

Lips thinning, Mamma looked between Nerissa and Denton, who looked right back at Mamma with a blank stare. "Is that so? What, exactly, happened?"

"Later, Veri. We're ready to fall asleep on our feet."

Mamma acquiesced, but not without warning them she'd be pursuing the topic after they rested.

Somehow, Nerissa found herself falling into step with Denton. The exhaustion muddling her thoughts shadowed the skin beneath his eyes, and his steps dragged.

If they were attacked, none of them would be of any help.

"Are you certain you're okay?"

He grunted an affirmation before rubbing the back of his neck. "Nerissa, I know you thought I wanted to discuss your shortcomings, but I didn't."

It took a long minute for that particular memory to be retrieved. "I had forgotten about that." Humiliation wasn't something she enjoyed experiencing, yet Denton determined to bring it up again and again.

His voice was quiet. Almost soft. "I wanted to tell you the most courageous people are those who face danger even when they're afraid."

Tears stung her eyes at the simple statement. Did his detective skills allow him to notice things others didn't, or was she just transparent? "I don't know why the Beginning keeps sticking me in these situations."

"Do you really think He cares what's going on?"

She looked over to find him studying her. Was that doubt in his eyes, or did she simply imagine it? "I do. The Scripts say that, for all who love the Beginning, 'all things work together for good, for those who are called according to His purpose'. That good doesn't necessarily equate to what *we* think is good, but what aligns with His plan."

Denton huffed. "You honestly think someone you've never seen or met is in charge of everything? That He cares?"

"I do."

"Even after the atrocities you've witnessed, you believe that." The same incredulity in his voice furrowed his brow.

"I do. It's not easy at times, but I do."

If you really believe it, then why do you fret so?

Nerissa ignored the question even as her heart sank at the implication in his words. "You don't?"

"I don't know what to believe," he said in a raw voice. "I think He chooses His favorites and if you're not included in that, then you're left to wander whatever path fate chooses for you until you die."

The impulse to hug him—soothe his fears and hurts and scarred heart—almost forced Nerissa to grab his arm and do just that. Instead, she touched his elbow, only speaking when he stopped and looked at her.

Her heart broke at the hurt in those blue eyes. Whatever haunted his past had done more than cause him pain. It broke him. "Do you remember our conversation about finding beauty in everything?"

"I recall it centering more around the danger in everything, but yes."

"This is like that, Denton. We only see what we look for. If you seek out the bad in life, that's all you'll find. But if you know the Beginning will never leave or forsake those who believe in Him, then there is comfort in that. And creation exhibits it. What some see as coincidences are actually examples of His mercy. Chicks and foals are a reminder that new life is a blessing from Him. The new shoots of grass after a fire are a reminder of His grace and compassion—that good can come from the bad."

"I haven't seen much good." He looked away, jaw working.

Nerissa took his hands and pressed them between her own. "It can be hard to see beauty in the ashes, but it's there."

"I can't, Nerissa," he rasped. "I don't deserve to see any beauty. Not after I've destroyed it."

The questions mounted, but the words kept pressing. She could interrogate him later. "If you are a believer, that has been wiped away. A new creation, remember?"

Sadness deepened the blue of his eyes and the burden he always seemed to carry. "A new creation doesn't always mean a wanted or remembered one."

Tears stinging her eyes and nose, she reached up and brushed errant hairs from his forehead. "The Beginning does not forget His creations."

"He's forgotten about me."

"Denton—"

"We should get going. Your family hasn't realized we're not right behind them."

And then he turned, walking away.

A rogue tear slipped past her efforts to keep them constrained. A month ago, she would never have considered praying or even helping this outsider, but now, all she wanted was him to see the truth.

"Denton, wait."

He stalled.

Nerissa covered the distance, gathering him into a hug and ignoring his grunt of surprise. "He first loved us, Denton. He *is* love. The Scripts say He is, 'abounding in steadfast love and faithfulness'. He doesn't forget. We're saved. That means those sins are no longer held against us. He doesn't turn His back on us. He doesn't cast us aside because of our past. We're *His*. Daughters and sons."

When he said nothing, she looked up. The weariness, loathing, and longing in his eyes almost undid her. What had tainted his perception of being wanted? Loved?

He cupped her cheek, his hand warm against the late-afternoon air. "That may be true for you," he rasped, "but it can't be for me."

A gaping hole opened as he turned and walked away for the second time, defeat in his gait and the slump of his shoulders.

More tears escaped. *Please, Beginning, show him. Remind him he is Yours.*

"Whatcha looking at?"

It wasn't the fact that Elberta asked the question that drew Nerissa's suspicions. Nor was it the fact that her sister had just been playing with Noko, Daffy, and two of the rescued children before deciding to, for some reason known only to Elberta, pester Denton.

No, it was that innocent calm in her voice. *Too* calm.

Too innocent.

Nerissa peered over her shoulder just in time to see Denton give Elberta a wary look from where he sat on the steps leading to the cabin's back door.

She couldn't blame him. Mud streaked Elberta's face and hands, and there was always a possibility the rascal had a handful of mud tucked away somewhere, just waiting to be thrown at some unsuspecting victim.

"Mamma says it's rude to ignore someone after they ask you a question."

"Just like you ignored Nerissa earlier when she asked you to keep out of the mud?"

Elberta sniffed. "That type of question doesn't merit an answer."

He shook his head. "First, you're eight. How do you know what *merit* means? Second, there is an answer to every question, and your answer should have been respecting your sister's request instead of ignoring it."

"I didn't ignore it."

"You're covered in mud. You ignored it."

Nerissa set down the pan of banana bread and leaned against the table. Mamma insisted on hosting a meal for some reason or the other, and Nerissa sought refuge in the cabin. Specifically, guarding the banana bread from thieves—like Edver and her uncle—who sought to eliminate the entire supply before the meal began.

Elberta repeated her question.

"I'm looking at a map."

"Why? Isn't that boring?"

"For someone who claims to be the smartest person on Marteris' coast, you don't understand the necessity of maps."

"Why should I when I know where everything is?"

"Careful, Elberta. Being all uppity usually leads to a painful lesson in reality."

It was time to rescue the poor man. Wiping her hands on her apron Nerissa approached the back doorway.

Elberta looked up, an ornery glint in her eyes. "Why don't you use Nerri's nicknames? Do you think they're ugly?"

That child was in for a massive consequence. She wouldn't be smirking when she found her chores tripled.

Denton laughed softly. "To the contrary. Your sister's name is too pretty to shorten."

Heat seared Nerissa's face. Just how was she to respond to that? Did Denton know she could hear him?

Elberta grinned. "Ner is pretty, isn't she?"

"And you are just slightly annoying. Why don't you go play with Noko? He looks lonely."

Elberta huffed, but puttered off, and soon her voice rose as she taunted Noko to a game of tag.

Nerissa counted to three hundred as she bustled about the kitchen, banging pots and pans so Denton would think her too busy to have heard his reply.

He thought her name was pretty. No one ever said that. Elberta's was unique. Daffy's was adorable. But Nerissa's was just average, a name commonplace for the girls in her generation.

Finally, she worked up the courage to approach the man who had so unexpectedly fit himself into her life.

Praying her face didn't put a tomato to shame, she eased onto the step beside him. A map she'd seen in Chief Talart's office was spread out on his lap, and he studied it like it contained answers to all of life's questions.

"If you're interested in geography, Yald has one depicting this region's topography."

"I don't need that quite yet." He shifted closer and angled the map. "Would you mind showing me the attacked villages' proximity?"

Such a morbid request for a night that was to be filled with laughter and camaraderie. "Here's one." She pointed. "And the other two. These three are the most recent. I know two others are…here and here. But I don't know about the rest. Marteris villages look close on the map because you don't see the cliffs and terrain separating us."

Denton's brow furrowed. "So they're in these areas?" He pointed. "Are you certain?"

"Yes."

"Has this happened before?"

"About one hundred years ago, Marteris was at war. Along the coasts, primarily, though a few battles did occur near the cities, which are out west. The towers played part in those wars, as did the graveyard we passed on our way to Losibar."

"Do you know the cause?"

Nerissa shrugged. "The cause was never specified, I don't think. Or I just don't remember. I'm sorry."

A faint smile answered. "Nothing to apologize for."

Drawing up her knees, she braced her elbows on them. "Why do you ask?"

"This entire thing has been bothering me. Veerham didn't see attacks like this. Victims were kidnapped one at a time, usually through kidnappings when you least expected them. I don't know the methods used in Frilore or Halthdurn, but don't you think this is strange?"

Unease curdled in her stomach. "The entire thing is horrific."

"I concur, but they're not attacking the villages nearer Veerham. Now, they did take a load of kidnapped Veerhamers to a Marteris town, but that's the only time I've seen any southern area be involved. They're concentrating on this area and Losibar's region. Why? What's different?"

"Aside from the terrain? I don't know. I've never been down south."

"Who's been where?" Edver sauntered up, Afya on his elbow. Unlike every other gathering in the past, where he wore his usual garb, this time he was decked out in the tunic and pants worn to church.

Nerissa hid her smile. Edver was, indeed, besotted. And guessing by the way Afya returned his smiles, she felt the same way.

Their good natures slid off Denton as he offered not one hint of a smile. "What do you know of the southern Marteris villages?"

"I know they are high and mighty. They think just because they're closer to the cities means they're more sophisticated. I wasn't impressed."

"Are they intimidating? Do they wear weapons for show or function?"

"They rarely wear them if I'm recalling correctly. Why do you want to know? And isn't that Father's map?"

Denton rolled it up and stuffed it in its tube. "It is. He agreed to let me borrow it."

"Why would you care about a Marterisi map?"

"Why do you care that I'm looking at one?"

Edver glowered. "Uncle Morris and Father said you had something to tell Afya."

Denton exhaled and rubbed the back of his neck. "Now probably isn't the best time."

"Why?"

"This should wait until tomorrow morning."

"Please, I must know." Even after gaining confidence, Afya's voice remained as timid as a mouse's.

Another exhale preceded Denton's explanation. "Do you remember that woman in the tower?"

"I did not see her since I was with the children, but I remember something about it, yes."

Nerissa scooted to the edge of the stair in case Afya fainted.

Denton stared at his laced fingers. "I don't know if she was in there the entire time or if she somehow entered without my knowledge through some secret entrance, but a woman made her presence known as I prepared to lower the final child." He looked up, sympathy softening his handsome profile. "She claimed to be your mother."

Afya blanched. "What did she look like?"

"Around your height, skin a little darker than yours, with poofy black hair and mean, mean eyes. She wore a dress I'd expect to see in Veerham's court and thought she was more proficient with her knife than she actually was."

Afya swayed.

Edver tucked his arm around her shoulders. "What did she say?"

"That she'd let me live if I turned over Afya. I ended up knocking her out so the kid could escape."

Afya let out a low whimper before crumpling.

"How is she?"

Nerissa paused at Denton's question. He sat at the table with Uncle Morris and Father, an untouched plate of banana bread before him. The meal had gone on, but Mamma said Nerissa's and Afya's absences did not go unnoticed.

"She is shaken. Edver convinced her to eat, so that helped. Hauni said she didn't expect her to go into shock." Nerissa brushed escaped strands of hair from her face. "She wishes to speak to you."

Denton didn't move. "Is Edver going to skewer me?"

"Why would he do that?"

"For not telling his ladylove sooner? I thought he was going to smash in my head when she fainted."

Father snorted and Uncle Morris chuckled.

Nerissa shook her head. "Edver is protective over those he cares for. He won't hurt you. I won't let him."

She'd just ignore the sly look Uncle Morris shot Father, who looked less than thrilled.

Denton raised a brow, but pushed back his chair and stood. "After you."

Edver did indeed glower when Denton entered, but he kept quiet, only crossing his arms while trying to melt the outsider with his death stare.

Mamma, perched next to the bed, smiled. "She'll be fine, Denton. No need to look so worried."

Afya nodded, although the motion lacked energy. "Thank you for telling me," she whispered.

"I'm sorry I didn't sooner."

"Why didn't you?" Challenge edged Edver's words.

Denton sighed, but his answer came several minutes later. "I know what it's like to have a...less-than-optimal parent. I also know what it's like having those memories creep in when you're trying to survive day-to-day. You don't need those when you're attempting to just get by. I didn't withhold the information to be deceitful. You were already so shaken by the attack. I didn't want to worsen that."

Afya's gentle smile cut off Edver's protest. "Thank you."

Denton blinked. "For what?"

"For wanting to protect me. It's—it's been a long time since I've had anyone care." She cast a shy glance around the room, lingering on Edver the longest. "Thank you all."

Edver knelt and took her hand between his. "You know we'll defend you with our lives."

Mamma pressed her lips and looked down, a sure sign she struggled against laughing.

Nerissa coughed back her own amusement. "You'll find Edver emulating the nobility you read about in the novels of old."

Edver straightened. "I do think I'm quite chivalrous."

"You're quite arrogant, that's what you are," Denton muttered.

"At least I'm able to handle a sword."

"At least I can stay on a horse going faster than a trot."

Mamma chortled. "Boys, boys, that's quite enough. Afya, you'll stay here for the night. Tomorrow morning, we'll escort you back to Hauni and Doc's."

Well, there went a good night's sleep. Sharing a room with Elberta and Daffy meant enduring pranks, Elberta's whistling snores, and Daffy playing with her dolly well into the night.

"Denton, it's time to go," Uncle Morris called from the dining area. "Veri, I'm leaving the dog with you."

A squeal came from the girls' bedroom. "You mean we get a dog now?"

Father groaned. "Only for the night, girls, and you are going to let Bluet sleep. No dressing her up, no playing with her. All three of you will be going to bed at your normal time."

A chorus of complaints answered him.

"Bluet? Who named my dog after a *flower*? Who committed this unforgivable crime?"

Father laughed. "That's what you get for not naming the poor pup when you first got her."

"Nothing fit!"

"Well, now she has a name. A name she answers to. I'd like to see you try training her out of it."

"And you wonder why I threw you in the creek so many times as a child."

"And *you* wonder why I always put sand in your boots and stickers in your socks."

Shaking her head, Mamma swept into the other room to break up the fight.

Nerissa couldn't contain her laughter when Bluet ambled in and licked her fingertips. "You like your name, girl. Don't you? Yes, yes, you do."

The laughter died when she looked up. Denton watched her, an emotion in his expression she couldn't determine.

Edver cleared his throat. "I suppose it's time I get going. Please, milady, have a good night and don't worry about your mother. She sounds like a heinous villain and I'll make sure to protect you from her should your paths ever cross."

Afya giggled. "I know. You are, after all, quite chivalrous."

Edver puffed out his chest. "See? She says I'm chivalrous."

"Afya, are you certain you aren't suffering from shock?" Nerissa feigned checking Afya's temperature. "You are saying untrue, addlepated things."

"Nonsense. She speaks the truth."

"Nerissa's right." Denton smirked at Edver's consternation. "Be careful, Afya, or his ego will cause his head to explode."

Afya covered her smile. "That was a nice comeback."

"Thank you. I learned it from Red."

Edver harrumphed. "I don't think I'd like this Red."

"Don't worry—she wouldn't like you either. You couldn't handle her level of sass."

"I can handle any level."

"Keep believing whatever helps you sleep at night."

"Let me guess—another Red insult?"

"Yes."

The two continued bickering as they exited the room.

Nerissa perched on the edge of the bed. "Edver really likes you."

Red tinged Afya's cheeks. "I really like him." A sly grin replaced the blush. "And you really like Denton."

"Perhaps." Nerissa examined her nails. A few still had rough edges. Time to rectify that. "But he's so withdrawn. And he's hinted that he doesn't have the cleanest past."

Afya patted Nerissa's hand. "I don't have a lot of positive experience with people, but I recognize the pain in his eyes. I feel that same pain myself. You can't fake that. It's so raw and aching. Your soul feels like it's being shredded one sword slice at a time and you wonder if the hopelessness and worthlessness you feel is genuine or fabricated from the lies you've been told your entire life."

At the tears in Afya's eyes, Nerissa berated herself with a thousand lectures. Of course she would somehow make a bad day worse. "I am so sorry. I never meant to make you cry."

"These aren't tears of sadness, Ner. I just...I realized—truly—for the first time that I'm *free*. I'm free from that tower. I'm free from Mother allowing her child to be used in ways no parent should ever dream of letting happen. I'm *free*. And after your parson explained why we need the Beginning and what sinners we are, I'm not only physically free, but he prayed with me, and now I'm spiritually free. I've never been free before. And now I can't stop thanking the Beginning for it. I always thought I'd die in that tower, but look at me. I can walk on grass, pet a dog, and ride a horse. I even have a different dress. This freedom is unlike anything I have ever experienced."

"I know I do not speak for only myself when I say we will do anything to help you keep your freedom." Nerissa clasped Afya's hand. "I know Edver, especially, will fight with all he has to keep you free."

Afya ducked her chin. "He is a good man, isn't he?"

"He is." Ornery and obstinate and irritating at times, but still a good man.

Just like Denton.

Nerissa tossed the thought away. The seeds of what could be more than friendship were there, but Denton's secrets remained a chasm between them.

She stood. "I should help Mamma put the girls to bed. Have a good night, Afya."

Yet, as she listened to Elberta's whining and Daffy's protests, one thought remained, continuously looping through her mind.

Despite his claims, Denton hadn't studied the map for mere curiosity. There was something more—deeper—to his inquiries.

But what?

Chapter Twenty-Three

DENTON

HE NEVER UNDERSTOOD SUNRISES. The day ahead might witness storms, tragedy, and death, yet the sunrise was always bright and brilliant and breathtaking. A false herald, that's what they were. A lie offering hope that the day would go well, when in reality it could make some wish for death.

Perched on the corral's top rail, Denton watched the colors slowly bleed into the sky. Nerissa's words from a few days earlier shouldn't be replaying through his mind, yet they were. She was wrong. There couldn't be beauty in everything. Fire was not beautiful. Blood was not beautiful. Pain was not beautiful. Willing his limp brother to regain consciousness wasn't beautiful. Nor were what he'd anticipated being his last thoughts—the horror of leaving Red and the little girl unprotected during the fight to rescue Carter, Chamonix, and the other victims.

"Beauty in the ashes..."

The light and warmth from fire could be beautiful, the way candlelight lit the stables in the early morning as he prepared for another day of training horses.

The blood covering Carter hadn't been beautiful, but it meant he was alive and fighting. And Carter's gasping breaths as fresh air entered his lungs and drove out the smoke had caused relief like none other to wash over Denton.

A foal, the sheen of a glossy coat as a freshly-groomed horse trotted through a field, and a freshly-oiled saddle could be considered beautiful.

Perhaps beauty could be found in some circumstances, but not many.

Dewy grass squeaked beneath weight.

"It's something else, isn't it?" Morris leaned his forearms on the rail. "Never ceases to amaze me."

"You like sunrises?"

"I do. They remind me that, as the Scripts say, 'His mercies are new every morning'."

"Do you really think the Beginning has mercy?" Denton stared at the sunrise. If only the answers were written in the colors or clouds. He'd even take them written in waves.

"The Beginning is mercy, son. He's justice, truth, mercy, and love."

Denton did nothing to silence his scoff. "I've heard He's infinite, but does that extend to all of His attributes?"

"What do you mean?"

"Is His justice so vast that those who are kidnapping and harming children will suffer for their crimes? And if He is truly just, doesn't that mean everyone who's sinned will be punished?"

At the lack of immediate response, Denton looked over. No censure darkened Morris' expression. Instead, what looked like shrewd understanding was displayed.

"The Beginning is justice, Denton. That is why we have no hope of getting in Heaven by our own merit. We are fallible, sinful beings. Imperfection cannot coincide with perfection. A sacrifice had to be made in order for us to ever have hope of residing with Him. To allow evil to go unpunished goes against the very concept of who He is. Sometimes that punishment occurs here, but even if it doesn't, don't think the Beginning has turned a blind eye or forgotten about it."

"How will we know when our punishment will come?" Perhaps that was why the Beginning all but abandoned him. He was too vile to even have hope of being accepted and loved.

"If you are a believer, your punishment has already been given." Morris' bushy brows bunched together. "That sacrifice wipes away a believer's sin and makes us a new creation. As a new creation, you are a son of the Beginning. You are His."

"I don't feel new." Instead, he felt as dirty and wretched as before. "And His love can't be infinite."

"Oh? Why not?"

Denton waved a hand. "How could He love us?" *How could He love* me? The words spilled from him, unending and incapable of being stopped. "My father hated me. I was a stain upon his existence. If he couldn't love me, how can the Beginning?"

"Boy, the Beginning cannot be forced into a manmade box. He is not defined by human error. He is the Beginning, and that means what He says He'll do, He'll do. And if He says you are a new creation, you're a new creation. If He says you're not saved by your own works, but because of His mercy, then you know those words are true."

"But how can He possibly love me?" Denton slid off and faced Morris. There was no way to articulate the longing burrowed deep in his chest. The longing to be loved. The desire for unconditional acceptance and the knowledge that, no matter how terribly he failed, he would never again be discarded.

"My own father *hated* me. He wanted me gone. If he could go back in time and stop me from ever coming about, he would have."

"Denton—"

"*No.* Don't you get it? I'm incapable of being loved. That means not even the Beginning can love me. So stop...stop telling me He's infinitely loving or whatever. He's not. He can't be."

Denton backed away as tears stung his eyes. It *hurt.* The truth hurt so, so badly.

Love was conditional. As long as he refrained from disappointing people, they would accept him. But the minute he slipped up, they would retract that love.

And he would be left alone once again.

Perhaps he should escape into some unpopulated part of Veerham and survive on leaves and edible plants until he died. That would be better than this destructive concoction of pain, loneliness, and constant reminders of his past failures and sins. At least on his own, with only Cinders for company, he could dwell in his self-loathing in peace.

A strong grip clamping onto his shoulders drew Denton from the mire of thoughts and half-baked plans. Morris glared up at him, gaze fierce and countenance set. Spine stiffening, Denton steeled himself. He'd never seen Morris raise a hand, but if he was pushed too far, he may prove he was just like Father.

Closing his eyes, Denton turned. This way, he wouldn't receive such bad whiplash when the fist landed. And, though shorter he may be, Morris was sturdy and could incapacitate a man with just a few, well-placed punches.

"Oh, son. You're fitting the Beginning into a manmade box again."

Common sense said the blow probably wasn't coming—at least not yet—but intuition warned him once again about being taken by surprise. A busted nose wasn't what he sought to acquire on this journey. Endeavor. Whatever it was.

"Come on. Let's check on the horses as we talk." After wrangling Denton into the pasture and beginning an amble along the perimeter, Morris clasped his hands behind his back. "We are finite. The Beginning is infinite. We are but a vapor in the timeline of history, yet the Beginning created the very beginning of this world. We are imperfect. The Beginning is without one sin. He cannot sin. The Creator of everything—and by everything, I mean *everything*—is, and was, and is to come. You can fit each man into certain categories based on their personalities, flaws, and beliefs, but you cannot force the Beginning, who created *you*, into something you designed by your own fallible merit.

"Our experiences shape how we see the world. And, to an extent, they shape how we view the Beginning. Jarrel and I had a good upbringing, so it wasn't difficult for me to accept that the Beginning is our Heavenly Father. Because that's what He is to believers, Denton. Tell me, are you saved?"

"Yes."

"Why? What compelled you?"

Denton's throat thickened. Perhaps fate would be on his side for once and he would die where he stood so his secrets couldn't be revealed. It wasn't like anyone would miss him, and Cinders would quickly adapt to her new life in Marteris. "I've...I'm...I've messed up. Royally." Would he ever forget those innocent little faces?

Faces he helped condemn?

"And?"

"And I recognized I needed forgiveness for that. Parson Gil explained I had sinned against the Beginning, and soon he helped me realize how lost I was."

The repentance hadn't been enough, though. He still hadn't earned the Beginning's favor.

"You can't earn His favor, Denton."

Only additional weariness flowed through him at the realization he'd spoken the thought aloud.

"The Scripts make it clear our salvation comes by grace through faith. It doesn't come from our works. You are the Beginning's. His child. He loves you. Your sins have been covered and there is nothing you can do to either earn or lose his favor."

Morris couldn't be right. Such a notion was implausible. "There is no way the Beginning would love or want me."

"I don't see anywhere in the Scripts saying, 'I love and want all of my children except Denton Yindell'." Morris sighed. "I know you're hurting, son. I see more than you realize. But, what *you* must realize is the Beginning transcends humanity's attempt to whittle Him down to our size. Our standards. You see the Beginning as Someone who will never be pleased and who will neither want nor love you. When, in reality, He sees you as His own."

"How?" The word more resembled a frog's croak. "How could He possibly want *me*? I've allowed children to be harmed. I'm not worth saving."

"In whose opinion?" Morris' words turned sharper than Red's knives. "Yours? You, who know very little about anything? Or the Beginning's, Who knows everything about everything because He created everything? Do you see what I'm trying to say, boy? We can let our perspectives define how we view life and the Beginning, but they can't change the truth. And the truth is you are His. You are His son. Nothing you do can change that. He makes wretches heirs and turns sinners into saints. You are saved. Your past cannot compete with His mercy."

Denton risked looking at Morris. "Are you sure?" Oh, how he wanted to believe it. "I just…for most of my life, with the exception of Stepmother, I've been told I'm not wanted."

"By men. The Beginning is the Beginning." Morris' voice softened. "Denton, there are many misconceptions about love—romantic, filial, agape, almost every type. What many call love is not, actually, love. Real love does not turn away when flaws are exposed. Real love seeks to help you become the man you were made to be. Real love does not give you up. The Beginning is real love. He will never let you go."

Denton couldn't say he understood everything, but the earnestness in Morris' eyes, combined with Parson Gil's sermons and his and Nerissa's discussions, formed a key that fit perfectly into the lock he'd crafted around his heart.

"Promise me you'll think on it?"

"I promise." And he would. He would think and pray and, when alone, rejoice.

For maybe Morris was right.

Maybe he really was loved after all.

"Did something happen?"

Denton glanced up as Nerissa settled beside him, leaning on the corral's post and watching the horses graze.

Funny how he stood in the same place as this morning—only this time, hope—instead of continuous devastations—brushed his heart.

After she repeated her question, he shook his head. "Everything's fine. Why?"

"Something is different." She searched his face, brow crinkling. "Are you coming down with something?"

The last person who asked if he was sick had been Stepmother. "No, I'm fine." Denton stared at his hands as he braced his forearms on the rail. So many things to say and no words to say with which to say them. He couldn't tell her who—what—he was, but maybe...well, he didn't know what he hoped for. Only that he wanted to spend more time with the quiet Marterisi.

"Do you know when the chief will be free?"

"I don't, but I can ask. Why?"

"I need to find Jonah." And it was high time that man—that lying rat-faced cretin—stopped sidestepping the situation.

Nerissa shifted and what could be tension pulled her expression. "Denton, I—" She looked past him and blanched.

Following her gaze, Denton felt the blood drain from his face. Thick, black smoke rose in a column stretching for the sky. He looked back just in time to watch Nerissa sway, her eyes unfocused.

"Okay, nope. No fainting for you. Not today." His reflexes were subpar at best, and the last thing he wanted was her to sustain injury during the fall. Gripping her upper arms, he turned her. "Go to the village. Find any able-bodied man who can help."

"What...what about you?"

"I'm going to see if I can find the smoke's source." Calling Bluet, he dashed into the cabin, grabbed the loaned sword, and belted it on as he returned outside, whistling to Cinders.

The mare's ears perked before she trotted toward the fence and followed him to the gate.

Denton mounted Cinders and commanded her to a trot. Cantering would do no good with the copious amount of bushes he'd need to duck, and getting knocked off would only create more problems.

Please, Beginning, let me find the source.

In hindsight, he should have gone with Nerissa instead of trundling off by himself.

Keeping an eye on the smoke, Denton reined Cinders along trails skirting the village proper and weaving between smatterings of cabins.

The acrid stench burned his nose, and tiny flecks of ash and red-hot sparks drifted from the sky.

Lungs aching as he neared the smoke, he offered another prayer.

Bluet barked at the sinister cackle of flames feeding off their source.

Heart plummeting as they entered a clearing, Denton jumped from Cinders. What could have been a cabin was reduced to a flame-consumed, lopsided skeleton. The outer buildings burned as well, and the stench of burnt chicken and pig almost drew a gag.

Sword drawn, he advanced. "Hello?" Perhaps the homeowner hid in the nearby trees. "Hello? Anyone there?"

"Always search the ground. It often contains the smallest—and vitalist—of clues."

Red would murder him and kill him again for not recalling her advice sooner.

Denton scanned the ground. Divots uprooted many shoots of grass and the imprint of horseshoes littered what ground wasn't dug up. A few dead chickens smoldered near what could have been the coop, and charred lumps of what Denton assumed was once the garden's crop marked more devastation.

He spun at the ominous cadence of heavy footsteps.

Talart, Morris, Edver, Nerissa's father, and a bevy of other men thundered into the clearing, followed by Nerissa and Hauni.

Nerissa blanched and Hauni gasped and covered her mouth.

Mouth pressed in a grim line, Talart surveyed the area. "Morris, Edver, Jarrel, search for Kanni, Lloyd, and the boy. The rest of you, look for any indication of who did this."

Denton repressed the urge to spew breakfast as he continued scanning the ground. "There weren't a lot of them. I'm only counting three or four different boot prints."

"One of those had to be Lloyd."

Kneeling, Denton touched the imprint of a hoofprint. "Do all Marterises shoe their horses with wider horseshoes?" Fragments of a memory jostled in the back of his mind, but he couldn't fit them together and determine their importance and relevance.

"The plainsfolk do. We use standard horseshoes. They work better with the terrain, and the wider ones are heavier."

A shard moved into place. He had seen these type sof prints while tracking the Marterisi who had stolen Topeka, a child Chamonix all but doted on. "Did the residents have a horse?"

"No. They borrowed from Morris when they needed to prepare the fields."

"Then there was at least one horse from this area." Denton pointed at the imprints. Tuning out the other men, he tracked them. Who knew Red's lessons would come in handy in such a way?

"They merge on this path." The scuffed dirt indicated the horses had both arrived and left via the slender route.

Morris and Mr. Wessen emerged from the trees, wearing expressions that deflated hope and more mud than a pig. "We found them."

Talart fisted his hands. "And?"

"They didn't stand a chance."

Gut churning, Denton dragged a hand down his face. Once again, evil struck. What if he had paid attention? Could he have saved these poor, unsuspecting folks?

"What of Jonah?" another man asked.

Denton's blood froze and an incessant ringing filled his ears as numbness swept over him. Surely it was just a coincidence. Surely Marterises used that name as well.

He convinced his wobbly legs to turn. Morris and Mr. Wessen warily stared at him like he was a rogue predator about to attack. Talart hissed what probably wasn't a word befitting a man who claimed faith in the Beginning, and Edver studied the ground.

"No sign of the boy."

Iron encased his legs with the weight of ten horses each, but Denton managed to step forward. "Who is this Jonah?"

Only the cackling flames answered.

Heat collided with the numbness, and every heartbeat felt exaggerated and too forceful. The ringing loudened. "Who. Is. This. Jonah?"

Again, no verbal answer.

Heart balancing on the precipice of outrage and disbelief, Denton directed his attention to Nerissa, who stood near the chief. "Who is he, Nerissa?"

She shook her head, hunching her shoulders. "I—I..."

No. It couldn't be true. All this time Jonah had been within his reach, yet they kept him from the boy who deserved to be returned home.

And people thought *he* was the monster.

"We only meant to keep him safe."

The words would be a betrayal no matter who spoke them, but coming from Morris? The man who, just that morning, fervently spoke of the Beginning's love and power, and to whom Denton was beginning to look up to?

It was nothing less than treachery.

Smoke-laced breaths did nothing to quell the tightening in his chest. "You knew. All this time, you knew."

Nerissa's wide eyes met his. "We didn't...at first we weren't sure of your intentions."

That he could understand, but, "And after that? All those so-called *promises* of me helping in return for information? Information you never provided? For a deal you broke so many times?" A lump grew in his throat. "Nerissa, how long did you know?" Horses and horseshoes, he hoped it wasn't the entire time.

The apology in her eyes declared otherwise.

Being pierced by arrows was a pain beyond description. But this? From the woman he was beginning to care for? From the man he admired? From those who claimed to want what was best for the trafficking victims?

It made the pain from his past wounds look insignificant and dull.

Soul shredding, he scanned the group.

No one met his gaze.

"I bled for you people. I almost *died* for you. And you still withheld this." Unbelievable. He wasn't the coward. They were.

Skirting the group, his surroundings blurred in his peripheral as he reached Cinders. Mounting, he reined her toward the path the attackers took.

"What are you doing, son?"

Son. He hated that word. Father spoke it, lips dripping venom and hatred. And now Morris, coating it in lies and false care.

"Denton..."

"I'm going to find Jonah." He already broke his promise once. He wasn't about to again.

"You saw what those spawn of evil did. You don't stand a chance."

"Then at least I'll die doing what's right." Maybe then his penance would be paid.

Chief Talart's voice thundered after him. "Stay where you are. We'll gather a posse."

Denton glared over his shoulder, patting Cinders' withers to keep her from becoming too antsy. "I don't want your help. Chances are you'll only put Jonah in more danger."

At his command, Cinders leapt into a canter, the drumming of her hooves drowning their calls.

Tears blurred his peripheral vision as the land passed in a smear of colors. To think...no, it was foolish to think anyone could ever care about him.

After all, Father hadn't.

Why would these people who uttered lies like Red wielded insults?

Every effort to shove away the sting of betrayal failed. The sensation left in his chest a weight so heavy it may crush his heart and lungs.

Even after proving himself, they thought him dangerous. Unworthy of upholding a vow.

Grinding his teeth, he allowed the volcanic heat within to blaze to life. He had failed Jonah twice.

He wouldn't fail a third time.

Chapter Twenty-Four

NERISSA

HEART LODGED IN HER throat, Nerissa jumped from her spot at the table as the thunder of pounding hooves rumbled from just beyond the trees.

After Denton fled the carnage wrought upon Kanni and Lloyd's property, Chief Talart sent Uncle Morris and four other men after him.

They hadn't yet returned.

Elberta bounded into the cabin, swinging the basket of eggs as haphazardly as if they were pebbles instead. "Edver's here. And he's riding like a swarm of hornets is chasing him."

That meant little. If Edver even so much as thought he smelled banana bread, he'd come riding.

Wiping her hands on her apron, Nerissa slipped from the cabin. Before she could stop herself, she glanced toward Uncle Morris'. No matter how often she looked and pinched her arm, reality remained. Denton was gone, their deception—*her* deception—driving him away.

Please, Beginning, bring him back.

The tears she'd cried in private had watered the deep ache residing in her chest, until roots formed and permanently attached the moroseness. She couldn't name what had been growing between them, but now it was gone.

Crumbled and blown away in the winds of time as though it was ash in a gust.

Edver reined his horse to a halt near the porch. "They're back. And they have Jonah."

They were *back*. Maybe now reconciliation could begin and Denton would forgive them—her—and stay so whatever had been between them could continue.

"Here." He offered his hand. "Mount up behind me. We'll get there faster than if you walk."

Tossing orders over her shoulder to Elberta, who responded with a list of complaints, Nerissa allowed Edver to pull her up.

The irony. Riding a horse to meet the man she swore made her never want to ride again.

"Are they okay?"

"They look like it. A few cuts and scrapes, of course, and Jonah won't stop clinging to Denton, but I think they're fine overall."

The trees and rocks whipped past them in a stream of color, yet every step felt like one hundred years.

Stomach in knots, Nerissa offered a continual string of prayers until they reached the village. Skirting the crowd of villagers, she and Edver made their way to the front. The men were handing their horses over to the younger lads, who eagerly scampered away, likely hurrying so they could return and not miss whatever stories were yet to be told.

She laced her fingers and scanned the area. "Where's Denton?"

Edver craned his neck, his superior height offering him a view over almost everyone else. "There he is. Coming from the infirmary."

Heart leaping, Nerissa stepped forward. Denton strode from the building, Jonah's hand within his. A grim expression did not bode well for the upcoming interaction, but perhaps he was just tired and hungry, and hiding only minor bruises beneath his stained and smudged shirt.

Jonah caught Nerissa's eye and offered a timid wave. Like Denton, mud and grime spotted his clothing and face. No visible injuries marked the child, and Nerissa sent another prayer of gratitude.

"Are you okay?"

Edver shrugged.

Denton's gaze sharpened, and Nerissa's breath caught when those piercing blue eyes fell on her. Nothing amiable crossed Denton's face. Instead, what could be animosity honed his visible displeasure.

"Neither of you are injured, right?"

"We're fine," Denton ground out. "No thanks to you and your village."

Her heart accepted the words like they were a barbed quiver. "What do you mean? We rescued him and kept him safe."

"You knew full well I was looking for him, and for some reason—no, not for some reason—because even after all I've done for this hypocritical place, you still think I'm a monster—you lied to me. You and your precious chief and *wonderful* fellow villagers."

The heat of the anger simmering from him made the desert look cold.

Every instinct demanded she step back, but part of diminishing her worry-wartish ways was to reduce cowardice. "I don't think you're a monster."

"That's not what your actions indicate." Bitterness coated his tone. "Now, please move."

"But I—"

"Come one, Ner." Edver's hands on her upper arms gently eased her to the side. "He's not budging."

Still retaining his grip on Jonah, Denton stomped past them, pausing only long enough to glare up at Edver. "Your self-righteous ways won't fool everyone."

"What self-righteous ways?"

Lip curling up in a sneer, Denton shouldered past Edver. "Where's Noko?"

Though tears stung her eyes, Nerissa refused to look away. *Please, Beginning, stop him long enough so he can listen.*

Silence befell the village, until even the waves sounded muted.

"Where. Is. Noko?"

Uncle Morris stepped forward. Dirty like the rest, at least he looked lucid and free from pain. "Why do you want to know, son?"

"Patronizing me will get you nowhere. Now, I want my question answered."

Chief Talart crossed his arms. "You're acting awfully uppity for an outsider."

"I'm King Calvin Seyden's royal detective. I could put on a lot more airs than this. Now answer the question."

Voices rose in protest at the disrespect, but Chief Talart held up his hand and advanced toward Denton.

Who promptly shoved Jonah behind him and drew the sword.

"Lower your weapon, boy."

"Where's Noko? Or have you taken and hidden him, too?"

The tears burned hotter. She understood he was hurt—she would be too—but must he be so cruel?

"It's okay, Ner," Edver murmured.

"Maybe I can try talking to him again. Maybe he'll listen."

"Honestly, Nerissa, I think that'd be the worst thing. You're the last one he probably wants to talk to right now."

A few months ago, the words wouldn't have hurt. But now they burrowed deep, causing unimaginable torment. "Why?"

"Because of what he felt for you. Now he probably sees our actions as destroying those feelings. He likely thinks you didn't feel the same, when he thought you did."

A hiccup announced itself. "I don't even know what that was."

"I don't think he does, either, but there was something there. Everyone saw it."

Uncle Morris tried again. "Denton..."

"Detective Yindell. Answer my question. Where is Noko?"

Chief Talart's glare deepened, but he didn't motion for Denton to be arrested or dragged to his office. "Hauni, would you please fetch Noko?"

"And his belongings." Denton's tone left no room for argument.

Nerissa clutched Edver's arm. The ground dipped a little and the dirt felt like it was sinking inwards, as though it planned to collapse at any minute.

Denton was leaving.

The man she was beginning to care for…was leaving.

After Uncle Morris was rebuffed three more times, no one said another word to Denton until Hauni returned with Noko, who carried a bag.

"Where are you taking him?"

"They're both coming with me. I'll ensure they are returned to their families." Denton sheathed his sword and spoke to Noko in a voice too quiet to hear. After the boy scampered off, Denton again swept the crowd with a harsh, icy glare.

Nerissa hugged herself when it landed on her. Up until the attack, she hadn't regretted withholding the information. Now…now it had splintered something delicate. Something promising.

She opened her mouth, but nothing came out.

For the briefest of heartbeats, what looked like hurt flashed through Denton's eyes, but it vanished when Noko returned, a horse ambling along behind him.

She squinted. "Isn't that the horse we brought back from that one rescue?"

Edver grunted an agreement. "Guess no one wanted it."

The horse was the ugliest equine Nerissa ever saw, but it was sturdy and calm. Why no one wanted it went beyond her.

Sparks kindled in her chest.

It was the village's fault Denton was leaving. If someone claimed the horse, he wouldn't be taking it. Without two horses, surely he and the boys couldn't travel.

Please stop him, Beginning.

Denton hoisted Noko onto the ugly horse before doing the same to Jonah onto Cinders before mounting behind him. With a brusque command, he guided Cinders away, Noko and his ride following.

The plea for him to stop lodged in her throat. Why must he go? Why couldn't he let her explain?

Please, don't go.

But she couldn't vocalize the words.

Denton rode on, never once looking back.

Never once offering her hope that he would return and her breaking heart could mend.

Once they disappeared from sight, Nerissa's knees buckled and the tears broke free.

Clumps of dirt flew in the air before raining down, plunking off her head and back, but Nerissa ignored them as she stared at the weeds demanding extermination. Plucking another one, she placed it in her overfull basket.

"How are you?" Mamma snatched the weed Nerissa reached for.

"It still hurts."

"It will for some time, Nerri."

Had she loved Denton? Not yet. Not fully. But she had been getting there. His gentleness with Noko, his protective nature, his stunning eyes and handsome smile, and the way he had, almost off-handedly, stated his belief in the Beginning was renewing...

Yes, she was close.

Had been close.

"It was a losing battle." She grit her teeth and yanked a stubborn sticker weed from between two tomato plants. "Tell him, and he would have taken Jonah and left immediately. Not tell him, and look what happened."

Mamma placed her hand over Nerissa's. "Perhaps he wasn't the one for you, dear."

"It's stupid, feeling this way."

"No, it is not. The heart is easily bruised, yet for the pain we suffer when it breaks, the love and care and devotion it produces is worth the potential aftermath. Denton was a good man. But, for some reason, the Beginning allowed him to leave."

"Is it silly to miss him?" She'd even take a riding lesson—at full gallop—if it meant bringing him back.

"Oh, dear girl. No, 'tis not silly at all. It's been three days, darling. The heart does not mend so quickly." Mamma beat her to another weed. "Why don't you deliver some banana bread to Hauni and Guy? We still owe them for looking at Daffy's foot."

Yes, because Daffy just couldn't stay away from the creek, where slippery rocks abounded. She shouldn't have been surprised when she slipped and caught her foot between two unforgiving rocks.

"Yes, ma'am."

"Nerissa?"

"Yes?"

Mamma offered a smile full of understanding. "I know your dream is to be a wife and mother. The Beginning will send along the right man in His perfect timing."

A wispy hint of a smile was all Nerissa could offer before she washed up and retrieved the banana bread. "Elberta, out you go. Mamma needs your help in the garden."

Elberta pooched out her bottom lip. "But I was babysitting Daffy."

"I don't need babysitting." Daffy scowled, though with her pudgy cheeks, she couldn't pull off the disgruntled look. "I'm fwour."

Nerissa picked up the whiny child and deposited her in the chair on the back porch. "It's *four*, Daffy, and yes, you do need babysitting. Now, sit here and tell Mamma your letters and numbers as she weeds, okay? I'll be back in a bit."

"Where are you going?" Elberta crossed her arms, the epitome of defiance.

"I need to deliver something."

"You mean you're gonna go hang out with Edver and Afya while me and Daffy have to work. That's not fair."

Nerissa shook her head, bid Mamma farewell, and left, Elberta's whining hounding her footsteps until she exited the clearing.

The crisp scent of pine, combined with the sea's salty tang, filled her lungs as she made her way to the village. Mamma was right, but the healing process was taking too long for comfort.

She missed him terribly, even if he did insist on putting her life in danger through nightmarish horseback rides.

Come back, Denton.

But he wouldn't. He would return home and never think of her or her home again.

After giving the Talarts their bread, Afya stopped by Hauni and Guy's.

Guy patted his belly when she handed the loaves to Hauni. "Your family can keep injuring yourselves if it means being paid in banana bread."

Hauni tsked and snapped her towel at him. "Really, Guy. That's hardly the correct mindset."

"Well, I won't have the correct weight either after we finish this tasty treat, but you don't see that stopping me."

Shaking her head, Hauni motioned Nerissa out the door. "Such a rascal, that man. If you wish to speak with Afya, she is in the back tending to the garden." The lines framing her eyes softened. "Perhaps it will do you some good, dear child."

"Yes, ma'am."

Truthfully, Nerissa had no idea what she and Afya would speak about. She liked the young woman, but it was terribly dull constantly listening to Afya sigh about Edver's positive attributes. Somehow, in the midst of admiring his strength and kindness and on and on, she forgot he could down two loaves of banana bread in one sitting, screamed like an enraged baby whenever something unidentified brushed the back of his neck, and had no common sense to speak of.

Love was blind, Nerissa supposed.

Afya smiled from where she knelt over an herb patch. "How are you?"

"I'm alright." Nerissa knelt and began helping. "And you?"

"I feel like I may sprout wings at any minute and begin flying." Afya hid a giggle behind her hand. "Edver asked to court me this morning."

"He did? And the big lug didn't tell me?" She was so putting three cups of salt in the next banana bread loaf she made specifically for him. Then he wouldn't be tiptoeing about with his chicanery.

Afya tucked springy curls behind her ears, a bashful expression adding a twinkle to her eyes. "We wanted to tell you together, but I just let the fish out of the net, I suppose."

Nerissa laughed and reached over to hug Afya. "Regardless, I'm excited for you. Please let me know if you need any help thinking up ways to keep him on his toes. I know a few of his secrets we can use against him."

"Oh?"

"Mmhm. He hates sand in his boots, for one."

Afya pulled away from the hug, a sly grin overtaking her smile. "Do go on."

"Yes," a deep voice rasped. "Do go on."

Blood icing over, Nerissa leapt to her knees and spun. A tall, dark-skinned Marterisi with more height than Edver and bulkier arms than Chief Talart leered at them from the garden's edge.

Her knees quaked as he advanced, sword drawn.

"Stay right where you are, little missies. One scream and I'll let you water your little plants with your own blood."

Nerissa closed her eyes as cold iron brushed the underside of her jaw. Of course this would happen the moment she let her guard down.

Worry may be wrong, but at least it kept one prepared.

"Come on now, little missies. Where did the chattering magpies go?"

A shriek tore from Nerissa when thick fingers clamped around her arm. This couldn't be happening. She and Afya weren't about to be abducted and sold into slavery.

"Let go." All fervored pitch had drained from Afya's voice, and once again she sounded like a mouse.

"No. You two are going to help us."

Us? There were *more*?

Skirts tangling about her ankles, Nerissa struggled to keep up with the man's league-long strides. Prayers cramped in her mind, begging for release, but she couldn't find the strength to utter them.

The man led them through the village without anyone noticing. How was that possible? How could they be so unaware of what went on around them?

"Here they are." He thrust them toward a familiar, tall, slender woman with light blonde hair and sunburned skin.

She smiled and patted Nerissa's and Afya's cheeks. "Oh, don't look so frightened, darlings. No one will sustain injury as long as you comply."

"What do you want?" Afya asked what Nerissa could not.

Haether waved her hand, the motion causing the sleeve of her deep purple dress to sway. "You'll find out in a minute, darling. Now, Pearce, do call the rest of the villagers. We haven't all week, you know. And do release the girls. They won't be going anywhere."

Bile burned Nerissa's throat as she glanced at the four bulky guards standing behind Haether. She and Afya weren't particularly speedy, and the men could easily catch up and detain them.

Clearing his throat, the man released them and faced the village. Cupping his hands around his mouth, he hollered for Chief Talart.

As villagers streamed from the buildings, some armed and others empty-handed, she caught Afya's next question. "What are you doing?"

"Why, darling, you needn't worry your pretty little head about it."

Chapter Twenty-Five

DENTON

The birds chirped, the boys conversed, and hooves drummed against the packed road, but neither noise nor impact reached the frozen muscle he called a heart.

If something sounded too good to be true, chances were it was.

Truth was something to spit on and trample.

And hope was no more tangible than a wisp of fog.

He swiped his sweaty palm on his thigh, Jonah's and Noko's chattering filling his ears. Just as well he left when he did. They would discover his past sooner or later, and he had no desire to die by being tossed from the cliff or pummeled to a pulp by Talart.

He'd take Jonah to Veerham and get Red to find the boy's family before taking Noko to Halthdurn. And after that? What then? No home awaited. No one cared if he returned.

A dash of color in the sea caught his eye. The flotsam drifted with neither anchor nor steerage, only going where the waves carried it.

Denton swallowed. Like that flotsam, he could only travel the tides of life. The current could not be resisted, and his destination would forever remain unknown.

That night, he settled them in a grove of hideous bush-trees. With plenty of grass in the area, the horses would be free to munch away, and the sliver of a brook would provide enough water to refill their canteens.

"Why did you come for me?" Jonah's bright eyes pierced Denton as he scarfed down another piece of dried rabbit.

Denton would never win Hunter of the Year award, but he managed to use Morris' tips to work up a snare. The three rabbits would have to suffice until he procured more game.

Jonah swallowed his bite. "You and the wolfman said you'd never let them take me again, but they did. And then you didn't come for a long time. I thought you'd forgotten about me."

Oh, how well he knew the pain of abandonment, although his had been emotional instead of physical. "I didn't forget about you, and I came as soon as I could." Denton split his portion and handed the halves to the boys. "After you were taken, there was a fight. Two broadheads caught me, and I wasn't allowed to travel until the physician cleared me."

In response, his scars throbbed. He'd take physical pain any day over this raw grief grating his heart and soul.

Jonah's jaw dropped. "How are you alive? I didn't think anyone could live after being shot."

Noko shook his head. "You can. My da was hit three times during a battle, and he's still alive far as I know." The boy's swarthy complexion paled. "You do think he's still alive, right, Denton?"

It wasn't the responsibility of two extra lives weighing on Denton's shoulders like a pasture of draft horses, nor was it the task of returning the boys to their families. No, it was the trust and admiration with which Noko looked at him, like he was some kind of hero.

Swallowing a lump, Denton offered the closest thing to a smile he could conjure up. "Your people are hardy. I'm sure he's fine."

The potential lie tasted as sour as unripe apples, and lingered long after the boys had tucked in.

Denton slipped over to Cinders and rested his forearms on her back, staring at the star-speckled sky. Morris had participated in the lie about Jonah, but had he lied about the Beginning too? Just because one spoke falsely about one thing didn't mean they did on everything.

Was he right?

The key had unlocked the gate guarding his heart, but that left it vulnerable to probable heartache.

Call him a wimp, but he didn't know if he could handle more.

"Just because we don't understand His plan or see what we think is evidence of His existence doesn't mean He's not real. Human expectation does not define Him."

Or so Parson Gil said. Morris had mentioned something similar.

The Beginning wasn't confined to humanity's understanding of Him.

"He can't be put in a box, boy."

Denton laced his fingers and bowed his head. The Beginning was perfect, according to Parson Gil. That meant He did not act like Father. The Beginning also was the definition of mercy and love. That meant He knew how to *be* those things, right?

One half of Denton's heart struggled toward the promise set before him—a Heavenly Father who had made it so he could have eternal life. The other half rebelled, struggling against the pull, bound by chains constructed of past fear and pain.

Denton had no idea how deep the deepest well in the world went, but he was certain the ache within went even deeper. A visceral longing so fierce he sometimes thought it would knock him off his feet.

I don't know how to do this. Did he pray? Speak aloud? Use fancy vernacular? Was there a specific format? A particular set of words?

"You are His child, my boy. A child who can approach his Father whenever and whyever. There is never a time when He will not hear you."

Father always slammed the door shut in his face or verbally listed a long string of select phraseology to express his displeasure whenever Denton attempted to speak with him about something other than business.

Is Parson Gil right?

He must be. He studied the Scripts every day and had been preaching them for longer than Denton's age times two.

Just how did he approach the Beginning, though? He'd never been able to with Father.

Chamonix always just walked up to King Calvin and began speaking with him in normal, conversational tones. Calvin had adopted the method as well, his confidence something Denton never thought his brother possessed.

He couldn't exactly just walk up to the Beginning's throne. And the Maker of all was to be feared and revered at a level an earthly king would never deserve.

How did Parson Gil and Morris begin their prayers?

Dear Beginning...

Halted and hesitant, he formed the prayer. Was he doing it correctly? Would any errors be held against him?

Errors.

Despite his efforts to atone for his past, it still lurked. Jonah hesitated every morning before allowing Denton to hoist him onto Cinders. His past had destroyed all chances at continuing his dream—taking Father's business and changing it into a profitable horse training venture that didn't rely on stolen funds.

"You are a new man now, Lord Yindell. You are no longer stained with crimson. Instead, you are now as white as snow."

Did that mean the Beginning fully forgave him?

A whisper of weight upon wild grass shattered his introspection.

"Why did you come?" Jonah's whisper cut the air.

Denton ran a hand through his hair. "You have every right to doubt me, and I don't blame you for it. I came because I couldn't let you remain a slave. I made a promise, and I needed to keep it. No child should be forced to endure what you've been through." He knelt before Jonah and risked reaching out to put his hands on the boy's shoulders.

Jonah didn't flinch.

"I know you thought I broke the promise. I swear I did everything I could to begin looking for you as quickly as possible."

"What about the wolfman?" Tears wetted Jonah's voice.

"He and his friend were called away, but I'm sure he wishes he could have upheld his vow."

"I was so scared," Jonah whispered. "I thought they were going to break my arms. And the chains were too tight. I couldn't feel my hands most of the time. When Chief Talart rescued me, I overheard him and Mister Guy saying I could lose my fingers because of bad circulation." A whimper threaded its way through his words. "I don't even know if my parents miss me anymore. D'you think they still miss me?"

Cursing and berating himself a thousand times over, Denton copied Nerissa and Chamonix and drew Jonah in for a hug. The boy's skinny frame trembled as tears soaked into Denton's shirt.

"I know they still miss you."

"How?"

"Because they are good parents, and good parents never stop looking for their child."

"I just wanna see them again."

"I will do everything to ensure you will."

And this time, he wouldn't fail. He wouldn't let the promise lapse.

He would do whatever it took to fulfill his vow.

Marteris wasn't known for earthquakes, so why was he experiencing one?

Denton grit back a complaint and rolled to his stomach. Nothing was around to fall on him. He would just endeavor to sleep through the stupid thing. Rest was a precious commodity, and soon he'd need to arise and continue toward Veerham.

The earthquake continued, accompanied by two spots of pressure on his shoulders and a squeaky rumble in the distance.

Thunder didn't squeak, nor did it pitch upward.

It also didn't call his name.

Cracking one eye half-open, Denton managed to grunt a response to the unusual chaos.

"There's smoke."

Who cared if there was smoke? They were by the sea. If flames came their way, they'd just take a few steps into the man-eating waves. No one could outrun a wildfire, and it was better to drown than burn to death.

"Denton, wake up." Noko's voice joined the cacophony.

Peeling both eyes open, Denton returned to his back and blinked at the two children staring down at him. Against the sun, which shone brightly against the fading colors of dawn, their faces were shadowed and darkened.

Noko hiked a thumb over his shoulder. "There's a fire somewhere. A big one. That's a lot of smoke."

Thoughts slowly organizing themselves, Denton pushed himself to a seated position. The haziness of sleep faded at the sight of a thick, black cloud of smoke billowing into the air. It was too concentrated to be a wildfire, so what was the source?

"Mister Guy's village is the nearest to us, right? Maybe they could help."

"I think that's between us and them." Chances were, the fork-tongued liars had already seen the smoke and were on their way to do their daily good deed.

"We hafta go help." Noko yanked Denton's arm. "Come on. One time, a nearby clan was on fire, and if we hadn't gone, everyone would have died."

"This will delay our return to Veerham."

Jonah bobbed his head, red hair in dire need of a trim flapping with the movement. "I know. But Mother and Father would want me to help. That's what a gentleman does—help others."

Stumbling to his feet, Denton brushed off his cloak. The campsite was clear and the horses already saddled. "You two are serious about this."

"Yep. We found a rock and stood on it. I checked the cinches and everything, just like you showed me." Jonah beamed.

Patting the kid on the head, Denton dug through his saddlebag before tossing the boys their breakfast. "We'll have to eat on the way."

And eat they did. Before half a league was covered, Denton was fairly certain seagulls would spot the crumbs left by Jonah and kill Denton in their efforts to retrieve the paltry morsels.

The smoke still rose the next day.

Noko's expression twisted. "What if the people are already dead? What if we're too late?"

The thought of the boys seeing such carnage did not settle well in Denton's stomach. "You two must promise to do whatever I tell you, alright?"

Their reluctant agreeance matched Red's when she was determined to pacify others so she could sneak away and carry out whatever hair-brained plan was forming in that insane mind of hers.

If only Red and Carter were with him. Red's orneriness disguised a caring attitude toward those she deemed worthy, but she would protect the boys with her life. And Carter didn't cotton to innocents being mistreated or harmed, even if he hadn't done a thing to rescue himself from Father's clutches.

After two more leagues passed, Denton's heart sank. They still hadn't reached the smoke's source, and Nerissa's village was only a few leagues away.

Perhaps the smoke was beyond that place.

His gut warned otherwise, however, and Red said to never discount that intuition.

Please, Beginning, let it just be a brush fire.

Smoke thickened the air as its acrid stench burned his nose. Just like when he arrived at Kanni and Lloyd's, ash drifted down. While no flames flickered through the trees separating them from the village, tension hung in the air. No wildlife twittered or chirped and nothing moved.

The hairs on the back of his arms prickled.

Please, Beginning.

What he prayed for, he didn't know.

Denton slid off and drew the sword he'd not thought to remove when grabbing the boys before leaving. "Stay here. In fact, go into the trees. Keep the horses quiet just like I showed you, and only come out when you hear me call for you, understood?"

Without waiting for their replies, he crept through the trees, locating a path Edver showed him during his first week.

Premonition slugged him in the gut and the hairs on the back of his neck joined those on his arms. Now so thick it settled like an unwelcomed fog, the smoke choked the air from the area.

Sand crunched beneath his boot when he finally emerged onto the beach.

His heart stalled.

Flames consumed the area where the church once stood. Thick Marterises fed logs to the fire while others, weapons drawn, guarded the villagers, most of whom sat.

A woman in a pale-yellow dress paced back and forth. When she made to turn, she looked in his direction and paused before lifting her hand. "Seize him."

There were tales where the heroes defeated their foes singlehandedly. Denton always hated those stories due to their illogical nature.

Five men rushed him.

If he fled, they might find the boys. If he met them, he'd likely die.

He brought up the sword to meet the first man's blow, but nothing protected his ribs from the fist plowing into him like it had a personal vendetta against ribs in one piece.

Breath fled his lungs.

Another blow sent his head snapping back.

Dark smudges dotted his vision as bruising grips latched onto his upper arms and yanked him forward.

"We found him," a man bellowed.

Found who? Talart? Edver? Morris? Another village fighter?

Hands devoid of weapons, all he could do was be dragged toward a woman whose identity hovered at the edge of recognition.

A familiar face snagged his attention.

With Daffy in her lap, Nerissa sat next to her mother, who held Elberta. Grime and weariness streaked Nerissa's pale visage, her haggardness matching the rest of the villagers'. Coughs ripped from several of them, no doubt their lungs protesting the smoke.

Denton tore his gaze away and set his jaw as the distance between himself and the woman diminished.

The woman offered a smile devoid of warmth when Denton was brought before her.

He ground back a snarl. A fortnight ago, he'd had the displeasure of meeting representatives from the village of Keller when they came to retrieve one of their children. The lass had been rescued in the latest round, but hadn't acted like she was particularly enthused to see the woman before Denton, who introduced herself as Haether.

At Haether's gesture, he was forced to face the villagers.

This was madness. Sheer madness. And if Denton wasn't soon let go, he would show them what a furious Veerhamer looked like, with a heavy coating of Red's favorite insults thrown in for good measure.

"It's about time you got here." Haether drew a knife and tapped the flat of it on her palm. "I have a proposition for you, Denton Yindell."

"How do you know him?" Ice coated Talart's tone.

Haether smoothed her skirt with her free hand. "My husband was murdered by the Veerhamer before you."

Cold washed over Denton. Before coming to Marteris, he'd only killed some of the traffickers during the fight near the Queen's Forest. He wasn't a murderer—took no pleasure in spilling blood.

"My husband was desperately attempting to save a little Marterisi girl, but this man gutted him and left him to perish a slow, wretched death. That girl was forever lost to us, and now her family mourns her every day." Haether wiped her eyes. "A fellow villager was there that day and witnessed my husband's demise. He saw a group of your people traveling with this man and promptly reported the news to me. I apologize for the destruction to your building, but it was the only way we could lure this man in without wasting valuable supplies."

Because a church wasn't valuable. Because wood and the hymnals and Scripts weren't valuable.

Because *truth* wasn't valuable.

Haether sniffled. "It was obvious he cared for this village. Playing on his sympathies and concerns was the only way to begin the process of retribution."

The process of *what*?

Haether's voice turned as venomous as Frilore's rattlesnakes. "And since your village harbored this murderer—this criminal—you are complicit as well. Not only in protecting a man who murdered one of your own, but a man who is also a wanted criminal in his own land."

Denton jerked. Horses and horseshoes, what was this woman talking about?

"He is the son of a notorious trafficker and black market operator. He helped his father and brother kidnap and traffic children, and is suspected of having ties throughout the lands. His family has already paid for their crimes, but somehow this man wheedled himself out of his punishment."

The rest of Haether's words faded into the distance as Nerissa's gaze locked with Denton's. Even though at least seven people separated them, he could detect the sheen of tears in eyes wide with betrayal.

She thought him guilty.

She believed Haether, even after that mindless woman threatened Nerissa's family's lives and demolished the church.

The mending pieces of his heart shattered.

Swallowing moisture into his dry throat, Denton retained eye contact. "She's lying. I didn't—"

His lungs were again forcibly emptied of air as a fist the size of an anvil silenced him.

Fingers clutched his hair, nails digging into his scalp as Haether dragged him up from where he bent over, gasping for air.

"This man has slain in cold blood, helped kidnap and traffic children like your own and Keller's, and *you* have protected him. That is in direct defiance to Marteris' law. No criminal or wanted man may be assisted by any village, lest that village suffer his same punishment."

Morris began rising, but a skinny woman beside him yanked him back down.

The villagers murmured, their voices quieter than the flames, but somehow louder than a thunderclap.

"Since he's not one of our own, however, I will offer a choice."

A cool blade dug into the juncture of Denton's jaw and neck. "Your life for the village, or theirs for your own?"

"You'll just kill them after you kill me." He wasn't that stupid.

"I will not. They assisted you, but that does not mean they knew your past. A punishment must be given, but since there is a chance they are innocent, their fate is not mandatory."

So said a viper who looked over the villagers with loathing in her eyes.

Denton grit his teeth. "You have the wrong man. I'm not a—"

Every effort to protest was silenced, until his pulse throbbed in time with the agony blooming in his ribs.

Did it really matter, though? They wouldn't believe an outsider over one of their own countrymen.

More words were exchanged. The tears tracking down Nerissa's cheeks hurt worse than any punishment Haether would ever inflict.

I didn't do it.

But that mattered little. His fate was already decided. He couldn't let these people—liars though they were—die.

"Well? What is your decision?"

He never imagined he'd offer himself up to die.

People aren't worth it.

Father was wrong. Little Daffy, feisty Elberta, the other young ones…

Nerissa.

Afya.

The two pregnant women who would soon bring forth new life.

Beginning, please save the boys.

"Get him out of here," Haether commanded. After bidding the villagers a casual farewell—like she hadn't just obliterated the most important building in the village and wasn't dragging an innocent man toward his death—she mounted a horse one of her henchmen brought her before flicking her hand.

Denton wheezed as he was tossed onto a mud-flecked dun. Hands bound to the saddle horn and a foul-tasting rag gagging him, he could only look over his shoulder as the horses plodded toward his doom.

I didn't do it.

But when had he ever mattered enough for anyone to care?

I didn't do it.

Perhaps Haether was right, though. He *had* turned a blind eye, and that made him complicit. He *had* guessed something shifty was going on, but hadn't said a word. That made him just as guilty as the actual participants.

He hadn't said anything when Carter was beaten up by Father and Antony, either.

Maybe...maybe this was his punishment. His recompense. Maybe this was how the Beginning was punishing him.

When the trees closed in and blocked the village from sight, Haether uttered another command.

A fist connected with Denton's jaw, and the explosion of dark spots soon coated his vision, blocking everything from sight and hearing.

While recuperating from being shot, Denton had wished away time, willing it to speed up so he could return to walking, riding...being *normal.*

As though normal could ever be achieved in the aftermath of Father's and Josiah's choices.

Now, as he slumped against a tree, bound to the trunk with more bruises than Red had freckles, he found himself slipping into the practice.

Willing away every minute. Wishing each second would pass at ten times the speed.

Parched didn't begin to describe the dryness tormenting his throat, and the ropes securing his torso to the tree cut into him with every breath he attempted. Feeling in his hands had long fled, and heat throbbed through his face.

Probably a good thing the boys weren't around. He probably looked like a monster.

Haether pranced over and inspected him before snapping her fingers. The two largest brutes stomped toward Denton, knives bared.

"Remove his gag. I want to hear his pitiful pleas before he gets what he deserves."

Denton squinted the best he could when the sunlight caught the gemstones decorating Haether's fingers. Once the gag was removed, he worked his jaw to ease the stiffness. "Does Lady Riley know you're wearing her jewelry?" The words scraped his raw throat, but the wrath and rage darkening Haether's expression was worth it.

Denton mustered all the defiance he could and copied Red's smirk. "What did Riley bribe you with? More gaudy rings and necklaces? Land? Money?"

His neck cranked to the side at the impact of palm against cheek, but if he was going to die, might as well go out in a glorious display of aggravating the soulless wretch before him. "I bet you haven't been fully paid. Did you know Riley died last year? He was hung and buried in the criminals' graveyard."

Right next to Father and Josiah.

"Shut up," Haether hissed, "or I'll cut out your tongue."

Denton coaxed his swollen lips into a sneer. "You wouldn't because that'd keep me from screaming."

Another slap.

At this point, his head would be removed with a slap.

What a pitiful way to go.

"How long did you work for him? Had to be at least three or four months to supply all those Marteris children."

"Al, silence him."

Gasping for breath, Denton doubled over as Al—a gargantuan Marteris with the build and personality of a sea-weathered cliff—put his fists to good use.

He swore he heard his final, intact rib break.

A meager amount of tears stung his eyes. Perhaps it was the dehydration, or even the exhaustion.

"Coward."

He'd prove Red wrong. He'd go out fighting the best he could. He'd not die as a coward.

"Bet…bet you weren't happy that your husband disagreed with you," he wheezed. If his theory was correct, then Haether's equally-despicable spouse had been the man attempting to kidnap Topika. The same man who injured Red.

If only the spitfire detective were here. She'd give these bloated fish corpses a piece of her mind and then some.

"Al, if he says one more word, knock out his teeth."

Looked like he'd be dying toothless, then. "Did you know he tried reclaiming a Marteris girl? One who was actually born in Veerham? Said Marterises didn't deserve to be slaves."

Haether's nostrils flared, and at her signal, Al yanked Denton to his feet.

He groaned and hunched. The sheer agony shooting through his middle stole the bit of air left in his lungs.

Beginning, please let it be quick.

Was it unmanly to not want to suffer?

Haether's fingers, topped with fingernails that could pass as a falcon's talons, dug into his chin. Dull blue eyes spit venom. "I can tell you're thirsty, you worthless piece of trash. How about we fix that? Al, to the cliff."

The crash of waves coming into contact with the cliff and rocks sent a bolt of raw terror through his veins. The remnants of his adrenaline humming, Denton wrangled up enough energy to try writhing from Al's grasp.

A solid blow to the back of his head dissuaded those efforts.

No. He refused to die by drowning. Those waves—those man-eating waves—would not claim him. He refused. He *wouldn't.*

Haether's chuckle was like a rattlesnake's warning just before a strike. "I see you are no fan of the beloved water. Unfortunately for you, you're about to become very much acquainted with it."

Foam-capped waves surged below, and while the cliff wasn't the highest, it did tower over spindly rocks that could easily impale or break him.

His empty stomach heaved. This really was how he would die. *Please, Beginning, no. Not like this.*

Warmth, followed by stinging pain, spread across his arm.

Haether withdrew a knife, the edge shiny with crimson. "Just in case any sharks are nearby." Wildness claimed her eyes as she yanked his head back. "You Veerhamers may hold no allegiance to your own, but we Marterises don't tolerate folks killing our loved ones. If you hurt one of our own, you will pay. And you killed my husband." Her breath hissed in his ear. "You will suffer, and I'll exult over your death."

"Coward."

He wouldn't be a coward. He'd be strong.

But those waves...

"Now what?" Al's voice, accented and rough, struck a distant memory.

Denton jerked his head up.

"I'm not Cinders."

"Hand over the sword."

"Throw him in."

Denton's lungs failed as Al hefted him, then tossed him into the hungry waves below.

Cold water consumed him, and as the salt stung his eyes and threatened to enter his airway, he could only use the last of his energy to pray one more time for Nerissa's and the boys' safety.

CHAPTER TWENTY-SIX

NERISSA

VOICES CHATTERED AND TOOLS hammered and clanged, but the buzzing in Nerissa's ears kept her from understanding what was being said.

Two days had passed after the raiders left and Denton's identity was exposed.

It both made sense and didn't. He didn't have the eyes of a trafficker—a killer, and his care toward Noko was not fabricated. But he also refused to reveal his secrets, and that loathing in his eyes had so often been directed at himself.

No, Denton was no senseless murderer.

And he had given himself up for the village.

But that didn't mean he hadn't been a trafficker at some point.

Nerissa groaned and dropped her head into her hands. He had looked so innocent, up there and caught in evil's clutches. And he had come back, armed and—dare she hope—ready to help save them from the sudden appearance of malice and poorly-disguised contempt for her people.

Haether Cauth, Keller's crowned drama queen and one of its many resident nasties, had never liked Nerissa's village. Her attempts at entering had been blocked up until she arrived to retrieve a rescued child. After witnessing the calloused destruction of the most sacred building in the village, Nerissa didn't doubt the rumors that Haether had been seen speaking with those suspected of trafficking.

And that decaying seagull of a woman had seen how many children were ripe for the kidnapping.

Weariness washed over her as she lifted her head and stared at the organized chaos. Reconstructing the church had been top priority, but after Chief Talart learned Nerissa and Afya had been caught by surprise, he ordered the women and children to always be in the village square so the men could guard them.

It made housework tricky and gardening and caring for the animals difficult, but there was no denying the cloud of premonition hanging over the village.

Something was coming. Nerissa felt it in her bones.

Clutching her churning stomach, she rose from her perch on the infirmary's steps and weaved her way to where Afya helped the cobbler's wife teach the children their letters and numbers.

"How are you doing, Nerri?"

She blinked the postmaster into focus. Yald's thin hair did little to obscure the growing bald spot overtaking his scalp, and the skinny man carried a hammer larger than he was. "I am fine." The words poured forth in a wooden, monotone voice she didn't recognize as her own.

Yald shook his head. "Such a shame about that outsider. I truly thought he was on our side for a time."

Nerissa squinted. Haether's accusation remained disjointed. Something was off. "She lied," she murmured, "and she twisted the context of that law."

"Beg your pardon, Nerri?"

"Just speaking to myself. I thought you always disliked Denton."

Wiping an arm across his forehead, Yald shrugged. "I did at first, even though the emblem on his introduction letter was genuine. Your father and uncle seemed to like him, so I trusted their instincts." He shook his head. "Always knew in my gut that boy was a rotten fish."

Nerissa mumbled some unintelligible excuse for leaving and dashed away. Tears burned her eyes. Part of her wanted to believe she'd been blind and tricked into believing Denton was on their side, evidence suggested the contrary.

But he'd given his life so her people could live.

Please, Beginning, help me make sense of these jumbled thoughts and emotions.

She slid in next to Mother, who sat in a circle with other women peeling the passels of wild potatoes dug up earlier. Accepting a paring knife and potato, Nerissa set to work.

The familiar, boring motions dulled the wild tempest that was a culmination of her emotions. "How are you?" Mamma murmured.

A lump lodged in Nerissa's throat as she scanned Mamma's features. Short, graying strands of dark blonde hair hung in Mamma's face, which exhibited no sign of stress or worry. During being kept on the beach for two days straight, not being allowed to get up or move about, she had soothed Daffy and Elbert and remained calm, leaning on Father as he wrapped his arm around her shoulders.

The stories emulated queens and women who charged into battle with swords bared, but those weren't the strongest women to ever live. No, that title went to Mamma. Maybe most didn't see being a wife and mother as glamorous professions, but they were the jobs the Beginning called Mamma to, and she carried them out with grace, faith, and gentleness. Wrangling Daffy and Elberta while keeping up with the chores was not easy, and more, she had done her best to emulate a Beginning-honoring life. With the Scripts she taught her two older daughters to read. Through songs she helped Daffy memorize verses. And through her actions she illustrated just how a woman who feared the Beginning was to act and respond to any event, whether good or bad.

Mamma was so stalwart and strong, and Nerissa was such an emotional wimp.

"Ner?"

"I'm okay," she murmured.

Mamma bumped Nerissa's shoulder with hers. "Do you miss him?"

"I do." The question didn't surprise her. Not really. She had come to gradually enjoy Denton's snappy wit when facing off with

Edver, and he was so patient with the girls. Not to mention brave when rescuing the children, and during the last few days, she thought she saw his faith strengthen. She missed his laughs—rare as they were—and the way his eyes softened when he smiled.

She'd gone from wanting him gone, to wanting him to stay, to her initial fears coming true.

Denton had brought ruin upon her village.

"I'm sorry, starfish."

Nerissa shrugged. Nothing could assuage the situation.

"If it helps, I doubt he committed those crimes."

"He's not a murderer, but what if he was, at one time, a trafficker or kidnapper like what Haether accused him of?'

"Haether is so consumed by her revenge and oversized self-worth that she will say anything to make someone else look like bad."

"I know." Nerissa scanned what she could see of the forest. "I don't think that was the end of it, though. And if he was innocent, he died falsely accused."

Mamma's lips pursed. "No one thinks that's the end of it, dear. No one."

Arms burning, Nerissa wrung out Daffy's dress before snapping it to eliminate wrinkles. Despite being kept under the entire village's scrutiny, Daffy somehow managed to locate the only puddle and immerse herself in it. Thrice.

"I'm bored," Elberta whined. "It's been three days. Can't things return to normal?"

"That's for Chief Talart to decide." And by the chief's stiff stance and growly expression, now wasn't the time to ask.

"I wanna go home. I wanna *stay* home."

"I know. We all do." Nerissa hung the dress on the makeshift clothesline. Clothing of various sizes and colors fluttered in the breeze, and the scent of cooking fish overwhelmed the air.

Probably not the best thing to make on laundry day.

"Nerri?"

"Yes?"

"Who does that horse belong to?"

Heart plummeting to the pit of her stomach, Nerissa followed Elberta's finger. The tension coiling in her shoulders and neck relaxed. "That's Sir Marlin, remember? You named him."

Elberta squinted. "I suppose I recall that event. Not the brightest name I concocted."

No, but it was better than Magpie.

Nerissa exhaled at the memory before more tears took a sudden appearance. She watched Denton be hauled away, but she hadn't comprehended to *where*.

He was dead. Denton was dead. Haether intended to kill him, make him suffer for his supposed crimes.

Her chest collapsed at the thought and what felt like a hole in her soul opened. *Please, Beginning, if he didn't survive, let his end have been swift and painless.*

The prayer brought no comfort.

"Nerri?"

"Yes?"

"Do you think they really killed him?" Elberta's wide eyes tracked Nerissa's every movement.

She managed a shrug. "I have no idea. I pray not."

"I'll pray that too. I like him. And he *like* likes you."

Heart too wounded for such a discussion, especially with her eight-year-old sister, Nerissa hung over the next garment before ushering Elberta toward where Mamma mended clothing with most of the other women. "Why don't you help them instead?"

"But I was helping you."

Nerissa wouldn't call rubbing salt on the wound, *helping*.

She sighed and rubbed her forehead. "I think I just need some quiet time, Elberta. Please?"

Shoulders slumping and a sour expression on her sunburnt face, Elberta trudged off.

Sniffing away the latest round of tears, Nerissa commenced her work. She needed to be strong like Mamma and quiet, yet steady like Afya, but she didn't appreciate the trials she had to endure to get that way.

Why couldn't she just become as mature and strong in her faith as she needed to be without the tests and troubles that came with it?

Her heart jumped as a scream pierced the air.

For a mere second, silence descended before Chief Talart roared for the women and children to find shelter.

Pulse pounding faster than a galloping horse's, Nerissa located Daffy and swept her up before meeting Mamma near the shore. Women screamed and children yelled as men shouted over the battle cries rising from the trees.

Cold energy pulsed through her. There was nowhere to run. Nowhere to go. Venturing toward home would result in them being taken, or even killed.

A scream of her own joined the melee as a thick, dark-skinned Marterisi emerged from the forest, his gait all too casual for attacking an innocent village.

Because he knew they could not outrun or hide from him.

Please, Beginning.

Clutching Daffy, Nerissa inched back. The paring knife tucked in her pocket would do no good, and she hadn't the aim to place it in his eye. No horses lingered about, so she couldn't put Daffy and Elberta on one and send them to tentative safety.

Please, Beginning.

Mamma snarled, shoving Elberta behind her and placing herself between her daughters and the oncoming menace. "Get away from them."

The man's scythe cut through the air as he rotated his wrist.

Nausea rose as two more men, both shorter though no less terrifying, joined him.

Crashing blades coming from the village's main area offered dark assurance the men were already engaged in combat.

The only possible way to escape was to take down the enemy herself, but with no weapons, how could she manage such a feat?

Perhaps running toward them like a madwoman? Acting crazing and touched in the mind? It mattered little if she died if her blood secured Mamma's and her sisters' freedom.

The men advanced. Nerissa placed Daffy next to Elberta and slid her hand through the sand. She'd always enjoyed the soft grains and overall lack of pebbles and shells, but now that proved a detriment.

She curled her fingers when they grazed something pointy.

Mamma drew a knife from her skirt.

The men closed the distance.

Beginning, please guide my aim.

At their next step, Nerissa sprang upright and flung her handfuls of sand and seashells. The foremost man hissed, cursing as he clawed the sand from his eyes.

The other two lunged toward them.

Snatching another handful, she sent it flying toward the man to her right as Mamma did the same to the other.

Sand crunched.

Elberta screamed.

And an unbreakable hold pinned Nerissa's arms to her sides.

"Let go!" She kicked at where she thought his knee would be, but only met air.

Another man, a spindly towheaded Marterisi, grabbed Elberta and Daffy as the two survivors of the initial sand attack contained Mamma.

Hot tears stung Nerissa's eyes. No matter how hard she writhed and squirmed, she could not escape. In fact, her efforts were so pitiful and paltry that the man holding her didn't have the decency to sound out of breath while speaking to the two forcing Mamma's hands behind her back.

Rough fingers gripped her jaw and forced her to connect gazes with the man she first flung sand at. Bloodshot eyes burned with the hatred lining his voice. "She's young enough. Take her and the kids."

Mamma struggled against the men. "Hands off, you—"

Daffy wailed as fist collided with cheek and Mamma sagged.

The man holding Nerissa howled as she ground her heel into his instep. Father put her through a basic self-defense course a few years ago, but very few of those moves would work in this situation.

"Try that again, you infernal brat, and I'll—"

Nerissa threw her head back. Pain and a satisfying crunch rewarded her efforts.

A flurry of curses greeted her ears before she was wrenched around and sent to the ground.

Hot pain blooming in her cheek, she could only blink into vision Daffy being thrown over a man's shoulder.

"Get up."

A bruising hold forced her to her feet and yanked her toward the village's north edge. Daffy's and Elberta's cries rang in her ears, coupled with the beginning cackles of new flames and the enemy's barked orders.

Please let this be a dream.

In the village center, those who weren't dead were forced on their knees, their hands on their heads. When Mamma was thrown down beside Father, he popped to his feet, fists swinging, only to be taken down with a swift punch.

The sobs lodged in her chest escaped, and Nerissa could do nothing to stop the tears. Why was this happening? Why did the Beginning allow this? Why were none of their allies coming to their aid?

"Move."

The push sent her stumbling, and she struggled for one last look, peering through the trees and the attackers ushering other children and young women to their doom.

The last thing she saw before the forest swallowed her was a sword arcing downward toward Uncle Morris.

Chapter Twenty-Seven

DENTON

WHY DID HIS SKIN feel like it was ten sizes too tight? And what was that rhythmic swooshing in his ears?

Cool moisture brushed across his face and dampened his lips before something wooden forced liquid down his throat.

He coughed as his throat resisted. The spasmic seizing in his lungs constricted his chest until it felt like he'd never draw another breath.

"C'mon, breathe."

The voice came from so very far away. Perhaps it was Carter's? Denton heard his brother's voice at one point during the journey back to Veerham. Not that Denton expected Carter to even worry too much about him. After all he'd done—allowed to happen—the only place he deserved to stay in was the prison.

"Wake up, Denton. Please?"

That wasn't Carter's voice. Come to think of it, nor was it Red's or Federigo's.

"Wake up." A sob punctuated the words.

No, that voice belonged to a child, one who did not reside in Veerham.

Convincing his fingers to move, he faintly registered the texture beneath him.

He wasn't in his bed.

Was he still in the wagon, struggling not to scream against the excruciating pain as the conveyance lurched back and forth on an uncharted path?

No, there was no scent of weathered wood mixed with blood, nor did the jangle of tack and the groaning of wagon wheels fill the air.

Gentle hands did not smooth hair from his face. Murmuring voices did not tell him to hang in there, to fight the infection and blood loss.

He wasn't in Veerham.

"Please wake up."

Grit sealed his eyes shut. What had he been doing? Rolling in mud puddles like Red?

"You should dump water on him."

"Why?"

"I don't know. It always seems to work. When Da was knocked out, that's what our tracker used to wake him up. And Da's much bigger than Denton. If it worked on Da, it'll work on him."

The words hadn't fully processed until cold water splashed on his face and all but drowned him.

Spluttering, he jolted upwards.

Only for the blurry smear of tan and blue-gray to tip topsy-turvy as his stomach decided right then was the best time to retch.

Gut twisting and grit still crusting his eyes, Denton exhaled and lowered his head. A deep, throbbing ache radiated from his very core, settling with particular vengeance in his bones and muscles. Even his face felt as stiff as a frozen horseshoe. Almost drowning again hadn't helped, either.

Again.

Fists, a cruel smile, and twisted details about his past swirled through his sluggish memory.

Forcing his eyes fully open, Denton reached for his sword. Whoever awakened him could easily be a friend, but foes were in plentiful supply too, and he had no desire to be skewered so soon after once again evading death's clutches.

Empty space met his fingers.

"You're okay? You're okay. How alive do you feel? How many fingers am I holding up?"

A child-sized hand drifted into focus, close enough to poke out his eyes if that was the desire.

"Three," he croaked. "Three fingers."

As for how alive he felt, well...he felt like a runover worm that had been pecked at for a week then trampled a thousand times over.

"What's with the fingers?"

"I don't know. My ma always does it after we hit our heads."

Neck muscles screaming in protest, Denton turned his gaze toward two kids who should be leagues away. "What are you doing here?" The words scraped across his throat, likely laced with the roughest grains of sand known to mankind.

Noko crossed his arms, his mulish expression and defensive stance a younger version of the wolfmen who helped with last year's investigation. "We saw them take you away, so we followed the best we could."

Jonah nodded. "You would be dead if not for us. We pulled you out of the water. You were this close to dying." He held up a thumb and forefinger, with hardly a sliver of space between. "But now you're better, so we can go back for the others."

His skull and ribs protested every movement with concerning vehemence, but Jonah was right. Intuition warned Nerissa's village wouldn't be left alone. And Red said to never ignore intuition.

A groan tore from him as he attempted convincing his legs to work. Despite his numerous pleas, they remained unwilling to acquiesce.

Beginning, please give me strength.

Good thing Father wasn't here. He'd be both gloating and irate. Gloating how he was right about Denton being a weakling, and irate that Denton was too weak to be of any use.

Twigs snapped and sand crunched, and Denton twisted himself just enough to peer over his shoulder.

Through the swirling in his vision, he managed to make out a dark face.

"Boys, get behind me," he rasped. A leg muscle twitched as he forced one knee beneath himself, then the other. He couldn't protect them in such a sorry state, and the Marterisi was likely laughing all the way to Veerham and back at how pathetic he looked.

"Be at ease, boy."

The voice held a modicum of familiarity, but whether good or bad eluded him.

Denton squinted as the man came closer. A vague recollection reminded him he had no weapons save his fists, and those couldn't be considered weapons in his current state.

"Get to the horses."

"I recognize him."

Noko was a bright kid in most aspects. Good survival skills, had a way with animals, and could set snares Denton only dreamed of replicating. But his hearing had been poor as of late.

"Go," he ground out.

"He helped us rescue the others. Vittor or something?"

A rumbling laugh. "Valti. And yes, I did assist. Now it looks like you require more of that assistance. Here, allow me to help you up."

Hands gripped Denton's elbows as Valti continued issuing orders. "There is a full water flask in my saddle. Fetch it, please. And he will require sustenance."

Sustenance was not a good idea. With the building nausea, the food wouldn't stay down for long.

"I must look at your eyes."

Denton attempted to keep his eyes open as the world spun. Dark eyes stared back, calm despite the occasion.

Footsteps, then, "Will he be okay?"

"See this bruising on his face and his dazed reaction to everything? It is wise to assume he has a concussion at the very least."

Valti harrumphed. "Your wrists are raw. Where else are you injured? Wait, I think I know. You are wheezing, and not just due to the bruises around your neck. Lift your shirt, boy. If your ribs are broken, you won't be rescuing anyone anytime soon."

Somehow Denton managed to grab his shirt's stiff hem and force the material upward.

Someone let loose a strangled gasp while another asked what could cause such damage.

"Mhmm. I see. I can't ascertain if any bones have been snapped, but that bruising is extreme. I would be surprised if there aren't any breaks."

Denton let the material drop. If only he too could heed gravity's pull and take a decade-long nap. "I need to get going. I don't think they'll be left alone for long."

"You will go nowhere without food, water, and a fresh change of clothing. While that will not ease your discomfort, it will go a long way in making you feel human again. Noko, I saw some yarrow near where my horse grazes. Fetch it, would you? If we can make a salve, it will help his bruises."

The boys scurried off, leaving Denton to wither beneath Valti's stern gaze. It wasn't like Father's when his anger was stoked. No, this was more akin to the look Halda gave Red when the detective did something the lady-in-waiting disapproved of.

"Just what happened?"

Denton's shrug sent his neck off on another protest. He'd need to work out the stiffness before returning to Nerissa's village or he'd be of no help.

Valti grunted. "You'll be wanting to return to Talart's, I imagine."

"Yes."

"I have bad news for you, boy. There may be nothing left to return to." Valti hiked a thumb over his shoulder. "Smoke has been rising from that direction for the past two days. I was sent to take a look."

"You're no match for the soldiers I saw there before this happened." Denton gestured to his wrists and neck."

"Soldiers?" Valti squinted. "I do not know this word. Is it an insult?"

Right. Marterisies and their odd terminology. "I meant warriors. There were several."

"Ah. I see. No, I did not go to fight. Merely to scout. And I am an accomplished scout. No one would know I was there unless I wanted them to."

There was a verse in the Scripts about pride preceding a fall, but too much haze still swirled through Denton's mind for him to accurately recall the precise wordage.

"Here's the water." Jonah's tone carried the fear reminiscent of when Denton first met the lad. No child should be afraid. No child should suffer the way Jonah and Noko had.

And now Nerissa and her sisters may be caught in the very same webs of evil as the two boys Denton swore to protect.

He already struggled upholding his promise to Jonah and Noko. How could he possibly help Nerissa, Daffy, and Elberta?

"Drink slowly, small sips at a time. You will become ill if you disobey me."

Muscles protesting the simple action of lifting the water flask stoked more than Denton's chagrin, but Valti was right. He'd be worthless if he didn't get something in him. Slowly, of course. His ribs couldn't take more dry heaving.

The lukewarm water could have been from the coolest spring for how good it tasted.

Jonah darted off again, only to return at the same time as Noko, one boy carrying Denton's extra pair of clothing and the other thrusting at Valti a handful of what looked like weeds.

Denton bit back a wince when Valti patted his shoulder. "We'll give you some privacy so you can change, then we'll get this salve on your injuries. Come along, boys. Let me see what weapons you have."

The Scripts made clear lying was wrong, but at that moment, Denton was tempted to deny the pain ricocheting through his ribs as Cinders picked her way through the forest. While Queen's Forest contained rutted paths and tree roots emerging from the ground to create a tripping hazard, it was flat, or mostly so.

Marteris' forest was all hills and jutting rocks, roots, and other dangers. One misstep and Denton would go flying, meeting his fate at the base of some granite-hard trunk or something.

What a way to go.

"How are you?"

"I'm good." As good as one could be when the world was swimming and nausea claimed its reign. If this didn't soon end, his stomach would be as empty as when he first awoke on the shore.

"You don't look good. You look really sick. If Ma were here, she'd make you take a long nap then have you drink all types of herbal concoctions."

Noko. Ever the encourager.

"I'm fine. I promise." Denton tossed a weak grin toward where he thought the boys rode. Any sharper movement and he'd topple off.

"I hope you are right," Valti said, "because we are coming upon the village."

Or what remains of it.

The sharp unpleasantness of smoke and charred wood mingled with sea salt, and only the clomping of hooves and the low murmurs of the sea created any noise.

Denton's arms and spine tingled.

"Boys, why don't you stay here? Keep an eye out for anyone or anything suspicious. Holler if something is amiss. Denton, come with me."

The impact of his feet hitting the ground buckled his knees, but now wasn't the time to give into his body's unimportant demand for rest.

Denton staggered after Valti, who crept from tree to tree with sword drawn.

Cursing himself for not pulling a Red and hiding weapons in his clothing, Denton held his breath as they entered the village.

Or, what remained of the village.

Pale tendrils rose from smoldering heaps. Deep brown stained the sand and dirt and weapons and other tools, like hammers, kitchen knives, and even fire pokers, lay scattered. Only the letter office and the scorched stone buildings remained upright.

Icy fear clamped around his lungs and throat in a chokehold stronger than any man could replicate. "It still stood when I was taken."

Valti clenched his fists. "This is what happened to every village attacked by the traffickers, only this time it looks like they took everyone instead of murdering the men and leaving them to rot."

Bile burned Denton's throat. "We have to find them." Pushing aside the agony claiming every bone, muscle, and ligament, he limped toward the path leading to the Wessen's. Valti joined him, pointing out signs of attack as they went.

Please, Beginning, let them be hiding. Let them be safe. Please keep them from harm.

The utter destruction wrought upon the Wessen cabin defied his prayers. The outer buildings were flattened, the livestock either slain or missing, and the cabin a ruined heap.

The chokehold tightened, and Denton gripped the branch of the nearest tree as his legs threatened to give. This couldn't be happening. The village was strong, with good soldiers and enough weapons and supplies that they could hold their own.

Or so he thought.

Please...

The prayer fizzled at the sight of smoke drifting from Morris' cabin's location.

Everything was destroyed. Everyone was gone.

Why, Beginning? Why?

"Come." Strain thinned Valti's tone. "Let us search for clues."

Denton grit his teeth. Yes. Clues. Clues were important. Red would say looking for clues was second only to seeking survivors.

"Careful," Valti called as Denton began poking through the cabin's remains. "They may still be hot. Embers can retain warmth for a long time."

While the topmost boards were cool, the ones trapped beneath were still warm, some too warm to touch. Growling and ignoring the dizziness, Denton found a stout stick and began pushing away the debris. Ash flew and smoke stirred, lazily spiraling upward.

The fireplace's hearth, scorched and blackened, offered no clues. Nor did the stone foundation.

Sight bleary and limbs ready to give way, Denton stepped back. Sweat itched as it traced numerous trails down his face and neck, and so much soot coated him he could easily blend in during nighttime.

"Nothing's here."

Valti emerged from the path a few minutes later, a solid mass of black. Only his teeth and the whites of his eyes indicated this was a living person and not a statue carved from sooty obsidian. "I found nothing either, but I did not get to all the buildings. Or what remains of them."

Denton ran his hands through his hair. Halda always scolded Red for looking like a drowned raccoon that rolled in mud then picked a fight with a rabid coyote, but he was fairly certain his appearance easily rivaled Red's worse day.

"Did you find any tracks?"

"There are some on the shore, but the waves eroded most of them. I have the boys gathering the weapons and organizing them by type. We will need to replenish our supply."

Why wasn't the Beginning helping? This was a noble cause. Many in the village were believers. Wasn't the Beginning supposed to take care of His people?

Heat warmed the back of his neck as the clouds shuffled away to reveal the sun. How typical. On horrendous days the sun shone, and on good days rain obscured it.

He grimaced and looked away as a flash of brightness threatened to blind him.

"Is something wrong? You look to be in more pain."

"I'm fine." Sidestepping, Denton squinted in the brightness' direction. Everything should be coated in grime and ash. How was it something shone? "Do you see that?"

"See what?"

Grabbing his stick, Denton poked around the area before kneeling. Levering the stick beneath a pile of boards, he raised them.

Beneath lay a familiar shape, all but the topmost part of the handle obscured by residue.

"What is it?"

"Nerissa's key." Denton fetched the object and hefted it in his hand. Slightly warm, the neck was a bit misshapen, but from what he could tell, bore no other signs of ruin. "It goes to Losibar's gate."

"Ah. The wall. Yes, I remember her receiving it. A high honor for one so young."

"Why was she chosen?"

"Chief Talart recommended her. Her family is one of the few he completely trusts. She is responsible and mature, and my chief instantly recognized why Chief Talart suggested her."

Denton wasn't surprised, but the key struck another broken chord in his heart. Would he ever be able to return it to her? Would he ever get the chance to explain his past?

Or would she think of him as a wretch, the worst of the worst, for the rest of her life?

Please keep her safe.

Valti patted Denton's shoulder. "Your discovery made things easy on us. We can now go through the gate instead of by sea. That will save us much time."

"Too bad there's not a falcon we can use to deliver a message to your people."

"Why would we use a falcon?"

Denton blinked and tore his gaze from the key. Oh, right. Marteris and their difference in delivering missives. "We use that method in Veerham."

"We have letter deliverers for that." Valti's eyes narrowed and he tapped his chin. "The letter office still stands. Its side is a bit scorched, but that is the only damage I could tell."

"That's unusual."

"Indeed. I believe this was a coordinated attack. In a few weeks, Talart planned to take most of the men on a fishing endeavor—they do it yearly. During that time, they also visit other coastal villages and gather information about recent kidnappings and what goes on in the rest of the lands. Then they relay that to us."

An image of a map flashed through Denton's memory. "Are you their strongest ally?"

"We are."

Tucking the key into his pocket, Denton returned to the village and letter office. True to Valti's claim, little damage touched the building, an unsettling surprise given how every other structure was now reduced to nothing.

Calling to Jonah and Noko, he went inside. Based on his last time within the building, nothing looked out of place.

The cabinets in the front area revealed nothing of use, nor did the ones in the back room. Exhaling, Denton entered the bedroom off to the meeting room's right. A bed, dresser, and nightstand crowded in the minimal space.

Normally, going through someone's personal belongings would leave a sour taste in his mouth, but the unease crawling up his spine demanded manners be set aside.

Besides, he was a royal detective, albeit a lousy one. He could pull that title if anyone had a quarrel about his current actions.

Where the first few drawers held clothing and personal items, it was not fabric he saw when he opened the bottom drawer.

Withdrawing the precisely-folded pieces of paper, he placed them on the bed before pulling out an object that unfolded into a map. After calling for Valti, he spread it on the dresser's top.

"What is it?" The giant of a Marterisi stomped into the room, spreading ash and dust all over. Jonah and Noko followed.

Denton waved at the bed. "I found those papers and this map."

"What does this have to do with the fire?"

"Read that opened letter."

Silence passed Valti read, then growled unintelligible words. "That bloated shark's corpse. I'll find and gut him, then feed him to the fish."

"I was studying Talart's map a week or so ago and noticed something. I didn't think much of it at the time, but now…" Denton smeared soot on his finger and used that to circle the villages he remembered being attacked. "See this? It looks like they were eliminating all nearby allies."

Still muttering, Valti took his own sooty finger and circled numerous areas farther north. "These are the ones near Losibar that have been attacked in the last two years." His eye twitched, the first physical sign of the warrior's ire. "They are reducing our allies so we have no assistance. See how they have created a horseshoe shape of attacks? Aside from the villages who helped with the tower rescue, there is no one within a ten league vicinity."

Denton drummed his fingers, ignoring how the action dirtied the furniture. "Losibar and this village are the strongest, right?"

"Of the coastal villages, yes."

"So if they eliminate you as well, there will be no one to hinder their trafficking route."

Valti snarled. "We must warn my people."

Denton rolled up the map. "We also need to rescue Nerissa and her family," he said quietly.

Stance stiff, Valti fingered his sword. "I will look at the tracks. We may be able to catch two fish with one net. Get some water, boy, and find yourself a few weapons. We'll have to make good time if we're to save your woman and my people."

Chapter Twenty-Eight

NERISSA

COLD SPRAY FLEW THROUGH the open window as waves crashed against the tower's exterior. No shutters or curtains blocked the sight of the deep blue storm clouds gathering on the horizon. While they looked leagues away, they would reach the tower before nightfall.

Nerissa shuddered and closed her eyes. The waves responded to the wind's command, and if the storm was as fierce as it looked, the waves would surpass the tower in height. If too much water splashed into the room, they would all drown.

She bit her lip to keep the tears at bay. To her right, Daffy and Elberta curled up, sleeping. To her left, Afya stared at the floor, a vacant look on her face. Other children and young women from the village, along with six or seven she didn't recognize, filled the rest of the room. Those who weren't asleep wore despondent expressions.

Shifting to regain some circulation in her legs, Nerissa pulled her knees to her chest and rested her chin on them. Thick ropes bound her wrists, rendering her fingers about useless due to the tightness, and her shoulders and neck ached from being jostled and thrown around.

Emotion welled in her throat, as thick as the approaching storm clouds. Her parents and Uncle Morris had to be okay. They *had* to be. No other option was acceptable. And Edver, Chief, Mrs. Talart, and Hauni and Guy...they couldn't be dead.

Yet a sword had struck Chief Talart and Uncle Morris.

"Stop fighting the ropes." Afya's monotone voice sent chills down Nerissa's spine. "It'll only tighten them."

"How are you?" A ridiculous question, but Nerissa could think of nothing else to ask.

Afya shrugged. "I should have known I could never escape Mother."

"What do you mean?"

"Haether is her friend, but I never knew she was with Keller until that day."

That day.

The day, now one of many, haunting Nerissa. "I don't think he could be a trafficker," she whispered.

"He is not." Afya turned dulled eyes her way. "I have seen traffickers and have watched kidnappers do their worst. Denton is not one of them. He may not have a spotless past, but he is on our side."

"He *was* on our side." The words tasted bitter. "Now he's dead."

"That is the way of the world. Death consumes the innocent." Afya returned to staring at the floor. "Best not to fight. Whatever they do…just don't fight. That will only anger them, and then they are even worse."

"I'll not let them take the girls from me." The words sounded brave, but they were a mere façade for the empty hole gnawing on her heart. Her family was splintered. Destroyed. Her parents and uncle were murdered, and her sisters—so innocent and young and impressionable—were at the mercy of heartless spawns of evil.

Please protect them.

The plea rose, fractured and slow and hesitant. The Beginning hadn't answered her cries during the attack. Surely this too wasn't part of His plan.

But what if it was? Could she remain trusting Him even when the tides of life destroyed everyone and everything she loved? Could she remain steadfast when her world was obliterated?

She wasn't strong enough for such tests.

And neither were her sisters.

Please, Beginning, help them. Remove them from this evil.

Afya sighed, the sound so full of helplessness that Nerissa felt it sink into the very marrow of her bones and erode the fragment of hope she clung to. "This is evil's territory, Nerissa. No one—not your family, not Edver, not Denton—is coming to help us. We're on our own now."

Nerissa gazed out the window, the colors blurred by the hot tears burning her eyes. Was it true? Were they on their own?

"I will never leave you nor forsake you."

A verse she had read in the Scripts, but only skimming with passing reassurance. Now, however, the words felt so very real. The Beginning did not lie. That meant He would, as the verse said, never leave nor forsake her.

But that didn't mean He wouldn't allow her to walk through trials, to be broken and beyond the end of her rope.

More tears came, and Nerissa buried her face in her skirt. The nightmare was just beginning, and already she was so weak. *Give me strength. Please protect us. Please stay true to Your word.*

There was no comfort to be had in the unfeeling tower. No safeguard against the storm.

Only her faith, as fragile and terrified as it was, could sustain her.

You are the anchor no matter what storms life throws at me. You are the only One who can save us. Please, please help us. Help me. Help my sisters.

Bright sunlight filtered through the thick, pine needle-laden branches woven overhead. Squirrels, chipmunks, and birds flitted about, their joyous trills and chirps at odds with the decimating heaviness gripping the group of captives.

Nerissa adjusted Daffy on her hip and smoothed the little girl's hair as she whimpered. Daffy had run about wherever she pleased at home, but she could always stop, rest, and grab a bite to eat and drink. Now, they were given two short breaks during the trek's duration, and water and food were hoarded like precious commodities.

"Pick up the pace," a slithery brute snapped from his place near the back.

Marterises, both dark and light, guarded the captives. Some as gargantuan as Lemuel and Chief Talart, and others as short as Uncle Morris and Guy. They all carried weapons. They all had no qualms about pushing others around. And they all were in a hurry.

Mind fuzzy from the heat and thirst, Nerissa blinked Afya's back into focus. Ever since the seaside tower, she hadn't said a word, only complying in silence.

Countless steps later, the leader, a bearded, dark-skinned Marterisi with a glower comparable to the ill-tempered Friloran bears Nerissa had read about, ordered a halt just after they reached a set of caves.

Nerissa bit back the need to bring forth her last meal, scant as it was, when more Marterises emerged from the caves. Dressed normally, one wouldn't think twice about their appearance on any other day. Men and women both, all of whom scanned the captives like they were mere animals.

Clutching Daffy, who remained asleep, Nerissa willed herself to become like the chameleons she'd read about and change color to blend with her surroundings.

"This is the latest batch?"

"Yes. Fresh catch from the coast."

Raucous laughter accompanied the leader's comment.

A woman, lithe and petite, ambled along, a man by her side as they murmured to each other. Finally, she selected seven children—five girls and two boys. "The others should be sold to the mines. The older ones you may find suitable for other professions, but I heard a few mine owners are meeting in Jalla in a few days. You may be able to catch them."

The leader waved his hand. "Just take your pick and move on. We have a schedule to keep. Lady Susann awaits her delivery."

Afya emitted a slight gasp.

After more discussion, the leader called out the command to continue. Willing her numb arms to retain the strength to carry Daffy, Nerissa shuffled onward. Each step battered her tenuous grasp on the shard of remaining hope.

"Nerri?"

"Yes?"

"I'm scared." Daffy's tear-and-dirt-streaked face peered up at Nerissa.

How many times could a heart break in two days? "I know, sweetie."

"Where're Mamma and Father?"

"I don't know."

"Will we see Denton? He'll help us."

How could she tell Daffy Denton was dead? Slain by those who wrought destruction upon the innocent? "I don't know, Daf."

"I miss him. And I miss Mamma and Father and Uncle Morris and Bluet."

"I do too."

"Where's Elberta?"

Nerissa nodded toward Afya. "She's just ahead. Go back to sleep, Daf."

Daffy blinked, sheer exhaustion lowering her eyelids, but she stubbornly remained awake. "Nerri?"

"Yes?"

"Is the Beginning with us?"

"*I will never leave you nor forsake you.*"

The words stuck in Nerissa's throat. "Yes, Daf. He is. He is always with us, even when life is scary." Her voice broke at the end. How difficult it was to believe. Of course, believing in the good times was easy. But in the hard? The unsure? The petrifying?

"I will never leave you nor forsake you."

Father always said to praise the Beginning whether in sunshine or storm.

It was so, so difficult to praise during the storm, though.

Lifting her chin and willing her fragile heart to remain steady, Nerissa took one more step, then another, then another.

Help me believe. Help me remain steadfast.

A dull throb pounded through her head, matching the cadence of her weary heart.

Forcing her eyes to focus, Nerissa found herself gazing at a dull gray ceiling joining with equally dull gray walls.

The kidnappers always drugged them out before depositing them into the tower. Was the entrance so secret that such an unhealthy use of sleeping herbs were necessary?

At the sound of broken sobs, she gradually turned her head toward where a woman with poofy, curly black hair placed her hands on Afya's shoulders.

"Isn't it good to be back home, darling? Where you're safe?"

Afya tried backing away, but the leader drew his sword and nudged her shoulder with the tip.

The woman tsked. "Dear me, I think all that time in the sun has dried and shriveled your mind to look like a raisin. I know you're traumatized, darling—being kidnapped by those pesky villagers will do that."

Afya shook her head, the tears on her cheeks glistening in the sunlight.

"Your room is prepared. Why don't you go rest? I have business to take care of."

Again Afya shook her head, but at her mother's stern look, plodded past Nerissa's line of sight.

The woman brushed off her hands, expression momentarily curdling like something unpleasant remained on her palms and fingers. Then she turned, a cunning smile morphing her face into a sinister visage. "Get up, girl. I know you're awake."

Blood chilling, Nerissa met the woman's cold gaze. So this was what it was like to stare in the face of evil.

Huffing, the woman snapped her fingers.

Harsh fingers grabbed Nerissa's arms and dragged her upward.

Breath catching in her lungs, her limbs froze as the woman advanced. She should fight, should defend herself, but the self-defense actions she knew fled her mind.

Beginning, please protect me.

The woman crossed her arms, tapping her fingers on her bicep as she circled Nerissa. "Hm. Plain, but decent enough features. That hair is beautiful. Average in height and build, probably not that strong. Depending on who places the final offer, you'll go for anywhere from a high-middle to mid-high price. Yes, I know a few different purchasers who will be interested in you."

Nerissa bit her lip to dissuade the gathering tears from falling. Predators thrived off prey's fear, and the last thing this woman needed was to be even more emboldened.

"Don't worry, child. Perhaps you'll be able to stay by the sea. You coastal villagers have such a strange attachment to it."

Because the sea was everything Nerissa knew? It was her home? Because the waves' rhythmic whooshing often calmed her anxious heart?

The epitome of condescension, the woman patted Nerissa's head. "Do try to go back to sleep. I do so dislike it when people yawn. It's so unmannerly and rude."

Said the one kidnapping and ruining lives.

Pursing her lips, Nerissa reclaimed her spot and stroked Elberta's hair. The emotions still warred, but a numbing layer was settling over. She couldn't protect her sisters and Afya if overwrought with emotions.

Please help me.

She couldn't do this by her own strength.

The woman and leader sat at a table in the corner, eating and speaking in hushed tones.

Perhaps they were right. The tower seemed impenetrable, with its lack of stairs and entrance known only to the enemy. No one could rescue them.

And if her entire village was slaughtered, no one would know what happened.

Closing her eyes to ease the tightening band around her chest, Nerissa pressed her bound hands to her mouth and stifled a sob. If only the options were as simple as dying so her sisters could live and go free.

But they weren't. Not yet, at least.

In the past, the storms of life, while terrifying, had passed with relative lack of aftermath. This storm, though, threatened to drown her—smother her in the waves of fear and guilt and doubt.

Be my anchor, Beginning, because I can't do this without You.

Chapter Twenty-Nine

DENTON

A SOFT CLICK WAS the only indication the key still worked.

Exhaling, Denton withdrew the object and looped it back around his neck. Although realistically weighing no more than a pebble, the key felt heavier than one hundred horseshoes.

"Now what?" Jonah's small voice stabbed Denton's heart.

"We keep going." Denton offered what he hoped was a reassuring smile. The boys were so brave, but it wasn't difficult to glimpse the fear beneath their courageous veneers.

Denton didn't blame them. The situation was such that anyone would have nightmares for weeks.

During the rescue mission for Carter and Chamonix, he'd looked to the older men for guidance and wisdom. His stomach roiled at the thought of being viewed the same way he thought of the older men. Failing others when they expected nothing extraordinary from him was bad enough. Failing those who depended on him? Viewed him as knowledgeable and trustworthy?

Even worse.

Beginning, please guide me.

The prayers were coming easier now that he realized he wasn't just talking to a vast, cold expanse and being ignored.

After everyone was through, he closed and relocked the gate. Mounting Cinders, he took Dancer's reins from Noko and set his jaw as they resumed their journey. How the kidnappers got the captives past the wall was beyond Valti, but all that mattered was there were tracks.

Beckoning Cinders to a trot, Denton scanned the area. No torn material scraps, no blood, no nothing. Whoever was responsible, they kept it clean.

Fire burned within his chest. He would pursue Nerissa, her sisters, and Afya until his dying breath. He refused to again fail.

Days passed, with the tracks eventually fading. As the campfire flickered, somehow smokeless from a trick Noko knew, Denton sat against a tree, one hand pressed against his ribs. The warmth helped the ache, and it was the only time he could truly rest them.

It was getting harder to draw a deep breath, indicating the injuries were not healing, but he wouldn't tell Valti that. The man would leave him somewhere, chained to the ground until he recovered.

Three more nights passed much the same way, and with every new sunrise, the sensation of loss and mourning hit Denton harder.

Every day lessened their chances of finding the captives. Every day lessened the chance of Nerissa and her sisters emerging unscathed.

Please keep them safe.

Three days passed until Valti held up a hand. "Stop."

"Denton?" Jonah pointed as his voice wobbled. "Are they going to kill us?"

Fingers curling around the borrowed sword's hilt, Denton sat straighter as he eyed the men slinking through the surrounding trees. What was it Nerissa said? "No. This is their customary greeting."

Dark-skinned Marterises armed to the teeth swarmed the horses, and hands helped Denton down, handling him like he was a fragile dish. Likely due to Valti's passing comment about "the injured outsider".

A weathered old woman Denton vaguely remembered from his last visit hauled him to a building smelling of herbs and clay. Gesturing to a counter in the middle of the room, she told him to hop on and remove his shirt. As she hummed and poked and prodded, more men than Denton thought possible crowded into the small room.

The chief frowned as he eyed Denton up and down. "You are not fit to travel."

"I won't stop until they're found."

"Itti, what do you think?"

The woman clucked her tongue. "He is in bad shape. His breathing is raspy and he cannot stand straight due to his injuries." She peered at Denton, brows crunched together and an expression of abject disapproval multiplying her numerous wrinkles. "You are fortunate you do not have any broken ribs that I can tell."

Broken ribs or not, poor posture or not, he wouldn't stop until he found Nerissa and the rest.

The men began speaking in a flurry of sentences, with the chief taking the lead for most words vocalized. The conversation went 'round and 'round, and Denton soon lost track. Not only did they mix common language with their own, but their thick accents butchered some of the words to the extent he couldn't understand them.

The light outside dimmed when the chief finally called the meeting to a close. As the men filtered out, Valti came to Denton's side. "You look confused."

"What just happened?"

"They called a meeting and decided to assist you in finding your woman and her people."

"I thought meetings were more formal." His head spun. In Veerham, decisions were rarely reached in a few hours' time.

Valti chortled. "In your land, maybe, but we Marterises are people of action. We'll not sacrifice lives for the sake of comfort and fancy settings."

"Right." Denton admitted he didn't know much about Marterisi culture, even after spending over two months immersed in it. But he tried not to show his discomfort whenever his home was mocked. Just because Veerham placed more value on less rustic settings didn't mean they were willing to "sacrifice lives" for it. But now wasn't the time to take Valti to task. "What's the plan?"

"Tonight, the plan is to sleep."

"Excuse me?"

"Sleep." Valti crossed his arms and raised a brow, likely daring Denton to argue.

A dare he accepted. "That's ridiculous. Every hour helps turn this situation to the kidnappers' favor. How many leagues can you cover in an hour? Three? That's three more for them and three more *we'll* have to cover."

Valti's amusement turned to annoyance. "The chief knows what he's doing, and I suggest you somehow manage to comprehend that. You will be worthless if you do not rest. As it is, you are ready to topple. We require time to prepare and send messages. A search and subsequent attack cannot be conducted in a moment's notice. We will do your woman no good if we are unprepared."

The rebuke stung, and every fiber within chafed at the concept of more waiting—more wasting time—but he couldn't find Nerissa without help, and at the moment, Losibar was his only ally.

"Valti is correct." The chief reentered, his looming presence similar to Talart's. "You know little of what ensures a successful mission. Now, where did you get that key?"

Surely Valti already told the condescending man. "We found it in the rubble. It was Nerissa's."

The man's eye twitched. "You are unauthorized to carry it."

Horses and horseshoes, these people would drive him into the sea.

Easing to his feet and ignoring the swaying room, Denton mustered what he hoped was an acceptable replica of Red's deepest, stormiest, and fiercest glare. "I have been on missions before, and I have the scars to prove it. I may not have your experience in planning or expertise with weapons, but one willing heart is worth more than one hundred apathetic ones. I'll adhere to your plans—so far—because you know more than me in this area, but I will not allow you or anyone else to stop me. As for Nerissa's key, I will return it to her as soon as possible, but we have to find her for that to happen."

At home, that tone would gain him copious bruises and a broken rib or seven. But he was tired of being worthless. Tired of standing by doing nothing while wrongdoers wrought havoc and pain upon the innocent.

He may only be one man—and a pathetic one at that—but he would uphold his promise.

The chief only stared at him until he called to Itti. "Give him something for the pain." To Denton, he said, "Get some rest. We will move out tomorrow morning."

Itti shook her head as the men exited the building. "Very few get away with addressing Chief in that manner. Here, boy, drink this."

Denton eyed the steaming cup before gulping it down. His throat screamed at the abrasive liquid scraping across the rawness, but if less pain meant a more optimal performance, then he'd deal with it.

Itti puttered about, shoving a biscuit in his hand. "If you need something warm, I have clam chowder ready to be served up."

"I'm fine, ma'am, but thank you. Do you know where they took the boys?"

"Chief's wife took them in. The dear woman has a soft spot for children, especially those who have endured so much. Now, do go on and eat. You outsiders are much weaker than us Marterises."

Because, apparently, Marterises did not require proper nourishment after almost dying followed by four days of hard travel.

Such arrogant people. Denton almost preferred Veerham's court.

He bit into the biscuit and fought back a gag as revulsion swept across his taste buds. Pale, flakey filling inhabited the biscuit's center.

Itti beamed. "Do you like it? It's a Marterisi special. Fish-stuffed biscuit."

Denton swallowed both the nastiness and a groan. "It's definitely unique," he choked out.

"Excellent. There are more over there if you need."

Denton did not need. "Thank you."

"Indeed. When you're ready to bed down, that cot is yours. Have a good night, and if you need anything, just holler." With that, the plump woman snatched a few biscuits for herself and toddled on out.

Forcing down the rest of the biscuit, Denton attempted to drown the taste with herb-flavored water, but nothing scrubbed away the foulness.

What did Red call it? Taking one for the group? Team? Something?

Whatever. And not like they viewed him as part of anything.

Fatigue smacking into him like a horseshoe to the face, Denton eased onto the cot.

Please, Beginning, help us find them before it's too late.

Soft, yellow rays of sunlight streamed through the pine needles, causing a dappled shadow-and-light pattern to decorate the path. The crisp scent of pine and salt filled the air, and the brisk morning was similar to those back in Veerham, when he took Cinders for early-morning rides.

That brief encounter with tranquility bore few similarities to the setting in which Denton now found himself. He still rode Cinders, and the morning was still cool, but that was where it ended.

Tack jangling, hooves thumping, and weapons shifting as leather sheaths rubbed against belts decimated whatever calmness the morning once held. Gripping the knife Valti insisted Denton add to his "collection", Denton eyed the men in front of him. Their brawn made most of Veerham's strongest soldiers look puny, and they rode with the ease of experienced horsemen.

"We have marked every possible clearing and outlet," Valti said in a low tone. "Three other villages agreed to assist. We'll cover the ground as quickly as possible."

Scouts had been sent. Apparently, letters had too. While a trot was the most conducive pace for covering large amounts of ground, it felt too slow.

Please, Beginning.

"Our scouts are seeking any sign of activity," Valti continued. "Like Chief said, we cannot guarantee we will find our allies, but we will do our best."

"How could you spare so many men with an attack imminent on Losibar?"

"We have safeguards in place, and half of our men remained home."

Denton estimated fifty Losibar men total joined the efforts. Groups of ten went their separate ways, keeping in touch with each other via crows. Valti mentioned he thought over seventy men from other villages joined as well.

Still, that number netted no finds.

Father's choice expressions lingered on the tip of Denton's tongue as he paced the latest clearing. No sign of captives or kidnappers, and the only towers they'd come across were abandoned.

Where were they? How could the kidnappers and their victims just disappear?

Denton shoved his fingers through his hair. Surely they hadn't murdered and dumped the bodies into the sea.

"I think I know what you're thinking, boy." Valti reached into his saddlebag and withdrew a biscuit, taking a bite. "And no, that's not what they did. Not with the women and children, at least. They're worth too much to just slay and cast away."

That comprised part of Denton's worry. Nerissa would be a commodity because she was beautiful and young. How quickly would buyers attempt to enslave her? And after that, what would they do to her?

Carter had told him the traffickers' plans for Chamonix, and that was likely Nerissa's fate if Denton didn't reach her in time.

"You are terribly anxious to rescue someone who lied to you."

Denton groaned and slid down the tree until he sat. "How did you know?"

"Noko and Jonah told me."

"She may have lied, but I..." *I still love her.* "I can't let this happen to her."

Valti stroked his beard and eyed Denton. "It takes a man of integrity to offer such forgiveness."

"I'm no man of integrity."

"Perhaps you should reexamine yourself again. I believe you would recognize the error in that statement." With that, Valti stood and ambled away. "You best get some rest. I'll awaken you when our scouts return."

The scouts never returned.

At the chief's command, they saddled up and prepared to ride out.

Denton kept the prayers flowing as he navigated Cinders behind Valti's sturdy dun. The green, brown, and gray surroundings blurred until a sudden stop lurched him from the haze.

Valti dismounted and, with three others including the chief, dashed into the bushes, only to return minutes later with a thunderous expression. "We found the scouts."

Denton needn't ask what happened. Valti's snarl told him everything.

"We are tracking the blood," the chief curtly announced. Rage simmered from his very being, and his huge fists clenched and unclenched.

Feels personal now, doesn't it? Denton hadn't wanted any from Losibar to die. The scouts, from what he could tell, were good men with genuine desire to rescue those in danger. Their deaths were senseless, but perhaps that knowledge would spur the chief into moving a little faster. If they had kept riding last night, maybe death would not have been the men's fate.

"We will avenge them," Valti snarled. "Then their families will know they did not die in vain."

Steel against leather rang through the air as the ferns to Denton's right rustled. He drew his own sword and steadied Cinders. She was fast, but only a small animal could slip through the underbrush. To get away, she'd somehow have to squeeze by the horses in front or behind.

A familiar brown face emerged.

The relief flooding his heart almost drowned him. Dismounting, Denton crossed to where the grime-covered mutt stood. "Bluet?"

The dog barked.

"You know this dog?"

"Yes. She's Morris Wessen's."

"Do you have anything of Morris'? Or your woman's?"

Denton dug through the saddlebags and withdrew a piece of cloth Morris gave him to rub down Cinders. "The scent may be too faded."

"Never underestimate a dog's nose. Tell her to sniff it, then find."

Denton knelt beside Bluet and scratched behind her ears. The dog whuffled his shirt before whining, her tail thumping.

"I know, girl. You're tired and hungry and in desperate need of a bath, but the fight's not over yet." He held the cloth to her nose. Chances were she'd lead him straight to Cinders. "Bluet, find."

Bluet's ears perked and her tail wagged with such enthusiasm it smacked Denton in the jaw. Cocking her head to the left, she sniffed before putting her nose to the ground and taking off at a trot.

Mounting Cinders, Denton urged her after Bluet, skirting the other horses to come in the lead.

"Keep an eye out," the chief ordered as he drew alongside Denton.

Denton didn't know if they rode ten paces or ten leagues until Bluet stopped and barked before growling.

"Dismount. Carl, Xandr, hide and guard the horses. Be ready for an expedient getaway."

Adrenaline coursed through Denton, urging him to bolt headlong into whatever upset Bluet.

That wasn't what a good detective did, though. Red always said to measure one's breathing and count heartbeats before jumping into a situation.

Not that she obeyed herself, but do as she said, not as she did, right?

"Steady, boy," the chief whispered as he placed a heavy hand on Denton's shoulder. "You'll do no one any good if you die by recklessness."

Was that pity or understanding in the man's tone? Wonders never ceased.

"They have to be alright." The words escaped him without warning.

"Beginning willing, they will. Come." After issuing hushed orders to his men, everyone spread out.

Denton inched through the underbrush. Bluet had been sent ahead as a distraction. Hopefully, she could take a few bites out of whatever aggrieved her.

He slipped behind a thick pine tree and peered around the edge. His breath stuttered in his chest. In a clearing, bound and gagged and bloodied, huddled the adults from Nerissa's village. The elation morphed into dread as he counted the guards. No way could the small rescue group take on fifteen and win.

Please, Beginning, help us.

Yald, who lounged near the horses, stiffened when Bluet stalked toward him. "Kill the dumb mutt."

"I don't kill dogs," a man armed with a scythe said. "Never hurt an animal unless it's life or death." He knelt and whistled to Bluet, wiggling his fingers before drawing a piece of what looked like dried fish from his pocket. "Here, girl."

Bluet barked before slinking back.

Denton's heart dropped when she waded through the captives until she plopped next to who could be a bound Morris. The man's swollen and bruised features and blood-stained beard obscured his identity.

Bluet whined.

"That's the nice thing about dogs," another man said. He stood from where he stirred a pot over the fireplace. "They're loyal to the end. She'll be crying about her master's death for a long while, even if you do adopt her, Mason."

"You should just kill her. She'll cause nothing but trouble." Yald glared at Bluet.

"I said I don't kill dogs."

The other men murmured in agreement.

Denton flexed his fingers. They may not want to kill Bluet right then, but they would after she bit the smithereens out of them.

Mr. and Mrs. Wessen sat near the edge, Mr. Wessen doing his best to shield his wife from the attackers. His shoulder sagged at an odd angle, and though it was slightly obscured from Denton's perspective, it looked like Mrs. Wessen's foot pointed the opposite direction it ought.

Those two wouldn't be making a speedy exit anytime soon.

Bluet whined.

An attacker circled the perimeter. "When do our instructions arrive? Those scouts won't be missed for long."

A wiry Marterisi with dirty blond hair and numerous knives gestured toward the path. "We don't move on until we've heard back. Haether said she heard Losibar is involved now. Somehow someone escaped us."

"Couldn't have been the whelps in the towers. They're kept in line."

Bluet barked.

A bird's trill drifted through the air.

The nearest attacker stiffened. "It's the wrong time of year for—" He toppled, a blade piercing his chest as Valti leapt from behind a tree and ended him.

Denton raised his sword and charged as the rest of the Losibarans rushed from the trees. Ducking a swinging enemy, he let Valti take the man down. Halting before the first captive, he sawed through the ropes binding the woman's wrists and helped her to her feet, shoving a knife into her hands. "Go free the others."

He continued, setting loose those who weren't blocked by the fight. When he reached the Wessens, defeated eyes met his.

"We'll find your girls."

Mrs. Wessen shuttered. Her split lip and vacant gaze stoked Denton's ire. These people had lied to him, but they did not deserve this.

"They took some to the cliffs," Mr. Wessen rasped. "To kill them."

Denton glanced behind him. Every single Losibar warrior was locked in a fight. He'd be going in alone.

Handing a knife to Mr. Wessen, he took off toward the vague path pointing east. Deep scuffs gouged the dirt and cracked weeds and twigs littered the edges. Whoever had been taken, they didn't go without resistance.

His boot snagged on a protruding root, and he flailed his un-occupied arm as he pitched forward.

Something halted his fall. "Easy, boy."

Denton found his footing and righted himself. A man barely above his height frowned at him, fingers tapping the hilt of a worn sword.

"I don't recognize you. Who are you?"

Denton slammed his fist into the man's jaw, dull pain throbbing through his knuckles. The man dropped, creating a soft thump.

Exhaling, Denton dragged the man off the path before con-tinuing. One man against however many attackers couldn't do much, but perhaps he could free a few captives and they could overwhelm the spawn of evil. One captive, at least, still had some fight in him.

Voices drew him behind a tree trunk as he neared a gap in the trees. Beyond the smattering of bodies prone on the ground stretched a green-gray mass reaching for the horizon.

"Grab him. We don't have all day."

Denton peered between a cluster of pine needles as two men grabbed a dark-skinned Marterisi's arms and hauled him to his feet. The man's knees buckled, but he yanked against the hold and tried smashing a knee into the left attacker's middle. The tears adorning the man's shirt showcased numerous injuries leaking fresh blood.

"Get him under control," a familiar voice barked.

"We're trying."

Denton sliced through the nearest captives' bonds, motioning the gaping villagers to silence as he passed out his last knives.

Breathing a prayer, he dodged into the fray of attackers swarm-ing Edver and began introducing his hilt to their skulls.

Valti would be proud it only took him two tries per noggin. The man had despaired of Denton ever catching on, even though a five minute lesson wasn't enough time for even the most intelligent of individuals to become even mediocre swordsmen.

And, as Red always illustrated, it was best to go in fighting and not stop until you were beaten. Even then, the detective bared her teeth and used her claws whenever possible.

Blinking away the sweat and ignoring the weariness claiming his muscles, he blocked a half-aimed strike before punching the man into unconsciousness.

Fire raced through his back, and he whipped around, sword up. Most of the attackers were either on the ground or cursing the freed captives, except for the ugly behemoth glaring at Denton like he was a wasp to be crushed.

"Stupid outsider."

"Hope your sword is sharper than your insults." Oh, Red would approve of that one.

Denton braced himself as the man swiped with his equally-gargantuan sword.

The blade never completed a half-arc.

"And that's for Mother!" Edver smashed a double-fist-sized rock one last time into the man's cranium, savagely smiling as the man collapsed.

Edver faced Denton and raised a brow. The wary and doubtful expression just didn't have the same intimidating effect as when his face wasn't swollen and bruised.

"You're supposed to be dead."

"Sorry to disappoint you."

A smirk didn't dim the ferocious glint in Edver's eyes. He thrust out his hands. "Cut me free, please. How did you get here?"

Denton sawed through the ropes. "Losibar. They're occupying the rest of the group in the other clearing."

"Great." Edver rubbed his wrists, calm as could be despite looking like a battered piece of meat. "I heard where they're taking the girls. There's a port not far away, and if we don't intercept them in time, we'll never see them again. You up for it?"

Did this man actually want to ally with Denton?

Sweat dripping down his face and neck, Denton gasped in lungfuls of dust-laced air. "Did you hear if they're going to attack Losibar?"

"Haven't heard a word. Doesn't mean anything, though." Edver picked through the scattered weapons like Carter perused horses—deliberate and indicating his displeasure with grunts and mutterings. "Ah, here we are," he announced as he hefted a sword. "Brainless minnows thought they could steal my sword."

"I didn't see your father anywhere."

Edver's fierce grin returned. "That's because he's right over there."

Denton turned. In the corner of the clearing, blood soaked Talart's shirt, but he held steady as he badgered two attackers with a thick branch. "He looks horrible."

"He's losing blood." Grim determination lined Edver's tone before he snagged one of the captives in better shape and ordered him to bind Talart's wounds once the attackers were sufficiently branched to death.

After helping his father dismantle the attackers, Edver spoke with Talart for a minute before returning to Denton. "Beginning, please keep him safe," Edver muttered as he motioned. "Come on. I know where the attackers keep their horses."

Sticks and pine cones crunched beneath their boots. Denton ignored the intuition screaming how this was a suicide mission. Two men, both injured and in less-than-optimal condition, were no match for blood-thirsty lunatics. The only reason the attackers were overwhelmed was because the captives rallied their strength and managed to fight back.

The horses were tethered to trees, munching from feed bags. Average in breeding, Denton didn't see how the equines would be of any use if a long-distance escape proved necessary. One favored its left hind leg and another bore a nasty gash on its fetlock.

Just one more reason to despise the scum who caused this trouble in the first place.

"Not that one." He blocked Edver from reaching for a dingy sorrel. "She's going lame. Pick that one."

"That one looks like it faced a shark and barely won."

The horse could be a twin to the one Denton claimed after the attack on the tower. "It's good stock and is sturdy. If you want to rescue Afya, you'll select that one."

Edver clenched his teeth but listened.

Every rib made their existence known as Denton hauled himself onto Cinders. Gritting his teeth to keep from wheezing against the pain, he patted her neck. "Does your father know where we're going?"

"Yes."

Good, because Denton hadn't been able to tell Valti. The kidnappers in the first clearing were a tougher lot than the ones wanting to make Edver fish bait.

"This way," Edver rasped as he directed his mount. "I heard them say the nearest tower."

"And you know its location how?"

"I study maps."

So reassuring.

"You do know we'll probably die, right?"

Edver glanced over his shoulder, determination etched into his countenance. "Afya's worth the risk, and I know you think that way about Nerissa. Plus, I know where I'm going if that happens, so I'm not afraid."

Denton didn't bother answering. The fact Nerissa thought him a monster and unworthy of trust still pushed the barb from his past deeper and deeper, but he couldn't hold a grudge. Not when she was in danger.

Besides, Parson Gil once said holding a grudge went against the Scripts.

And, despite his countless flaws, Denton wanted to do better at not being a disappointment to the Beginning.

Cinders and Shark Bait trotted along, the drumming of their hooves drowning out all other noise except the rushing of his pulse in Denton's ears.

Please, Beginning. Help us. Keep them safe.

Chapter Thirty

NERISSA

"Give your canoe to the Beginning, young one, and relinquish your grip on the oars."

Some good Hauni's advice did.

Ignoring the urge to press her fingertips to her bleeding lip, Nerissa stared at the big, broad back in front of her. If only her surroundings would blur and her cognizance of time fade. Each plodding step brought her and her sisters closer to their doom. Each time she inadvertently slowed brought more pain to Afya.

She'd tried giving her canoe to the Beginning, and what had He done? Thrown her and her sisters in the mother of hurricanes and allowed them to flounder in pain and confusion and fear.

You say you'll never leave or forsake us, yet where are You?

Instead of being reassured by a strong anchor as the waves battered her, it felt like the anchor had been eroded into nothingness.

Tall pine trees swayed gracefully in the wind, immune to Daffy's exhausted cries or Afya's sharp gasps of pain as chains dug into her raw wrists.

Nerissa tamped down her own whimper. The metal, so heavy and thick and rough, pressed into the wounds created by days of friction caused by coarse rope. After her "stunt", as Afya's mother called it during an attempt to help Daffy and Elberta to escape, ropes were too good for her and Afya. They couldn't run or cause trouble if manacles added the weight of five hundred anchors to each step.

The stuffiness in her head throbbed in time with the pulse in her cheek. The latest backhand lent a permanent spin to her vision, and if it didn't soon stop, she would empty her already-hollow stomach.

"Stop here."

Nerissa blinked as she dragged her gaze upward. The wind no longer trundled through the pine trees, its whistle replaced by the gentle crash of waves upon rock.

"We'll camp here tonight," Afya's mother announced. She dismounted her mare with the grace of the nobility Nerissa read about in tales. "Begin the fire, would you? I'm famished."

Nerissa dutifully sat once the chain was attached to a stake drive into the ground. The grass' warmth seeped through her skirt, but it did nothing to quell the ice coating her veins. There was nothing she could do to rescue Daffy and Elberta.

Hopeless.

She was just a worthless worrywart who excelled only in fretting about the future.

And her sisters' futures were condemned.

If only she waited a few more days, then she could have snagged them and made a break for it during a trek—without getting caught.

"I want Nerri," Daffy wailed as she strained against a guard holding her back.

Afya's mother tsked. "Your sister is in bad trouble, darling. She is serving her punishment."

"Nerri did nothing wrong." Elberta glared at the woman. "You're the bad one. The Scripts say not to take what's not yours, and you've taken us. We don't belong to you."

The woman laughed. "Such a fiery spirit. You'll not be an easy one to train, will you? No, little fire ant, you do not belong to me, but you soon will to another."

"You're a lying, good-for-nothin', decaying possum."

Nerissa closed her eyes. Of all the times for Elberta to repeat an insult she learned from Denton, who apparently learned it from his Red friend.

Denton.

The thought of the handsome outsider with captivating blue eyes and a gift with horses threatened to drown her in the sorrow bringing tears to her eyes. Had his end been swift? Painless? Had the Beginning granted him that mercy?

Please forgive me for lying to him.

"That mouth of yours, child. You best learn how to temper yourself before it lands you in worse trouble. Now, do be quiet or I'll gag you."

Late summer always unleashed the hottest days. During that time, it was a struggle to keep the plants alive, and one could almost see them withering before their eyes.

Nerissa felt like those plants. Withering beneath the harshness, desperate for a reprieve but with no hope of receiving one.

Only a corner of her heart remained unbroken, and a bit broke off that corner when, once again, Elbert and Daffy were kept from her. Would she never hug them again? Soothe their fears while masking her own? Wipe away their tears? Tell them stories from the Scripts?

Oh, Beginning, protect them.

Why couldn't she be more like Mamma? Strong and unwavering?

Instead, she was a puny little weed, flattened by the mildest of storms.

"I am sorry," Afya whispered from where she huddled against the base of a thin pine. "This is my fault."

"It's their fault." Nerissa forced her dry tongue and dryer lips to work. The fresh taste of copper alerted her the cut in her lip had reopened. "They're such greedy mongrels they'll do whatever is necessary to gain more coin, even if it means harming others."

"Quite right, darling," Afya's mother sang as she withdrew a waterskin from her saddlebag. She then procured a strip of thick cloth and sashayed toward Nerissa. "Do hold still. If you bit or kick or flail, then I'll simply be forced to remove one of your sister's fingers. Slaves can easily get by with just nine, you know."

Nerissa remained as still as a frozen turtle as the woman gagged her. If increased misery meant lessening her sisters' suffering, she would accept it without resistance.

The kidnappers scarfed down their meal, fed some to the younger captives, then set up the rest of camp. Closing her eyes, Nerissa willed sleep to arrive. Endless darkness was the only break granted from the desolation of knowing she was helpless to rescue her sisters and the soul-rending possibility her parents were slaughtered.

"His ways are higher than our own," Father once said when Daffy asked a hard question. *"He knows all. We don't. And while we may not understand, we can rest in the peace granted by the knowledge He is always in control."*

This didn't feel like control.

"Peace, I leave to you..."

The verse was wrong. There was no peace to be had. Not in this place. Not ever again.

Clanking bowls and the scent of roasting fish drew Nerissa from the welcoming darkness into the harsh light of day. When had the sunlight become so repulsive?

"Time to arise," Afya's mother trilled as she preened and fixed her hair. Her gown's deep crimson color was fitting. How much blood had she caused to be spilled?

"Now, darlings, listen closely. We're going to play a game. I'm going to ask Nerri some questions, and she receives one tally mark for each question she refuses to answer. Once she gains five marks, something bad will happen. Now, we don't want that, do we? No, we don't, so why don't you just encourage your sister to comply and behave?"

Daffy's bottom lip quivered and Elberta drew her close.

Her sisters shouldn't be trembling with fear. Not at their tender ages.

Nerissa prayed for the Beginning's mercy and help as Al dragged her to her feet and hauled her toward the fire, plopping her down on an overturned stump. The woman removed the gag before settling down before Nerissa, well without of kicking range, but close enough to keep her voice at conversation level.

"Now, Nerri, do tell. Who is your village's strongest ally?"

"I don't know." The words clung to Nerissa's parched throat.

The woman shook her head.

Nerissa recoiled as she drew a knife.

Instead of plunging it into flesh, the woman carved a mark into the ground. "One tally. Better rethink your little rebellious stint, girl."

It wasn't rebellion. Nerissa truly didn't know.

But she did suspect.

Losibar, by far, was the strongest nearby village. But they were finicky at times, and likely wouldn't be an ally in everything.

"How many allies did your village have, and who were they?"

"I don't know." And she didn't. Father never told her such things, nor did Edver ever offer up the information.

Another mark.

"How often did that outsider correspond with Veerham?"

"I don't know. Never, I think." The words lodged, resisted being uttered, but what did it matter? Denton was dead and Veerham wasn't known for its warfaring capabilities.

A third mark.

"You are much stupider than I anticipated. Which chiefs did Talart meet with most?"

"I don't know." Oh, how she loathed those words.

A fourth mark.

The surroundings pitched to and fro and only Al's harsh grip kept her upright. What if she didn't know the final answer? What would happen?

"How large do you estimate your total number of allies to be?"

Nerissa shook her head as tears stung her eyes. Save her sisters or condemn others to the same fate. Why must she be forced to choose?

Beginning, this isn't right.

"Al, fetch the youngest one."

The youngest...Daffy was the youngest.

"I don't know," Nerissa cried. "I don't, I swear. So many villages have been destroyed in the past few years, and I was never told who was or wasn't an ally."

Al continued walking toward a screaming Daffy.

"I promise I speak the truth." Her voice edged upward, and a distant part of her mind noted she sounded rather hysterical. "I promise, I promise I don't know. I'm not lying."

Al reached Daffy.

"No!" Nerissa's voice cracked. Panic swelled within, seizing her chest and squeezing the words from her struggling lungs. "I answered your questions. I didn't lie." She rose on unsteady legs. She would stop them. Somehow, someway.

The woman sneered. "I said nothing would happen if you answered. Ignorance is still a refusal to answer." She tapped her pointed chin. "You did put effort and heart into it, which I appreciate. Therefore, nothing will happen to the child. Younger ones are easier to train, anyway. Al, grab the middle sister."

"No!"

Elberta writhed and squirmed and kicked as Al threw her over his shoulder.

Nerissa charged, her feet catching on her skirt's tattered hem. "Leave her alone."

Al caught her shoulder and threw her to the side.

Two other guards latched onto her arms, one attaching the chain to the manacles.

The woman flicked her hand. "Gather the others up and prepare to commence travel."

"What are you doing with her?" A hundred different possibilities flashed through Nerissa's mind. *Please, Beginning, spare Elberta. Rescue her. Please, I beg You.*

A wide hand smashed into the side of her face. "Shut up."

Nerissa poured every ounce of energy into fighting, but she couldn't escape the harsh hands dragging her toward the path. The woman and Al remained by the fire, Elberta still screaming and resisting.

When they reached the intersection of path and cliff, the woman held up a hand. "Say farewell to your sister, because this is the final time you'll see her alive. Al, toss her over the cliff."

A piercing scream came from far away and emptiness filled Nerissa.

No. No! "Don't! Throw me over instead. Please!"

The woman pinned Nerissa with a look dripping with venom and hatred. "This is what happens when the weak resist the strong. Learn your lesson. This brat wouldn't have brought in substantial income anyway. One less weakling to weed out."

The trees blocked Nerissa's view.

Her knees locked, and she crumpled.

Elberta's last seconds were accompanied by Nerissa's sobs.

"Silence her and let's go. We have ground to cover."

A gag was once more inserted.

Fingers dug into her arms as she was forced to find her footing. Everything blurred as scalding tears poured forth. The ache in her chest was no longer a hole, but a vast pit so deep it would never be assuaged or filled.

Why, Beginning? Why?

Chapter Thirty-One

DENTON

THE SCREAM RENT THE air, rising above the frantic thrumming of Denton's heart as it struggled against his chest's confines. While he never desired to come face-to-face with a mountain lion—the infamous felines stalking Frilore's mountains—he rather that instead of a human be the scream's source.

But gut instinct warned him that wasn't the case.

If only the tower hadn't been empty. If only the captives had still been trapped within the cold stone walls.

Nothing but a smear of dried blood greeted him and Edver when they finally hauled themselves into the accursed prison.

The tracks, at least, were a blessing. The dew dampened the soil enough that the imprints were a beacon, leading them straight to the nefarious wretches who did their best to destroy innocent lives.

Please, Beginning.

The prayer had become his mantra. Please that he could remain upright when agony shafted through his ribs. Please that they would find Nerissa and the rest. Please that no one innocent would die.

"We should dismount here."

He reined Cinders to a stop and slid off as another scream arose. "Tell me this place doesn't have screaming seaweed or something equally weird."

Edver sent him a look suggesting Denton was a few horseshoes shy of a full set. "What are you talking about?"

"Just making sure Marteris doesn't have screaming seaweed or deranged cats that sound like humans."

"You're an odd one, Yindell."

"Just making sure that's a human."

"It's human." Edver cracked his knuckles. "And whoever's causing that will soon become fish bait. Come on, outsider. Follow my lead. I know this area better than you."

No kidding.

Perhaps Red's bad habits were rubbing off on him. She always exhibited increased sarcasm during stressful moments.

After tethering Cinders and Shark Bait off the trail, Denton followed Edver as they crept along the path. Hadn't Red said it wasn't the wisest idea to take the actual path?

Then again, she always had been one to do her own thing.

Nausea rose and his stomach heaved when they reached the clearing, the path tucked back enough that they couldn't see the left edge. The man who threw him overboard was now hauling a struggling Elberta toward the edge of the cliff. The woman he encountered in the first tower stood near a firepit, inspecting her nails.

Another scream.

Elberta was tossed.

Heart clenching, Denton shoved his sword at Edver, yanked off his boots, and rushed forward.

"You colossal fool. What are you doing?"

Edver was strong enough to deal with Floofy Hair and Big and Nasty. Elberta was too weak to withstand the current and waves' strength. He couldn't stand by and let her drown.

Al snarled precisely one curse as Denton tore past him. Fingers grazed his shoulder just before Denton's feet left solid earth.

Hindsight was both ally and enemy.

As he hurtled toward the foaming waters swirling around jagged rocks, common sense caught up. Perhaps it would have been best to look before diving so he could land in a spot not inhabited with pointy people-impalers.

"A good detective always thinks before acting."

Another claim Red didn't follow.

Well, too late now.

The knowledge he was about to be swallowed once more by the sea smacked him just before cold water enveloped him.

Gasping for air, Denton clawed at the water's choppy surface. "Elberta?"

"'M right here."

Spluttering as a wave slapped his face, Denton squinted through the waterfall of salty water dripping from his hair and stinging his eyes. With his luck, a shark lurked below the surface, contemplating if it'd like to gobble up its early-morning snack in one gulp or numerous bites.

Whatever a shark was.

"Right here, Denton."

He paddled toward the voice before locating Elberta clinging to one of the rocks. "Are you okay?"

"I'm tired, hungry, and half-drowned. I'm the okayest okay in the world."

Alright, then. Not okay. "Let's get you back to dry ground."

"You're supposed to be dead."

"So I've heard."

Horses and horseshoes, how could struggling to stay afloat be so draining? "Here. Hold on to my arm."

"I can swim."

"What?"

"I can swim." Elberta flicked a strand of sodden hair from her face. "I'm a Marterisi, Denton. Everyone knows how to swim. Those rotting possums just didn't think before throwing me in."

Oh. "Still, we should get you ashore. Then you can tell us where the others are."

Her face crumpled.

"Come on, Elberta. First thing's first. Let's get back to land."

She clutched his arm despite her claim about swimming. "I knew you wouldn't die."

"Oh?"

"Yes. That would make Nerissa unhappy, and I know you like her and wouldn't want her to be unhappy. And Uncle Morris calls you stubborn. That means you wouldn't let yourself die."

"You're terribly confident," he grunted. Muscles burned and the wound on his shoulder, although scabbed over, stung with the movement.

Please, Beginning.

"There aren't any inlets. Anyway, yes, I am confident because I am always right."

"You wanted to name Cinders *Magpie*."

"Magpie is a good name."

"Do you even know what a magpie is?"

She sent him a crusty glower.

Shaking his head, Denton diverted the remnant of his energy into surviving the swim. His lungs constricted to the point where breathing sapped his remaining strength and his limbs threatened to lock in place.

He was in the sea. Amidst man-consuming waves. With who-knew-what swimming beneath and out of sight.

The first time he'd ever interacted with the water, it hadn't gone well. He could only pray this time wasn't the same.

"How will we get up?" Elberta had ceased kicking and now let Denton pull her along, providing no assistance.

He couldn't be irritated even with the fear locking him in a chokehold.

Gasping a prayer of gratitude when they reached the cliff, Denton latched on to a nearby rock. "Edver!"

"What?" Edver's dark face peeked over the edge.

"Throw a rope, please."

"Do I look like I can haul your skinny hide up by myself?"

Someone was cranky. "Attach it to Cinders."

Although Edver's response didn't reach his ears, Denton could imagine the other man grumbling and grousing.

Soon, a serpentine object fell down, smacking the water about ten feet away.

"That's not close enough."

"That's the best I can do," Edver hollered back. "Now get going. I know where they took the others."

Praying for strength, Denton hauled Elberta to the rope and helped her tie a loop so she could sit in it. "Have Cinders pull," he called.

After a moment, the rope went taut and Elberta rose in the air.

Denton pulled in an anemic breath after another wave crashed upon him. If Edver didn't soon cast down the rope, there would be no need.

The last meal he ate—a paltry, stale biscuit with too much fish and not enough dough—arose. Spray peppered his face and surely he hadn't imagined something brushing his foot.

Did sharks have big teeth? Lots of teeth? Or did they have tentacles, like the squids he remembered Stepmother reading about from her book of lore?

The waves increased in size and choppiness.

Please, Beginning.

He rather face the entirety of kidnappers by himself than drown.

Something smacked the top of his head before kerplunking into the sea.

"Come on, Yindell. We don't have all day."

Hands trembling and fingers as steady as soggy flatbread, Denton grasped the rope, squeezing his eyes shut as he was lifted from the water.

Hands latched onto his drenched shirt and hauled him onto the cliff.

Denton gasped for the first fulfilling breath since he decided to court death.

"That wasn't so bad, was it?"

The sarcastic tone drew his bleary gaze upward. Edver stood, fresh blood soaking into his shirt. "The woman ran and the man beaned me over the head out before taking off. At least we don't have to fight anyone right now."

"Right." An unsettled lurching sensation in his gut accompanied the answer.

Elberta clung to Edver. "They have Nerri and Daffy," she whimpered. "They took them that way."

"Why did they throw you over?"

"They asked Nerri questions she didn't know the answers to. After five questions, Afya's mamma got angry. She said Nerri was having some type of punishment." Edvera trembled. "They hurt Nerri and Afya."

Denton staggered to his feet. A good thing the saddle had stirrups, or he'd not stay on. "We'll do our best to find them. You said they went that way?" He pointed at the northern edge.

Elberta nodded. "They might be far away by now."

"They're hurrying."

Denton jumped at the voice.

Noko and Jonah sauntered from the trees.

Horses and horseshoes, he was going to give those two a lecture they'd never forget. "*What* are you *doing*?"

"Helping." Jonah patted the oversized hunting knife at his hip.

"Yes." Noko brandished a child-sized bow. "We're men, and men are to protect the womenfolk. That's part of the Halthdurn creed, you know."

Denton cared little what their "creed" claimed. "You need to return to Losibar."

"Can't. It's under attack. They were beating the bad guys, though. Whoopin' them good."

Denton pushed his fingers through hair gritty with salt and sweat. The boys couldn't come with them. It was too dangerous.

Bad enough he would need to protect Elberta, who needed more care and love and hugs than he could provide.

"We're going with you." Noko set his stance and crossed his arms, actions Jonah copied. With the Veerham boy's twiggy frame, he didn't look intimidating in the least, but the mulish expression was one Denton saw Red make numerous times.

Perhaps stubbornness coursed through ever Veerhamer's veins.

He just hoped enough filled his. He would need it for the upcoming fight.

He looked at Edver, who shrugged. "Fine, but you must obey *everything* we say, alright?"

The boys nodded.

Elberta wiped her eyes.

"She can ride Sir Marlin," Jonah offered. "And I bet that ugly horse we saw with Cinders needs a name."

Edver ushered the boys back to where they left their horses. Denton placed a hand on Elberta's shoulder. "We'll find them."

"I know. You're a royal detective. Isn't that your job? To find missing things and people?"

Denton swallowed the lump amassing in his throat. Why must she look at him like he was a hero? He wasn't. He was a pathetic coward. A man who allowed his brother to be abused and beaten because he was too weak to stand up. "It is my job," he finally managed to say.

Elberta wiped red, watery eyes, saying nothing until Denton pulled back on his boots. "Nerri likes you too, you know."

Denton's chest ached as his heart soared before dropping. It couldn't be healthy to experience such a dramatic shift in that short amount of time. Nerissa didn't still "like" him. That much he knew. "Let's go rescue your sisters."

"I count twenty of them."

Denton glanced up from where he cleaned Cinders' hooves. Edver had snuck away not ten minutes ago to spy on the men congregating in the nearby clearing. He returned wearing a look boding ill tidings.

"I see Daffy and some of the other youngers, but not Nerissa or Afya."

An invisible clamp fused itself around Denton's chest. "Did you see any blood?"

"No, and no sign of a scuffle. Something's off about the cliff line—perhaps there's a tower there? I've heard of towers carved into sea-facing cliffs. They were used as lookouts when rumors were swirling about attacks from the lands across the sea." Edver hissed as he rotated his shoulder. "I'll deny ever saying this, but I can't take on two men right now, much less ten."

"Nor can I." Lowering Cinders' hoof, Denton stood and kneaded the tension from his back. "Let me see the clearing."

"No way. You're too pale. You'll stick out like a sea bream among cod."

Denton had no idea what a sea bream was but he did know he wasn't pale. Not with the major sunburn. "I'm going. If we're to rescue them, you need to realize I'm not some incompetent ninny who screams at the slightest scare and will give us away."

Edver harrumphed, but jerked his head. "Come on, then."

Holding his breath and willing nothing to snap beneath his weight, Denton crept through the forest until coarse voices grated his ears. A good thing the kids hadn't accompanied them, else their ears would be subjected to the roughest of language.

Edver's count proved true. Twenty criminals milled about, some drinking, some eating, and others huddled in groups scheming who-knew-what. Edver's observation regarding the cliff line also proved true. An unnatural hump disturbed the otherwise flat edge.

The odds didn't exactly inspire a rousing burst of courage, but Denton refused to let numbers dictate the outcome. They *would* succeed and they *would* rescue the captives and find Nerissa and Afya.

"Father should be here in a day. He said he'd come as soon as possible."

Marterises were insane, but at least they were sturdy. Aside from Captain Bedros and probably King Calvin, Denton knew of few Veerhamers who could endure their injuries, dehydration, and weakness and still charge into battle.

Still, tomorrow was too late.

"Be careful where you put the saddle blankets," a familiar voice snapped. "I refuse to be thrown off because you simpletons placed them in a bed of sticker weeds."

The accent sent blades of fear up Denton's spine. Al hadn't just tried to kill him twice, he attempted to murder an innocent little girl too.

Please, Beginning, give us wisdom.

One wrong move would ensure their deaths.

Something crunched beneath his heel when he stepped back, and he looked down to see a rumpled sicker weed. At his motion, Edver followed him back to their makeshift camp.

"You're plotting something. I can tell."

For the first time in countless days, he offered a genuine grin—albeit an impish one much like what he'd seen Red give when brainstorming one of her crazy ideas. "I have an idea."

"This is a horrible idea."

"It'll be a great idea if you don't muck it up." Denton drew a knife and inched toward where the unsuspecting victims snored their hearts out. The guard hadn't seen Edver's fist, and he was now snoozing beneath the tree branches, tied to a tree with no way of escape.

"Why am I the one to handle their stinky boots?"

"Because I know horses. You're just lucky to stay on when your mount's going faster than a trot."

"I take offense to that."

Despite his grumbles and growls, Edver hefted his pack and tiptoed toward the camp.

Denton made his way to where the tack was sprawled over low-hanging limbs. Taking his knife, he reached for the first saddle cinch and began sawing through the leather. Completely severing the band would alert the villains, but he could weaken it to such a point that, when they attempted to saddle the horses, the cinches would break.

No cinch meant no saddle, and from what Edver said, few found riding bareback a thrilling endeavor.

Cinch after cinch he weakened, praying with every stroke no one would awaken. The children were chained in the middle of the camp, and undoing their bindings would cause too much clanking and awaken the enemy, so a rescue right then and there was out of the plan.

But this plan would work. It had to.

And Denton's efforts were Plan B. Edver's were Plan A, and after that came Plan C.

After he finished sabotaging the cinches, he approached the horses. The first, a stately buckskin gelding, huffed.

"None of that," Denton whispered. He held out his hand, let the gelding whuff at it, and stroked the animal's neck. He hated harming any animal, particularly horses, but it'd be more unpleasant for the rider in the end. "Sorry, boy. You won't like this if things come down to it."

Opening his own makeshift bag, which was just a looped and tied shirt, he withdrew the first sticker burr from the bag. Gently placing it on the saddle blanket, Denton then moved on to the next horse, made friends with it, and proceeded to sticker up the nearby blanket.

Most thought him wacky for "making friends" with horses, but a horse that trusted you was less likely to alert others to your presence. There would be no shrill whinnies, no uneasy stamps, no loud snorts.

When the final burrs were in place, Denton motioned to Edver, and they slunk back into the trees, not saying a word until they reached where the boys and Elberta slept beneath Bluet's protection.

Come morning, the evil sots would stick their socked feet in their boots, only to be greeted with sticker weed leaves. If that didn't deter and throw them into a tizzy, the busted saddles and burred saddle blankets would certainly throw a crimp in their plans.

Edver clasped Denton's shoulder. "Pray this works."

"I have been." He rubbed his eyes. Exhaustion begged to pull him under, but he couldn't give in. Not when victory was so close. "Now all we have to do is wait."

And pray.

Always pray.

Pray Talart and his men would soon arrive. Pray Nerissa and the rest were okay. Pray the captives could be rescued.

Please, Beginning.

Parson Gil was right. Sometimes, praying was the most powerful weapon.

CHAPTER THIRTY-TWO

NERISSA

ONLY A WEAK BEAM of moonlight snuck into the tower that night.

Nerissa shifted the best she could, causing the connected chains to clink and clack and make more ruckus than Haether and Afya's mother—whom Haether called *Joan*—would like.

Her ears still rang from the last time she caused too much noise. She hadn't felt the blow, though. *Couldn't* when everything was numb. Empty.

Elberta was dead.

At least two people she loved were dead. Four if Mamma and Father were murdered, and five if Uncle Morris had been slaughtered as well.

This couldn't be happening.

But it had. Elberta's screams repeated through her mind with incessant clarity. The panic, the wrenching fear...

It had happened.

And she, once again, was powerless to stop it.

After they left the clearing where Elberta was killed, Haether intercepted them. Minutes later, Joan and Al appeared, Al muttering something about revenge and a man attacking him. Fresh blood stained his shirt, but he said no more about the incident, although Joan constantly looked over her shoulder, saying something about one being better than two.

Nerissa hadn't cared about Haether joining, and she didn't care about Joan and Al.

The only care remaining was toward Daffy and Afya. Even then the pieces of her heart struggled to meld back together.

Was this what deep, rending loss felt like?

I can't do this, Beginning.

Afya moaned in her sleep, wincing as she turned to her side. The chains were no more her friend than Nerissa's, yet somehow Afya fell asleep almost right after they were deposited on the floor.

The thick gag pressing down on Nerissa's tongue stole any chance of slumber.

Daffy was still outside with the rest. Was she cold? Hungry? At least Joan wanted the children in good condition for the auction.

Auction.

How could one human sell another?

Shuddering, Nerissa leaned against the wall. She and Afya wouldn't be attending that auction. No, they'd already be sold.

At least, that was what Haether said.

Nasty, evil woman. If only Nerissa had listened to her worry, to her gut. No one from Keller meant any good, and Haether's and Al's involvement indicated as such. How the two regurgitated pieces of seaweed ended up partnering with Joan, she didn't know.

Even if she did, there was nothing to be done. No one was coming, and even if they were, they wouldn't know how to access the tower. At high tide, the sea concealed most of the natural steps carved into the cliff's side.

The Scripts contained many chapters where believers were stuck in undesirable situations. Some capitulated. Others stood strong.

She wanted to stand strong, but nothing remained of her strength.

"'Stand firm in the faith,'" Uncle Morris always quoted when hard times rolled in.

"My flesh and my heart may fail, but He is the strength of my heart..."

So said the Scripts.

I can't do this. Her flesh and heart were, indeed, failing. *But I know I'm not alone.* And she did. But it was hard. So hard. And it hurt. A devastating stabbing boring deeper and deeper into her soul with each passing hour.

Elberta wasn't mine.

The realization caused her heart to skip a beat.

All her life, she struggled to keep her sisters safe. Struggled to control the environments they found themselves in. Never any danger or hardships, not if she had any say. They were to grow up safe and sound and secure.

But human machinations capitulated to the Beginning's will, and her plans were blown away in the wind when they conflicted with His.

Her control, her desire to safeguard her sisters...they weren't hers to do that with. Protect, yes, as that was her job as the eldest. But to practically lock them up?

Couldn't I have learned that lesson some other way? An easier way?

The prayer was too late, but still no less true. Why must the most important lessons hurt the worst?

And, just as she had been forced to relinquish control over Elberta, so must she do the same with Daffy.

She's Yours. Not Nerissa's. Not even Mamma's and Father's. *Yours and Yours only.*

Life was a vapor, a mere breath in the passage of time. She could not control which paths were trod, nor which outcomes awaited.

Only You determine how things end.

How loved ones passed.

How her own story would end.

Only Yours, Beginning.

A tearless sob jerked her weary frame. The realization both comforted and frightened her. Her family, should they perish, would go to their true home. It was the pain experienced by those left behind she wanted nothing to do with.

I don't know how to relinquish control and surrender myself. Please help me.

Not a sparrow fell without His knowledge. He already counted every breath her family members would breathe. Not one less, not one more.

Only You know.

Still trembling, Nerissa closed her eyes. The knowledge of the Beginning's omniscience would be her bedrock—her anchor—as the storm worsened.

Only Yours. Only You know.

Only He knew.

And that was comfort enough.

"How do I look?"

"Like you are ready to make a sale."

Haether and Joan giggled like foolish schoolgirls as they finished fixing their hair and dusting off their clothing. They had opted to sleep in the tower, declaring they would need space and time to prepare for the nearing business arrangement.

Because Nerissa and Afya were mere goods to be traded.

Nerissa glanced at the other woman. Afya stared at the floor, gaze empty and posture slouched. Twigs decorated her hair in a messy array and pine needles and dirt clung to her dress.

"This is your fault, darling." Joan knelt before Afya and began plucking out the twigs. "If you had stayed with me and not ran off in a fit of childish rage, then you could still be at home, safe and comfortable. This is what happens when you allow yourself to become ungrateful."

What a manipulative old vulture.

"Now I must sell you. Actions have consequences, you know, and I simply cannot keep you, even if you brought in a decent amount of income."

Afya shuddered.

Nerissa forced down the nausea at the thought of what Joan forced her daughter into.

"You have become more trouble than you are worth, and your little adventure has cost me precious time and money. I have no use for a rebellious brat, not when I could raise another who won't put more gray in my hair."

If looks could kill, Nerissa would slay this woman on the spot.

"I do hope you two aren't prone to seasickness." Haether glided over and began removing debris from Nerissa's hair. "That can be a rough journey, and the shipmaster is not the kindest man."

"Your new owners may be, though, so do be on your best behavior." Joan shook a finger at Afya, like she admonished her for filching a cookie before suppertime.

How could they be so casual? They weren't selling horses or fish or even dogs, but *people.*

There had to be a way to escape. Had to be a way to save Daffy.

A shout belted through the air, soon followed by several more, many laced with vulgar profanities.

Joan huffed. "Whatever could be causing such a ruckus?"

When the chaos did not stop, she motioned for Haether to check on the scoundrels above. "Please make sure they are not harming the merchandise."

Someone screamed as they hurtled past the window.

Haether recoiled. "I'm not going up there. It sounds like a civil war."

"Stop being a ninny and go. You are Al's new wife, and he dislikes cowards. They won't notice if you poke your head over the top."

"As you so astutely stated, I am the wife of Keller's new chief. This is below my station."

"And I'm the one determining how large a cut you receive from these sales. Now get your empty-headed self up there and stop those buffoons from killing each other. We still need them."

Haether snarled before spinning, her skirt swirling out in a bright sea of pale yellow. She clambered out the window and disappeared.

Joan stood and brushed off her hands. "There. You both are of good age and decent appearances. Your youth will be what brings in the high prices. Oh, don't give me that look, Nerri dear. You were the one who fought and resisted. If you behaved yourself, I would have let you spend your last night with your sister. But, as I said, actions have consequences."

Yes, they did. And when Joan stood before the Beginning one day, she would receive her comeuppance.

"Joan!"

"What now?" The older woman stomped to the window. "What is it, Haether?"

"You need to see this."

"Oh, for the love of—I don't have time for this. What is it?"

"Just come here."

Snarling about incompetent fools, Joan eased out the window and onto the thick edge below the window.

A woman screamed, the sound backed by the faint collision of what could be weapons.

Rubbing her cheek against the stone wall until the gag loosened, Nerissa spit out the foul-tasting cloth. "Afya, we can escape."

The hopelessness in Afya's eyes broke Nerissa's heart.

"We must escape. Surely your mother has an extra key."

Afya shook her head. Following Nerissa's lead, she worked free her gag. "There is one key, and she keeps it with her at all times." Choking on a sob, she lowered her head, her matted locks providing a curtain to her expression. "All those years I thought she truly cared. I remember her taking me from my real parents, saying they weren't taking care of me and used me to pay a debt.

She promised me a comfortable bed, warm food, and more dresses than I could imagine. It sounded like a dream. Where I grew up, we weren't wealthy, but looking back, I realize I had enough food and sufficient clothing."

"She manipulated you."

"I was a fool," Afya whispered. "When I reached the appropriate age, she claimed I needed to pay her back. That's when...that's when I realized something was wrong."

A woman screamed.

"I thought to escape," Afya continued, gaze distant. The slavers caught me, and that's when Edver rescued me. And to think I had a chance at freedom."

Another body plummeted past the window.

"You still might have that chance."

"No, that is impossible. I know the man coming to transport us. He is punctual. We have no hope, Nerissa, especially with Mother having the only key."

"Never fear, ladies."

The stuttering in Nerissa's heart couldn't be healthy. Her mind was playing tricks on her, a side effect of dehydration and no sleep. She hadn't just heard Edver's voice. Wasn't imagining his round, dark face, complete with his typical infectious and sometimes-obnoxious smile.

"Why are you frowning? You should be smiling. Unless you like this stuffy little stone hut?"

That was something Edver would say.

"You're not real," Afya whispered.

"Oh, honey, I am real. And I'm going to get you out of here."

Nerissa stared at the man hauling himself into the tower. This was impossible. Edver was dead.

"Stop looking at me like that, Ner. You know it'd take more than a few cuts to bring me down."

That was also something Edver would say, in that precise, peeved tone.

"You're dead," she numbly said.

He looked at himself then spread his arms. "I know I look like I was just dragged through a sticker weed patch edged with sharks, but I don't look *that* bad. Now, where's the key?"

"On Mother." Afya shook her head, likely attempting to dislodge the same shard of hope Nerissa felt worming its way into her own heart. "You can't be here."

"I'll leave if that's what you want."

"No, I meant you're *dead*. I watched them throw you down and stab you."

Edver held up a finger. "First, it took *three* of them to take me down. Second, they stabbed *at* me. And missed, Beginning be thanked, else I wouldn't be here." Drawing a knife from his belt, he limped forward. "Let's see if this works."

He knelt before Afya, pressed a kiss to her cheek, then commenced poking at the lock. After what felt like decades, a belligerent click sounded.

"Ah, the beautiful sound of freedom." Removing the chains and manacles, Edver helped Afya stand.

She wobbled, mouth ajar.

Nerissa couldn't blame her. While Edver was as stubborn as a sticker weed and twice as difficult to get rid of, she hadn't expected him to survive.

Thank You, Beginning.

"What of my parents?"

"They lived last I checked. Your mamma has a broken ankle and I think your father's arm is out of socket, but they're alive."

"How did you get here?"

Edver strode over. "That's a long story. Suffice to say I believe you'll be surprised in a good way."

Nerissa cataloged his features as he began working on the lock. Bruises swelled his face and numerous slices stained his shirt with blood, but he lived and looked fine. Definitely hiding his pain, but fine.

A shadow flitted across the wall, but Edver's oversized frame blocked the window from Nerissa's view.

Afya gasped. "No. Go away."

Bile burned Nerissa's throat as Joan backhanded her daughter. How had she snuck in here?

"Edver, behind you!"

He stood, but not fast enough to block the knife from entering his thigh. Crimson immediately splattered the stone floor.

Edver fell to his knees.

Nerissa scooted forward as far as she could, tugging at her skirt's hem. The material wouldn't tear.

"Afya, did you really think I would abandon and allow you to ruin my plans?" Joan placed her hands on her hips, somehow looking as clean as she did before leaving. "You certainly are intent on making things worse for yourself. Did you know I can control who bids on you?"

Hands fisting, Afya pulled herself to full height. Her bottom lip quivered, defying her attempted bravery. "I won't let you kill him. I won't let you hurt me and Nerissa."

"Oh? I'm the one with a knife. You have nothing."

"I'm a Marterisi. I'm resourceful."

Joan laughed. "You cannot be resourceful when you have nothing to be resourceful with."

"Get away from her," Edver growled. His legs buckled when he again attempted to stand, and more blood pooled on the floor.

With a wrench, Nerissa yanked a strip from her skirt. The material was more dirt and muck than anything, but it would stem the bleeding.

She hoped.

Please, Beginning.

"Let me see that wound."

Once the injury was within reach, Nerissa waded the cloth and shoved it in.

Edver screamed.

Please, Beginning, help him. Help me.

After ensuring Edver wouldn't die, she'd help Afya with Joan. Somehow.

Edver groaned Afya's name.

Nerissa tore another strip and continued packing the wound the best she could. Edver's continuing screams rang in her ears, and he thrashed as much as his weakening body would allow. If only she could use his belt for a tourniquet, but that would require removing his weapons and making them that much easier for Joan to grab.

Tearing three more strips reduced her skirt to a raggedy mess hitting just above her ankles. At least it'd be easier to run if she ever got out of the tower. She patted his hand, taking short, shallow breaths to keep her panic from showing. She had helped Hauni with injuries, but never any so severe. "You'll be okay. You have to be okay. You didn't come this far just to succumb to blood loss."

Edver groaned. "Gotta...gotta stop..."

"I'll help Afya. Don't you worry, Edver Talart."

"You're not that great with a knife."

True, but *not that great* was better than no effort at all.

After securing a strip around the packed wound, she snatched his largest knife. The chain kept her from taking more than four steps, which helped Afya none, but she could pray and guard Edver.

Calling Afya's name, she slid one of Edver's knives her way.

Afya dodged Joan and scooped up the knife. "I refuse to be the victim."

"Suddenly growing a spine, now are we? Wasn't it just a few minutes ago when you told Nerri there was no hope?"

Afya raised her chin. "I forgot how hope can come in many forms. I won't let you hurt him. I won't let you near me and Nerissa."

Joan trilled a blood-curdling cackle. "You've only ever peeled apples and potatoes. You couldn't stick a worm, much less your mother."

"You're not my mother."

Joan slashed her blade, catching Afya's shoulder. "You should stop now, child, before I'm forced to maim you. That would result in a loss of profit, and a loss of profit irritates me."

"I don't care what irritates you. Not anymore." Tears thickened Afya's words. "I was so stupid and blind."

"Yes, you were. As I've always said, actions have consequences, and this is your consequence. Such an ungrateful child you are."

Afya stumbled back, her foot snagging on the manacles Edver freed from her wrists.

She kicked them aside.

Nerissa scooped them up. All she needed was Afya to lure Joan closer.

Joan swiped, knocking the knife from Afya's hand.

Afya screeched when Joan grabbed her hair, but she struggled toward Nerissa, and the younger woman's momentum dragged Joan within reach.

Afya's eyes caught Nerissa's for the briefest of seconds before the dark-skinned Marterisi went to her knees.

Nerissa swung the manacles.

A solid thump preceded Joan crumpling to the floor.

Afya sobbed as she undid Nerissa's manacles. "How...how will we get him out?"

"We'll think of something."

A third body hurtled past the window.

"We have to get Edver out of here." Afya paced from one side to the other. "We can't carry him, can we?"

"No."

"I'll go to the surface. Maybe...maybe we can find a rope or something. The chains aren't long enough."

"We still can't haul him. He's too heavy." Nerissa felt Edver's pulse. Weak, matching his breathing.

Afya eased out onto the edge. "It's cracking. I don't think it will hold my weight for long. Don't come out yet. The cracks are worsening."

Nerissa turned her attention to Edver once Afya disappeared. "Stay alive, Edver Talart. You hear me? Stay alive."

A cracking noise rumbled from outside.

Nerissa reached the window just in time to watch the ledge crumble and a man hit the churning waters below.

He popped up one breath later, bobbing about like a fish that forgot how to swim. "Throw down a rope!"

That...no, it couldn't be...could it?

Afya joined her, gaping at who very much looked like a certain outsider. "He's alive too?"

The Denton could-be inched closer to the tower's base. "Is there a rope you can throw?"

Surroundings spinning, Nerissa located a thick coil tucked in the corner and tied the end to the hook she'd been chained to. Fingers cold despite the day's humid warmth, she fumbled the rest of the coil before heaving it out the window. It tumbled down, almost giving her rope burn, and landed in the water with a loud plop.

She tied the end to the hook she'd been chained to. Edver still breathed, but his clammy skin meant he wouldn't be long for the world without proper medical attention. Joan, too, was still alive, although blessedly unconscious.

Nerissa ignored the blood smeared across the floor from where the woman fell.

The rope went taut, and she again peered out the window. An apparition looking just like Denton awkwardly scaled it, much like he had during the first tower rescue.

It couldn't be. She was going delusional from dehydration. Imagining things in her grief.

Haether wanted him dead, she made that much clear. No way would she allow any chance of Denton's survival.

Yet he pulled himself into the tower, arms shaking but expression determined.

Nerissa's legs gave. She must have a fever, for this wasn't...it couldn't be.

Denton, blurry and sounding far away, said, "The ledge broke, else we could do this the easy way."

Easy way? The easy way would be to remove her from her misery. She could believe Edver survived, but Denton?

Warm hands framed her face, calloused fingertips brushing away strands of hair. "Breathe, Nerissa. This will be a lot harder if you pass out on me."

"You're dead."

"I've been getting that a lot. What happened to Edver?"

"Joan...Joan stabbed him." The words wouldn't come. Those blue eyes were the same. He looked the same.

But he was dead.

"I take it that's Joan?"

"Yes. I—I hit her over the head with the manacles. And Afya said she'd find help for Edver."

A ghost of a smile quirked his lips. "Red would approve."

That was the same, too, saying Red would either approve or disapprove.

"Are those manacles still operational? It'd be best if we lock Joan up. I don't want her hurting Edver while we wait for technicalities to be figured out."

At Nerissa's mute nod, Denton's gaze softened. "Elberta is alive."

"What?"

"She's alive and needs you, so the sooner we get out of here, the sooner you can reunite with your sisters."

"What about Daffy?"

"Fine, but scared. Your parents are alive as well."

"How do you know this?" Surely the ringing in her ears and the fading of her peripheral vision didn't have anything to do with these revelations—if they were indeed true and she wasn't in some fever coma.

"I saw them." He picked up the manacles. "Do you know where the key is?"

"On her, I think."

"I'll just lock it with the knife."

Denton secured the manacles onto Joan and hooked the chain to the loop Afya was chained to, then motioned for Nerissa to join him at the window.

"The ledge is broken, so you'll need to just slide down until you reach that stain right there, then begin angling yourself to the right. There are grooves carved into the side you can use as steps once you reach them."

Nerissa blinked. "You can't be real."

"I'm real, Nerissa." Hesitation lurked in his motions as he scanned her face. "We can discuss that later, though. It's time to go before Poofy Hair wakes up. Follow my lead."

At least Joan couldn't reach Edver. The woman would surely murder him.

Denton grabbed the rope and began lowering himself. Nerissa bit back the nausea. Heights never bothered her before, but now...

Now, if she fell, she could very well meet her end at the tips of the jagged rocks below.

A soft sawing reached her ears as the rope strained.

She spun to find Joan sawing through the rope.

The final fibers snapped, and the rope whipped across the floor.

Denton's yell was brief.

No. No, no, no.

She couldn't look out the window to see if he made it. Chances were she'd watch blood mix with the water.

"Not that you'll ever use this lesson when you're a slave, but you can only unlock manacles with a blade—not lock them. The mechanism doesn't work that way." Joan sneered as she kicked aside the manacles. Her steps stumbled and a crazed expression glinted in her wild eyes. Blood oozed down her face and her speech slurred, adding to her unhinged appearance.

Prayers swirled through Nerissa's mind. Would this nightmare ever end?

Scooping up Edver's discarded knife, she braced herself for Joan's attack.

The woman's momentum carried Nerissa backward. No knife flashed in Joan's hands, but that meant nothing. Joan could easily strangle her to death.

"I've worked too hard to have my plans destroyed by a bunch of impudent children," Joan hissed.

The bottom windowsill caught the back of Nerissa's knees.

And then she was falling.

The water welcomed her with what felt like a thousand needles, and the impact forced the breath from her lungs. When she was little, Father sometimes tossed her into the sea, but into gentle waves, not ones threatening to drown her.

Years of swimming kicked in, and soon she resurfaced, gasping for air. Foaming waves surged around her, and deep blue storm clouds were settling in and blocking the sky from view.

An arm wrapped around her waist. "Come on. A cove isn't too far from here."

She twisted, treading water. Denton's hair hung in his eyes and he eyed the water with the disdain of a cat, but it really was him.

"You're alive."

"Yes, for now." He cast a look toward the cliff. "I can't tell if the fighting is still ongoing, so we should get out of sight before we find out the painful way. I don't fancy being shot while defenseless."

Though her skirt dragged her down, the cove wasn't that difficult to reach. Shrouded by high sides, thick pines, and plenty of underbrush, it would make a delightful getaway spot in any other circumstance.

Her legs gave as soon as she tried standing, and the world tilted as the fatigue she'd held at bay flooded over her.

"Are you okay?"

The bleariness barely cleared when she looked up. Denton watched her, concern etched in his face.

One sob, followed by another, came with brute force, propelled by the maelstrom of conflicting emotions and sensations.

She was so tired. So scared. So pathetically wimpy. Her family was alive. Edver was alive. *Denton* was fine.

"Hey, it's okay. You all are okay." Strong arms tucked her into a broad shoulder, and she clung to Denton's shirt as the tears unleashed in full force.

"I'm so sorry," she choked out. She had lied to him time and again—helped mislead him—yet he had been prepared to give his life for her and was still as sweet as could be.

"We'll worry about that later." Denton again brushed clinging strands of hair from her cheek. "All that matters is you're okay."

Yes, she was okay. Her family was too, according to Denton, and he had no reason to lie.

Nerissa released a shuddering exhale and looked up. Tears marred her vision, but not enough to disguise the yellowing bruising mottling Denton's face. "You're hurt."

"I'm okay." He took the hand she reached up and squeezed it.

Nerissa closed her eyes as he wiped away her tears. While she fretted about the future, she never contemplated just how safe being at home made her feel. Now, after being vulnerable and exposed to the very evil her village attempted to eradicate, she relished being safe, even if it was on a shore far away from her family and home.

"You're safe, Nerissa."

She leaned into his hand, ignoring the unnamed flipping sensations occurring in her stomach. "I know."

Crunching sand drew her eyes open. Al stormed toward them, sword drawn as another familiar figure appeared from the trees edging the left side, sliding down the slope.

"Denton, behind you!"

CHAPTER THIRTY-THREE

DENTON

"THAT SWORD IS MINE." Denton scrambled to his feet and placed himself between Al and Nerissa. No way would he allow the decaying fish to go near her.

"Finders keepers." Al bared his teeth in what Denton assumed was an intimidation tactic.

"No, pretty sure you stole it from me after you tried killing me on that beach."

"Not my fault you couldn't keep your nose where it belonged. If you hadn't poked around, you wouldn't have gotten a little booboo."

Denton wouldn't call the wound that gave him the impressive scar a *booboo*, but now wasn't the time for semantics. "Not my fault you were careless and allowed the body to slip from your grasp. Nor is it my fault you left your mark out for all to see."

Al drew Denton's sword. "Squeal all you want. You're uttering your last words."

"Captain Bedros gave me that sword, and he rarely loans those out. He won't take kindly to news of the theft." Denton loosened his borrowed blade. He couldn't take this man on, not even with the numerous injuries dotting Al's torso and legs. And it wasn't like he could just run away.

Carter may be on the slimmer side, and not as strong as, say, the wolfmen, but at least he was a fast runner. Denton just puffed along like an out-of-shape bulldog.

Movement shifted behind Al.

Haether emerged, knife in hand.

Just great. Perhaps he should request they wait so he could commission a plaque saying, *"Denton Yindell's last stand took place here. The outsider meant well, but was woefully unprepared when it came to actually participating in combat."*

Yes, that sounded quite adequate.

Maybe Carter and Red would miss him enough to bring flowers.

He doubted it, though.

Al swung.

Denton blocked. The shock reverberated through his arms and seeped into his muscles, weakening their already-questionable strength.

Within a few minutes, sweat dripped into his eyes and his arms trembled.

Beginning, please help me. Please let Nerissa be okay.

He couldn't face both Al and Haether at once. He wasn't a wolfman with enviable talent.

Haether screeched, and Denton danced out of Al's reach just long enough to look over. The villainess was doubled over, clawing at her eyes as she called Nerissa a wide variety of crude names.

Al growled.

Denton brought up the sword just in time to ensure he kept his head for another minute.

A flurry of harsh blows pushed him to the water's edge.

Al sneered. "Nowhere to go, eh, outsider? You should have just stayed in your uppity little kingdom."

"I think Veerham would disagree." Denton sidestepped Al's thrust and slammed his palm into the man's nose, his ribs screaming from the motion.

Al reeled back, clutching his face.

Denton drove forward, tackling him to the sand. Before Al could react, he planted his fist into Al's nose once again, followed by an awkward blow to his throat.

Al went limp, eyes rolling up in the back of his head.

Heart thundering, Denton rolled off. The final vestiges of adrenaline faded, leaving behind unsteady limbs he doubted he could move.

"Are you okay?" Nerissa fell to her knees beside him.

"I'm fine." Denton gulped massive lungfuls of air. He reeked of sweat and the sea, but he and Nerissa were alive. "You?"

"Yes." She scanned his face. "Haether didn't like the sand in her eyes."

"You threw it at her?"

"Yes." A blush spread across her cheeks.

"Where is she now?" That wouldn't have knocked Haether out.

Nerissa's smile wavered. "Uncle Morris and Chief Talart secured her. Uncle Morris looks terrible. They said they have Joan in custody and preparations are being made to retrieve Edver." She grabbed his hand and squeezed it. "You were right. They're alive."

Denton worked up enough energy to smile. "Wouldn't lie t' you."

"I know," she whispered. "I know."

Morris materialized behind his niece. As battered as Cinders was when Carter first brought her home, he limped, one arm pressed to his chest and wearing a fierce scowl. "They'll learn not to mess with us. Nerri, your sisters are waiting up on the ridge. All the cowardly good-for-nothings are bound and ready for transport."

Denton groaned and let his head flop back onto the sand. Thunder boomed and lightning flashed, but he could take a year-long nap where he lay.

"I know you're tired, boy, and heaven knows you deserve a rest, but there's still work to do. Scrape up some of that Veerhamer stubbornness and let's get to work."

Morris could do his own work. Somehow, a grudge was all too ready to form against the rest of the village. This man had lied to his face while simultaneously speaking about the importance of following the Beginning.

Chamonix has forgiven them."

Carter relayed the information with a stunned tone when he told Denton the goings-on during Denton's stint in bedrest.

They had captured Chamonix, prepared to sell her for horrifically barbaric purposes, yet she still forgave.

"The Beginning didn't say it would be easy, but we are to forgive our enemies and those who have wronged us."

Denton grunted. He wasn't at the forgiveness level quite yet, but he would do his best to make the Beginning proud.

Somehow rising despite his weakness, he nodded to Morris. "Lead the way."

Turned out "things to do" was Morris code for, "Criminals to drag to Losibar, clam chowder to eat, and stitches to receive".

Dragging the criminals to Losibar, which looked just fine despite the attack? Doable. Preferable, even.

Eating clam chowder? Denton passed, even though his stomach begged for sustenance.

Receiving stitches? Well, he would have passed on those too if Valti hadn't physically held him down while calling in Jonah and Noko. The slippery fish knew Denton wouldn't fight when the boys expressed interest in "seeing how skin was sewn."

Add to that Jonah's helpful, "Wow, Mrs. Itti. That's kind of how my mother sews squares for her blankets," and it was a right fine week.

Not.

Denton rubbed his shoulder. During the scuffle, the gash gained from rescuing Edver had reopened, gradually bleeding throughout the short jaunt to Losibar. According to Itti, who gave Denton a pursed-lip look that rivaled Halda's, the cut needed stitches.

Balderdash. It would scab up. Eventually.

"Stop your complaining," Edver groused. He hunched over Shark's saddle, one hand gripping the horn as the other clutched Shark's coarse mane. "It's a splinter compared to my injury."

"Itti offered to give you more pain medicine."

"I'm fine."

"Sure you are. You look like you're about to faint. You're not even supposed to be riding."

Edver scowled. "I don't faint."

"Oh, right. You *pass out.*"

The chief's son speared Denton with such a snarly glower Denton expected to find himself six feet under.

"Look, Talart. One, Afya isn't paying attention. Two, she was there when the injury occurred. She knows its severity. Three, everyone expects you to be in pain. No use denying it."

Edver grumbled something about aggravating outsiders.

Denton stroked Cinders' neck. Bittersweet anticipation kicked his heart rate up a notch. A few horses away, Noko and Jonah jabbered on with Elberta, who held the hands of Daffy, who sat behind her. Nerissa and Afya rode side-by-side, occasionally peeking at Edver, although Denton wouldn't tell him that. The man's ego was large enough already. He needn't know Afya gazed at him with admiration.

Behind them, Mrs. Wessen rode in a travois, which Itti made as comfortable as possible. Others too injured to ride did the same, while the rest led horses bearing what supplies Losibar and fellow villages could spare.

Scrawled on their expressions was the eagerness to return home.

Denton ignored the pang in his heart. He had no home to return to. Yes, it would be great to once again be in Veerham, but what then? There were no more children to hunt down unless something happened during his stint away. Red, certainly, did not want him intruding upon her status as royal detective, and Carter did not deserve to deal with him, not when Chamonix had been three months pregnant when Denton left.

No, there was nowhere for him.

But at least he knew he was loved by the only One whose love mattered.

That knowledge was a balm on his broken soul.

Silence befell the group as the horses entered what used to be the village. With the exception of Yald's office and the stone buildings, nothing remained.

"Was there anything salvageable?" Hauni's voice cracked.

"The stone buildings probably are, but I don't know about their foundations. Yald's might be the best place for the injured to rest up."

"I still can't believe that snake," Edver hissed. "To betray his own...he got what came to him."

Similar sentiments had been expressed during Yald's trial. Four villages, counting Losibar, had convicted those who participated in the kidnappings. What their fate would be, Denton didn't know. Even after helping rescue Marterisi children, he hadn't been allowed within the makeshift courtroom for more than to give his testimony.

He hated trials. At least that time, he didn't have to worry about being convicted.

"How long until we can rebuild?" a man asked.

Talart ran his hand along a stubbly beard. "If every able-bodied person participates, we can get the church rebuilt and stay in there as we work on dwellings."

Part of Denton nagged at him to stay, but it was time to go. Aside from helping, there was nothing for him in Marteris.

Ignoring the ache in his heart, he watched Nerissa help Daffy down. She still moved like an octogenarian, but Hauni and Itti said it would take time for her—for them all—to gain the full rest they needed.

So much pain. So much heartbreak. So much destruction.

But his girl was strong, and even though she wasn't a fighter like Red, she wasn't a damsel in distress who only knew how to cower and scream.

His girl?

Get that idea out of your mind, Yindell.

Nerissa was no more his than he was anyone important to Carter and Red.

After grooming the horses and securing them in Morris' pasture, where the other equines still grazed, unconcerned with their master's disappearance, he joined the others in sifting through the rubble. Tomorrow he and the boys would begin their journey to Veerham.

"It's all gone," Elberta muttered as she and her sisters and father stared at the heap of what remained of their cabin. "Even my doll is gone."

"So's mine." Daffy clung to Nerissa's skirt. The lass could put a tick to shame for how she refused to be separated from her eldest sibling.

Denton withdrew the thin rope from around his neck and held out the key to Nerissa. "Here. I forgot to give this to you back at the gate." The weight had become a reminder to uphold his promise, and now he felt too light without it."

Icy fingertips brushed his as she retrieved it.

"It was the only thing that survived aside from the hearth. It was how we reached you all so quickly."

Her lips trembled. "It should have melted."

"Yes."

Mr. Wessen placed an arm around Elberta. "The Beginning works in mysterious ways."

That He did.

Before awkward silence could fall, Denton bid them farewell by way of a nod and turned to return to the village proper. Before he could take one step, Elberta called his name and slammed into him, wrapping thin arms around his waist.

Watery eyes looked up at him. "Thank you for saving me, and for letting Bluet stay with us while you and Edver fought."

Denton hadn't even remembered the faithful dog, but when he staggered into the area where they left the boys and Elberta, Bluet was standing guard.

The three had been fine, if not a bit unnerved by the commotion. But they had obeyed, and that was what mattered.

He patted Elberta's shoulder. "Thanks for keeping the boys in line. They can be rascals at times."

"Do you really have to leave?"

Her question shouldn't tear at him, but it did.

"I do. Jonah needs to return to his family and it will be quite the journey to get Noko back to Halthdurn."

"But you're hurt too. You shouldn't travel."

"I've traveled with worse injuries before."

Elberta sniffed as she stepped back. "Can you at least let me rename Cinders? So you remember us?"

She wanted *him* to remember them? Him, an outsider? A man most of her village wanted dead when he first arrived, no matter how inadvertently?

Was it unmanly for tears to sting his eyes at the declaration? "Tell you what," he said, throat thick. "I'll make that her middle name. Cinders Magpie Yindell. How does that sound?"

Elberta beamed. "I think it sounds like a perfect name for a hero's horse."

Yep, those were definitely tears.

"I'm not a hero." Before she could argue, he scuttled for safety. He wasn't prepared to handle the emotions, the concept that she thought him a man to be lauded.

He'd just done what needed to be done so a wrong could be righted.

The second he stumbled into the village square, Talart cornered him. "We need to talk."

Denton said nothing. Why must everyone want to speak with him when he was too tired to comprehend how to correctly respond?

"Jonah…when we first found him, it was through one of the rescues, much like the one you assisted with when Edver was shot. He had withdrawn and spoke to no one, and it was a long time before he willingly consumed an adequate meal. When he did trust us enough to speak, he said those who said they'd protect him had let him be taken. Then you showed up, and we made the connection." He held up a hand to stall Denton's response. "I'm not saying we were in the right by lying. I am just telling you the thought process behind our actions."

"If you had been honest with me, chances are half of what happened could have been avoided." Denton watched the boys find sticks for a fire. "Yes, I was one of the ones who broke his promise, but as soon as I was cleared to travel, I made my way here and began looking for him. I broke my promise, but that didn't mean I would do nothing about it."

"We didn't know that."

"Not at first, but didn't I prove myself? I bled for your people. I pushed myself beyond what was healthy."

Talart's jaw ticked. "A few years ago, an outsider entered our lands. He claimed to be searching for villages to trade with, saying he was a traveling merchant. He gained our trust and ended up bringing about decimation to several villages because they refused to give him their entire bounties. He refused to realize they needed those bounties to trade for real, important supplies. Not worthless trinkets."

Denton ground his teeth. "I understand your hesitation, but I could say all Marterises are bloodthirsty brutes who only want the destruction of the innocent. My brother and friend almost died because of your people and a Marterisi assisted in my sister-in-law's kidnapping. Just as the majority of you are not like the ones who hurt my family, I'm not like the man who destroyed your villages."

"We know that now—"

Denton backed away, grasping for any excuse to flee. "It looks like someone needs you."

Talart didn't call after him as he hustled toward the trees.

"What do you need help with?" he asked after running into Morris, who was hauling buckets of water from a nearby stream.

"You can help with these, if you're able."

Denton filled a bucket and joined Morris, helping wear a path from the stream to the village. Hauni and some of the younger girls scrubbed the infirmary down while others set up supplies for the night. Dusk tinted the sky a muted mash of orange and pink, and the nighttime birds sang.

Perhaps in a different life he wouldn't have minded Marteris.

"I'm sorry, Denton." Morris halted and scratched his chin through his overgrown beard. "I know an apology doesn't heal the wound, but it needs to be said all the same."

"Did you share their opinion? That I'm dangerous?"

"I did at first, but it wasn't long before I caught glimpses of what you really are."

"And what's that?"

Morris speared him with a look so intense Denton took a few steps back. "You, Denton Yindell, are a young man with a wounded heart and soul, who is trying to learn who is worthy of trust and who isn't. You want to atone for your past while longing to realize the truth."

No one ever dissected him in such an accurate way. Red called him a coward. Carter likely exulted when Denton left, despite allowing him to keep Cinders. Father and Antony often spoke of how much easier it would be if Denton no longer existed.

This...this peering into his soul wasn't an experience Denton desired to endure ever again.

"Like I said, words can damage, but they can't heal. Still, I need to apologize. I said nothing despite knowing Chief and the others were in the wrong."

Never had Denton imagined someone apologizing to him. "I accept," he stiffly replied.

After handing over his bucket, he escaped to Cinders' side and spent the rest of the night watching the stars blink from their stations so far away.

Marteris experienced its fair share of wind and thunderstorms, but Denton never heard of it enduring a dust storm.

And that was exactly what hurtled toward them.

"What are we gonna do?" Jonah clutched Sir Marlin's reins with such a tight grip the gelding sidestepped in protest.

"I don't think that's a storm." Noko squinted. "One time during a drought, my pa had to go defend our water source from another clan. When they returned, their horses kicked up so much dirt it looked like a cloud came our way. And it looked just like that."

"Are they more traffickers? Should we tell the others? Maybe then we can say goodbye."

Denton ignored the passive-aggressive comment. He'd had the boys up and ready to go at the first touch of dawn, well before the first villagers stirred.

His heart wanted to bid Nerissa farewell. It wanted to recapture the unexpected feeling he'd dealt with at the cove when she cried into his shoulder and exhibited concern for his welfare.

His heart. Such a traitorous thing. It wanted to love and be loved. It wanted to tell a certain Marterisi woman what he could feel for her if only a wall didn't separate them.

His mind remained on the opposite side. Love hurt. Love was fickle. Nerissa didn't think of him the way he thought of her, and it was best to spare himself the humiliation and leave without more interaction.

The mind won.

"I see red and gold. Do kidnappers wear red and gold?"

Horses and horseshoes. "No, they don't. I think this group is friendly."

Only Veerham's royalty and ambassadors wore the royal colors during travel, and Denton could guarantee King Calvin and Queen Isadora wouldn't be leaving their daughter's side, not with the grandbaby well on its way.

Soon the dust's cause skidded to a stop mere horse-lengths away.

Denton copied Noko and squinted. Delirium was definitely setting in, because he wasn't really seeing who he thought he saw. *"Carter?"*

"Denton." Carter sat atop Gus like a king viewing his conquered enemies for the first time. A sword strapped to his hip and bracers on his forearms indicated he hadn't gotten lost on a leisurely ride.

"Is that chainmail?"

"It is, and I don't recommend it."

Captain Bedros rolled his eyes. "You know why you need it. With you being the Seydens' son-in-law, you're a target now."

Carter shook his head.

Denton rescued his jaw from the ground. "What are you doing here?"

"Saw a lot of smoke and figured you were the cause." Carter's eyes twinkled with merriment. "Actually, aside from the smoke, we received a missive from a trader stationed somewhere between here and the Veerham-Marteris border. Said trouble was afoot and rumor had it a Veerhamer was causing mischief."

"I wasn't the one causing problems if that's what you're insinuating."

Carter shrugged before nodding to Jonah. "How are you? We've been concerned."

Denton wasn't the only one picking his jaw up. "You're a prince?" Jonah breathed. "Why did all the cool stuff happen when I was kidnapped? Should I bow? I should probably bow."

"You're fine."

"Yes," Bedros chortled. "He refuses any manner of respect."

"Because it's unnecessary."

"You're related to the crown now, boy. It's necessary."

Denton placed a hand on Cinders' neck, not so much to steady her, but to ground himself. "You're here with twenty soldiers because you thought I was causing trouble?"

"No, Denton. I'm here with twenty soldiers because I thought you were *in* trouble."

Not one ounce of sarcasm laced Carter's tone.

He was serious.

Carter had been concerned about *him.* The man who did nothing while Carter was targeted by Father and Antony.

Carter dismounted and stretched. "So, what happened?"

Denton exhaled. "First, allow me to introduce a special friend. Noko, this is my brother, Carter. Carter, this is Noko. He was kidnapped and needs to be returned to his home."

Carter greeted Noko then fixed an intense stare on Denton. "Sounds like a lot has happened."

At least he hadn't corrected Denton. Most would cringe at being called his stepbrother much less his brother. "Yes, a lot has."

"Do you think they're here to help rebuild the village?"

Jonah's whisper could awaken a corpse.

Carter raised a brow. "What village?"

"It's a long story."

"We have time."

The villagers hadn't known what to think and say when Carter and his crew sauntered in offering their assistance, but the help was welcomed, and within a week's time, lodgings were rebuilt and most of the village was reconstructed.

During that week, Denton steered clear of Nerissa. The tumultuous feelings raging within required more energy than he could spare, and there was no way she'd ever think of him what he thought of her. That much was clear.

Cold water splashed across his shirt, yanking him from the monotonous task of hauling wooden planks.

"I am so sorry."

Denton met Nerissa's wide-eyed gaze. Why did heat rush up his neck?

She lowered the bucket. "I didn't see you."

"I was the one in the way. I should be apologizing."

Nerissa set the bucket down and wrung her hands. "I...I need to apologize for more than...than that." She inhaled. "I shouldn't have withheld the information about Jonah."

"Talart already told me your reasoning behind it."

"No—well, yes, at first I agreed, but after a while, you proved you weren't what I feared." She hunched and looked down. "I know my participation hurt you, and I cannot apologize enough for that."

"Why didn't you tell me?" The apology scraped away the layer of indifference he'd built up.

She bit her bottom lip. "I was afraid. That was part of it. You...I didn't mind you after a while. And I just grew used to you being here. I don't think I wanted to see you go, and if I told you about Jonah, you would have left. Not that I wanted him to be separated from his family," she hurried to say. "But he was safe. And I didn't want him to be hurt again. And I dislike change. No, I *loathe* change. Any type of it. And this would have been change. It was wrong of me, and I am not attempting to explain my way out of it. I just wanted to apologize."

"He accepts," Carter said as he ambled past.

Denton glared.

"It sometimes takes a while for his mind to work, but I know my brother, and he does accept your apology."

Nerissa dipped her chin in deference despite Carter repeatedly telling the villagers to treat him "normally".

Carter stopped next to Denton, hands in his pockets. "Why doesn't your family return with us to Veerham?"

Nerissa gaped.

Denton was pretty sure he did as well.

"We don't have an ambassador for this area, and Father's been wanting to establish connections with the northern area for a while now. I've already spoken with your family about it. Why don't you go add your input?"

Nerissa opened and closed her mouth multiple times before retrieving her bucket and fleeing.

Denton crossed his arms and faced Carter. "What was that about?"

"What was what about?"

Oh, he was getting better. Taking lessons from Red, no doubt. "Why did you invite her?"

"You know you wanted to."

"Yes, but you heard her. She dislikes change, and I can't—and won't—ask her to leave the land she loves."

Carter tilted his head, blue eyes shrewd. "You like her."

"You're absolutely brilliant, you know that?"

"You *like* like her."

Denton scowled. What if someone overheard? He'd be staked and gutted for daring to like Nerissa that way. "What's your point?"

"I wasn't lying about Father's wishes regarding this region, and I'm doing you a favor."

"I do *not* need you meddling in my love life."

"What love life? You're avoiding it like Red avoided the wolf-men."

Oh, if only he could wipe that smug grin off Carter's face. "Stop trying to matchmake. You're terrible at it, and the last thing I need is for you to pull a Red."

Carter smirked and clasped Denton on the shoulder before saying in a low tone, "Then, to borrow one of Red's favorite expressions, don't be so obtuse."

Denton glared at Carter's back as his brother beat a hasty exit from the area. "What am I being obtuse about? Carter? *Carter!* Carter Blayn Brendhal, you answer me."

Carter's laughter was the only answer Denton received.

Chapter Thirty-Four

NERISSA

GRAND HALLS AND STRONG walls adorned with red, gold, and white tapestries rose above Nerissa as she shuffled into the palace.

At least, Denton called it a palace. The structure, with its clean atmosphere, baked-bread scent, and ornate furnishings didn't match the description Nerissa read about.

Servants bustled about, not acting like thralls enslaved to cruel masters, but everyday folk happy to go about their work.

They were so clean, and she was so frumpy and dirty.

Days of travel stained her clothing and clung to her, making her smell like sweat and something else unpleasant. She hobbled from days of riding, her efforts to just stay on hindered by Denton's barked orders to "drop her heels, relax her posture, and lose the tension in her shoulders".

Clearly, Doc's concoctions to battle pain weren't working.

When Mamma heard her muttered complaints, she could only smile and said that was his method of flirting.

There was no reason for Denton to flirt, and decidedly no reason for him to be interested in her, a village girl who'd never before seen a cow or town.

Father hadn't budged when she argued against coming. It was safer, he said, and he wanted Mamma to have the best chance at healing.

Like traveling in a wagon, no matter how lined with fluffy blankets, assisted Mamma's broken ankle.

But Father's word was law, and so they went.

Lord Brendhal proved to be an amiable man. Quiet, but easy-going and good with Daffy and Elberta. Denton, on the other side, was so pent up even a man named Captain Bedros commented on his "unusual" behavior.

A strange look crossed Lord Brendhal's face at the comment, but he said nothing.

Now, as her family followed a dignified woman named Halda, Nerissa wanted nothing more than to shrink away and go hide in a hole.

"Here we are, and please sit." Halda moved aside to reveal a grand room with white sofas, pale pink curtains, and a stunningly-engraved mantle above a large fireplace.

"Oh, we can't." Mamma encompassed them with a wave of her hand. "We are covered in filth."

"Trust me, ma'am, those in worse condition have perched in this room." Wryness entered Halda's tone. Was she thinking about the infamous Red, whom Denton and Carter mentioned on numerous occasions?

"In fact, at one time, Queen Isadora came into this room drenched in mud and who-knows-what else. Please believe me when I say all will be fine."

Once they gingerly sat on the cushions, Halda swept away, saying something about tea.

Daffy giggled. "It's like sitting on a cloud."

"Please don't do that, dear." Mamma wrung her hands. "You must all be on your best behavior. King Calvin and Queen Chamonix are even higher than Chief Talart, and they rule a kingdom instead of a village. No disrespect at all. In fact, it may be best if you say nothing."

Father framed Mamma's face and kissed her forehead. "Relax, love. I've been watching Denton, and he's not one bit nervous about this."

"Denton knows these people."

"Yes, and when he's not trying to inch away from someone, I know he's fine with them."

Nerissa exhaled. Her stomach grumbled, but a bath sounded lovelier than food. Would the king and queen hold their appearances against them? Halda was just a servant. What would she know?

A maid hastened in bearing a tray laden with sandwiches and tea cups. "Their majesties say to please eat your fill. They will be in in about half an hour."

Daffy and Elberta had no issue downing their portion.

Despite her grumbling stomach, Nerissa struggled to swallow one bite. What did her family's future hold?

Please help me trust in You no matter what.

Her family was the Beginning's. The time in the tower taught her that much.

All too soon, the door opened and Halda helped the same maid clear the table, brushing aside Mamma's instance at helping. "Nonsense. You are injured. And don't you even think about standing when their majesties enter. They'll have none of it."

And indeed they didn't.

Nerissa clamped a hand over Elberta's mouth to keep the precocious youngster from speaking when the king and queen, followed by Carter and a pregnant young woman, entered.

"Please, do not try to stand." Queen Isadora placed a hand on Mamma's shoulder. "I wish I had been told the extent of your injury. You would have been taken straight to Federigo."

"I am fine, your majesty," Mamma squeaked.

"Nonsense. And please do not feel like you must partake in every type of formality known to mankind."

Queen Isadora, with her red hair and stately stature, was beautiful. Her husband, King Calvin, stood tall and commanding, but the faint lines around his eyes and the gentle set of his mouth belied his stern first-impression. Carter still wore the dust from travel, and his wife, Chamonix, had her father's golden eyes and her mother's red hair.

"Your eyes are yellow," Daffy piped up.

Nerissa slapped her other hand over the child's mouth.

Instead of frowning or bursting into a fit of rage, the nobles laughed. "Indeed they are, little one," King Calvin said.

Queen Isadora hooked her arm through her husband's, gave him an adoring smile, and then directed her attention toward Princess Chamonix. "Where is Redwyn?"

"I do not know—I have not seen her all day."

"What of Denton?" King Calvin asked.

Carter shrugged. "He said he was going to clean up. I think he fell asleep. He'd been yawning since we started for home. That or he's babying Cinders. Probably giving her a bath then a four-course meal."

"That does sound like him."

At the queen's motion, everyone sat. Daffy snuggled into Nerissa's lap, playing with her pigtail as she stared at the royal couple. Elberta pressed against Nerissa's arm, clinging to her wrist. "Carter calls you *Father*. Why doesn't Denton call you that? Aren't they brothers?"

No laughter came from the king this time, and Nerissa again covered Elberta's mouth, opening her own to apologize.

Carter and the king exchanged a glance before Carter spoke. "If you want to be technical, Denton is my stepbrother. I only call King Calvin *Father* because I married his daughter."

"But Denton's still your brother." Elberta pried Nerissa's hand down. "Why can't he call him that too?"

Another glance. "Denton may if he wants," King Calvin said, "but that is something you'd have to ask him."

"That is something you'd need to tell him he's allowed to do," Queen Isadora murmured. "He would not think of such a thing on his own."

"He may not be ready for that, yet. He's still healing."

Silence descended at Carter's words.

Until Elberta, bless her heart, decided to speak. Again.

"Healing from what? His injuries are almost fully fine, and the gash he got when we first found him is a scar now. I don't think he's hurt anywhere else."

Queen Isadora gave Elberta a gentle smile. "Some people have injured souls and hearts, dear one. Denton has suffered many physical injuries, but his heart and soul were hurt the most."

"Who hurt him? I'll feed them to a shark." Elberta stood and planted her fists at her hips. "He's been nice and rescued us from all sorts of problems. No one gets to hurt him."

"Those people are dead, little one. And does Denton know he has an admirer?"

Carter chortled. "He knows, but it's not the admirer you're thinking. And he's too obtuse to realize it."

Princess Chamonix shook her head. "Now you sound like Red."

"I've known her for over thirteen years. Can you blame me?"

After small talk consumed another hour, Queen Isadora commanded Mamma be ushered to the physician and the girls shown their room. "Chamonix, would you mind showing them?"

"Certainly." With Carter's help, the princess stood. When he continued hovering, she batted him away. "Oh, stop. Red already hounds me enough to drive me mad. I do not need you evaluating my every breath as well."

"I just want you to stay safe."

"I know."

Nerissa looked down as the two lost themselves in the other's eyes.

Finally, Princess Chamonix motioned them toward the door. Once in the hall, she fell in step with Nerissa. "Would you prefer your own room?"

"I am fine sharing with them, ma'am." Or was it *your majesty*?

"That makes me feel old." No censure infected the princess' smile.

Daffy leaned her head on Nerissa's shoulder. "How old is the baby?"

"Almost four months, by Mother's and Halda's estimations." Princess Chamonix flushed as she laid a hand on her belly. "We're hoping she doesn't inherit her aunt's penchant for locating trouble. Oh, here we are. If you require anything, please just let us know. A maid will be up in a few minutes to take you to the bathing chambers."

"Oh, but—"

"It is no trouble. Traveling is wearisome and we want you to feel welcome."

The baths passed in a blur of convincing Daffy they weren't meant to be swam in and making sure Elberta didn't tangle her hair in an uncontrollable rat's nest. After hastily scrubbing away all traces of dust and travel, Nerissa, with the patient maid's help, ushered the girls back to the room.

The bed, expansive and softer than even the settee, pulled her straight into sleep.

Soft candlelight illuminated the chapel sanctuary. Simple and elegant, its quietude offered Nerissa a place to sit and pray.

Only, the words wouldn't come.

So she sat, closing her eyes and thanking the Beginning for bringing her family back together.

After what could have been ten minutes or ten hours, Nerissa rose. What would it be like to attend church in this place? Did Denton come?

Her heart about escaped her chest when she turned. A woman waited in the doorway, her skirt not flaring out like Princess

Chamonix's and her hair, even with the distance between them, an obvious mess.

Hadn't Denton said something about Red having perpetual bad hair days?

Once her eyes accustomed to the light filling the foyer, Nerissa found herself looking at a woman around her age with out-of-control, curly red hair, as many freckles as the shore had sand, and numerous smudges adorning her dress garment. Thing. Whatever it was.

"You must be Nerissa Wessen."

Nerissa nodded. She had faced traffickers and fire, kidnappings and unspeakable fear, yet she couldn't muster her courage to verbally answer this woman with three knives attached to her person.

"I am Red."

"Denton spoke of you."

"I'm sure he did." She shook her head. "What did he say? That I have bad hair, a bad temper, and even worse fashion sense? It's okay to tell me the truth."

No animosity shone in Red's eyes, a darker blue than Denton's. "He did mention the hair, but he said you are a good detective and would have dismantled the traffickers in half the time."

Red snorted. "I don't know about that. Walk with me, would you?"

This would either end terribly or with Nerissa making a potential new friend.

"Why are you here? I thought you Marterises preferred your sea to our trees."

"We do. Carter—Lord Brendhal—invited my father. He said something about an ambassador?"

"Your father is not ambassador material."

Red was nothing if not blunt. "No, he isn't."

"He would do well working for Uncle Calvin, though. If he knows fish, he could help trade. Right now, the fish we're receiving are nearly unfit for consumption."

"How do you know this about Father?"

Red flashed a saucy smirk. "I met the rest of your family earlier. The little ones are adorable."

"Denton said Elberta reminded him of a younger you."

"I can see why."

Just as Nerissa could see Red's limp. "Are you alright?"

Red waved a hand. "I'm fine. Federigo says I'll likely always gimp about."

"What happened?"

Red eyed her, saying nothing as they passed from the courtyard, past the wall, and into a meadow lined with deciduous and pine trees. "You like Denton."

Heat seared Nerissa's face. "I...it wouldn't work between us."

"Why not?"

No good withholding the truth. From what Denton said, Red was tenacious enough to wrangle it from someone else. Exhaling, Nerissa relayed all of the past few months' events.

They emerged from the meadow, and Red leaned on a split-rail fence, staring at the pasture and horses. "Do you know the story behind Denton's scars? The one on his abdomen and the other on his thigh?"

"He alluded he was shot with broadheads. Why?"

"I'll leave his history for you to ask him, but let's just say Denton wasn't always the type to fight against evildoers."

"I've seen the self-hatred."

"Which is completely ridiculous that he's still beating himself up for what happened, but Denton is Denton. Anyhow, Cater, Char, and several local children were kidnapped. During the rescue, Denton not only saved my life twice, but he helped pull Carter from a burning building, and also jumped from Cinders onto a wagon and beat the stuffing out of the two traffickers before taking on two more. He was shot in the process and almost lost his life. It took multiple months for him to recover, and at one point, we weren't certain he was going to."

Red snickered. "You should have seen him on the crutches. We almost ruined Char and Carter's wedding because we tripped over the rug."

"You were on crutches as well?"

"Yes, and together we were a disaster."

"Are you related?"

"To Denton and Carter? No." Red laughed. "Though I can see why you'd think that. No, I am not blood relation to the Seydens, although they raised me from a young age."

"What do the feathers in your hair symbolize?" She'd seen numerous young servants wearing the white feathers too.

Red reached up and brushed her fingertip along the red feather, which haphazardly remained attached to her hair. "Red means you are a noble. In this case, I wear it because I am the crown's ward. White means you are single."

"Denton doesn't wear them."

"We didn't send Denton with his feathers because they can be a bit conspicuous, and he needed to be opposite that. As for the red feather, he hasn't worn that since his father and brother were convicted and sentenced for their crimes."

Processing the information, Nerissa closed her eyes as a bird trilled and the breeze whispered through the grass. There was a different type of beauty to this place. More sophisticated and soft, but still...nice.

"Denton is a good man," Red said quietly. "He has his demons, but he's come a long way in the past year. Stubborn mule just doesn't always recognize what's right in front of him."

"Do you know him well?"

"Well enough to know he regrets his past and has a hard time recognizing he's wanted." Red faced Nerissa, one elbow propped on the top rail. "He loved his stepmother—Carter's mother—but his father and brother were the lowest of low. Looking back, I realize Carter wasn't the only one they beat up."

Nerissa swallowed bile. "He always looks so lost."

"He's gone through a lot." Red studied her some more until she simply said, "You're good for him. Just remember to give him time for everything to sink in. He still has a lot to sort out and probably won't say anything for awhile."

When Red looked away, Nerissa followed her gaze to where a familiar black-and-white horse rounded the far building's corner, an equally-familiar rider sitting astride.

Red laughed again as Cinders took off, Denton staying on like a professional. "He must have some things burdening him if he's riding her so soon after traveling."

With her red hair and red undershirt, Red stuck out like a blue whale among minnows. "I'm surprised he didn't notice us."

"He and Carter are similar that way. They go riding when they need to think things through, and when they're focused, they don't notice much. Right now, Denton is shouldering a lot of guilt, most of which he's taking upon himself."

"How long will he be like this?"

Red shrugged.

"Where is he going?"

A sad glimmer gleamed in the detective's eyes. "I'll show you."

CHAPTER THIRTY-FIVE

DENTON

THE WIND RUSHING PAST his ears and the familiar cadence of Cinders cantering across the meadow threatened to dull the past and erase the future. Was it so bad to want to remain in the present? To never want a moment to end?

At the time, Denton hadn't thought anything about going to what used to be his home, taking care of Cinders, then crashing after a quick wash. To pull up Stepmother's blue quilt and sleep in his own bed felt like a temporary dream come true, and he would have slept for another day if one persistent thought hadn't hounded him into awakening, drenched with cold sweat and gasping for breath.

This wasn't his home anymore, and he had just waltzed in like he still had the right to live there.

Technically, Carter hadn't kicked him out yet, but Denton was still trespassing.

Pulling on a fresh change of clothing, he had bolted from the house, ignoring Aldyth's call about lunch, saddled Cinders, then took off.

"Worthless."

He wasn't worthless. He was the Beginning's.

"Stupid waste of time."

The Beginning had saved him. He wasn't a waste.

"Coward."

He still was a spineless wimp, but he was trying. With the Beginning's help, he would get better and not let the chains of fear hold him back from doing what was right.

"You're no longer my son."

Perhaps not, but he was the Beginning's child now.

What was it Parson Gil once said? Something about nothing ever separating believers from the Beginning's love?

A wave of what could only be peace flooded him, calming the rest of the tempests. He was a failure. A sinful wretch, but he was saved. He was loved by the only One who mattered, and that love wasn't conditional.

Real love wasn't conditional.

Thank You.

The tears did flow, then. Straight from his raw and breaking heart, drying almost as fast as they escaped.

One hurdle had been overcome. Jonah would depart for his family in two days after he rested and ate three times his weight in pastries.

Nerissa and her family were safe. That was another relief.

Noko had taken a shine to Red after asking to see her knives. Chances were the kid was hounding her steps right then.

Carter was happy, beaming whenever someone mentioned Chamonix, and strutting like a peacock at the prospect of soon holding his little one.

Denton didn't begrudge Carter that happiness. He deserved it.

And it only stirred up a longing for a family, a longing that only worsened whenever Denton was around the Seydens and Carter and Chamonix.

To be part of the Beginning's family was enough, but he couldn't deny the draw of belonging to an earthly one as well.

Slowing Cinders, Denton dismounted when he reached the cemetery. Stepmother's grave was, as always, tended and adorned with a fresh batch of flowers.

He knelt before the weathered headstone. Words never came easily when he visited, but somehow he felt better when he left. As long as his visits didn't coincide with Carter's, all was well.

"I'm back," he said quietly. "It was quite the adventure. Pretty sure Carter already told you this, but he and Chamonix are about to have a baby. I think Red will murder him if the little one doesn't share her name in some way." He eased until he sat, arms around his knees. This always took him back to the days of childhood, sneaking out in the middle of the night to visit, knowing what would happen if Father or Antony caught him.

"I guess I thought I would feel different, you know? Braver, maybe. Or even less cowardly, if that's a thing. But I don't. I feel the same. Better, I guess, in that some things were explained about the Beginning and I understand them now, but also emptier. Veerham is home, but there's nowhere here for me."

Nowhere to go, either, but he wouldn't turn maudlin at Stepmother's gravesite. "Cinders is doing well. I don't know how I would have made it without her. It's silly, I know, thinking of a horse as family, but that's what she is."

"It's not silly."

Denton scrambled to his feet, hand out and sword drawn. He had buckled it on by habit, so used to being wary of kidnappers potentially lurking behind every tree.

Carter stood a few paces away, shoulders loose and hands in his pockets.

Denton stepped back. Was it possible to die from humiliation? "You heard nothing."

"I heard everything. Unintentionally, mind you, but still. Do you really think that? That there's no place for you here?"

This was not how he wanted the visit to go. "There's not, and I really need to go—"

"Denton."

The gravity in Carter's tone froze him. Carter was—what? A duke or something?—and had the king's ear. If Denton messed up again, Carter had every right to complain to the king.

"I don't hold you accountable for Draymond's and Antony's sins."

"I helped."

"No, you didn't. Yes, you were passive at first, but do you really think, after your bravery and heroics in the Queen's Forest, that I consider you responsible?"

"I said nothing, Carter."

"And you almost gave your life to defend others. That's not cowardice. That courageous. You know, Elberta called you a hero, and she's right."

"I'm not."

"You are, and it's high time you accept that." Carter advanced, determination etched in his brow. "I *never* held you responsible. I thought you were wishy-washy, yes, but you were never cruel like Draymond and Antony. And then you went after Jonah of your own volition when we weren't even certain Marteris was where he was. You almost *died*, Denton. Twice! And yet you think you're not worthy of respect or the befitting title?"

Denton grit his teeth. "I could have stopped them from hurting you."

"No, you couldn't have. Not when you yourself were equally battered." Carter rubbed the back of his neck, gaze more intense than Denton ever before saw. "You did well on this mission, Denton, but you're not cut out to be a detective. You know that and Red and I know that. Your gift is with horses, and when I say gift, I mean *gift*. I've never seen someone calm a terrified horse the way you do, or watched anyone else win over a horse everyone else thought broken. Yes, the manor is mine, but it's also your home. Do you really think I would kick you out?"

"It's your right. We did invade it."

"You were a year older than me. Hardly capable of deciding whether or not to *invade,* as you put it. You are my *brother,* Denton. Blood doesn't turn away blood. And your father and brother don't count. They were, to borrow from Red's terminology, despicable, bloated louses with not one ounce of moral compunction."

Denton couldn't help but huff a laugh. Red had spewed that particular insult many a time.

"I want you to run the family business, Denton. The crown will be needing more horses soon, and there's no one else I trust more than you. Plus," a sly look crossed Carter's face, "that manor is big enough to raise a bunch of children in if you ever find your spine and propose to Nerissa."

"That's complicated, Carter. She's not interested."

"Really? Because every other sentence is *Denton this* and *Denton that*. The girl's in as much love with you as you are her, and you can't deny she's perfect for you."

Denton tucked his chin and looked down, though that did nothing to disguise the heat burning his neck and ears. Nerissa's strong faith and gentle, yet steadfast demeanor drew him, and she had the prettiest eyes. She was patient with little ones and worked hard to help her family.

Yes, he was, as Carter termed it, *in love.*

"There's too much between us."

"Then talk about it. That's what rational adults do, anyway."

"Bold of you to assume I'm rational."

Carter snickered. "Come on, *brother*. Let's go home. I saw Red and Nerissa riding around, and who knows what trouble Red's getting your girl into."

What began as a calm ride soon turned into an all-out race, but this time, *freedom* pulsed through him.

He was home.

Chapter Thirty-Six

NERISSA

"Do you think you could be happy here?"

Father's question drew Nerissa's attention from mending Daffy's torn stocking to where he sat at the desk in the palace library.

Could she be happy in Veerham?

Gazing out the nearby window, the answer struck her like a sudden summer storm hit the coast.

"Yes. I could be."

Because happiness wasn't where a building stood, nor where the sea brushed the shore and shimmered like a million diamonds when the sun hit it just right. Happiness was wherever her family was, whether that be back home, amidst Veerham's many trees, or even Frilore's frigid mountains.

"Good. Because King Calvin offered me a job and I accepted."

Somehow, the news didn't surprise her. "I assume Mamma knows."

"Yes. We spoke and prayed extensively before accepting. Morris is on his way, and I hear he's already secured a job helping a certain detective train horses."

Nerissa ducked her face to hide what she was certain was a blush.

"Nerri, life is too short to let what is already forgiven still stand in the way. Your mamma and I already know you two are head over heels for each other. Just talk with him. Give each other a chance." Father raised a brow. "I hear he's testing a new horse out in the field."

Her parents never had been subtle. "Do you like him?"

"I trust him." Father pinned her with a steely gaze. "But no man, and I mean not one, will ever get away with hurting my daughter. One wrong word, one wrong move, and I'll gut whoever harms you."

Laughing, Nerssia placed her mending in the basket and handed it over. "I'll be sure to let everyone know."

"You do that."

Still chuckling, she made her way from the library, down steps now familiar, and outside, where warm air carried the scent of summer. Father was right. Life was too short, and love—both familial and more—was too precious.

When she and Red arrived at a cemetery of all places, Denton and Carter were talking, something Red said shouldn't be interrupted. So Red took Nerissa on a sightseeing tour, pointing out notable buildings, which consisted of the common law office, the physician's, and dry goods store.

The detective certainly had her opinions on the definition of "important" buildings.

She copied Red's pose and leaned against the fence as Denton took a stunning, pale palomino through its paces. He looked so at peace, her outsider.

Her outsider.

One, he wasn't hers. Two, now she was the outsider.

He stopped the horse when he saw her and dismounted, leading the equine over. "Is everything okay?"

"Everything is fine."

He worked his jaw before motioning for her to join him. "I think I know why you're here."

"Oh?"

"Yes. Haether's accusations."

The accusations had fled her mind once he rescued her from the water.

"I'm not a murderer."

"I know."

"Those men—they were trying to hurt innocents. That…that was the only way to stop them."

"Denton." Nerissa held up a hand. "Red explained what happened that day. Haether was wrong. You are no murderer. Elberta termed it correctly when she said you were a hero."

His face turned as red as Veerham crimson.

"Red also said something about your father and brother."

Denton exhaled and shoved his fingers through his hair. An odd mix of grief and fear claimed his features. "I know you've noticed mine and Red's limps." At her nod of affirmation, he went on. "About a year ago, Carter and I uncovered my father's shady dealings. He actively participated in not only the black market, but in the trafficking ring as well. Carter was kidnapped due to his snooping around, Chamonix was taken to be sold, and an attempt was made on Red's life. It took some time, but we hunted the kidnappers down. Once we dragged them back for interrogation, the link between my father and brother and the ring's activities—not to mention orchestrating Carter's assault and kidnapping—was explained to the king and they were rightfully declared guilty and sentenced to death by hanging."

The sorrow permeating his voice and countenance made her want nothing more than to draw him in for a hug. "I'm so sorry."

"They broke the law and willfully harmed others. They deserved it." He sighed. "I was complicit, though. I knew they were up to something, but did nothing until Carter was taken."

"Red said you're a hero."

"Red says a lot of things. Doesn't always make them true."

Nerissa held out her hand. The stubborn Veerhamer caught the hint and took it, his own warm and strong. "What about the feathers? Red explained their meanings and why you didn't wear them to Marteris. Why aren't you wearing them now?"

Denton shrugged. "Honestly, I forgot about the white feather. Which is ridiculous since I've been wearing it since I was sixteen."

"What of your red one? I was told you were a lord's son."

"Father usurped Carter's land, home, and title. After he died, that was rightfully restored to Carter. I am no noble."

"It doesn't look like Carter bears you ill will." When he sent her a wary look, she explained. "Red and I saw you two racing."

Denton's shoulders slumped. "Carter is a good man. I don't deserve his forgiveness, but he offered it anyway."

Nerissa planted her hands on her hips. It took Denton a few paces to notice she no longer accompanied him, but when he did, he hastened to her side.

"What's wrong?"

What was she going to do with him? Was it possible to simultaneously hug and slap someone? "Don't you think Carter's the one who should determine whether or not you're deserving of his forgiveness? It is his to give, after all."

He stared at her for a long moment before opening his mouth. "I..."

"You act like you are unworthy of forgiveness, yet others offer it without hesitation. You have repented and changed. Stop believing you are still the same man as you were last year. You're not."

He swallowed. "I just—"

"Denton."

After a long stretch of time, his stance relaxed, and something in the lines of his expression told her he understood.

Only after they resumed walking did Nerissa continue the conversation. "How did you learn Yald was working against us?"

"He was always too eager, for one, and always insistent on copying everything. Plus, he knew where the enemy would be, giving just enough information to convince you all to agree with him, but not enough to arouse suspicion. Then I found evidence in his room, and you heard him confess at the trial."

"I heard you say something about a mark to that other man."

"Al? Yes. I noticed this last year during the Queen's Forest rescue. Some of the horses were branded with a particular mark.

I don't know how to describe it. Red has a sketch and will be investigating. Anyway, I saw the same mark imprinted on the inside of Al's wrist when he stole my weapons on the beach. A few others, including Haether and Joan, wore the mark in some way, and it was drawn on the upper righthand side of Yald's map."

"You really are a detective."

He again went red. "Not a good one."

They walked in silence, following the fence and occasionally waving to other palace stable hands as they exercised the horses.

"Father was asked to work for King Calvin."

"What did he say?"

Nerissa stopped and faced Denton. All those months ago, she never thought she'd consider him a friend, much less view him as potentially *more*.

Denton's throat bobbed with his swallow. "Do you think you could be content here? Without your sea and friends?"

"I'll miss Edver and Afya, but in a way, there's nothing left back in Marteris aside from my fellow villagers."

He swallowed again. "That didn't answer my question."

Nerissa took a breath to calm her jittery stomach. "Yes, I could be content here. More than content, actually. The Beginning taught me a stern lesson that happiness is not dependent on physical situations. My family is safe and happy, I'm learning to like it here, and all these different trees are stunning. Yes, I could be more than content here." Her voice threatened to give when he took a step closer.

"Do you think you could be happy?"

"More than."

Denton opened his mouth before closing it. An amusing silence fell before he muttered something about horses and horseshoes. "But you hate horses."

"I don't hate them. I'm simply...unknowledgeable about them. But Uncle Morris is on his way, and I'm sure he'll be enthusiastic to share his knowledge."

"We don't have a sea."

Nerissa framed his face with her hands. "That's fine—I don't need the sea to be happy, and I rather like the way the grass bends in the wind. It's a type of sea unto itself. Yes, the waves and crisp salty air are part of me, and they always will be, much like Veerham will always be part of you."

Denton captured her hands. "I—I'm not a perfect man, Nerissa."

How was it possible for her both love him and want to smack him? "No one is perfect, and you know full well I have my flaws."

"I've been speaking with Parson Gil."

"Yes?"

"He said...he said a husband and wife are a team. I think we'd make a good team."

"I do too." Why did she feel so breathless? It wasn't like she just ran a league.

"I'll have to ask your father."

"Her father approves," Father shouted.

Face as hot as a fire, Nerissa looked over to see her family, plus Red, leaning against the fence and obnoxiously listening in. Even Mamma managed with her crutches.

Nerissa smiled up at Denton, whose color likely matched her own. "See? You have his approval."

"And ours," Elberta hollered.

"And my sisters'."

Denton lowered his voice, but made no other move to secure more privacy. "Do I have yours?"

"Depends on what you're asking."

"I don't have a ring unless you want me to dismantle a bridle."

"I don't need a ring."

Eyes locked with hers, Denton lowered himself onto one knee. "Nerissa Wessen, would you do me the honor of being my wife?"

Nerissa prepared to answer, but before she could speak, Elberta yelled, "Yes! She says yes!"

Everyone in the vicinity erupted with laughter.

Nerissa framed Denton's face after he rose. "Yes," she whispered. "I do say yes."

Denton grinned, taking her breath away, before pressing a kiss to her cheek, then a short, yet gentle one to her lips. "Hopefully Red doesn't insist we name our first child after her," he whispered.

Nerissa couldn't contain her chortling, even as Elberta and Daffy made disgusted noises at the kiss.

She was home.

For home wasn't a house or land or a certain geographical location.

Home was where your family was, and her family was in Veerham.

Thank You, Beginning.

Chapter Thirty-Seven

DENTON

THE WELCOMING SCENTS OF horses and hay surrounded Denton as he brushed down a new acquisition to Carter's stable. The young filly—an elegant buckskin—possessed an even milder disposition than Cinders. She would make a good mount for a young noblewoman or an elderly grandmother.

"How are you doing?"

Denton looked up as Red entered. Like him, her limp was more pronounced toward the end of the day. "I'm fine, and you? Finally cleared to cause mischief, I see."

"I do not cause mischief. I merely willingly partake in it."

He snorted. "What's this about you telling Nerissa so much about me?"

Red leaned against a stall door, arms crossed and nose snootily pointed in the air. "I'll have you know I said very few negative things about you."

"How reassuring."

The detective rolled her eyes. "Obviously it didn't dissuade Nerissa from accepting your proposal."

"You heard about that, did you?"

"How could I not? I was right there and it's circulating the grounds. The council is proclaiming it a 'brilliant step into forming a secure relationship with our new ally'."

Denton shook his head and resumed grooming the filly. "Marteris is hardly our ally. They're neutral. Nerissa's village may be our ally, but I can't see the villages getting together to vote on the matter. They're rather hard-headed."

"Then you should fit in just fine with them."

"Har har."

"I thought so." Red offered Denton a slight smile, the action so rare he almost toppled over from shock. "I haven't always liked you, but I am beginning to respect you more. You're no longer a coward, Denton Yindell." She held out her hand. "Welcome to being a royal detective."

Denton shook her hand, although why he didn't know. "I'm not staying in that position, Red. I'm not cut out to be a detective."

"From what I heard, you did well in Marteris."

"There was little detectiving that went on. Most of it anyone could figure out."

Red tilted her head. "Regardless of your opinion on the matter, you did far better than I expected."

"Thanks, I think."

"I'm serious." Red ambled over and petted the filly's neck. "What's her name?"

"Elberta wants to name her Carnation."

"That's actually not too bad."

"Better than Magpie."

"Definitely."

Denton grabbed a hoof pick and lifted the filly's leg. The mundane chore solidified the fact that he was back. He was home.

Carter hadn't taken no for an answer, and Denton's fingers still carried the ink stain from when he accidentally tipped over the inkwell after signing his name next to Carter's as co-owner of the stables. Morris would make a good foreman and already five requests had come in for dependable saddle horses.

If only his younger self could have known what his future held.

Then again, would I have realized my need for You?

The filly nickered and nudged his shoulder with her nose.

"Looks like you've made a new friend," Red remarked.

"Looks like." It wasn't the only thing he had made, nor the only thing he gained.

"Don't tell Red this, but we're giving our baby the middle name of Red or Redwyn, depending on if it's a boy or girl." Carter grabbed another halter and began buffing it. His grin, which had grown brighter and wider during the past few weeks, lit the stable.

Denton smirked from where he oiled a saddle. "I'll let her be surprised."

Soon, a little Brendhal would be brought into the world. While Veerham wasn't perfect, it was a good place to be born and raised. And the baby would be loved, spoiled, adored, and spoiled some more.

Neither Carter nor Chamonix need know Denton planned to teach the little one how to ride as soon as the baby reached the appropriate age. Carter was a fine rider, and even though Denton was the only uncle, he wanted to be the *cool* uncle.

Yes, he'd spoil the little one rotten. Carter and Chamonix would hate him and his niece or nephew would love him.

"Surprised about what?" Red sauntered into the stable, Noko—her ever-present shadow—following.

"Nothing. And who says we were talking about you?"

She rolled her eyes at Denton. "My superior skills, that's what."

Carter set down his rag and leaned against the stall door. Some protested at the princess' husband helping with such "menial" chores, but Carter would have none of it. "What's going on?"

Red lost her amusement. "Noko and I will set out for Halthdurn in three days. We'll need your best horses, Denton."

"Cygnus isn't behaving?"

"Cygnus is a brat."

"Like rider like horse."

"I take offense to that."

"More like you *represent* that."

Red scowled. "Fine, then. If you're sticking me with that ornery best, then Noko still needs a horse."

"He can take Dancer." Denton nodded to the red roan grazing near Cinders. "He's dependable."

Carter sent Red a snarky grin. "It could be worse, *Redwyn*. You could be stuck with Kline."

"*No.*" After trying to kill Carter with a glare, she returned her attention to Denton. "Aren't you supposed to be preparing for your wedding?"

"What time is it?"

"Noon."

Denton threw down the rag and took off across the yard. Horses and horseshoes, how did time move so quickly? He'd had a few hours to catch up on chores before suiting up for his nuptials, but now he would be *late* if he didn't hustle.

A hasty, yet thorough wash and the quickest clothing change ever saw him attempting to secure his shirt's top button as he and Carter ran for the chapel, sliding in just in time for Parson Gil to give them a crusty look.

"It does not bode well when the groom is almost late."

"I'm here."

"Barely," Red hissed from where she stood in a pale blue dress. How had she managed to change so quickly?

Elberta and Daffy lingered nearby, baskets of small flowers in their hands. Some type of Marteris tradition or something.

"Breathe," Carter commanded as he took his place behind Denton. "Won't do you any good if you pass out."

"I don't pass out."

The music began, and the doors opened to reveal Nerissa and Jarrel walking down the aisle. Denton's collar went tight. Not from fear, but from...elation? The chance to begin anew? The opportunity to finally have a family?

His bride's shy, radiant smile nearly dropped him as they took hands and recited their vows.

This was real. This was happening. From this day forward, he would be the husband to the most amazing woman the Beginning ever created.

"I now pronounce you husband and wife."

Elberta gagged at the kiss, a common theme for that one.

"She won't be doing that on her wedding day," Denton whispered to Nerissa.

She burst out laughing. "No, she won't be."

Chatter and exultations filled the chapel as attendees congratulated them—and Red gave Nerissa her condolences. Denton tucked his arm around Nerissa's waist and watched the crowd. A storm waylaid Edver and Afya, but it hadn't halted the letter declaring their own upcoming wedding. Jarrel—*Father*—patted a weeping Vari on the back as Morris hoisted Daffy in the air.

King Calvin stared at Queen Isadora like it was *their* wedding day, looking at his wife with pure adoration as she conversed with a gaggle of women. Carter had joined Chamonix, who sat with a glass of ice water in hand.

Perhaps soon Baby Brendhal would have another cousin.

"I'm proud of you, son."

Denton turned to find Parson Gil looking up at him. "Sir?"

"You've come a long way from the trepidatious boy who first crept in here during one of Parson Gary's sermons."

Denton swallowed. What could he say to that? "Thank you for mentoring me."

"It was one of my greatest pleasures." After a few more words, Parson Gil moseyed off and helped himself to one of the cookies Vari—who told Denton he could call her *Mother*—insisted on baking for the occasion.

He looked down just in time to catch Nerissa's smile his way. Squeezing her, he rested his chin atop her head.

She was right. Home wasn't a building, but wherever your family was.

And he was home.

Home.

He was finally home.

Thank You, Beginning.

For sneak peeks, exclusive giveaways, early-bird book news, and
other fun events and updates, you can subscribe to my newsletter
on my blog, madismusingsblog.wordpress.com.

If you enjoyed *KEY*, keep reading for a sneak peak into the next book, *POISON*, which arrives to bookshelves October 2023.

POISON

A Sneak Peek

WHOEVER TRACKED MUD INTO her library was going to die a slow, painful death.

Sara rested her hands on her hips and scowled at the mess marring the rug. Once crisp and pale- blue, now it was a disturbing mucky color, one she couldn't name. Clumps of mud, pine needles and leaves clumped in various areas, and streaks of mud destroyed the stone floor the maid just cleaned.

The audacity.

Oh, yes, there would be retribution.

Grabbing her skirt, Sara stalked from the foyer to the room containing more books than most could dream of reading in five lifetimes. Light streamed through the windows, falling upon the rows of gleaming spruce bookcases. The rug—this one too smeared and soiled—muffled her footsteps.

Her heart twisted as a thread of common sense penetrated the aggravation guiding her actions. What if the messy visitor was a criminal seeking a hiding place? Or someone intending to cause trouble? What would she do then? A hasty scan indicated no maids were within sight. No way to send someone for assistance should a problem arise.

This is why you think before you act, Sara. You should know this by now.

Sara swallowed and stiffened her spine before hastening her speed. She would discover who infiltrated her library, then take the appropriate actions. Nothing more, nothing less.

Mother will be quite displeased with me.

She couldn't ascertain Father's reaction. Half the time he laughed at her "antics", and half the time he joined in on Mother's displeasure.

Slipping into the nearest book row, Sara peered through the spaces between the shelves. Her time of ensuring the library was kept into tip-top order paid off—no half-shelved books obscured her view of the back of a gray shirt smudged with who-knew-what.

She pursed her lips and eyed her surroundings. Nothing more substantial than a thick book with a hardwood cover, but that could be a weapon should she require one.

Grabbing the hefty tome, she slipped to the row where the intruder so brazenly lurked. Steeling herself, Sara stomped into the row, her skirt swishing about her ankles. The rapscallion didn't even notice her.

Dark hair littered with a few pine needles combined with a strong profile hinted at a distant memory, but she shoved it aside. Many Frilorans had black hair, and there were only so many types of noses in the world. Surely at least a sixteenth of Frilore's population had a straight nose.

Still, he did look vaguely familiar.

He adjusted the book in his hands and turned the page.

Heat boiled in Sara at the grime coating his hand. How dare he desecrate her precious books with such filth!

Placing the heavy book on a nearby shelf, she crossed her arms and tapped her toe, barely restraining herself from murdering him with her glare. "So *you're* the one who's messed up my library."

The man looked up, his blank expression and dirt-streaked face making him look like a racoon caught in the henhouse. "What?"

Mother instructed her to always be ladylike, so that meant no clobbering him. Unfortunately.

Huffing, Sara gestured at him. "You are covered in filth and mud, yet you had the audacity to enter the library. Do you not know this is a sacred place? It should be kept clean. *Clean.* And didn't you see the rules about wiping your boots *outside*?"

He blinked. "No. My apologies."

Oh, he'd be apologizing, alright. And after that, she would discover why he sparked a distant memory. "Why are you even here?"

"Research."

"For what?" It better be for a good reason, or she'd have him dragged from her father's lands by his toes.

Audacious Rapscallion and Destroyer of Books returned his gaze to the book in his hands. "I need to find a cure. Do you know where the herbal section is? These old wives' tales won't help."

"And just why do you need a remedy? Are you planning to poison all of Frilore?"

That gained her his full attention.

Exasperation deepened his voice and narrowed his eyes. "Why would I do something like that?"

Because you, sir, look like a shyster. "That is what I'd like to know."

He closed the book and stood, crossing his arms over a broad chest. Sara's younger sister would be swooning at his thick, black hair and intense gray eyes, but Sara was not a woman swayed by physical appearance, no matter how handsome the man.

And she'd admit this one was...*attractive.* Well, he could be if he was clean-shaven. And hadn't attempted to decimate her library.

Those gray eyes flickered with irritation. "I heard Montagne had one of the best libraries in Frilore. I need answers, so I came here. If those rumors are unfounded, tell me now and I will leave."

"While I would certainly appreciate you vanishing from this region and never returning, the rumors are true. We do have a grand library."

He closed the book with a soft slam, never once breaking eye contact. "Good. If you would so kindly point me in the direction of medicine and herbs, I will continue seeking the answers I need. The sooner I find them, the sooner I can leave."

First he dirtied her library, then he slammed a book. She ought to have him thrown in a cluster of poison sumac.

Gritting her teeth against an unladylike reply, Sara pointed in the proper direction. "They are over there. Five rows down, to your left, and two bookcases in."

After placing the book on the shelf, he nodded. "Thank you, miss."

Sara glowered as he slipped past. He couldn't be the son of a neighboring lord—he would recognize her as Lady Sara Admusen if he were.

Still his elegant sword and arrogant bearing hinted at aristocracy, and his boots hadn't born the scars a working man's did.

She crossed her arms and drummed her right fingers against her left elbow. She would uncover this man's identity before he left, then she would pen a scathing missive to whomever he worked for. No one harmed her library and got away with it.

Sara exhaled and retrieved the damaged book. Hefty, it weighed almost as much as her impromptu weapon. A few dirt specks soiled the cover and she brushed away the dirt left behind on the pages before gently closing the book and inspecting the front cover.

Elegant, faded penmanship scrawled across the cover's middle in black ink. What room wasn't claimed by, *A Guide to Remedies and Cures from Healers of the Past,* was decorated with sketches of leaves and flowers.

The man called this a book of wives' tales. Was he so obtuse as to not realize many remedies and cures originated from these "wives' tales"?

Hmph. *Ignorant, uncultured crow.*

"Miss?"

Heart relocating to her throat, Sara shrieked and spun, bringing the book into a swinging arc that was interrupted by the impact of cover against resistance.

She stumbled back, pressing a hand to her chest and struggling to regain control of her lungs, which refused to take in sufficient air.

The rapscallion groaned and doubled over, clutching his face.

Crimson dripped to the carpet.

"What happened?"

Another male voice, accompanied by the soft zing of a sword being drawn, caused the mixture of fear and shock to furrow even deeper within Sara. She held the book in a defensive gesture as the second man appeared, although not even the hardwood cover would protect her from the terribly sharp and shiny sword.

Beginning, please protect me. What type of kerfuffle had she gotten herself into?

The second man stepped in front of the first, sword pointed at Sara. Cold green eyes narrowed. "What would you have me do with her?"

"At ease, Lyndon." The first man placed a hand on the second's shoulder as he stood. A bruise already swelled his left cheek and a gash spanned from the top of his forehead to the corner of his eye. "She's not a threat."

"Not a threat, my foot," Lyndon muttered. "She walloped you!"

"I scared her."

Disagreement scrunched Lyndon's expression.

Sara backed up. She could run decently fast even in a skirt and slippers, but she could not outrun the two men before her. "You honestly did frighten me." She adjusted her grip on the book. Her heartbeat still hadn't slowed to normal pace and forget about inhaling an adequate lungful of air.

"Easy, Lyndon," the first man grumbled as the second started after her. "Calm down."

"*Calm down?* She's not even remorseful. Back home, she would be arrested at best for this."

Was it possible to feel color drain from one's face?

"Lady Sara?" The head librarian's voice cut the tense silence. "Sara, where are you?"

What would the men do when Ludie reached them and realized what happened? What would *Ludie* do?

After what felt like centuries trapped in a staring contest with Lyndon, a hand settled on Sara's shoulder. One glance at the plain, well-worn ring adorning the left ring finger indicated Ludie stood behind her.

Instead of launching into a lecture about disrupting the library's sacred quietude, Ludie released a strangled groan. "Oh, Sara, what have you done?"

"Whatever do you mean?" Sara kept her attention on Lyndon. The first man remained holding a hand to his face. Blood oozed between his fingers and dribbled down his hand to his wrist before soaking into his sleeve.

She patted Ludie's hand. "Why don't you fetch some bandages? That way you won't have to see the blood." It wouldn't do for Ludie to pass out again at the sight of an injury, especially in this circumstance.

Ludie moaned. "It's not the blood, you daft girl. Come here."

Then, with strength one would not anticipate Ludie's narrow frame of possessing, she hauled Sara backward to the end of the row, all the while sending terrified glances toward the men.

"I can't believe you," she hissed. "What possessed you?"

Sara clutched the book to her chest. Just who were these men? Ludie only exhibited such flusterment when someone wreaked havoc in the library. "What possessed me? He scared me! I'm surprised my heart is still in my chest."

Ludie pressed the heels of her palms against her forehead and released another drawn-out groan. "Sara, use your eyes. Look at them."

Oh, for the love of tea and thick books.

Sara squinted at the men. Lyndon glared back, all the while muttering what had to be curses upon her. "I am looking at them."

"What do you see? *Who* do you see?"

"I see two men who look like they've been dragged through the muddiest pigpen. I see one who likely wishes he could skewer me right now, and I see another who may require stitches." Did she feel bad about delivering such an injury? Yes. Should he have frightened her out of her wits? No.

Ludie's eye twitched. Her graying hair, pulled back in a tight bun, only made her severe expression all the sterner. "Do you recognize either of them?"

"No. Should I?"

"Are you certain?"

Sara pursed her lips to conceal her need to sigh. Such a thing was unladylike, and Mother would be most displeased if she acted any more unladylike than she already had. "Quite certain. For the love of tea and thick books, just what are you hinting at?"

Ludie threw up her hands. "Sara Admusen, you are either the blindest woman in the entire world or you are the daftest. Young lady, that man you so cavalierly walloped is Keaton Ryson. *Prince* Keaton Ryson. Your betrothed."

If you enjoyed *KEY*, I would very much appreciate hearing your thoughts through a review. Reviews are authors' lifeblood, and they encourage both fellow readers to pick up our books and immerse themselves in another world.

Acknowledgments

As always, to my family. Thank you for pushing me to write even when I possessed neither drive nor energy to do so, and for putting up with me as I stumbled around in a sleep-deprived daze, no doubt muttering to myself about plot holes, expanded word counts, and deadlines.

To Lil' Sis, alpha reader extraordinaire.

To K.R. Mattson and Faith Gilliosa, for answering my medical questions.

Once again to K.R. Mattson for being willing to beta *KEY* on a super-duper short time frame.

To the WTCC girls: your encouragement was such a driving force in me finishing this project on time.

Most importantly, thank You, Lord. May this story bring honor and glory to You. *Soli Deo Gloria.*

About the Author

Madisyn Carlin is a Christian, homeschool graduate, blogger, voracious bookdragon, and author. When not spending time with her family or trekking through the mountains, she weaves tales of redemption, faith, and action.

Want to connect? https://linktr.ee/madisyncarlin

THE REDWYN CHRONICLES

WHERE FAITH, DETECTIVES, DANGER, ROMANCE, AND BAD HAIR DAYS ABOUND.

AND
MORE

THE
SHATTERED LANDS

A SERIES OF CHRISTIAN FANTASY FAIRY TALE RETELLINGS
FILLED WITH FAITH, HUMOR, REDEMPTION, AND ROMANCE.